The Spiraling

Book One of the Tunsealiorian Saga

L.A. Garnett

To Vivian, may your life be full of stories.

Prologue

Marin

"The keys," the old woman said, holding them out in her shaky grip. Marin took them delicately, half believing they'd be ripped from her grasp at the last moment. She stared at the rough metal, the leather loop worn and frayed, and allowed herself a soft smile. Finally, finally, she had a home.

From here on the stoop she could easily see that the building itself was disheveled, the brick walls chipped and almost crumbling in places where the wind had whipped down from the docks and pummeled it over the decades. It'd be work, maybe more than she expected, but it was all hers now. She couldn't wait to write home and tell everyone. No, she reminded herself. Write back to her family's home. This was where she lived now and this was where she could say that she had put down her own roots and truly built something. It never would have happened back there, not really. Her family had been close at hand and her friends were pleasant enough — she'd just felt as though something were missing. She'd wanted to travel; her father had said that the road was calling to her, and she couldn't disagree. She had to find a place where she wasn't someone's daughter, sister, or aunt — here, she was just Marin. A baker.

"Treat it well and it'll love you back," the woman, Katia, said with a wily grin. She clapped a wrinkled hand onto Marin's shoulder. "I left some things out for the evening customers — pass them out, will you? I told them you were coming."

"You aren't staying?" Marin asked, a slight frown creasing her brow. Katia had been one of the first people she'd met in Erengate when she'd moved here almost a decade ago, and she'd grown accustomed to the old Veden's sharp and often crass humor. "At least stay the night — the sun is already beginning to set."

"Oh no. I have an hour or so before the dark falls, and I've been stuck up in this frozen wasteland for three hundred years too long. Now that this business with the rebellion is good and squashed, I think I'll head back east. I miss lakes, and true mountains," she said, her voice going distant. Marin could understand the sentiment. She could appreciate the sea now — it still felt so new — but compared to the sprawling forests and snow-topped mountains of her own homeland it felt very flat in comparison. The west had some mountains, she supposed, but they weren't nearly as grand as those that used to stand just outside her door.

"Thank you, Katia, for everything," she said, feeling it wasn't nearly enough. The old woman grinned and shook her head.

"I think you'll do just fine, dear. I'll send word when I've settled, and you better write to me," Katia said, wagging her finger in front of her face before setting off toward the harbor. That was the best farewell she'd get, Marin knew. Katia had never been one for goodbyes.

Despite the unique smell of the shoreline that she didn't think she'd ever get used to, Marin allowed herself a moment of peace on the stoop. Her stoop. It was in disrepair, much like the building itself, but she didn't want to think of work right now. She had a bakery, just as she'd said she would, and it was going to be magnificent. The only thing left to do was convince Katia's old customers that she was just as good as her predecessor.

The people here didn't hold with strangers very well, but she was determined to prove herself to them. Erengate, the northernmost port on the far western shore of the continent, was isolated on the best of days. Summer was the busy season, when the docks were packed to the brim and foreign sailors and fishermen flooded the streets and mingled with the locals. Those days were her favorite. They almost reminded her of home. The sun lingered and its warmth brought out a friendliness from her neighbors that was sorely missed through the rest of the year. Winter, on the other hand, was a terrible beast. She'd expected ice and snow, as Sienma was known to be a frozen country, but she hadn't entirely realized just how much its people matched the landscape.

She couldn't help but laugh at the choices that had brought her here. It had been many years of wandering but Erengate had finally begun to feel like home. Sometimes her father would put a sprig of pine or a maple leaf in his letters to remind her of her roots, and she'd reassure him that she had in fact made some friends. *Katia had been chief among them*, she thought with a sad smile, *and I'll miss her*. She didn't know where the old woman planned to be—probably the nearest inn for a night of foolery for now—but she wished her well all the same.

More of a conundrum, however, was her newest friend —if she could even call him that. Lord Silas Zavalynn worked for the Karkas family, who ruled the city on behalf of Sienma's king. He looked after the properties in the Harbor and Trading Districts and even with all her charms, he hadn't allowed her to purchase one of the nicer buildings. Those, it seemed, were reserved for the more established Eilvyn and Iokans. Katia had been kind, helping her with her little cart that she ran by the docks. It had taken all her savings, years of toiling, to give Katia what she deserved for the place. Still, Silas hardly left her alone. If she were honest with herself, his continued patronage was half the reason she'd been able to build up any savings at all.

Zavalynn's help wasn't innocent, and she'd been around long enough to recognize his advances for what they were. Her heart just wasn't in it. He was a fine man with a high position in the court that allowed him respect and no small amount of responsibility; he also made her nervous. There was something else going on with him that she couldn't quite put her finger on and his disapproval of her selling to humans didn't help matters.

Casting aside her often troubled thoughts of her would-be suitor, Marin instead made a mental list of everything that had to be done before she could truly rest for the night. She stepped inside, taking in the warm tones of the bakery itself, and smiled. Katia had left out cloth bags, made bulky by their contents, and she could imagine what was inside. She made rolls, cookies, a variety of different breads, and fruit-filled hand pies that were so popular she'd rarely had leftovers. Marin knew that today Katia had made extra as a final goodbye.

A knock on her door and the jingling of the bells hung on the handle drew Marin's attention from her thoughts and she put on her best smile as she stood to greet her first customer. He was Human, as Katia had said he'd be, and he barely could make eye contact as he shuffled through her doorway.

"Evenin' miss," he said, gripping his worn patchwork hat in pitch-stained hands.

"Good evening. Katia left some things out for you," she said, ushering him closer and moving behind the counter. She handed him the first bag, and his eyes widened at the heft of it.

"She was mighty kind," he said, peering inside before digging into his pocket. "Here, miss. Katia said you'd be taking over from now on?"

Marin knew what he was really asking, and she nodded even as she felt the small hexagonal gemstone drop in her palm.

"Yes, I'll be opening tomorrow morning, just as Katia would. You and anyone else is more than welcome to come by at any time," she said. He nodded politely and bid her goodnight, giving her one last appraising glance before he stepped out.

She couldn't help but smile at his retreating figure, playing with the small caliot. Katia had told her that some Humans insisted on paying properly, with the highest value currency they were paid, but others would prefer a trade of goods. She didn't mind.

Human dockhands and servants knocked on her door well into the evening on their way home from a long day's work, whispering shy greetings and leaving with whatever Katia had prepared for them. She used that time to explore the small kitchen and get accustomed to how things were situated. Katia had let her use her ovens these past couple of years, as her cart had none and her own home wasn't equipped for the workload required, so she already knew she'd be changing a thing or two. As the evening went on, she eventually opted for what she hoped was a comfortable and welcoming silence. They'd grown to love Katie; given time, she hoped they'd do the same for her.

She accepted various payments—small bags of flour, charcoal and carved quills, and even a handmade knitted scarf that she couldn't help but stare at well after the customer had left. *If only they were allowed to sell in the central market*, she thought sadly, *they'd make a fortune.* She could bring it up to Zavalynn, but she knew what his answer would be. Humans were restricted across Tunsealior, a result of thousands of years of persecution, but Sienma had some of the strictest laws in the Coalition. Competing with Iokan or Eilvyn merchants was out of the question.

Her door's small bells chimed again, and she carefully stowed the scarf far from her floured table as she looked up; Marin froze in a moment of surprise, her hand still clutching the soft yarn. The Human who had ducked inside wasn't alone. With her was a woman she slowly placed as an Azha, albeit an Azha the like of which she'd never seen before. Their kind were usually broad-shouldered and larger than life, their innate gift with fire making them cocky and aggressive — at least, that had been Marin's experience with the few she'd ever met. They were rare where she was from, and even more so this far north.

This woman, however, was wrapped in dirty wool and visibly injured; she hunched to the side and lurched with each step as though every muscle in her body were stiff and strained. Her wide, chiseled face was scuffed and her dark hair, pulled back into a loose braid that left wisps around her face, was caked with dust from her travels. She must have only just arrived in the city.

"Miss," the young human said in greeting, her wide eyes darting between Marin and her newest customer. "Erm... she was asking for food and I thought since you're the only one still open that maybe you could help?"

"Of course, love, I'll take it from here," she said, smoothly coming around the counter to hand her a bag and holding the door open for her as she made her escape into the darkened street. It closed firmly and Marin directed her gaze, and her smile, onto the newcomer. "So, what can I help you with?"

The woman looked around the bakery curiously. She wasn't young, per say, but she certainly wasn't old either. Marin found it difficult to place the age of any of the four Iokan peoples. As they were blessed with the powers of the natural elements and with long lives, it was anyone's guess whether someone was sixty or three hundred. Her own people, the

Eilvyn, were like that too, so she figured this woman would have similar issues trying to see where Marin fell.

"You serve humans, then?" she asked, her voice raspy and dry as she nodded her head toward the few remaining bags on the counter. Marin almost had to lean forward just to hear her and the woman grimaced as she took an unsteady step back.

"Is that a problem?" Marin asked, unable to keep the sudden edge out of her voice. Most of her peers disapproved, and she'd heard numerous tales from Katia of how difficult it had proven to be for her business and had told Marin that she'd lost plenty of customers once the other Iokans and Eilvyn found out. Marin figured it would be the same for her, but it had been one of Katia's terms of sale. She wouldn't send the Humans away.

The Azha shook her head slowly. "No, that's not what I meant. I'm just surprised. Could I buy one?" she asked, gesturing at the bags. Marin handed it to her wordlessly, but her mouth dropped open when the woman pulled out a small pouch and she heard the rattle of stones and coins. As she picked through it, clearly looking for the right amount, Marin could see her hands bore thick scars that trailed up into her sleeves. They looked as though they'd only recently healed, and the new patches were shiny against her warm skin.

"It's just one caliot if you've got it," she said quickly, not wanting to see how much she had. No average traveler would carry that much money on their person unless they were intent on settling down. Not that anyone would dare rob an Azha — that was a death sentence just waiting to happen. Still, she'd never seen an Azha injured or even scarred. She'd heard that they healed faster than most, faster than even she did as an Eilfe. Clearly she'd heard wrong if one could end up in this state.

"Know anything about lodging?" the woman asked,

handing her three caliots. Her skin felt flushed to the touch and she retracted her hand from Marin's quickly.

Marin's smile almost turned to a frown as she thought, looking down at the coins. She'd overpaid, perhaps in exchange for information? The woman needn't have bothered; Marin would have helped her regardless. "There are more than a few inns and some are better than most if you've got the money. The Dancing Clover is the cheapest, although I wouldn't necessarily recommend it." She wouldn't go there if they paid her to, but this Azha could probably handle it just fine. "What brings you to Erengate?"

The woman shrugged and winced. "Looking for a change," she said, her eyes landing everywhere but on Marin. "I stopped by an inn closer to the gate but it didn't seem like a good fit."

If it was the inn that immediately came to mind, Marin wasn't surprised they'd turned her away, even if she was an Azha. Most places that catered to Eilvyn had strict dress codes, after all, and reputations to uphold.

"Why don't you stop by in the morning?" Marin said, surprising the woman into eye contact. Her eyes weren't normal for an Azha; she'd heard that they had gray eyes, oddly warm and bright but still solid through and through. The oddity was one of the few ways you could easily identify an Azha from Humans, if they didn't make it obvious by using their element first. This woman's eyes were speckled with orange and red and reminded Marin of smoldering coals. "I was new to the city not too long ago and I know how these people can be. It's helpful to have a friend."

The woman's eyes narrowed as she took Marin in and thought about her offer. She eventually nodded. "That'd be fine." she said. "Thank you." It was an afterthought, just the barest courtesy, but Marin let it go and smiled brightly.

"Lovely. I'm Marin Agata," she said, holding out her

hand. The woman looked at it, let it hang there, and Marin eventually let it fall back by her side.

"Tamora," the woman said as she turned on her heel and left both the bakery and Marin, who stared after her, a pensive frown growing on her face.

Chapter 1

Tamora

From the tree line Tamora could look out over the fields and take in Erengate in all its gray and frozen glory. Winter, the months of Dakelt and Yatés, had not been kind this year. The grim stone wall that surrounded the city rose out of the snow-crusted fields like a mountain, towering over everything in the surrounding valley. She could make out the torches of the guards that monitored the wall, flickering out against the darkness as they waited for sunrise. Tamora's hill, as she'd often considered it, started well in the dark forest and allowed her to walk at a slight decline much of the way to the northern gate. The only issue, she reminded herself with a grimace, was that it'd be a slower uphill walk on her return journey.

She set out. Her body's natural warmth cleared the snow with every step and where she'd paused was a circle of melted snow that she knew would refreeze shortly. It'd make the return journey all the more difficult, she was sure. When she'd chosen Erengate as her new home she hadn't realized that ice would prove one of her strongest opponents. She'd never had to consider it before — it had simply melted away in her presence. Now the icicles that hung off her cottage's roof were nearly two feet long and there was little she could do about it. Many years ago she'd realized it was best to stay inside for the season and pretend the cold didn't exist.

The guard on duty preferred napping to his post and she cleared the main gate easily, simply nodding at the half-asleep Iokan man. She wasn't quite sure which of her kind he was, but it hardly mattered. He wasn't Azhan, and that was all she cared about. She'd only seen a handful of her mother's people this far north and most thought her insane for leaving their far warmer homeland. Given the region he was likely Veden, as Erengate was originally a Veden city before the Eilvyn invasion and subsequent settling, or perhaps Mago. Upon second thought, she doubted that. Her father's people were, as their element, stout and earthy people. The guard didn't seem the type.

Tamora stifled the smells of the city with the edge of her hood and stepped carefully over the cobblestones as she made her way past the outer wall. Aged and uneven, these stones had been her downfall too many times for her to trust them now; she could still feel the burn of embarrassment from the first time she'd slipped on the ice that tended to cling to the streets well past the official end of winter. Besides, she didn't need to look up at the buildings to know where she was going. This time of day they were wrapped in a thick haze, the fog that rolled off the sea filling the streets with salty brine. Most of the buildings in this district were at least two stories, a mix of older stone establishments and newer wooden homes and storefronts, and they all loomed overhead silently and shuttered until daybreak.

The city still made her hair stand on end, even after more than seventy years. It smelled like the sewer had flooded the streets one too many times and during the day, when all the merchants and traders shouted over one another, it was impossible to hear your own thoughts. She found the early morning to be the most bearable.

A gust of wind caught Tamora's hood and she swore,

trying to force it back over her face as her hand went to the dagger on her hip. The people in this city preyed on the weak and she hadn't been thought of as dangerous for decades now. She glared in the direction it had come but there was no lingering sign of any wind at all. This patch of the main street was grimy and covered in a fine layer of sand, and just inside the alley on her small stoop was a woman who looked out at her with outstretched hands. Her porch was clean of any dirt and the woman smiled apologetically and wagged her fingers in greeting.

"Sorry, ma'am, didn't mean to catch you off guard," she said, her voice too loud for the quiet peace of the early morning. The woman turned away and continued to wave her hands loosely around her. Small tendrils of air, visible only by the dust they carried with them, whipped up and swept a night's worth of dust and caked mud from her entry. Tamora stepped quickly past, not wanting the mess to add to the disaster that already was the bottom hem of her cloak.

"Morning," she muttered as she wiped her hand across her cheek, seeing no evidence of dust or grime left over from the Tri's morning chore. They were always hasty to show off and with their element being air, it just made it so easy for them. She'd heard, years ago, that they hardly had to train to be able to harness the wind. It had been something she and her year mates back in school had never hesitated to bash them for. It just hadn't seemed fair.

The streets still smelled, although it was muted by the cold wind and snow that lay in the corners, now blackened and half melted. One thing that did surprise her was the lack of Humans; usually, even at this time of day, she would have run into a handful begging for caliots. It was the only form of money Humans were allowed to possess, the lowest form of currency in the Coalition. She passed by their usual alleys and peered in, despite herself, but saw that they were empty. The gate to the Harbor District was guarded in only the loosest of senses; the Eilfe waved her through with hardly a glance and she passed beneath one of the inner walls. Divided into uneven quarters, Erengate was unique in Sienma for its adherence to tradition. Eilvyn and Iokans could largely travel at will through the lower three quarters — Trading, Harbor, and Lower Districts — but the Upper District was reserved for nobility and their households. She'd never been past the Upper Gate and was not inclined to try. From what she'd seen, the nobility were more trouble than they were worth.

The harbor was more relaxed than the Trading District; the shop owners dealt mostly with sailors and locals rather than merchants and there was a general understanding that constant haggling and bartering would rarely end with everyone satisfied. Only a few people had managed to hold onto enough savings to make a difference here. Those who did, like Marin, had always looked out for the District. She'd certainly put in the work over the years, and Tamora was glad to see her enjoy some level of respect. Marin had been there the day she'd arrived in Erengate and she'd supported her every step of the way.

Tamora had just made it past the frigid docks, largely empty until spring officially arrived with the month of Maken, when she caught a faint whiff of Marin's morning bake. Her mouth watered and she picked up the pace as best she could, the lure of freshly baked bread, sweet molten jams, and spiced cakes enough for her to push through. Marin's treats had that effect on people.

The four stone steps of Marin's stoop stood in her way but Tamora, as always, refused to let them best her. Still, she leaned heavily on the wrought-iron rail as she stepped up to the door. She pretended that it gave her a moment to admire the handrail. Marin had insisted on it, something Tamora had always teased her for as the woman couldn't even bear the touch the damn thing. She had to admit that it was a beautiful work of art, with its vines and carefully shaped flowers, and even the most hesitant of Eilvyn would agree. Most still refused to trust the thick lacquer encasing it that theoretically protected them. Marin had always been more fanciful than she probably should be.

The stained glass in the door's small window rattled slightly in its fitting as Tamora knocked. *Lark really should fix that for his mother*, she thought, waiting a moment before rapping on the wood again. The calm of the street made her wait easier but her stomach was already growling, despite the breakfast she'd had just an hour earlier.

She knocked a third time.

A woman's soprano voice rang out from within. "We aren't open yet. At least wait for the sun to rise."

Tamora knew that voice and she could picture the scowl that likely accompanied it. Eloise Wyatt hated a great many things and pushy customers were high on the list.

"Eloise, let Marin know I'm here," she called back.

She heard shuffling from inside the bakery and a heavy drop, accompanied by muffled swearing. The door swung open. Eloise ducked her head out, her brown skin flushed from the heat within, and looked up and down the street and noticed the few servants out cleaning porches before smiling broadly up at Tamora. The warm gust that rushed out behind her smelled of baked bliss.

"Come in, come in, before anyone else sees you," she urged. Her hair was stuck to her forehead and her breath was sharp; she ushered Tamora in and closed the door heavily behind her. The bells on the handle rang, a clear and crisp sound that always made Tamora feel welcome. "We can't let them know we're willing to open early."

"I'm sorry to interrupt—" she began, feeling suddenly guilty.

Eloise cut her off with a shake of her head as she locked

14

the door. "Ma'am, I'm so sorry. We aren't really ready for customers yet and I thought you might be someone else," she said, her smile creasing her pale eyes and bringing a warm glow to her soft rounded features.

"Someone else? At this hour?" Tamora teased, but Eloise's smile dimmed slightly and she snapped her mouth shut, saying nothing. After an uncomfortable moment, Tamora cleared her throat. "Well, in any case, don't call me 'ma'am', you understand? I delivered you after all," she reminded Eloise with a grin.

The girl blushed and glanced away. Such a Human reaction. "All the more reason, ma'am," she replied.

Tamora took her outstretched arm gratefully even as she rolled her eyes. Eloise was a grown woman now, approaching her twenty-fourth birthday, but she could still picture her as a newborn. Even then she'd had a delightful spunk.

"Even your mother doesn't call me that."

Eloise shrugged. "Just seems wrong to change it now. You're an important woman. Ma'am," she said pointedly, allowing herself a small smile before turning to her unfinished work. There was a mass of rolled and cut dough out, the countertop floured and waiting for her return. She hardly gave Tamora another look as she gestured to the aged table and chairs that sat to the left of the door. "I'm just finishing up this loaf, feel free to wait. Mistress Agata should be right down."

Tamora nodded and let the young woman run to her station. She flitted around the kitchen with the energy of a small bird; Tamora had to remind herself that she had the gift of youth. Not to mention good health.

"When do you get here, Eloise?" she asked, settling into her usual chair with a sigh.

"I've been here for a few hours now, just getting things ready. I have a key," she said proudly, laying into the mess of doughy braids with a concentrated frown.

"As you should," Tamora said, looking around. The place hadn't changed much since she'd come in on her first night, weary from travel and a stranger in a city she'd found surprisingly standoffish. It shouldn't have been that shocking — times had been tough back then. People had still been scared; Krys's rebellion, short lived though it was, had only fallen had seen rebels lurking behind every corner. The bakery was warm and welcoming, with scuffed wooden floors and a sturdy stone-topped counter that she'd watched Marin at for decades now. She watched as Eloise worked and marveled; Marin never made it easy for herself, or her employees for that matter. Eloise was the second, after the last assistant had grown too old and stiff in the joints to keep up with the pace. For years the woman's grandson had come by Tamora's cottage for ointment, paid in full by Marin each month.

Tamora idly rapped her fingers on the table, content to wait. Marin always started her own work as the sun was rising, never earlier. It was a far cry from how she'd begun; back then Marin worked day and night to keep the place running and to feed all the hungry mouths that came to her. Eloise's comment earlier came to mind as well. Who else would come calling this early? *If Zavalynn has been bothering Marin again I swear he'll regret it,* she thought sourly, almost wishing she'd run into him one of these days. Marin was never strict enough with the man — he came by whenever he pleased and bought her entire stock, something he'd gotten in the habit of doing in the fall when people needed Marin's help the most. He knew exactly who he was taking food from, and that Marin could do very little to stop him.

Her musings were interrupted when she realized what exactly Eloise was struggling with, finally seeing a recognizable shape in the dough. "Is that a Basana Loaf? Already?" she asked, frowning. The first day of spring was still many weeks away; winter was only just beginning to recede.

"Who on earth would order that now?"

"Special order," Eloise grunted, coaxing and stretching the stuffed dough into the intricate design.

Tamora snorted and her fingers stilled. *It must be an Eilfe, one of the nobles. Who else would break tradition so brazenly?* They ruled the city after all; Erengate hardly followed Coalition standards. It hadn't taken her long to notice, all those years ago, that most of the city council were Eilvyn, as were most of the guards. While the Coalition might dictate on paper that power was to be split evenly between the Eilvyn and the four Iokan peoples, it rarely played out that way in practice. Erengate had originally been a Veden city, back before the Eilvyn had come to these shores. Now Veden were frequently outnumbered in major cities. Her own people, the Azha, were a rarity here. Her only connection to anything approximating her culture was through the other Iokans, the collective peoples blessed by the goddess Ioka with gifts of elemental power, and this far north there were mostly the Veden, who held the gift of water and ice, and the Mago, with power over earth and stone. Hardly her kin, despite her mixed heritage. No one had yet noticed that she had any Mago in her at all, and she wasn't inclined to share her history. No, she was just the crippled Azha here.

"Was it an Eilvyn customer?" she asked after a little time had passed, unable to stifle her curiosity. The Basana Loaf was a dish traditional to the Mago, filled to the brim with nuts, herbs, and dried fruit, representing the earth reborn as summer was at its height. It was delicious, made more so by its rarity, and not something most people would order outside the season.

Eloise's braided hair, dusted with flour and coming undone at the base, fell over her shoulder as she looked over at Tamora.

"You already know the answer," she replied wryly. "One

of the Karkas ladies — sounds like they're having a feast. Ordered it yesterday."

"Of course it's a Karkas—" Tamora grimaced, the sound of light footsteps overhead silencing her next words.

"Is someone with you, Eloise?" Tamora heard Marin call, the squeaky board on the staircase sounding as she came down from her and her sons' apartment. Eloise returned to her task with renewed vigor. Marin's smile was already in place and illuminating her sharp features as she pushed open the door at the staircase's end. She was radiant, as usual. Her hair was braided atop her head and wreathed her in a crown of gold, bright against the chocolate long-sleeved dress she wore with an easy grace. Her warm eyes drifted across the bakery, assessing, and alighted on Tamora sitting quietly at the side table.

"Morning, Marin," she said softly, knowing she'd hear her well enough. Eilvyn always could. It was really for Eloise's benefit that she tried to speak up. Her voice had long ago lost its ability to carry, settling into something more befitting an elderly man than an Azha of her young age. She was only two hundred and twenty-three, after all.

"Tamora! I'm so glad you're here!" Marin exclaimed, practically floating across the wooden floor between them. "I was going to send Lark with some things for you, but this makes everything so much easier. This past week has been terrible, hasn't it? I was afraid we'd all freeze solid."

She rambled when she was excited and Tamora was content to let her keep going. She never tired of hearing about the minutiae of the bakery's day to day.

"I needed some things. Can't grow everything in my little pots, no matter how hard I try. How's Sorrell?" she asked, hoping for good news.

Marin threw herself into the chair opposite her with a

sudden exaggerated huff. Her porcelain skin was stark against her dress and the warm homey colors of the bakery, and the flickering lamp on the table cast small shadows across her face.

"Thank the Eight he's doing well and finally keeping down food. You have no idea how hard it was to watch him begin to grow thin," she said, shaking her head. She reached over, grasping Tamora's hand for the briefest of moments. "I truly can't thank you enough," she said, squeezing once before releasing her.

Tamora allowed herself to release a relieved breath. "I'm glad. It was a rough break, Marin, he's lucky. I'd love to talk to him later to make sure he knows what to expect. He'll have a limp." She hesitated to admit it, but it wouldn't help any of them to mince truths. Eilvyn healed fast, Marin would know that well enough, but her boys were half-Human. It was anyone's guess exactly how long it would be before he was on his feet again.

Tamora caught a flash of a frown as it crossed Marin's face before her mask of pleasant placidity settled back into place. It was unnerving, sometimes, to see her so unfazed. She knew Marin didn't like others to worry, but she'd almost been glad to see her upset the night of Sorrell's accident. At least it was something more than what Tamora suspected was often false positivity.

"I've already told the boys that they aren't to go back to those docks. Too many unreliable people, and moldy boards to boot," Marin said, shaking her head. Tamora said nothing, just nodding along. It wasn't her place to challenge Marin when it came to her sons. Still, the break didn't match with what Lark had said happened. She distinctly remembered him saying that Sorrell had tripped and fallen off the dock, his leg hitting a rock in the shallows. The bone had split his skin and she'd known immediately it would be infected; sure enough, she'd spent four days tending to him until the fever had broken. It'd been a week since she'd left them.

It was odd enough that he'd fallen, and stranger still that the boys were so quiet about the ordeal. They were both light on their feet, after all, and far from clumsy.

Marin sighed heavily, glancing back at Eloise to make sure the girl was still working. She'd moved on to sweet rolls, a specialty of Marin's that she'd spent years securing a stable supply of ingredients for. Even some of the merchants from the Trading District ventured this way to snag a few when they were fresh.

"It's so hard to keep an eye on them," Marin admitted, speaking softly. "Now that Sorrell is stuck at home it's been a little easier, sure, but I swear Lark has doubled his efforts. He's gone most of the day, rarely coming back before sundown, and I hate that I don't know the company he keeps."

"They are almost fifty, Marin," Tamora said gently. "You can't protect them forever." Her friend nodded with her own brand of long-suffering sighs.

"I know that, of course. But you can't stop a mother from trying," she said. She peered over at Tamora. "You wouldn't know anything about that... would you?"

Tamora snorted. Marin was always trying to weasel more information out of her about her past, something she'd never caved into. Some things were best left alone.

"Definitely not."

Marin sat back, disappointed. It was a hobby of hers to imagine all sorts of sordid deeds, past lovers, and no small number of illegitimate children scattered across the continent. Tamora had no idea what she'd done to make Marin think that any of that was at all possible. *If only she could know the truth*, Tamora thought ruefully, *then she'd understand just how impossible that all was.*

She decided to flip the tables, for once, and narrowed her

eyes at her friend. "So, I hear you often get some early morning visitors," she said. Marin looked sharply over at Eloise, who was suddenly very intent on her egg wash.

"Where'd you hear that?"

A shrug was all the answer she was going to get. "A curious old woman hears things," Tamora said. Marin's polite snort widened her smile.

"You aren't old, Tamora, I can tell. Not as old as I am, at any rate. You're just... well... different," she trailed off, as though she'd realized she'd begun to say something that could be insulting. She'd always been careful not to bring too much attention to the fact that she was curious, but Tamora knew well enough there was no sense in pretending. Everyone stared. Azha were rare enough, but a crippled Azha with no Guardian? She was likely the only of her kind in all of Tunsealior.

She laughed, letting Marin relax with relief. "You can say it, I know I'm no doll," she said. There was little point in hiding it.

She was average height for an Azha, towering over most Humans even crooked as she now was, and her light brown skin bore the scars of too many stories to count. Her tattoos were typical of any Iokan and she should have been proud to bear them for all to see, but the scars from her Spiraling on the Gwen Plains had marred her skin and rendered nearly every marking illegible. Now no one saw her without her full-length sleeves and a stiff collar that latched at her collarbones; she already drew too much attention simply by existing. She was lucky she hadn't scarred her face. Tamora leaned back in her chair, rubbing the joint of her hip out of habit.

"I suppose. Anyway, you wouldn't believe the number of orders we've gotten just in the last week. I thought we'd have a bit more time before things picked up," Marin said, easily changing the subject. She never liked to dwell long.

"Mhm. People just want to get outside again," said Tamora. The cold was clinging more than it usually did and as Marin has said, it had been a tough season. Her own mention of Sorrell drew her thoughts back to his injury. Marin should have been able to take him to the Physician's Guild; Tamora was far from an expert. Everything she knew had come second-hand and she mostly dealt with minor tonics and at most a sore throat or chill that refused to let up. If they'd been able to get him to the Guild, Sorrell might not have been caught by infection.

Marin stood, her fingers twitching as she looked at the dough still on the counter.

"Eloise, darling, I'm going to take care of this. Could you make sure we're looking put together?" Eloise hurriedly took off her apron and, pausing only to hang it beside the oven, set about sweeping the front room. Marin checked the oven, waiting a moment before she was satisfied.

"Did you see many folks this winter?"

"Just a handful. You know not many people want to make the trip," Tamora said, frowning.

"To your haunted forest, you mean," Marin scoffed. She mixed ingredients by feel and watched it all come together beneath her hands. It was immensely satisfying watching Marin work and Tamora never grew tired of it. She also knew, though, that working was Marin's best distraction.

"It isn't haunted," she countered, standing and limping over to the counter. "That's just a rumor to stop people from poaching, you know that as well as I do." Marin just shrugged.

Tamora knew she was worried, that she would drive herself into the ground if it meant helping her sons. Sorrell's injury had taken a lot from her, as had the rejection at the Upper Gate. Normally, Eilvyn and most Iokans could pass freely into the Upper District. Her boys, however, were *Joien*.

Half-Human and half-Eilvyn. Even in the largest of cities that was a dangerous thing to be, and in a relatively remote place like Erengate they were one, well, two of a kind.

She hadn't asked much when she'd been treating Sorrell a week earlier; she'd been too focused on his injuries.

"I'm sorry, Marin, I really am," she said softly. She'd seen the writing on the wall when the boys were born and had warned Marin that this might happen — she'd never wanted to listen.

Marin smiled miserably, knowing immediately what she was referring to, and leaned back against the counter. The batch of molasses cookies lay forgotten on the metal sheet. Eloise, sweeping the main room, was trying to melt into the floorboards.

"You know I don't regret it, not at all. William was the best man I've ever met. But it's hard for the boys and I'm not blind, I see it too. They have no friends their age, none of the Eilvyn children would ever play with them and now... now I just watch them struggle and there's nothing I can do," she said, waving her hands helplessly.

Tamora didn't say anything. She felt lucky to have known William; he'd met Marin ten years after Tamora had arrived in the city and the boys had come along almost a decade later. William had passed nearly twenty years ago now, well into his eighties. He'd loved to tell the tale of their marriage and the uproar it had created in Marin's social circles while drinking his nightly cordial, as though Tamora hadn't been there to witness it herself.

"In any case, if it was fated to happen, I'm glad it wasn't now," Marin said, shaking her head. "Everyone is getting antsy now, with the weather starting to calm. You know how the spring season gets. They might have locked us away for trying."

Tamora scowled. Every spring, almost like clockwork, Erengate's nobility embarked on a scouring of the city. A fresh slate, they called it. Anyone who stood out, especially Humans and those who catered to them, were at risk of drawing their attention. Seeing Marin's miserable expression, she swallowed the angry words that sat at the tip of her tongue and decided to lighten the mood.

"I'm sure Lark and I could break you out easily enough, he's a sneaky rascal. Got in and out of my cottage this winter before I even noticed, did he tell you? I turned around from the fire and suddenly your damn sweet rolls were on my counter," Tamora said, chuckling at the thought of him lurking in the shadows.

"He's crazy, that's for sure. Sneaking up on you is a death wish most days," Marin laughed. Tamora was just happy to see the light coming back into her friend's face. After a few moments of staring at the tray of rolls in front of her, Marin shook her head. "Thanks, Tamora, really. You've done more for me than I care to admit. Sorrell and I both owe you a great deal."

Tamora felt the discomfort of her smile stretch her face. "Anything for a friend," she said, truly meaning it. She hoped Marin knew how much.

They fell into comfortable silence, allowing Tamora to think over her errands. She wanted to be strategic and to spend as little time within the city's walls as possible. Her diet had consisted of mostly salted beef and Marin's rolls for some time now, and while they were delicious, it had gotten pretty old. There was also the matter of her pain; she needed more herbs for tinctures and balms, and only a few people in the city stocked them.

"Well," Tamora cleared her throat, "I guess I'll be off then. It's getting bright out there. Maybe some merchants have made the trip north; I imagine southern Sotwifas didn't have as tough a winter as us."

Marin's face fell at the mention of their neighbor to the east, a sprawling country that took up most of the western half of the continent of Tunsealior. It was a diverse land, with volcanoes to the southwest stretching toward Ozhansa and vast forests that stretched for miles before falling into deep ravines and lakes. Tunsealior was made up of the seven countries of the Coalition and, to the south, the Human country of Adbeter. Tamora had traveled most of it in her younger years. Those days were far behind her now.

"I doubt it," Marin muttered, frowning at Tamora. "You haven't heard? There have been riots in the south all through the winter, and before that up in Graenaka."

"What? That's an odd place to start something," Tamora said, frowning. Graenaka was an isolated country, sprawling and rocky, on the easternmost coast of Tunsealior. The Coalition of Eilvyn and Iokans, who had ruled over the continent for centuries now, had made their stronghold of Koren in the southernmost reaches of their Black Mountains and heavily patrolled the entire southern border. If Tamora had been in charge, she'd have chosen Erengate as her target. It was responsible for the production of one of their currencies, harvested from seashells native to the region, and they were far enough from Koren that it would take months for any sizable force to respond.

"Is it?" Marin asked, shrugging. "I think they burned down granaries during the last harvest festival, while everyone was celebrating. Ruined their stores for the winter, and the city had to borrow from the Coalition."

"I'm sure that didn't make them any friends," Tamora said, shaking her head. The last thing you wanted to do, if you were really trying to start a rebellion, was make everyday people your enemies.

"No, they've had a heavy Sentinel presence ever since,

from what I heard," Marin agreed. Tamora shuddered at the thought; one of the reasons she'd chosen Erengate had been the relative lack of patrolling from Sentinels, the Coalition's roaming peacekeepers. "Even though the Merchants' Guild has put out a bounty on them, since the Coalition made them cover for the granary, they are still causing trouble all across Tunsealior — it's just not safe anymore," she finished, shaking her head.

Tamora tried not to laugh; Marin didn't deserve it. In her opinion, it had never really been safe. She knew how tensions could rise at the drop of a hat, especially when the Coalition decided to acknowledge a threat. That kind of attention could set everyone on edge.

Marin continued, not noticing Tamora's reaction. "I think the High Council is going to take action soon—"

"That's rarely a good thing for anyone. They tend to burn things down first and ask questions later. Do people know what they want?" Tamora asked. Her stomach was tightening into knots.

"What they always want," Marin said, with no shortage of disdain. "The Council is being accused of negligence and cruelty; those do seem to be conflicting charges, no? They're spreading word across Tunsealior in whatever way they can, it isn't always a riot. Terrible things are scrawled on walls or shouted from a street corner."

"If you even see it before the person is dragged off," Eloise noted, her hand holding the broom loosely.

"I think it's time for you to sweep the stoop, dear," Marin said firmly.

"Sorry, ma'am."

Tamora frowned, partially at Marin and partially at what she'd shared. These rebels didn't seem very sophisticated, nor smart. None of her old friends would be so reckless. At least, she hoped not. As for Marin, she didn't seem nearly as understanding as Tamora would have expected.

"So, is it an uprising then?" she asked. She thought Marin's eyes would bulge from her face.

"I'd hardly say that," she snapped. "It isn't anything like the last, if that's what you're asking."

Tamora flinched at the sudden almost physical pain in her chest. "Why would you say that?"

Marin shrugged, turning to rotate the massive Basana loaf in the oven. "Because it's what's on everyone's mind. Believe in his cause or not, no one can deny that Krystopher Reene left a mark on Tunsealior and each of her countries."

Tamora couldn't argue with that, although his name dug into her heart like a knife. He'd certainly left his mark on her.

The bells on the door rang and Eloise burst in, quickly shutting it behind her.

"Pardon me, but they're here," she said, rubbing her hands together to warm them. Tamora gestured for her to come near and held her fingers with her own; it took only a few moments for her body heat to put feeling back into the girl's frozen hands.

Marin sighed again — frustration was something Tamora seemed uniquely capable of drawing out of her. "You don't mind?" she turned, sparing a small smile for her guest.

Tamora just chuckled and gathered her bag. She could take a hint. "Not at all, you've got a business to run after all. You've given me a lot to think about."

Marin snorted. "I'm sure. Stop by on your way out of town, alright? Sorrell will want to see you."

"Will do," she said as she opened the door. Gray morning light was coming over the wall and it was beginning to brighten the streets. She caught Eloise's watchful eye as she waved farewell. The girl looked at Marin, who gestured to her, and she wrapped her cloak around her with a sudden purposeful gaze.

"Wait, ma'am, just a minute," she said, catching the door and coming closer to Tamora than she thought the girl had intended. Eloise stared past her at the forming line, those at the front eyeing the open door hungrily, and closing it carefully behind her. "Um... could we talk? Somewhere private?"

Tamora ignored the antsy crowd, stepping down the stairs carefully. "This way, Eloise," she said, watching the girl try not to look anyone in the eye. The morning group were Eilvyn and Iokans, with few Human Guardians in the mix, and wouldn't bat an eye at seeing Eloise publicly disciplined for seeming rude or unwelcoming. Marin would never, but the threat was always there from others in the city.

She turned just down the street, far enough she didn't think Eilvyn hearing would be able to pick them out over the wind. "Alright, Eloise, what's wrong?"

A small shuffle brought the girl face to face with Tamora and she bent closer to whisper. "It's my father, ma'am. He's been arrested for treason, and I need your help."

Chapter 2

Marin

Marin said nothing as she watched Eloise run after Tamora. She knew that Eloise had been working up the nerve to ask someone for help; Tamora's arrival may as well have been a gift from the Wela. Her propensity for helping Humans wrongfully jailed was an open secret in the Lower District — Marin had tried convincing her of the danger, but Tamora never listened. Still, it was for the best. Bear Wyatt had been in jail for nearly a week now and Eloise and her poor mother had both been slowly unraveling.

She checked the Basana Loaf; it seemed to be browning nicely. Eloise had done well with this one; Adelina Karkas would be pleased. It was out of season but Adelina was a friend, and she'd paid a premium to cover the ingredients that had been more difficult to source. Marin looked around the shop, rolling on the balls of her feet, and debated letting the crowd in. It wouldn't do her any good to put it off. Now that Sorrell was bedridden all his responsibilities fell on Lark, and he'd have to make quick work of her deliveries if he wanted to have any free time at all.

Her conversation with Tamora dwelled on her mind as she opened the door and smiled broadly at the line of customers. She'd never met anyone who enjoyed arguing as much. That was a lie, she admitted to herself. William had been much the same. Perhaps that was why they had all gotten along so well. Tamora and William used to go at it for hours — nothing had been safe. It had made her life so vibrant.

Everything about William had made her life better. Early on in their relationship everyone she had known had asked her the same question; why? He was a Human, many years her junior, and their union would make her a social pariah. Her father, who still wrote her monthly letters, had even visited in person to try to talk some sense into her. She'd told him what she'd told everyone – she loved William. He'd captivated her from the first moment and she couldn't imagine a life not having known him. Now that he was gone, after a blessedly long life for a Human, she was just grateful for the time they'd shared.

Even as she filled orders and soothed hungry stomachs, she couldn't keep her anxieties at bay. Life seemed to contain so many unknowns. She'd planned on taking Lark and Sorrell down to Vasna years ago to start their formal education but life had always seemed to get in the way. Her parents had connections that could get them into the finest academy, after a few years of private tutoring, and she knew the boys were so excited to get out of Erengate. That had never been the issue. No, she'd kept them out of society. It was out of selfishness, she knew. She'd meant to let them attend school at the appropriate time, and she and William had frequently talked about what she'd do after he passed, but when it had come down to it she just hadn't been able to see it through. The thought of living in this house that they'd shared, all alone, simply broke her heart. Now, with the riots, she was second-guessing her plans once again. Next year would be fine. There was no rush. She'd known a man in her own class who hadn't started at their academy until he was forty-five, and the boys weren't much older than that.

The door swung open and shut just as quickly, the bells chiming loudly. "Eloise, could you help me with the pastries?"

she asked, before seeing the girl's face. Her eyes were puffy and her cheeks red. Marin excused herself from the man before her and came around the counter. "What's wrong?"

"I'm so sorry but I have to run home," Eloise said, her voice rough. "Tamora said — well, I need to speak with my mother. I can be back by mid-morning?"

Marin nodded, gathering the girl into a hug. "Of course, dear, whatever you need." Eloise practically leapt out the door, a quick thank you trailing in the air after her. Marin took a deep breath before straightening her spine and getting back to it.

.....

Marin managed the early rush and made sure each customer left happy, all too aware of how her popularity had grown since she'd first opened. Back when she started, this would have been a piece of cake, pardoning the pun. Now, though, managing without Eloise was difficult to say the least. New customers filled all available space, and she was at the end of her rope when Eloise finally did return. Despite her hectic start, she was glad that the hours passed in a blur of commotion and happy conversation. It made it harder to dwell on her thoughts.

She left Eloise to handle the much more reasonable crowd and leapt up her stairs, remembering as always to hop over the bothersome step third from the top. The moment of blissful muted quiet as she closed the door cleared her mind almost instantaneously, as it always did.

Her eyes were still closed when a finger jabbed into her ribs. "Oh!" she shrieked, immediately batting at the source. "Lark, I swear to Afina if you do that again I'll—"

Lark's eyes nearly glowed with devilish glee. "You're done with the morning rush?"

"And I didn't see you helping," she said, glaring up at him. He'd inherited her family's height. William had been so

31

small. She'd loved that about him. "There's nothing left for you, we've still got customers down there."

"Not even a scone?" he asked, his face falling.

She had to laugh at his abrupt disappointment. "If you aren't your father's son. How's your brother?"

Lark shrugged. "Well enough. He was trying to walk around, but I told him you'd break his other leg if you caught him." Marin chuckled as she walked through the hall down to their private kitchen. It was cramped and worn, but in far better shape than when she'd gotten the place. The previous owner had almost run it into the ground and it'd taken years of saving and elbow grease to get it to where it was today. Now it was small, and a little thrown together, and it was home.

"Sounds about right, thank you for staying up here with him. You know how I worry," she said.

"I know, Mother, I know," he said, leaning against the door jam and rapping his fingers on the aging wood. She'd have to get around to painting that soon. "I was wondering if I could go do my errands now? The regulars will be missing us."

She eyed him carefully. He was being extra careful, clearly trying to make her forget that she'd caught him sneaking back home in the small hours of the morning. He and Sorrell had gotten themselves wrapped up in something, she was sure of it, and now that Sorrell was injured she was getting concerned. "If I tell you not yet, will you actually stay here? Don't lie to me."

Lark's eyed flitted to the side — his usual tell. "Well... I suppose I could help Eloise—"

"Alright, alright. Go, but be careful. I can't have both of you hurt, how would I get anything done?" she said with a small smile. *Maybe Tamora's right, I can't possibly keep them here. Lark especially, he's far too excitable.* Besides, he was fifty-three, and Sorrell two years his senior. If they were Humans, they would have moved out decades ago and although Eilvyn had different standards for adulthood, they were well on their way. *I can't keep treating them like children... no matter how much I might want to.*

"I won't get hurt," he replied with all the bravado a young man could muster. "Did I hear Tamora earlier?"

He asked innocently enough, but the tension behind his smile told her he'd heard their entire conversation. She winced. "Ah... yes. I've been thinking, Lark—"

He cut to the heart of the matter. "You're not going to let us go to Vasna this year, are you? Look... I know I don't give you much to really trust in, but you don't have to worry so much. Sorrell and I know what we're doing," he said, grinning in that lopsided way of his.

"I do trust you, Lark," she said, not knowing how to explain what she felt. They hadn't been alive during the rebellion nearly a century ago, and while this wasn't at that level the rumors she was hearing were eerily familiar. "What's going on in the east isn't something you can just write off. If the High Council does get involved it won't end well, and Sienma isn't so far removed from everything that we can just ignore it."

The idea that Lark or Sorrell might get caught up in anything dangerous was too much. Vasna was a major city, bigger than Erengate, and it would be just like them to get roped into something that turned out to be more than could handle.

"Sure, I know that," he said, a frown bringing down his almost permanent good cheer. Marin shook her head; this wasn't the time. She was too scattered and she didn't know what she wanted to say. He couldn't spring this on her like this.

"Just go on, enjoy the day. Be back by dinner, alright? And no sneaking off tonight or I'm chaining you in up here," she said. Lark grinned from ear to ear and kissed her on the cheek, bounding past her down the stairs.

She could hear him clamber through the customers below and run out the door; a sense of quiet returned to the home. *I'm too hard on them*, she thought. *Sometimes they just need to be the young men they are. Paroi knows I had my moments in my youth.* She locked the door behind him and padded down the hall, her feet quiet on the worn carpet lining the hall. Lark's room was the smallest and the door was closed; she looked curiously at it but continued on. He'd know instantly if she peeked inside. Sometimes she heard banging and what seemed like barely controlled chaos from behind that door, but he always assured her everything was fine when she became worried enough to knock.

Sorrell's room was open and she poked her head through the door. It creaked and he looked up from where he lay on the bed, the book in his hands falling to the side. "Mornin'. How was the rush?" he asked, his voice still holding onto a bit of the sweet higher pitch of his youth. They were so different, her boys.

"Nothing we couldn't handle, Eloise's got it under control now. We went through all the basil rolls, so it seems they'll be a more permanent addition," she said with a smile. She'd always known which of her sons would take over for her if she decided it was time to retire. That was still many decades off; Sorrell was bright and a quick study, but he was far from ready. Not to mention the fact that she had no idea what she'd do with herself if she stopped baking. "How does it feel today?"

He shrugged. "Not great, but I'm not dying. Lark helped me with the bandages a few hours ago so I'll be fine until tonight. I think it's healing well but we'll have to wait until Tamora can come back to be sure," he said softly. He always spoke softly, her Sorrell.

"Maybe later—"

"She's coming back?" he asked, sitting straighter. "I couldn't be sure, I was having trouble hearing you."

Marin nodded. They always eavesdropped. "She'll want to see you, so she'll come."

Sorrell leaned back in relief. "Oh alright, good."

"The two of you are usually so attentive — my little spies," she teased.

"Not our fault that you all talk so loud," he said.

Marin smiled faintly. An Eilfe with exceptional hearing was not extraordinary on its own. For Lark and Sorrell, though, it was different. She'd never heard of a *Joien* inheriting that particular trait. Then again, she realized, she hadn't met many Joien. Not for the first time, she wished William had been able to join her on this path. He'd lived a good long life, for a Human, but she and the boys still had so many years ahead of them. It just didn't seem fair that he couldn't see them grow into the men he'd been so sure they'd become.

"You okay?" Sorrell asked, cutting through her thoughts and echoing his brother.

"Fine! Wela, the two of you worry too much," she smiled brightly. He just rolled his eyes.

"That doesn't work on us, Mother. Did Tamora say something?" he asked, truly putting the book aside.

"Why would you think that?"

"Sometimes she says things that you pretend don't worry you and then you're in a bad mood all day until you go find her and apologize for getting upset," he said. His eyes were like flint, the bluish gray that he and his brother shared cutting through the dim light of his lantern. They were so alike in appearance, those two, but so different in every other aspect. Marin couldn't tell if she preferred Lark's rush to action or Sorrell's more pondering nature — in this moment, though, she wished she'd raised a less perceptive son.

"I don't do that," she said quickly.

He raised his brow. "Sure you don't."

Marin crossed the room and sat lightly beside him, pushing back his sandy hair with a sigh. "You're too good at this, Sorrell. You should work up in the Palace District, for Lord Fredman or Mistress Diana."

"And get myself killed? I don't think so," Sorrell snorted. "Besides, I'm useless to them now. No one wants a spy with a limp — it's too noticeable."

"I don't want you to be a spy, Sorrell, I was thinking something more along the lines of a bookkeeper," she said, frowning. "You're too smart to be a dockhand." She toyed with the edge of his blanket. He was outgrowing this room. Outgrowing this house — this city. The thought filled her with dread.

He shrugged. "Well, that's behind me now too. Maybe the vendors have an opening — I could start up a cart of your goods." Marin tossed away the blanket.

"We've been over this before, I just don't know that it's worth it." It had taken her so long to get out of a cart and establish her own storefront, after all. She wanted to leave that behind her.

"But you could break into a different market. Right by the docks is a great opportunity, it's so busy there —"

"We have enough business now, Sorrell. I'm not going to risk it. There's only Eloise and I down there."

"You could hire—"

"No, Sorrell. I know you want to help," she added, seeing the flash of bitter disappointment in his thin features. He looked so much like his father. "But I just don't think I can manage it right now. There's too much going on."

"You mean Zavalynn," he bit out. His eyes had gone flinty again.

"He's a part of it," she admitted.

"We should tell Lark he's been coming by, he'd run him off faster than you could say—"

Marin cut off the swear forming on his lips; he looked unabashed. "You know that's why he can't know. Zavalynn is dangerous and his friends are worse. The only reason you know is that you're too observant for your own good," she teased, trying to distract him. Sorrell simply looked up at her.

"He's been after you for years, Mother, and we all know it. Lark and I are not blind to the facts. Zavalynn is a powerful man and he's growing impatient — he isn't the kind of man you want frustrated with you." Marin tried not to look surprised; she feared that she failed at that when he rolled his eyes. *When did he get so insightful? Or so knowledgeable about Zavalynn?* That thought scared her more than any other.

"Zavalynn is a nuisance, an old friend, nothing more. Please don't worry about me. I do have things under control," she said, standing and smoothing her skirt. It was, thankfully, relatively free of flour. Sorrell had always been particular about these things, probably a result of growing up above a bustling bakery. "On that note, I need to check on Eloise. I'm sure she'll be needing me."

"Sure. Please tell Eloise I said good morning," he reminded her, looking bitter. He picked up his book and flipped to an earmarked page. Marin felt utterly dismissed. The creak of his door echoed through their quiet floor.

.....

Something in the air had told Marin that the rest of the day would give her little reprieve; she was proven correct. Customer after customer were frustrated with something or another and she ended up taking at least three of them aside for their tone with Eloise. By midday she was exhausted and wishing desperately that Sorrell was well enough to come downstairs and help her. Not that she'd ever ask that of him right now.

The door opened with a slight chime and she wouldn't have looked up save for the audible gasps from her crowd of customers. Her eyes darted to the door and she sighed, wiping the flour from her hands and pausing. He'd come on his own this time — she supposed she should be honored. Silas Zavalynn, tall and thickly bundled in a coat of sable fur, glared around at the stares of her patrons until they scattered. He'd always been like this and she felt a fool, thinking that he'd ever been her friend. Accompanying him were three other Eilvyn, each wrapped in lesser quality cloaks that were still far more expensive than anything she could afford. He gestured to his silent companions to clear the room but he hadn't needed to expend the effort; her customers had vanished within moments of his arrival. One even left a full bag of produce on her countertop.

"Lord Zavalynn, to what do I owe this pleasure?" Marin said with a slight nod, the closest to a bow he would ever receive from her.

He stared across the counter at her as though offended. "How many times have I insisted, Marin? Please, call me Silas," he said, leaning closer. Marin had never been so thankful for the width of her countertop.

"Despite your insistence, *Silas*, we are not as close now as we once were. I would feel far more comfortable if we both adhered to what is customary," she said. He merely waved his hand, scoffing.

"Customs are so restraining."

"I have customers, Mr. Zavalynn," she said. She looked around and sighed. "Had customers. Please, I asked you not to visit me here."

He frowned. "But if not here, then where might I find you? You hardly leave the building," he admonished. Marin turned slightly to Eloise.

"If you would, my dear, please go check on Sorrell for me. I'm sure he'll be wanting a bit of lunch by now. I expect you back in an hour," she said, proud of herself for not allowing her frustration to show in her voice. She could hear Sorrell moving in his bed upstairs and she knew he'd heard their guest's arrival. Hopefully he wouldn't tell his brother. She almost paled at the thought of Lark returning now, while Zavalynn was here, but she had to get through on the hope that he'd take his time running around the Lower District. "Really, Lord Zavalynn, this isn't something one does. If you wish to make a house call you must notify me first," she said, turning back to him.

Eloise escaped without a word, only looking back once as she leapt up the stairs, muted terror and relief clear enough on her face.

Zavalynn scowled again. In recent years it seemed to be the only expression he was capable of. "If only you'd accept my invitation to dine in the palace, with myself and Lord Karkas. I know you'd enjoy yourself. I'd very much like the opportunity to get to know you again," he said, leaning on the counter.

Marin didn't dare sigh, or make any inclination toward her disgust with the idea. She hardly recognized the angry, vindictive man that Silas had become and she placed the blame for that firmly at the feet of Lord Karkas. He was a truly despicable man and the thought of dining with him made her blood boil.

"I don't know that that would be a good idea," she said, keeping her voice calm. "We've both changed, Lord Zavalynn. Neither of us are who we were when we first met and I fear we have little in common now."

His frown softened, almost regretfully. It was a brief

glimpse behind the formal cockiness he wore so comfortably.

"For the better, I'm sure. There are many benefits to my position now, Marin, and I'm finding that I would love to share them with old friends."

Marin looked at his stony-faced companions. "You have so many new friends these days, I think you may be more comfortable with them. As I am, here, with my boys."

"Ah, yes. Your boys. Getting close to the age where they should really be leaving the nest, don't you think?" He chuckled, shaking his head at her foolishness. Or so she imagined; the thought of him having any say at all made her insides twist in a knot. It took all of her self-control to not snap at him — as Sorrell had said, he wasn't someone to trifle with now.

"I'm aware how old my sons are, thank you. William and I made all the arrangements necessary for their schooling, but I do appreciate your concern."

At that, Zavalynn tensed; his new friends responded in kind. They seemed to read his every move. His pale hair, drawn back and slicked as it was, made his grimace all the more extreme. "Ah yes, your late husband. Human, wasn't he? Pity." He paused before grinning widely, so at odds with his previous expression that the hair on her neck stood on end. He was clearly not of sound mind — she supposed she could blame Karkas for that. "All the more reason to tie yourself into palace society, no? To be among your own people for a change. I'm sure the ladies of the court miss you greatly."

Marin forced herself to smile. "I just saw Lady Adelina last week; it was good to hear she's doing well. It seems that although she and the other ladies do miss my company, they understand that I am a mother and a business owner first. As should you. Now, Lord Zavalynn, you are disturbing my place of business. If you aren't going to purchase anything, I must ask that you please leave," she said, as politely as she was able.

He scowled. "Well, I was here on business actually." She hoped he was grasping at straws, but he continued. "You see — that girl of yours, the Human, is trouble, Marin," he said. Marin's vision clouded as she glared.

"I'm sorry, what girl? Eloise? That's absurd," she said harshly. Zavalynn simply shrugged. His companions, however, looked at her sharply as the energy in the room heightened in a way far from natural. She had little power over *Eiyer*; *Eiyer*, the energy that was present in all living and natural things, that could be manipulated by the Eilvyn. Marin was not as talented with it as her sister back home, certainly, but she still had some skills at her disposal. She forced her body to be calm, knowing that he and his men were far more powerful than she was.

"It's to do with her father — bad blood there, and damning rumors to boot. If I could question her, I'm sure we could clear up these concerns here and now," he said. She shook her head. It was disturbing that Bear Wyatt was known to Zavalynn; she hoped it wasn't because of her friendship with his wife and employment of Eloise but she had begun to fear in recent years, with Zavalynn's continued pursuit of her, that she might be drawing too much attention to their small family.

"Out of the question. She's tending to my son and she cannot be interrupted." She paused. "I must insist, however, that you leave. I can't have you questioning my employees and driving out my customers. No matter how well we might have known each other once."

"Very well," he finally said, his brows arched. One of the three with him seemed primed to protest but he simply gestured for them to leave. "But I will be back, Marin, and I expect an audience with your pet Human. I do suggest you take me up on my offer one of these days — things are getting very tense in the city, with the winter coming to an end, and I would very much hate to see you caught up in it. I could be of great help."

Marin shook her head, unable to keep her smile on her face. "I'm well aware that your particular brand of help is something that comes with attachments, Zavalynn. I am certain I can take care of myself."

His frown only deepened but he did leave, taking with him a few of her sweet rolls. Marin released a deep breath; it felt like she'd been submerged in a boiling pot and had just been taken off the heat. Zavalynn had always been ruthless, climbing over anyone and anything to reach the top. She supposed this was the natural end — he was in power and refused to let go. She looked down at her hands and saw they were shaking; she clenched them so tightly her knuckles turned white. Tamora would have a heart attack if she told her that he'd made another house call. She'd explicitly told Marin to tell her if Zavalynn did anything like this again, though Marin had no idea what she thought she could do about it. She was crippled, and a healer for Wela's sake. *I'm not going to tell her*, she resolved as she stared at her fists. *Not if she's going to do something foolish. She hardly needs encouragement from me.*

Hardly a minute passed before the door opened again, the tinkle of the bell making her heart race. *Back already? What's it this time, a marriage proposal?* But it was only one of her regulars, a slim young Eilfe with a shock of blonde hair. He leaned back out the doorway, gaping down the street.

"Was that Zavalynn? Are you alright, Mistress Agata?" he asked, his concern clouding his voice. She meant to hush him, certain Zavalynn could still hear, but just nodded. Anything more would certainly mean trouble.

Chapter 3

Tamora

Tamora's whole body heaved as she leaned against the rough stone of the nearest building to catch her breath, her lungs burning. No more than a few blocks from Marin's... this is ridiculous. She thought she'd worked up her strength over the last few years; she'd found that she was no longer content to simply remain in the woods. She wanted to explore, watch people as they went about their lives, and help as many of the ignored as she could. Speaking of which, as she rested she mulled over Eloise's predicament. Her father, Bear, was indeed a bear of a man. He was a pillar of the Human community in Erengate, a sturdy and reliable dockworker, and his home was the site of many gatherings both social and business alike.

From what Eloise had breathlessly explained, Bear was accused of the very treasonous activities that she and Marin had been chatting so carelessly about. He'd been in the harbor a week ago, going about his day, when he'd been placed in shackles and dragged off to the jail in the Lower District. She was sure Marin had known, and now she wondered why her friend hadn't mentioned it. She supposed it had been Eloise's story to share. It would be impossible to keep secrets in that house, as Eilvyn hearing was so sharp that Tamora entirely believed that Marin could be in her own room and hear someone sneaking a biscuit downstairs without even trying.

Tamora didn't believe that Bear was truly guilty of treason, although she didn't doubt he'd voiced his concerns about the treatment of Humans in the city. He'd never been a quiet man when it came to the safety of his family and those around him. If he'd been complaining again and someone had reported him or he'd been overheard by a nervous Eilfe or Iokan, she wasn't surprised that something had come of it. A week imprisonment, however, was far more than those typical complaints warranted. It was early and she had no doubt the guard on duty would be irritable because of it, but it was best to address this quickly. She didn't want Bear in there any longer than he already had been.

The weather had grown difficult during her time with Marin. People were out now, going about their mornings, but they moved quickly and with their heads down as the wind picked up and snow began to fall. Tamora glared at the skies as she made her way south, towards the Lower District. Passing through the gate was not difficult; the real challenge would be leaving later. The line she passed was at least thirty people long, Humans attempting to get to their jobs and run their errands, and threatened to grow even more troublesome as the day wore on and the weather worsened.

Tamora only glanced up at the buildings around her long enough to get her bearings. They were hard to look at, nothing like what was available even in the Harbor District. Grime coated their surface, making them all a mottled gray and black that made her shiver with disgust if she got too close. It had shocked her when she'd learned that it was considered better than the communities that cropped up around the fields south of the city. The gate behind her hid this from any passerby who may want a peek; they'd raised the wall after a short entreaty from the residents of the Trading District, when they'd built their buildings up high enough to see over.

It seemed that the sight of the southern half of the city made them uncomfortable. Tamora could make a few guesses as to why.

There were guards, too, more than Tamora cared to count. They patrolled these streets constantly, looking for anyone making a mess or who even looked suspicious. Simply being nervous for your first day could get you arrested, she'd found, and she kept her gaze firmly on the cobblestones. Not that she was at risk; she was Azha, after all. They knew better than to try.

The lower jail wasn't too far from the gate; its closeness made it easier for guards to spend as little time in the Lower District as possible. It was the largest building of its kind, almost a centerpiece for the district itself. The stone beneath the grime was gray and smooth and rang with the same energy as the city's walls. Tamora had spent more time here than she'd ever admit, even to Marin, though not for the reason one might assume.

She rapped her knuckles on the wooden door, set comfortably back into the stone in a way that offered some measure of relief from the growing onslaught of wind and snow, and waited for the small sliding window in the center to open. When it did she caught a whiff of whatever Gregory was eating for his breakfast and her stomach growled, setting her teeth on edge.

"Asken, I might have expected you - what do you want?" Gregory was Veden, her more water-logged brethren, and his breath stank of dried fish. Tamora found she was suddenly no longer hungry, a first.

"I expect better manners from you, Gregory," she replied, rolling her left shoulder under the weight of her bag. She refused to put it down; as it was her boots would need a thorough scrubbing upon her return.

"Don't talk like you're my mother, you ain't nearly old

45

enough."

"I beg to differ." From how Gregory had talked of his schooling in the past, Tamora had put together that he was barely over a century old. How he'd gotten a job like this at his age, she could only guess. *I could very well be his mother*, she thought dryly, nearly grimacing at the thought. That was one responsibility that wasn't for her; the idea of having children was enough to make her skin crawl. Watching Marin and William handle their boys' younger years had made her grateful that it wasn't a possibility for her, though she had grown to have a soft spot for them and Eloise.

Gregory coughed, a wet hacking sound that Tamora immediately recognized. She leaned back, not wanting him to breathe on her, but her interest was certainly piqued. "Why are you here? We didn't call you," he said finally, wiping his mouth.

"Someone else did. You got a man by the name Bear? Bear Wyatt?" she asked.

"Bear, huh? I don't think so—why?"

"I'm sure you've got him, look again." He was lazy, she knew that, and it was highly unlikely he cared enough to check the records. She managed to get a few men out of this hellhole simply by offering him a salmon pie just a few months ago.

Gregory hacked out another cough. "Oh, well there's enough of them that I don't know 'em all. We got half a dozen over the last two days alone; tracking 'em down has been about as much fun as a brawl with Kwim'wa." Tamora's eyebrow arched as he uttered the common oath; she knew what he meant but bringing up any of Dalka's lords was risky business. The Wela of the Dead didn't take lightly to oaths, or so she'd heard. *Oh, who am I to judge. I do it all the time*, she thought, sighing.

"Look, I'll make it easier on you, alright? Bear's a sick man and I don't recommend keeping him any longer," she said, feeling out the beginning of her story. She'd spent some on the way over crafting it. Gregory scoffed.

"Another sick Human, Asken? That's a load of shit. You came in just before winter to say the same about a whole cell—"

"They were, Gregory, and this one's true too. I was doing you a favor, didn't think you wanted Rocklung running rampant in your jail, especially with the cold front that was set to come through," she said calmly. She watched through the small slot as he visibly shivered at the thought.

"What's he got then?"

"Honestly, I'm not sure. No cough yet but he's shaky, pale. When I saw him just a few days ago he said his joints were on fire." She paused and Gregory leaned closer. "Truthfully, Gregory, I'm glad I caught you. I came because I was worried. I don't want whatever this is to pass on to you and the other guards — you know as well as I that the Guild won't make the trip down here."

Just last summer she'd been called to the lower jail when a man had simply broken his arm. The Guild refused to send anyone, and there'd been a terrible infection when she'd finally arrived. The guards here weren't prepared to let people die under their charge; those cells were in the palace. These people were their neighbors, or their neighbors' servants. It was hardly the same thing.

He nodded; she could see the bob of his head through the slot. "Well... his were really a minor thing, from what I saw in his file. A warnin', I think, would be as good as time in a cell." He paused. "Best to be safe, yeah?"

"I think so," she said seriously. "Let me in, then? I'll escort him home and see that he doesn't get anyone else sick."

"Yeah... give me a minute." Gregory stepped away and she could hear him scratching on a piece of paper. Then the door grated open and swung inward and she was greeted by the disconcerting smell of fish, old cheese, and more body odor than she'd ever wanted to smell. *Just like last time*, she thought grimly. Nothing like a trip to the jail to make you never want to eat again. A rarity for an Azha.

"Thanks, Gregory, I appreciate it. Won't be more than a minute," she said. The paper was shoved into her hands and while she tried to ignore the sticky residue on it, she delved into the jail.

"You know the way?" he shouted after her; she waved her hand in answer. *Like he said, I was just here for that whole cell block. Memorized the damn place after that. Never know when it might come in handy.* Double checking the paperwork, she turned down the right hall and walked as quickly as she was able. If Gregory's replacement showed up any time soon, she'd be in more trouble than she wanted to deal with.

Tamora reached his cell and peered in; it was dark, damp, and bone-chillingly frigid. Bear appeared suddenly, making her step backwards in surprise. "Damn it, Bear, don't do that," she snapped, shaking her head.

"Miss Asken?" He stepped further into the light, which strained down the hall from the single torch at her back, and she got a good look at him. He looked alright, given the circumstances. His beard was long and mostly tidy, and his eyebrows nearly touched his hairline. Nothing out of the ordinary. His parents had done right by him, name-wise. "Blessed Bensa, I knew you'd come. I told Eloise—"

"To let me know that they'd arrested you, even after I'd made the diagnosis," she interrupted him. He frowned, confusion evident in his clear eyes. He was in his late forties now, and he was still sturdy and in well health. Better than most of the Humans that he worked the docks with. She handed him the papers through the bars and reached for the key that hung on the wall a few feet away. "I already told Gregory that you're sick, possibly contagious. We're going to get you out of here where it's safe for you to heal."

He skimmed them slowly, parsing out words. Eloise had taught him to read Common after Marin had taught her. Tamora could still remember the day the baker had realized her new second hand didn't know how to read or write. It had started a whirlwind in the building, and even the boys had gotten involved. In fact, now that she thought about it, that might have been when Eloise and Sorrell had first spent significant time together. Something to bring up at Marin's expense later, she expected.

"This... my charges were dropped?" he asked shakily, looking up at her as she unlatched the door. "Miss Asken... I can't thank you enough—"

"Thank me when you're home, Bear," she said quietly. There was still a lot to be done before that happened.

The two walked back through the jail, past rows of cells that were far too full for her liking. She heard rattling coughs and smelled more than a little vomit, and tried to stifle her growing concern. The winter hadn't been kind to these people, confined as they were, but it would do little good if Gregory realized she was prying.

They reached the entrance and found Gregory, who'd returned to his usual post and was gnawing on some dried fish. Tamora tried not to gag on the smell.

"Alright Gregory, thank you for your understanding here," she said quickly. He peered over at Bear, who had the sense to try to look ill. He hung his head and coughed into his shoulder. Almost on cue, Gregory did the same. "By the way, how long have you had that cough?"

"Oh, this? Eh, about half a week. Think it's the chill that did it," he said, shrugging.

Tamora shook her head and flipped open her pack. "Hold out your hand," she instructed as she pulled out a jar from one of the inner pockets and shook out some pale green powder into his palm. She watched as his hand shook slightly, and he glanced between her and the powder. "Mix that with whatever drink you've got, I don't care if it's ale. Do it now." She waited for him to drop the stuff into his mug and take a sip, ignoring his grimace. "It'll help for today but you better go see the Guild as soon as you can. Don't delay." She didn't say the name out loud but she stepped back as soon as his hand had receded, and was careful not to touch him. She held back Bear as well. If it was what she feared Gregory would be bedridden in a day or two when the rash appeared, and then she gave him a fifty-fifty chance of making it through without lasting effects.

"Thank you, Asken, I'll do that," he said quickly. She could hear the sudden nervousness in his voice and nodded in what she hoped was a comforting way as they left. Gregory was a good young man, if a little dull. He didn't deserve to die just because the Guild ignored the Lower District and those who worked there.

.....

Eloise's family lived in the Lower District but Tamora had more trouble remembering the route than she'd expected, and was grateful that Bear was making a beeline for home. A few people were out and she recognized some of them, although she'd never be able to explain why or what ailments had brought them to her cottage. They all smiled briefly at her before looking away, usually towards the nearest guard, and walking off. The two hardly got a second look from those making their patrols; an Azha and a Human together didn't raise any alarms. Guardians existed, after all, and it was suicidal to accuse an Iokan's *viluno* of anything, unless you wanted nature itself to pay you back. The pressure in Tamora's chest released the further they got from the lower jail.

Bear came to a stop in front of a blue building, or at least a building that sort of looked blue beneath all the dirt and salt.

A lantern hung over the entryway and the metal that affixed it to the wall was elaborately shaped into a snake. Now that she saw it, Tamora did remember that Eloise's mother believed the animal watched over the family. Bear opened the door and his voice boomed through the entry.

"Miss Asken has saved me!" he shouted. Tamora winced and glanced back into the street. There was no one there, save a few Humans rushing off, and they turned away as soon as she looked at them.

"Bear? Bear!"

Tamora heard the shout and smiled; Eloise's mother Davina was a lovely thing. She had a warm softness to her that reminded Tamora of Selena, or how Selena had looked when she'd first met her. She'd grown hard and tough during their years together; they'd often laughed about her weakness at the beginning. It wasn't a bad thing, Tamora knew, just not what they'd needed at the time.

A door opened and a few unfamiliar faces peered out, saw Bear standing in the entryway, and closed themselves in again. Those would be the neighbors. Behind them, though, Davina appeared. She rushed down the hall, her dress bunched up at her calves, and launched herself into her husband's arms. He swung her around with a hearty laugh and Tamora suddenly felt as though she were intruding on a very personal, private scene.

He put her down and they grinned at each other, reminding her so much of newlyweds that she had to smile. She'd been there, at their wedding. Someone had fallen ill, she remembered, and she'd been at Marin's shop when Bear had rushed in and begged for her help. Apparently, he'd run half across the city to find her. She'd gone, revived the poor young man who'd fainted, and had been invited to the rest of the wedding ceremony. She smiled at the memory; it was one of her favorites.

It seemed to dawn on Davina what he had said, enough to move her eyes from her husband's face and look at the other person standing on her stoop. "Miss Asken," she gasped, grasping at her arms and pulling her inside. She pulled off Tamora's cloak, ignored her protests, and pushed her down the hall towards the kitchen. "We must thank you, how did you manage this? No, please don't tell me. Oh, I'm so grateful. Bear, start some tea. Eloise packed our good leaves on the top shelf of the cupboard—"

"You really don't have to," Tamora stammered. As she was ushered inside she got a look around; it was the first time she'd been there in years. *Since Eloise's birth? No, can't be, that was over twenty years ago.* It was cramped and packed with things of all sorts, generations of odds and ends. She saw old antiques that she assumed were someone's heirlooms next to dried fruit and herbs, and across from that were implements that she thought might be used for sewing in some way. Davina was a seamstress, after all, so perhaps that pedal contraption was hers? She had no idea, Tamora ultimately admitted.

Davina beamed up at her as she looked around. *Eloise looks just like her*, she realized.

"You're going to sit, love, and we're going to treat you. It's the least we can do," Davina said. Her smile made it clear that Tamora had little choice in the matter. "Bear, where's the damn tea?"

Davina wouldn't let her escape for hours; hours of little homemade cakes and small almost stale biscuits and more tea than Tamora could physically drink. It was wonderful. She heard stories about customers that Eloise had complained about and a few clients of Davina's who were surprisingly well-off in the city. Bear worked the docks and he had tales of his own, some borrowed from sailors over the years, and he had a captivating skill for storytelling.

The sight of the couple huddled together happily on the stoop was enough to bring a bit of cheer into her mood and she kept her smile as she made her way back to the gate; even the guard's questioning wasn't enough to dismiss it.

Chapter 4

Tamora

Tamora's nose warned her of the upcoming fish market and she turned the corner, finding it in all its winter glory. The street was, naturally, the main stretch of the Harbor District and right up against the docks, the space nearly as large as the city's central square up in the Trading District. Water lapped against the rock shoreline, which extended for an abnormally long stretch before ships could actually come into the docks. Years ago the city council had tried to dig out the stone and silt below the surface but it had done little good. Every Iokan knew better than to alter the natural state of the world more than strictly necessary. Reshaping the coastline was on par with attempting to move a mountain and neither were approved by the High Council — Wela, it wasn't even physically possible. Erengate had been left with an uneven shore, with deep pockets dotting the otherwise shallow stretch. It made it very difficult to install docks at even intervals, and most had resigned themselves to using small dinghies and rowboats to reach shore. There was the main dock, though, which extended out past the shallows into the sea itself, and it was the pride of the city. Well, not if you asked those who lived in the Upper District; but if you asked any true resident of Erengate, they'd be dead before they left it out. The maintenance it required was almost outlandish, as the wood was punished by the saltwater and frigid air, but the dock workers managed it with no small amount of pride.

The docks, and shallows, were alive and ready for the day with vessels already out for the day's catch and some of the local boys searching the shoreline for off-season clams and oysters. The stench of the bait being sold nearly made her reel back.

Tamora wrapped her cloak tighter as the wind came in off the sea and turned to walk along the row of closed shop stalls that sat out from the imposing wall of homes. While not as unpopular as the Lower District, this particular street was reserved for those without the coin to spend on nicer housing. Most rooms were rented out and they were popular among sailors who needed lodging for a few weeks at most, as the inns throughout the rest of Erengate were too expensive after more than a couple of days.

The wind whipped across her knuckles, sending a violent shiver through her. "And he said that warm weather was coming," she said quietly, shaking her head at the mental image of the city's Naturalismo preaching out from his balcony. He was just a crazy old Veden, that was all. He may have control over water and ice but he couldn't actually stop it from leaving the clouds, or predict when winter would break. His was a ridiculous title, and she couldn't believe he was considered a forecaster. That was something only the Wela could do.

She kept an interested eye on the docks while she hobbled along. It was always entertaining to watch the city's youth try to catch anything, but it looked especially miserable in today's chill. The water would be frigid and she wished she could do something to warm them. In the past she would have been able to keep a bonfire going, even from a distance, that they could use to warm their frozen fingers — not anymore. Tamora turned abruptly from the thought.

She passed a small cart, selling meat pies, that was run by one of her customers. The Human's wife was due any day now and he waved pleasantly. He'd call for her when she was needed; there were a few midwives in the Lower District, but she knew she was considered one of the best. The attention that her reputation had brought was uncomfortable. She was used to acting in the shadows; even during the rebellion, her title had shielded her actual identity from the world. Now, though, she was known by just about everyone to some extent. People had started recommending her to their children and grandchildren — she was pretty sure one of the young men that came by last year was actually a great-grandchild of someone she'd helped when she'd first arrive. Human lives moved so fast, it was hard to keep track of it all.

.....

Tamora felt she knew the city well — how could you not after seven decades in one place? Still, some things had clearly escaped her notice. She hadn't remembered so many shuttered windows and barricaded doors, nor had she expected guards at each corner. *I didn't even realize there were so many guards in Erengate*, she thought, feeling immediately foolish. Of course there were. They were a major city, and one of the only suppliers of inqu for the Coalition. That alone put them at the top of the list in Sienma, a relatively small country. Besides, Erengate had been the site of at least a dozen rebel raids during the last rebellion; they'd only stopped when the guard had nearly tripled and Krys had declared it too risky. She shook her head. Her conversation with Marin was making her recall things she'd long since cast out from her mind. It wouldn't do her any good to dwell on the past. Better to concentrate on the task at hand—the butcher, the spice shop, and then heading back to check on Sorrell.

The Lower Wall was short only in comparison to the main walls of the city, which towered overhead in the distance, ever-present on the city's horizon. Even still, the city's internal division must have taken many Mago to lift and assemble these massive stones. They were as long as she was tall, and it took only two blocks to form the full width of the wall. Guards patrolled the top, although she'd never seen them do anything outside of the Lower District. Her mind often wandered to think about what the builders must have gone through, far before the time of the Coalition and any form of alliance. *This had been a Veden stronghold, once. And back then, the Veden and the Mago were not kindred spirits*, she remembered from her coursework, so many years ago. She supposed that was one benefit of the Coalition; at least they weren't killing each other anymore. Even as the thought crossed her mind she felt guilty for it. They'd only pushed off their hate to other targets; she doubted any Human or Kit'ak would say the Coalition was in any way good.

Tamora could feel the energy seeping slowly out of the rocks and packed earth that held the wall together, a steady drumming up through her shoes and into the soles of her feet. It was present throughout the city, spread like a thin coating by the cobbled streets, but it tripled in strength as she neared any wall. *All those people, nearly two thousand years ago, put their souls into these stones*, she thought, tempted as always to run her hands against their surface. It distracted her as she approached and joined the growing line just outside the gate. It was open and wide enough for three people to cross through with ease, but two small swinging doors barred the way just enough for the guards to question those attempting entry.

This is new, she thought, a small frown creasing her brow.

"Papers." The grating voice pulled at her attention, and they weren't speaking with her. The man four people ahead of her was fumbling through his pockets, a dawning air of panic settling on his hunched frame. A Human, he had sandy hair and a ragged coat that looked as though it had seen far too many winters. The guard, a well-dressed Eilfe with bored eyes, stared down at him behind his short barricade just before the doors.

"I've got them in here somewhere—"

"Either show me your papers or get out of line," the guard said brusquely, gesturing with a gloved hand for the requested papers.

The man seemed to go through his last pocket. He swore quietly and started again; two other guards noticed the holdup and began to walk over. Suddenly he shouted in glee and whipped out a crumpled document. The guard sneered down at it.

"My papers," the man said in explanation. The guard took them gingerly, hardly touching it.

"Denied. Get yourself some new ones," the guard said, his voice colored with disgust.

The man looked as though the guard had just given him a death sentence. "But... but I need to—"

"Get going, Human. You bring that mess back here and I'll throw you in a cell until your family can bring you new ones," he said, his eyes narrowing above the scarf pulled high on his neck. He gestured for the line to continue. The next person pushed past the shocked man with impatience.

When Tamora reached him, still standing and staring down at his papers despondently, she didn't have the heart to say anything.

"Papers."

Tamora pulled them from her inner pocket and thrust the folded document at the man. His eyes darted along the lines.

"Tamora Asken." He folded it and handed them quickly back. The Eilfe had returned to his seemingly normal state of immense boredom. "State your purpose."

"I need to—" he looked quickly behind her and waved her forward, cutting her off.

"Fine, fine, go through."

Tamora simply nodded. He was on to the next before she'd passed him, the gravelly voice already asking for more papers. She glanced back at the Human; he was gone. His crumpled papers lay on the cold stone ground, the grime of the street already soaking through the blurred words.

.....

The Trading District was constantly crowded, even this early in the day, and was the largest of the four Districts. It stretched across the full width of the city, essentially cutting it in half and separating the Upper District entirely from the Harbor and Lower Districts. Eilvyn and Iokans who lived in the Upper District could go their entire lives in Erengate without stepping foot across the Lower Wall.

The eclectic nature of the Trading District never failed to surprise her. Merchants spent a large percentage of their earnings making themselves and their storefronts stand out and over the centuries it had resulted in a mishmash of patterns and colors that could be dazzling in the right light. The buildings were anything from orange to brown, reds and blues, to brilliant white and coal-black. Patterns of all shapes were tiled or painted or carved on their surfaces, often showing in some way what that particular store sold. There was an undeniable layer of grime and wear, but it was lively even on the slowest of days. They had guards here as well, posted on nearly every street corner and watching the growing crowds carefully. Tamora shielded her eyes from them as she passed, their presence sending a prickling sense of discomfort up her spine.

As she ducked out of the cold breeze, stopping into shops

and catching her breath in alley openings whenever possible, Tamora thought of these riots Marin had told her about. That, combined with the increased guard presence here and at the Lower Wall, was enough to convince her that Marin hadn't told her the whole story. *Tensions could very well be just as high as they were back when I first met Krys*, Tamora thought, frowning. Erengate had changed over the past few decades, although she didn't like to admit it. Many people had come and gone, winter the only real dependable thing, and the whole city had seemed to grow colder with each passing year. It wasn't just the weather either. The people were rough and detached, and even though that was one of the reasons she'd picked Erengate it did little to help her feel at ease in the city.

Another reason she disliked the city was the Karkas family. They were believed to be absurdly corrupt, at least from Tamora's perspective, and since Lord Severo had taken control the city had become more and more divided. Not twenty years ago, she'd been among some of the voices who had raised concerns over their practices of favoring their own stores and those of friendly merchants, driving the rest from the city. They built up the Lower District, claiming it would benefit the Humans who lived there, but then they'd raised rent and families had been forced to move in with their neighbors to save costs. It had led to more business for her, she thought ruefully, but an increase in sickness was nothing to brag about.

She sighed. *All this talk of rebels and uprisings isn't good for me*, she thought. She was still walking through the city, ducking into an alley here and there to avoid the crowd and the terrible wind that was picking up as the hours went on, and she couldn't help but notice she was leaving a trail of melted snow and puddles that would surely turn to ice soon. *Honestly, I'm a menace. Someone's going to slip and break their neck*, she thought, chewing on her cheek.

Tamora stepped out from the narrow alley and found herself swept up in a group of sailors coming from the Lower

Wall, cursing herself for being too caught up in her thoughts to look before she walked. They were Eilvyn, mostly, with a few Azha surprisingly among them. *I can't believe they willingly took a course this far north at this time of year,* she thought, looking for their Guardians. Human companions of every Iokan, a Guardian was essential for the survival of her people. Without a Guardian, an Iokan, paired during childhood by methods even she didn't fully understand, struggled to control their element. It was unheard of for any Iokan, no matter their element, to go unpaired.

The survival of an Iokan was also innately wrapped up in the safety and survival of their Guardian; if a Guardian were to die or be severely injured, the Iokan risked losing control of their element all together. *Where are their Guardians?* she wondered. It was rare to see Iokans traveling without them. *By the Wela, the Azha looks miserable.*

Tamora pulled her hood up to hide her face and her frown. They smelled of the sea and from their boisterous excitement she assumed they were on dry land for the first time in months. The noise almost immediately gave her a headache and she tried to hurry forward or find another alley to duck into.

She was in too much of a rush to pay attention to those around her. Turning out of the opposite end of the side street, she hit a stone at just the wrong angle for her hip and yelped as it gave out and she had to hop for a few feet, catching her bearings. She bumped a couple of Humans as a result, sending one smaller woman careening into a group talking in front of a jeweler's stand. She was clumsy, her arms taken up carrying her own day's shopping, and she plowed into two of the men, sending them into the stand's edge.

"Makmo's beard," the jeweler shouted, paying more mind to the necklaces and fine gemstones the men had displaced than the well-being of his customers. The others of the group, though, closed ranks and shoved the woman back. She landed sprawled on the cobblestones and her bags scattered.

Tamora tried to go to the woman's side and help her regain her footing but was pushed back herself, the Eilfe who'd been pushed into the stall shaking his head and pointing the others in his group to the woman. "Restrain her," he said, pulling back the hood that had hidden his face from wind and recognition and Tamora groaned. *Of course it's Karkas*, she thought, glaring past the Eilfe who'd stepped up to stop her.

"Let me past—" the man rested his hands on his belt, bringing her attention to his sword. She stepped back, watching with a feeling of impending dread.

The Human woman had tried to collect her things, small packages of food and the like, but was staring up at the group of Eilvyn who now approached her.

I know her, Tamora realized, although her name refused to come to mind. She'd visited the cottage some months ago looking for a tonic for a neighbor. *She paid with wool.*

"I— I'm sorry, Lord Karkas," the woman said, covering her face and bowing her head as he stepped closer. "I didn't mean—"

"Enough," he said, silencing her. Soren Karkas was heir to the city after his father and he lived up to their bastardized family name. They'd taken it up, corrupting the good name of Karkanwynn during the rebellion. She clearly remembered how Soren's grandfather advised the High Council to burn small villages and raid helpless outposts, using the opportunity presented by the conflict to rid their territory of those they deemed unfit. *Thankfully I killed him before they listened to more of his insane theories*, she thought with no small amount of satisfaction. Marin seemed to believe that the family cruelty had skipped the elderly Lord Severo, but Tamora had her doubts. In any case, he was sure to turn over the city and family legacy soon enough. He was growing old and Sienma was no place to live out your last days.

The guard just ahead of Tamora moved along but she saw him watch her from the corner of his eye, just as she watched him. He probably recognized her, she realized with a scowl that didn't help matters. She hadn't kept a low profile over the years and it certainly hadn't made her popular with the Karkas family. She was just lucky that they were unaware of the role she'd played in the rebellion.

Others had noticed the commotion and had come to watch. Tamora wasn't afraid to use her elbows to ensure she stayed at the front.

Karkas's features were striking as he glared around and brushed any trace of the woman from the expensive furs adorning him. It was something he shared with all of his Eilvyn kin; a face too angular, symmetrical, and harsh to be truly beautiful but unnatural in its perfection.

"Apologize to Lord Karkas, woman. I don't believe he heard you," another Eilfe, shorter than Karkas by only a few inches, walked purposefully to her side and pulled her up by the arm.

Silas Zavalynn had a high voice to Tamora's ears, too sharp to be considered pleasant. His fine furs did nothing to hide how he'd put on some weight, common to some of the Eilvyn of the Upper District but at distinct odds with the scarcity most in the city lived with. It didn't make him more popular. Or did his position as Soren Karkas's advisor; he'd set himself up to rule the city in his stead once the day of his coronation came, and the thought of living under Zavalynn's constant influence was motivation enough for many Humans to leave for greener pastures.

Tamora's lip curled at the mere sight of him. *I wonder if he's still bothering Marin. Maybe I need to break that nose of his again. I'd be doing him a favor.* That incident had been the true turning point between her and the city council, although it had been a long time coming.

She wasn't alone in her disdain; many others in the growing crowd looked upon him in a way they would never dare with Karkas. Zavalynn's position on the council was his only protection and he knew that well. His eyes darted around the crowd and he sneered back at them.

"You all Human-lovers now? Want to join her? She owes Lord Karkas an apology," he shouted as he yanked the woman's arm so hard she whimpered. A few people took a half-step forward but shouts from the three guards kept the immediate area clear. At a nearly imperceptible nod from his master Zavalynn was emboldened; he whipped his hand across the woman's face when she remained silent. "Apologize!"

Tamora winced and heard sympathetic muttering from the crowd. "Zavalynn!" she shouted, her voice rising above their indistinct chatter. "Don't you have anything better to do? She already made her apology."

His eyes snapped over to her; she saw the briefest glimmer of fear and it brought warmth to her heart. "Tamora Asken, our resident recluse," he sneered. She straightened as others turned her way and he sauntered over, releasing the poor woman. "One of your 'patients' then?" His fingers waggled in the air as he spoke, too close to Tamora's face. "A little friend? Stay out of this. She assaulted Lord Karkas and deserves just punishment."

"I think your presence is punishment enough," she replied, earning a laugh from the crowd. She smiled thinly over at him; she'd always felt it was clear who would win should the two ever come to blows. Even with her injuries, the prospect had never worried her. She'd met his kind of man before. He'd drop with one well-placed punch to the jaw. Tamora flexed her hand, hoping this was the time he'd step far enough out of line.

"I'll not have you insult my steward in my presence,

Asken," Soren Karkas said. The crowd was immediately silenced. He gestured at Zavalynn, who spared time for one final glare before heeding his call.

"It isn't her fault. I bumped into her first," she said, refusing to back down. Karkas sighed as though this were a great pain to him.

"And that, Asken, is clear evidence as to the superiority of our respective peoples. Your reflexes, while perhaps dulled with time and... experience, are enough to ensure your survival. This Human's are simply not enough." He almost sounded saddened by his words. He looked out at the crowd. "My good people, this is what I have been saying all this time. There is no denying that which we can see with our own eyes. Humans need our help; this world is no place for them. They are terribly weak and should be looked after."

Tamora tried to tune him out; preaching was a common pastime of his and she'd heard the arguments more than enough over the years. His beliefs were sadly common across Tunsealior and had been ever since the Eilvyn had first come to their shores. With the creation of the Coalition, over two thousand years ago, the veneration of all sixteen Wela had ended. The Eilvyn only acknowledge eight—the eight who existed before their own creation by Afina, their Silver Mother. Those who came after, be they Wela or mortals, were lesser. Karkas believed this strongly, as did his followers, and it meant that this protection he spoke of was little more than slavery. It made her sick.

The woman, Tamora noticed, was similarly frustrated. She saw a flash of anger across her pale face and it was suddenly very clear to Tamora that she was about to make a decision that could change her life, and not for the better. Silas was within arms reach as the woman rose up, unnoticed as Karkas stood in the crowd's spotlight. Tamora stepped forward, intending on stopping the woman from doing something foolish, but the guard had been watching and he moved in front of her and planted an arm on either shoulder. She tried to shrug them off to see what happened, but it wasn't necessary.

She heard the slap that broke Karkas's reverie; it seemed to echo through the crowded street. Silas yelped and clutched his cheek, Tamora pushed the guard off her to better see.

A sudden chuckle broke the silence and although Tamora saw an Iokan woman in the crowd clap her hand against her mouth, the damage had been done. Laughter cascaded through the gathered people like water through a broken dam. Karkas turned to the Human slowly, his normally grim mask cracked and revealing shocked surprise. The woman might have gotten away before, as he'd been so wrapped up in his speech he may have actually forgotten her presence.

The Human, Tamora noticed, returned his gaze coolly.

"How dare you strike my steward!" Karkas bellowed, his anger switched on in an instant. The laughter disappeared; no one wanted to draw his eye to them. His power physically swelled through the crowd and Tamora's head throbbed as he twisted the Eiyer around them effortlessly, the pressure in the air rising. She was not alone in her discomfort. Some onlookers fled from the edges of the crowd, determining the entertainment to come at too high a cost. The jeweler ducked behind his display and even Silas visibly braced himself.

It was too much for the woman and she tried to flee, but the crowd was no longer with her. Whether it was the tension and pain from Karkas's manipulation of Eiyer or their anger at her striking an Eilfe, Tamora didn't know. Most likely they simply vied for Karkas's favor and forgiveness.

"It'll be the Pit," a Human murmured to herself from beside Tamora. She looked down at the woman, frowning.

"We don't know that—"

"I need no reassurance from you," she snapped, physically leaning away from Tamora's presence. She stepped back and disappeared, quickly replaced by another curious onlooker.

"I meant no harm—"the other woman cried out, drawing Tamora's attention back to the terrible show. There was a fresh cut beneath her eye and her lip was beginning to swell as Karkas prowled around her.

"No harm? You've run into me, obviously intending harm, and then you attack my servant — an Eilfe! One of the Wela's chosen! This is a plot against my life, I swear it, and you will be punished for your treason," he snarled, a far cry from his normally refined air.

He had transformed from the noble figure he put forward into the man that Tamora had always suspected him to be. Soren Karkas had a reputation that had followed him all the way from Vasna, Sienma's capital. *I heard he killed another noble in a rage,* Tamora thought to herself, suddenly afraid he'd repeat the act here and now.

"Karkas, that's too far! I nearly ran into you myself, you think I also meant you harm?" Tamora shouted.

Karkas turned with such vehemence that she almost regretted it.

"Silence! You'll get your turn."

"And what, you'll throw me in prison? With what charge?" she snapped, pushing aside the people who had stepped in front of her. "This woman has done nothing wrong."

"She struck my steward!"

"We all know he deserves worse than that!" Her words were met with a few scattered murmurs; most simply looked between the two with thinly veiled shock. Karkas stepped closer. He was taller than her but she glared up at him. She met his dark eyes with her own, refusing to back down.

"I'll repay you for anything I damaged," the woman said softly. Karkas laughed with barely a glance back, all his attention on Tamora.

"Your little pet here thinks she has anything I want," he sneered. "You've gotten away with your treasonous words for too long now, *healer*, and I'm going to put a stop to it."

"You've no right." She willed herself to be calm. "You know the treaty — only my own people can charge me."

He leaned closer. "I can arrange that," he said, whispering as though the crowd couldn't hear him clearly. Tamora scoffed.

"I'm sure that would go over well. Lord Karkas, heir to the city, threatened by a crippled healer. You'll be doing wonders for your family's reputation," she said with a sneer.

He straightened abruptly, his terrible grimace disappearing. She paused, off guard. He switched it on and off like the flip of a coin; one moment he was murderous with rage and the next he was calm and poised. Silas watched him carefully, waiting for any instruction. *Or perhaps*, Tamora thought, *hoping he doesn't flip on him instead.*

"This was obviously an attack on my person by an illicit movement hidden within our very walls, the same group I have warned you all about on numerous occasions," he announced, turning away from Tamora and addressing the still-present crowd. A murmur rippled through the crowd. Tamora's frown only deepened as she was dismissed. She had no idea what he was talking about but from the looks being exchanged, most of the others did. *Maybe Marin's right, maybe I should come into town more often.* "May the Eight have mercy upon you during your sentencing; this treachery shall not go unpunished. We cannot allow Erengate to fall to the same terrible conspiracy as our western brethren."

Karkas made eye contact with as many individuals in the crowd as he could, seeming to look to each for the assurance that he was indeed correct.

"You can't sentence someone for walking into you in a crowded street," Tamora said loudly, again drawing his attention to her. "I tripped and bumped into her, it's as simple as that. It's hardly treason."

"You are obviously working with the woman, a partner in this crime—"

"If you expect people to believe that you're more insane than your sister," Tamora snapped. Karkas went white; it mottled his angry face. It was a well-known rumor that his sister, the very one who'd likely ordered the loaf from Marin, was as empty-headed as she was beautiful.

"How dare you—" he stepped toward her, hands outstretched.

"The Mother will protect me, healer," the Human interrupted, holding her chin high. "But I thank you for your words of support."

Tamora stared at the woman, blinking. She couldn't have heard her right. *No, no you stupid woman.* The Human smiled peacefully and turned to look at Karkas, who had straightened in malicious delight.

"Your false mother will do nothing," he said gleefully, gesturing for his guard. "Worship of your blasphemous 'Mother' is forbidden and as such you are under arrest." Tamora groaned, watching the woman be restrained and Karkas turn to the crowd.

"This woman is a traitor against the Wela, against the very gods who created and sustain us," he announced, to nods from those closest to him. Others were leaving, the show was over. Tamora stared at the woman who she'd unintentionally damned, gripping her bag so tightly she thought she might burn through it.

"I accept my fate," the woman said suddenly, standing tall as though the guards on either side weren't locking her arms behind her back. "I will join the Goddess and she will welcome me into her service."

Karkas sneered down at her, giving her only a single shake of his head. "Take her away. A pathetic creature such as her deserves no leniency," he said. He paused for a moment, thinking. "A trial will take place — on Itro. A fitting day for such an event," he declared, to the surprise of the crowd. That was only two days away.

Tamora scowled. *There's no good reason to tie this treachery to the will of the Wela. Itrodo represents truth, not this sham.*

The woman was led away swiftly, however Karas paused, sparing a moment to smirk at Tamora. "Don't think I've forgotten about you," he warned, coming so close to Tamora she could smell the peppermint he'd been chewing on. "What you've said here will not go unpunished."

"Sure, Karkas. I'd like to see you try," she replied, her anger and growing sense of guilt making her reckless. She knew it, and she knew she'd never hear the end of it from Marin. "I've faced stronger men than you." He swept his cloak out as he stepped away and his guard closed in around him. *Stronger men, yes*, she thought as she watched his receding figure. *But I was stronger then as well.*

Chapter 5

Tamora

T amora swore under her breath, sitting heavily on the stone steps that lined this particular street, and found herself filled with what she could only describe as an uneasy rage as she stared down at the Human woman's belongings. The crowd had dissipated, people going back to their day, but she couldn't just move on. Karkas was firmly out of reach, so she couldn't burn his face off no matter how much she might want to, and there was no way to free the Human from his grasp. She cursed herself for the whole mess—it was her fault, after all. If she'd been watching where she was going, or didn't have these Wela-forsaken injuries in the first place, that woman would be with her family safe and sound by now. Instead she would soon be rotting away in a cell, waiting for a trail that would ultimately lead to her death.

Why had she admitted to worshiping the Mother? Tamora wondered. It was outlawed, everyone knew it. Tamora's parents had secreted away their unusual interests, the least of which were their worship of all sixteen the Wela. They had also taught Tamora about other interpretations, wanting her to keep an open mind, and so she knew that the All-Mother, simply called the Mother in most cases, was revered in Adbeter, the Human country that lay to the southeast of Coalition territory. It was an isolated country and they were distrustful of non-Humans, for what Tamora felt were good reasons. The only influence they had on the rest of Tunsealior was this nagging belief in a single goddess and the anger it invoked in the High Council.

Tamora knew a lot about the Mother, something unusual among Iokans, even those as well traveled as she was. Her chest ached at the memory of her Guardian, Selena. Even the memory of her name brought her pain. Selena had been intensely private when they'd first been Paired, far older than was usual for Iokans.

Typically, an Iokan child was Paired with their Guardian only a few years after birth. The natural elements were unpredictable and often too powerful for a single individual to control; before the bond between a Human Guardian and Iokan had been discovered, it had not been unusual for Iokans of all kinds to lose themselves to their element. Tamora's parents had been curious about this old way of life, and had chosen to raise her and her brother without Guardians. They'd been discovered when Tamora was fifteen and she'd been Paired with Selena, and it had changed the entire trajectory of her life. It had been torture trying to get even the smallest amount of information from her; when Tamora had discovered her belief in the Mother she'd scoured the libraries for anything she could find on the goddess, desperate to connect. She'd grown up knowing that the bond between an Iokan and their Guardian, their *viluno*, was the strongest connection a person could experience. She'd felt she'd been denied that growing up, and now she was just sad that she'd had so little time with the most important person in her life.

She hated that her mind always ended up here. Thoughts of loss and regret did nothing to quell the burning anger in her core and only fed the fire that she normally kept restrained, coiled deep within her. The thought of it getting loose was like a splash of cold water on her face; something crossed between fear and gnawing desire rose within her.

Tamora stood abruptly, ignoring the screaming stiffness in her joints and the startled steps around her from those on the street. She'd spent too long here under the falling snow, sitting on the stone next to the jeweler, thinking about things best kept locked away. She'd go to Marin. She would know what to do.

Chapter 6

Marin

Word tended to spread quickly through Erengate, especially through the Harbor District, and Marin heard about the arrest almost as soon as it had happened.

"The woman threw herself at Lord Karkas, Soren that is, and thrust her knife right at him!" one older gentleman, Mago by the looks of it, insisted. Marin had a hard time telling the difference between Iokans, sometimes, so she couldn't be certain. If it weren't for the tattoos, she honestly couldn't tell them from Humans half the time. His Guardian nodded stoically beside him. "I heard it from a man who saw it himself! The young man had to fight her off while his guards rushed to his side! And the healer, Tamora Asken — she was there too! Said some nasty things to Lord Karkas, she did."

"I heard that he was waiting just out of sight for someone to trip, and then claimed she attacked him," another customer, a younger woman, asserted loudly as the other left. The man shot her a glare and she stared after him impassively. "I wouldn't put it past him. And that despicable advisor of his, Zavalynn, was there as well. Can you believe it?"

Marin outwardly said the right things, agreeable as always, and focused on selling bread and cookies. It would do her little good to make even more enemies than she already had. With Zavalynn making a habit of visiting her shop, often buying nothing, people were beginning to talk. The opposite sort of people who had talked about her for years for marrying a Human, and bearing two *Joien*. It was exhausting trying to keep track of it all.

After a time Eloise joined her, finished with whatever conversation she'd been having with Sorrell, her cheeks pink as she hopped down the stairs. Marin smiled at her, grateful for the distraction from Silas's actions. *And they think I can't tell there's something going on*, she shook her head at the thought. Eloise gave her an odd look.

"Everything alright, Mistress Agata?"

"Hmm? Oh yes, thank you. And thank you for checking on Sorrell, I'm sure he enjoyed the company," she said. The pink in the girl's cheeks deepened. *He's thirty years your senior*, she thought with a twinge of hypocrisy. *Who am I kidding; I was nearly two centuries older than William when we met.* If she were being honest, she'd give her approval if she were asked. Not that they needed any encouragement.

The door swung open when Marin was just assessing what was left of the day's goods; they'd had a busy time of it. Only a few odds and ends were left — just enough for her to make some bread pudding, she figured. She glanced up, a customer-ready smile plastered on her face, when she noticed the limping figure.

"Tamora!" she exclaimed. Her friend looked up with a cheeky grin, belying the exhausted look in her eyes.

"Told you I'd stop by, didn't I?" she said. Marin could only roll her eyes.

"I thought it'd have been hours ago. You're staying in

the city very late— you sure you're going to make the journey home?" She looked closely at Tamora, noting how tired she looked. "We do have a guest room, you know."

Tamora shook her head. Her collapse into the small chair, however, only accentuated her clear exhaustion. "No, but thank you. I'm probably going to stay at Lucrezia's." She grimaced, and Marin knew exactly why.

"I have a bed right here." She curled her nose. "Her place always reeks of perfume."

"I know, I know. And she hates my guts to boot. But I want to get a feel of the city... I feel like I don't know this place anymore," she said with a sigh.

"You mean the incident with Karkas? Don't you dare make my words the reason for your choices," Marin said, ripping up bread for the pudding. It also helped with anger, which she feared might grow after this conversation.

"You heard?"

She laughed, knowing it sounded hollow. "How could I not? You know how fast word gets around. I even heard that you were right in the middle of it," she said, watching Tamora out of the corner of her eye. Her friend looked more than tired; she was deep in thought. Conflicted, even. Had she not wanted her to know? *It's better that she tells me herself, rather than having me hear about it later from some random bystander*, Marin thought as she piled all the bread pieces into a bowl. She wiped her hands on her apron and went to the table. Eloise could finish that up in the morning.

"I may have been," Tamora admitted, finally. She looked around, assessing the room for the first time. "Where's Eloise?"

"She went back upstairs, with Sorrell. Probably the only reason he's not listening right now," she replied with a chuckle. Tamora's eyebrow arched.

"They're close." There was so much weight behind that,

as though Marin hadn't already deduced it.

Marin snorted, leaning back against the counter. "Oh, I'm well aware. It's funny how they don't think I see them sneaking around, leaving each other little trinkets and notes and the like. It's almost as bad as Lark, but at least he's sneaking off to go adventuring! Hopefully he'll be home soon," she said, looking at the door. Surely the sun had already set at this point; he was late. And he'd promised not to be.

Tamora laughed. It was good to see her do something other than brood. "They're getting older, Marin. I'm sure we'll see whether or not it's serious very soon." She had that knowing look that Marin hated to even consider. Sometimes she acted as though she were the eldest here, and most knowledgeable, but it was far from the truth. Marin thought she had half a century on Tamora, at least. There was no way to be sure, though, when Tamora never revealed anything about herself.

"I hope not. I wish they were still young," she said. "Young and innocent. This city is too dark for them."

"The whole world is," Tamora agreed and they fell into silence. Marin hated when Tamora did that. There was nothing she could say to lighten the moment, she could only move on. It was exhausting and it happened at least every other conversation. Perhaps this was why Sorrell thought they disliked one another. He was wrong, of course. She wouldn't keep talking with someone whose company she didn't like. Tamora was just difficult but that didn't make Marin care for her any less.

Marin cleared her throat. *Does Tamora feel it's a comfortable silence? Well, it certainly isn't comfortable for me.* "I'm not going to sit down here and mope. Would you like to come up? I've got a surprise for you I've been holding onto." Tamora's eyes had a sudden, slight twinkle.

"Why not," she shrugged nonchalantly. Marin frowned.

Did I imagine that? She's so hard to read.

.....

She tried not to watch Tamora hobble up the stairs behind her, wishing desperately that she could cure whatever had made her friend into this broken shell. Tamora never shared. But Marin had never seen her with a Guardian, so she'd been able to make some assumptions. She didn't know what happened to Iokans without their Human companions, but she could surmise that it wasn't anything good. All four Iokans, be they Azha, Mago, Veden or Tri, were still somewhat of a mystery to her. Before moving to Erengate and meeting Tamora, she'd rarely gotten the chance to talk to anyone who wasn't Eilvyn and from a very short list of approved friends. That had been one of the reasons she'd left home; after two hundred and seventy-five years, she had had enough of being second to her sister and fully surrounded by her parents' people. She'd wanted to see the world. Eighty years later and she was still learning.

"You've rearranged," Tamora noted as they stepped inside and Marin locked the door. Sorrell could certainly hear them now; after all, she could hear him telling Eloise to be quiet and could also hear the girl giggling. She didn't want to think about what they may have been up to. Giving the boys privacy was hard in a small place like this but she tried her best.

"A bit. What had it been, twenty years? Things can get a little stuffy," she said lightly. "Tea?"

"Eh. I've had a lot of that today, actually. You should move the bookshelf out from in front of the window, it blocks any chance of escape. You know, in case of fire," she finished quickly. Marin looked at her as she put on the kettle, but Tamora's face had gone carefully blank.

"Fires. Sure. I'll have Lark do it when he gets back,"

Marin said, gesturing for Tamora to take a seat. The room was so small the kitchen spilled out into their hosting space and the only option was the velvet armchair. Not that Marin hosted much, her friends had all but disappeared when she'd started seeing William. When she made the rare appearance at tea they picked up conversation as though she'd never left, of course, but they never visited her themselves. It was as though her home had become somehow tainted by William's presence. Tamora, though, was familiar enough with the ways things worked, although she never seemed entirely comfortable here. Not for the first time, Marin wondered what she thought of them. "So, tell me about this incident."

Tamora stiffened, but the story came spilling out all the same. Silently, Marin went to the kitchen and opened a cupboard, pulling out a dusty unopened bottle. The empty teacups were the perfect vessels.

"Is that *puhu*?" Tamora stopped her depressing rambling in sudden shock, somewhere between the woman's slap and her declaration for the All-Mother. Marin winced at the mere thought; if the High Council ever figured out how to read minds, Humans would truly be done for. It was a subject she stayed far, far away from with Eloise. She didn't want to know.

Marin smiled proudly, casting her dark thoughts aside. "I found it a little while back and there just never seemed to be a good time. I suppose this is as good as any?" she asked, shrugging as she struggled to open the corked bottle. "You know, I've never actually had this."

Tamora held out her hand abruptly as she was pouring. "That's more than enough. It's strong." She sipped and sighed in contentment. "Oh Wela, how I've missed this."

Marin followed her lead and sniffed the small glass first; it smelled strongly of cinnamon and something citrus she couldn't place. Nothing too bad, she thought as she sipped, but the drink itself left her gasping. "Why is everything you Azha make so… so harsh? It's so expensive I thought it'd be better," she coughed, sputtering.

"I told you it's strong," Tamora chuckled. She downed the rest of her small glass and exhaled. Marin knew that if she could do the same she'd practically breathe fire. "It's pure alcohol, save for a few herbs and spices. You know Azha aren't affected by alcohol. We make this for the taste," she said, her smile widening as Marin poured her another cup.

"Well, I'm affected," Marin said, squeezing her eyes together as she finished her cup. It burned on the way down, but the aftertaste wasn't terrible. "Alright, it's rough. Maybe not disgusting."

Tamora poured her a second glass with a knowing look. "Do you want me to keep going? I think I've said enough," she said. Marin knew it wasn't about the *puhu.*

"No, no. Karkas is cruel, I'm not going to argue that. You really shouldn't get yourself involved," Marin said. She shook her head at her full glass; she'd heard *puhu* was an Azha delicacy but now she wasn't so sure she wanted to try any of the others. *Give me some wine from Saltrol, though, and I'd be more than happy.* She was sure her parents still had a particular vintage she'd loved, but the last she'd had it was nearly a hundred years ago now. "You're going to get yourself killed, getting into it with him like that. His family already doesn't like you."

"Whatever gave you that idea." Tamora rolled her eyes.

Marin sighed. It was like she wanted to be driven from the city. "Adelina."

Tamora snorted. "Adelina Karkas is—"

"She's a sweet woman, Tamora. You don't speak kindly of her, and I don't really blame you, but she's no fool. It's not her fault that she's got a bastard for a brother," Marin snapped. Tamora sank into the armchair, sipping from her cup. "She has a gentle soul. A bit scattered, fine, but she doesn't deserve that," she said, gesturing at Tamora's face. She got only a frown in return.

"I didn't think she left the palace much, how'd you hear from her?" Tamora asked, clearly trying and failing to let it go.

Marin shrugged. "She holds tea a few times a month, I visit on occasion. What? It isn't a crime."

"I didn't realize you were so popular," Tamora said. Marin thought for a moment she might actually be pouting.

"I have some friends left. You asked a question; don't you want to know the answer?" She waited until Tamora's mouth snapped shut and seemed like it would stay that way. "Adelina mentioned something during a luncheon a few weeks back about her brother and... well, honestly, it just seemed like one of her little stories so I didn't think much of it. But after today... I'm not so sure. I think Soren wants you gone. She said something about Humans and Eilvyn holding the same company—of course she stopped that as soon as I spoke. I think she may have forgotten I was there," Marin said, frowning.

"I told you, she's not right in the head," Tamora said, rolling her eyes. "Doesn't sound like it has to do with me though."

"You heal Humans, Iokans, and Eilvyn," Marin said, shrugging. "Even the occasional Kit'ak, from what I've heard. You're the first person I thought of. Not to mention that business with Soren a few years ago—"

"That was hardly my fault," she said, wincing. Nearly ten summers past, Soren Karkas had come down with something that, seemingly, no one could cure. Lord Severo Karkas had ultimately, albeit reluctantly, reached out to Tamora. With how fast Tamora had cleared it up, the Karkas family became convinced that she'd somehow orchestrated the whole embarrassing event. Not to mention that Tamora hadn't been very scrupulous with who she'd told that Soren had been ill with a pox normally reserved for Humans and spread by intimate contact.

Marin held back a laugh at the memory; it had made for some entertaining afternoons in the palace, with the other ladies gossiping for years about Soren's misdeed. "Mhm. In any case, she did pull me aside and mentioned you specifically. She was trying to warn you; it isn't exactly something she can easily do in the company she keeps," she said, the thought of what Soren might do if he'd overheard them enough to make her heart race.

Tamora slammed the glass down, empty again. "I'm not going to stop seeing Humans, if that's what she was worried about." Marin eyed her hand clenched on the table, specifically the small stream of smoke that trailed up from it.

"If you burn a hole in my table I'll charge you for the repairs," she said lightly. "I'm just passing along a message. She's not so bad, you know. Once you get to know her."

Tamora snorted, pouring herself another glass. Marin let her top off her glass as well; the stuff was starting to go down a bit easier. She waited a moment before speaking, hoping it allowed Tamora to calm her nerves.

"You need to keep your head down. Stop getting involved. It's drawing too much attention," Marin said. She too was becoming overwhelmed; she forcibly stopped her fingers from tapping on the table and laid her palm down flat. If she had any control over Eiyer she was certain the pressure in the room would have skyrocketed by now.

"It was my fault, Marin—"

"I don't mean with the woman today," Marin snapped again, hating what Tamora brought out in her, "although I do have my own thoughts on the matter. I mean the Humans you've been helping in the jail. Not Bear, of course, but you freed an entire cell block. You're going to get yourself arrested."

Tamora's shoulders were stiff and her next pour took visible effort. "Those people were sick. They'd have infected the whole place."

She snorted. "Yes, with Rocklung. I heard. The group before had some sort of obscure flu from Sotwifas, and the woman before that had—"

Tamora raised her hand. "Okay, okay. I get it. I'm not about to let innocent people rot in a cell."

"You're going to get yourself killed!" Marin shouted. Her eyes darted to the door and her voice fell to a whisper; Sorrell was lying so close. Not that it mattered, she reminded herself. She wondered if he was relaying any of this to Eloise; the thought of the girl believing she didn't support her people was painful, but Tamora needed to hear this.

Tamora's thoughts were clearly elsewhere. "Fine," she ultimately said, "but those men with Rocklung really were all sick. That stuff travels." She sounded so petulant it was almost funny. Marin relaxed in her chair. That was as close to admitting recklessness as she knew Tamora would get.

"Why is this so important to you?" she asked, feeling like her skin was crawling beneath the stare of those odd gray speckled eyes. She wasn't Human. She was Azha, an Iokan, and her people were some of the most highly regarded people in Tunsealior. Control over fire was a dangerous and very lucrative thing, and there was no reason for her to push as much as she did. Every time something big happened in the city, Marin knew that Tamora would find herself in some way or another.

Tamora didn't answer right away, choosing instead to swirl her cup and stare at it as the particles settled.

"It just doesn't seem right," she finally said. Everything

with her was like pulling teeth.

Marin waited for her to elaborate but, yet again, Tamora said nothing. *This always happens*, she thought bitterly. *Why can't she just trust me with her thoughts? What more could I possibly do to prove myself?*

"Well," she said, breaking the silence. "I heard the Sentinels will be here soon and they can help."

Tamora huffed at that. "Sure. Hopefully they're better than the last."

"They're just doing their job," Marin said, shaking her head with a small smile. At least that was some reaction. "You did pull quite the stunt —"

"Why do people always bring that up? That was years ago!"

"That was hardly the first time, or the last time for that matter, that you insulted a Sentinel," Marin said, rising to her feet as she heard the door open below. Hopefully it was Lark coming home and not a customer; she could have sworn she locked the door but now she wasn't so sure. She'd been so distracted with Tamora's arrival that her normal routine was completely out of sync.

Tamora shrugged. "I don't even remember what I said anymore, you know how my mind is," she said. Marin glanced back at her, unable to tell if she was being honest. Tamora was always saying she was forgetting things, usually when it came down to why she knew some obscure fact about a part of Tunsealior she claimed never to have been to. She'd known, for example, the exact supply routes of Marin's favorite wines and had known the specific suppliers in Koren. From someone who didn't even drink the stuff, it was unusual to say the least.

"Well, I hope they can help out around here. Between what happened this morning and the news coming from the east...," she trailed off as footsteps creaked on the steps leading up. She and Tamora both watched as the door cracked open and a head poked through; her breath came out in a whoosh as she recognized the face. A single glance to the dark window told her all she needed to know. "Lark, you're late."

Lark grinned from ear to ear, not abashed in the slightest. He shoved something into his pocket, something that looked suspiciously like a letter, but shrugged nonchalantly. Marin's eyes narrowed. "We never actually agreed on a time — yeah, I'm late," he corrected, seeing her face. His own brightened when he saw who she was with. "Tamora! It's good to see you!"

Tamora's face lit up and Marin was glad to see it. Watching her friend get more and more riled up, when she was already wound up like a spring, was always painful. "Good to see you too, Lark. What's new on the streets?" she asked; even Marin could hear the teasing in her tone.

He shrugged. "Actually, that's why I'm late. There's tons of people out, it's crazy out there. Not sure why, given the weather."

"People? What kind of people?" Tamora asked, her voice going sharp.

Marin frowned. "Lark, what did you see?"

He looked between them. "Just... people? Eilvyn and Iokans, if that's what you're looking for." He shrugged again. It was his most used expression. A simple shrug could fill the place of hundreds of words; it could mean "Hey Mother, good to see you" or "I'm off to the market" or "I love you." Additional meanings seemed to be added by the minute.

Marin looked her son up and down, trying to determine what he'd seen from the look of him. He'd said he was going to the docks after his errands but if she were being honest, he was missing all the signs. No dried salt on his pants or stains on his cloak and although his cheeks turned pink in the cold, a trait he'd inherited from his father, he hardly looked as though he'd been outside. "Lark—"

Tamora cut her off, her mind clearly elsewhere. "Eloise is still here... she shouldn't go out alone," she said, looking at Marin meaningfully. Marin nodded, letting her own question fade. It could wait — it was family business, after all.

"You're right, it's not safe out there right now. Who knows what trouble Karkas might have stirred up," she said with a sigh. *Or Zavalynn, for that matter.* She kept that to herself. But, from what she'd heard, he'd played a central role in today's show. "Eloise should get back to her parents soon, or they'll try to find her themselves. I'd hate for Bear to get caught up in something, and so soon after... well, Tamora, she can't go alone, is what I'm saying," she said, reminded of Zavalynn's request to speak with the girl. The thought made her sick to her stomach. She was pretty and young, and Zavalynn's people had worse reputations than he did, no matter how unbelievable that might be.

"I'll take her home," Tamora said, rising to her feet. She always looked like she was in such pain. She held up her hand at Marin's open mouth, silencing her protest. "You take care of the boys... you need to explain some of this to them. Whatever you don't already know," she said, turning slightly to Lark. He shifted on his feet, his expression making Marin believe that her efforts to shield him from certain truths may not have succeeded as well as she had assumed. *I'll deal with that when Tamora's left*, she thought, suddenly grateful for her suggestion. Having her in the spare bedroom had been a good idea but Wela knew it made her nervous to think about her influence on Lark, if not Sorrell. He'd always managed to keep his head, while his younger brother was so much more impulsive.

"If you feel that's best, then fine," Marin said, letting Tamora go down the hall. She knew the way, after all. She eyed

Lark, who was still standing by the door as though he'd wished he'd kept his mouth closed. "This is far from over, young man," she said, gesturing at him. He, infuriatingly, merely shrugged.

Chapter 7

Tamora

Eloise was with Sorrell, sitting on the edge of his bed and staring down at the pages he held in front of the flickering candlelight. When Tamora pushed the door open she leapt back, brushing down her dress. Sorrell, however, simply put away the book calmly.

"I don't mean to intrude but someone's got to get you home," Tamora said, crossing her arms and smirking at the sight of them. Eloise groaned as she looked outside for what appeared to be the first time.

"Oh Wela, I hadn't noticed. They're going to be so upset," she said.

Sorrell reached for her hand and smiled. He had a calming presence on her, that much was clear. The girl was usually wound up tighter than a spring. "They'll understand, I'm sure. It's good to see you, Tamora. Even if it is only briefly," he said.

He had a measured voice, refined, though it was more pitched than his brother's. The two were hardly twins; Sorrell was two years his brother's senior and acted like it was a decade. Sorrell had dark hair where his brother was blonde, he was thin while Lark was muscular, and he preferred books and quiet conversation to exploring the city. It had been entertaining watching the two of them navigate their childhood and to see the trouble they seemed to get themselves into. They'd started coming to her cottage for remedies as soon as they'd learned the way, with little bribes so that she wouldn't snitch. She hadn't needed to. There were still a few things Tamora had never shared with their mother, but Marin was no fool.

"I'm sure you heard more than enough of my visit here tonight. It's best if I take my leave," she said, shaking her head. It was impossible to hide anything from him, especially now that he was largely bed-ridden. "Eloise, grab your things. There's something going on out there and I don't want to spend more time than we have to."

They bid farewell to Sorrell, Eloise's goodbye lingering longer than Tamora would have liked. She tried to give them space but ended up rushing the girl out all the same. She was going to see him tomorrow, after all.

"Does this have something to do with the arrest earlier?" Eloise asked. Tamora frowned as she tried to determine whether the hint of accusation was actually there or not.

"Probably."

"Zavalynn came by earlier," she said. Tamora sputtered and very nearly stopped walking.

"What? When?" She peered at Eloise in the relative dark; the snow was still falling and it made the torches that dotted the streets close to useless. She was wrapped up in her well-worn cloak and thin scarf, hunched against the wind.

She thought she saw a shrug from under the layers. "It must have been before you saw him in the market. He was looking for me, though," she said. Tamora could hear a shake in her voice and, for once, she was sure it wasn't the cold. "Why would he want to talk to me?"

Why hadn't Marin told me? If I'd known... Tamora

scowled. That was probably why. Marin wouldn't want her to be in any more trouble than she already was. "I don't know, Eloise. He was probably just trying to mess with Marin."

She hoped that was the case. Zavalynn was reaching, growing desperate. He had a prominent place in the city but it wasn't stable and Karkas was hardly a reliable supporter. He needed an alliance with someone loved by the people, and Marin certainly fit that description. When she'd first rejected him he'd thrown himself into his little gang, the Foxes, and they'd grown since Tamora had arrived; they weren't content with idle threats any longer. Tamora glanced at Eloise, who'd fallen silent, and hoped that Zavalynn was just getting under Marin's skin. The Foxes didn't have many uses for young Humans, but it never ended well.

The streets were empty save for a few guards at the larger junctions and the glass-encased torches that studded the walls. Tamora watched them warily, half wanting to pull Eloise closer to her. She didn't hear the crowds that Lark had mentioned — *maybe they've moved on? Or was he outside the Harbor District?* He would have been held up at the Lower Gate this time of night; the guards knew him well enough to know that he wasn't fully Eilvyn. They'd stop him on principle. Tamora and Eloise turned down a side street that would bring them to the gate faster. Eloise moved quickly out of habit and Tamora was happy to let her lead the way. She made this trip far more often, naturally, and she knew all the shortcuts.

"Oi, you there."

Damn. Tamora didn't stop at the rash voice, but shuffled a little faster. She grasped Eloise's arm and pulled her forward. "Keep walking," she whispered, glancing back. The street they'd turned down wasn't well lit and she could barely see the street they'd started on. *That was stupid,* she thought bitterly, cursing herself for getting distracted.

"I'm talkin' to ya." This voice wasn't behind them, it was

to the side. A hand grabbed her arm and pulled, and Tamora's ankle turned on the slick stone and she swore as she hit the ground hard.

Eloise yelped and Tamora squinted to see her; they'd pushed her up against the opposite wall. Her small frame was almost entirely obscured by the man holding her. There was a startling flash of light as another man's hand was set ablaze, a flame the size of an apple resting comfortable in his palm. She could see four men, two Eilvyn, the Azha, and his Guardian. The Azha peered down at her, his eyes widening a moment later.

"She's an Azha, we can't—"

"Quiet," snapped one of the Eilvyn. "They're out after curfew."

Tamora pushed herself to her feet, wincing as her joints protested. "There's no curfew in Erengate," she said quietly. "Leave us be, or I'll see you never walk again."

The man snorted, looking her up and down.

"Sure, I'd like to see you try," he sneered, his idyllic face narrow and stiff. "What good is an Azha who can't even see someone coming up on her?"

He took a step forward and Tamora held up a hand. He stopped short and she thought she might have seen a flash of nerves. "You can't touch me," she warned, keeping her hand raised. He didn't know she couldn't draw on her fire; no one did. *I'll bluff our way out of this. Just hold on, Eloise.* She still hadn't gotten a good look at the girl, but the man holding her had turned back to see what the fuss was about. "You know the treaty as well as I do. I'll report this and you'll be tried for assault."

"There's no one here to enforce it, bitch, Sentinels aren't due for another week," said the man as he shook his head. The street was bathed in a flickering warm light and it gave his face a shadowed pallor as the Azha moved away from him.

"We should go," the Azha said. His Guardian agreed and she could see the man step back towards the main street.

"Who's going to know?" the Eilfe snapped. Tamora felt the energy in the air shift as he pulled Eiyer inwards and thrust it towards his companion. The Azha's flame flickered out as he was thrown backwards and his Guardian lost his footing. She stepped in the direction of Eloise, hoping to reach her in the dark, but felt the cold touch of metal on her neck. "Take another step, Azha, and you're dead."

"How are you going to explain that?" she asked, biting out the words. "I'm well known here and I swear, I won't go quietly." These men were strangers, she had to believe that. They hadn't recognized her and, after today, she'd have thought that would be unlikely.

She felt pressure in her ears and braced herself, not a moment too soon. The weapon dropped away and she was flung back by another burst of Eiyer. It hit her like a solid wall, pushing her into the cobblestones, before dissolving into nothing. Her things went flying and she heard Eloise shriek; it was all she could do to scramble to her knees.

"How dare you," she snarled. A hand appeared before her and she looked up in abrupt surprise, her hand going to her dagger.

A man, broad-shouldered and heavily cloaked, removed his hand as quickly as it had appeared and held it out. "Allow me," he said quietly, helping her to her feet. He steadied her, his face cast in shadow, but a glimmer of light on fine thread caught her eye. The insignia on his cloak came into sudden relief, Tamora seeing it more in memory than in reality, and she flinched back.

"It appears we have a problem here," he said, his voice smooth and unperturbed. He patted her shoulder, stepped around her, and addressed the men. The Azha and his Guardian had regained their footing and their fire; it doubled in size as they tried to get a better look at the new arrival.

"We were just helping these ladies get home. We'd be happy to take her off your hands."

"Don't lie," Tamora snapped at the Eilfe, unable to help herself. The Sentinel, because that was so clearly what he was, glanced back. His expression was invisible in the shadows but he almost looked as though he were amused.

"You boys should really know better," the man drawled in an eastern accent, any hint of interest nonexistent. He spoke as though this were just an average evening. *It might be*, Tamora thought. *They aren't due to arrive for a week, though. Marin had been clear enough — even this group knew that. What is he doing here?* "It's against the First Ordinance to attack any Eilvyn or Iokan without provocation. Or their Guardians." He nodded his head to where Tamora knew Eloise was being held his mouth a thin line as he looked through the gloom.

"Damn it, man—" the Eilfe stepped forward but one of the Azha had, again, gotten a better look at who they were dealing with. He visibly paled and the fire in his hand dimmed.

"He's a Sentinel," he said, his voice cracking. The man holding Eloise turned sharply and Tamora got her first good look at her; her nose was bleeding and she fell to the ground slowly, her hand dragging against the wall as she tried to keep herself on her feet. The sight of Eloise hurt filled Tamora with rage and she took a shaking step toward her, no longer caring about anything else.

The men barely waited long enough to confirm what the Azha had said; they tried to run. The Azha and his Guardian made it the farthest and Tamora was almost nervous that they'd get away. The Sentinel, however, just sighed.

He waved his hand, almost lazily, and all four men were

thrown up against the side of the building. The Eiyer that was being manipulated added to the pressure behind her eyes and she could feel a headache coming; it had always done that to her. Tamora rushed, stumbling over uneven cobblestones, to where Eloise was trying to stand.

"Are you okay?" she asked, wincing as she saw the bruise already forming across the bridge of her nose. "Take this," she said, going through her pockets until she found something useful. Eloise stared past her, ignoring her words, at the men who were now hanging ten feet above the ground, suspended against the bricked wall.

"Eloise," she snapped, laying a hand on the girl's shoulder and giving her a shake. She shoved the cloth into Eloise's hand and brought it up to her face. She was obviously in shock. Tamora swore silently at herself. *This was a bad idea. I should have left her with Marin and gone to let her parents know, alone.* If the Sentinel hadn't shown up, she thought bitterly, they would have been in trouble. Especially once they'd realized she couldn't defend herself.

The Sentinel walked towards the men, moving with calm purpose. "You should have left the first time your friend here suggested it," he said, speaking as though his show of power had been nothing. It probably was, Tamora knew. Sentinels trained for decades, they were the best of the best, the highest-ranking soldier the Coalition possessed. It had been a long time since she'd felt so much Eiyer, and so concentrated. The feeling and the sight of the insignia brought her back and she shook her head violently, willing the memories back where they'd come from.

Eloise grasped the back of Tamora's hand and pulled it away, whimpering as it brushed the tip of her nose. The Sentinel paused and turned on his heel, as though he'd almost forgotten that Tamora and Eloise were there. His expression was hard to read in the dim light, but he looked at the two of them and frowned for a moment before seeming to make a decision.

"I will return for you once I have ensured these women's safety. Please, remain calm. I wouldn't want you hurting yourselves," he addressed the men, who shouted and writhed against his invisible restraints. He ignored them, and Tamora knew that if anyone caught sight of them strung up like that they'd run for it before helping them down.

"I suppose we owe you," Tamora said as he approached, with as much respect as she could muster. His face was coming into better view, especially as he pushed down his hood. He had smooth Eilvyn features, as she'd expected, but they were softened by a dark beard he kept short and a broadness not usually seen in Eilvyn. He was *Joien*, she realized, and that was enough to give her pause.

He either didn't notice her confusion or chose to ignore it, turning to look at Eloise with a concerned frown. "I apologize for waiting as long as I did to intervene. They should have known better than to threaten an Azha or her Guardian." He sounded apologetic enough. *How long were you watching, then?* she almost asked, but didn't want to seem more rude than she already was. She'd spent too long staring and putting pieces together already.

"I — I'm not her Guardian," Eloise said, glancing at the two of them. "Miss Tamora is friends with my employer." Her voice was stuffy and pained. Tamora shoved the cloth into her hands.

"Put this up against your nose, Eloise," she whispered, shaking her head. "And tilt your head back."

The Sentinel's brows creased, matching his frown. "Ah... my apologies. I made an assumption."

"It's fine," Tamora said, glancing back at him. She cared more for Eloise right now than any insult he may have offered her. "What are you going to do with them?" she asked as she helped support Eloise's neck. The girl was quivering like a leaf and she needed to get out of the cold. As soon as her nose stopped bleeding Tamora wanted to be on their way.

"Bring them to the jail, hold them overnight at least. I must uphold the Ordinances," he seemed to want to reassure her.

"Yeah, the Ordinances," she said, carefully clearing her face. She'd spent years trying to destroy those damn things and now they were playing in her favor. *Of course, I have no idea of knowing if he'd have done anything if we'd both been Human. Comforting thought.*

He held out his hand. "Racynth Naewynn, second-in-command of the Fifth Sentinella," he said, with an easy grace and confidence that he clearly felt were well-earned.

Racynth

The Azha looked at his outstretched hand for a moment before grasping it with her free hand. It was warm, rough, and calloused; not unusual for one of her kind. What she was doing this far north, at this time of year, was the real question. Adding that to her defense of a Human she had no real ties to — suffice to say, he was intrigued. *I think I have a good idea of who you are, Azha,* he thought. He'd heard enough of Della's review of the previous Sentinella's reports to be able to put the pieces together.

"Tamora Asken," she said with reluctance. "I feel I may be lacking in titles."

A smile cracked his face as his thoughts were confirmed, many of his previous questions suddenly answered. *An Azha, yes, but a crippled one. I imagine she couldn't have defended either of them — no one else would ever let such an insult slide, especially after the fool used Eiyer. Sabina will be pleased. The healer might be more willing to answer questions now that there's a debt.* "Well, Tamora of few titles, I am pleased to meet you. I recognize your name," he said lightly.

She frowned, the expression carving deep lines in her brown face, adding to the harsh angles already present. Her eyes kept flickering back to the men still resisting their invisible bondage. The girl, however, simply seemed stunned and he found himself filled with sympathy for the poor thing. It was far from the proper time of day for any Human to be out, especially in a city with a reputation like Erengate's.

"Some sort of note left by your predecessors, and theirs before them?" she asked. Racynth nodded, seeing no reason to lie to the woman. "Of course. Can't you people just let it go?"

"Please, don't see this as a reason for worry. I was simply making the connection," he assured her.

She adjusted her bags and seemed to accept that,

checking the Human's nose. It was clearly broken and would need to be readjusted if she wanted it to look anything like it had.

"I'd heard your Sentinella wasn't due for another week," she said. He could have put her hesitation and inability to meet his eyes down to simple intimidation by his station, which happened often enough. But she wasn't a simple farmer, nor a simple healer for that matter, regardless of what she might insist with each passing Sentinella. She was an Azha, clearly, and it took a lot for one of their kind to be injured. Not to mention, no one had ever seen a Guardian. That alone had been enough to make the Iokans in his Sentinella nervous and more than enough for him to find her interesting, if not necessarily suspicious.

There was, of course, also the matter of the Karkas report. He wasn't looking forward to that introduction. From what the last Sentinella had written, the heir to the city was a handful.

"We aren't, officially. May I?" He reached out a hand, offering to take some of her load. She shook her head.

"I'm fine."

Racynth bowed his head again, as he'd found it was often better to air on the side of formality when dealing with Iokans. *And Eilvyn, for that matter*, he thought. She noticeably chewed on the inside of her cheek when she was nervous, something Della's notes had mentioned. They were surprisingly accurate, so far. "Very well," he said, brushing down the sides of his cloak. "Where might I escort you both?"

She hesitated, but it took only a glance at the men still struggling against their bonds to convince her. He followed her gaze, frowning as the four men flailed. It was a drain on his concentration, but one that couldn't be helped. He wasn't going to leave these women alone, not after such a brazen attack. *And on an Azha, for Wela's sake*, he thought, turning back to the woman in question. *Those men were lucky she's in no condition to fight, or we would have found their ashes in the morning.* It was risky business attacking any Iokan, but the Azha were especially dangerous. Fire was more immediately harmful than a gust of wind, after all.

"I was escorting Eloise home, to her parents. It isn't safe to be walking alone tonight," she said.

"Clearly. I assume you're returning to the northern wood, after?" He shrugged at her scowl. "I see no reason to pretend that I don't know what I know, Miss Asken. I'm willing to drop pretenses, if you are."

Tamora frowned up at him a moment longer than he felt was necessary. "Fine. I appreciate your help but I don't need or want your escort after we've delivered Eloise to her parents. I don't particularly feel as though I would enjoy walking back to the forest with you in tow." She spoke frankly, as though relieved that she could do so. Racynth snorted, the noise escaping rudely from his throat. Her frown returned as she narrowed her eyes at him. The Human—*Eloise,* he reminded himself—stared at him openly.

"Very well, Miss Asken, that sounds perfectly reasonable. Eloise, please lead the way," he said amicably, stowing his hands in his pockets. He'd forgotten his gloves with the rest of the Sentinella, a terrible mistake in this region. He was almost glad for the Azha's company; even a few feet away she noticeably warmed the air's temperature just by virtue of being there.

Tamora Asken's eyes darted to his hip, likely looking for signs of his sword, but he saw no reason to make it so clear that he was heavily armed. It remained securely below his cloak, offering him better warmth; if he needed it, he could always buy himself time with Eiyer. In any case, it was unlikely to be necessary in a Coalition city such as this. *You'd have to be more of a fool than these idiots to attack a Sentinel,* he thought, looking up at the men as they passed below. He reinforced the Eiyer that held them and then largely cut off the connection, leaving only the smallest strand possible to maintain the bond. This allowed him to move freely and, if necessary, apply his power elsewhere without risking his previous work. It had taken many years to perfect the technique.

"Any particular reason you are both out so late? As you said, it's hardly the best time of day to be simply perusing the sights," he said.

He didn't enjoy silence and he had found over the years that the more he talked, the more people felt comfortable in his presence. It was useful, in his line of work, to have people trust you. It was also something hard to come by, as the Coalition's Sentinellas had developed terrible reputations during the last rebellion. Although it had been almost a century since, most of the continent lived far longer than that. It was hard to convince people that you were on their side when you'd imprisoned their family; harder still if those people were Human, and they'd grown up on tales from their grandparents of your terrible deeds against their people.

Racynth glanced at Eloise; the girl didn't seem too frightened. Cold, certainly, and in pain. But she didn't hold herself the way someone would if they were scared. *She seems more curious than anything else*, he noted, as he caught her looking his way.

Tamora Asken still hadn't answered and when she did her voice was so stiff he knew without looking that she was gritting her teeth. "I got caught up with friends," she said.

It's not as though I'm pulling teeth here, he thought. He wouldn't allow her to see him frustrated. Instead, he scouted the streets ahead of them. There were few sources of Eiyer, the energy that flowed through living things, in the immediate vicinity. He noticed on his earlier strolls, just after the sun had set, that even the guards seemed to avoid this part of the city. It wasn't in the Lower District, so he wasn't sure why that was. *Something to mention to Della,* he thought, adding it to the internal list. He turned his attention back to the detached healer. She was watching the shadows with a practiced eye; even if he hadn't been there she wouldn't be caught off-guard again.

"To answer your previous question more fully, the rest of the Sentinella does not arrive until early next week, and our rounds are not due to start for another few days after that. I feel it prudent to see any city we visit with unfettered eyes," he said, watching for a response. She seemed surprised at his willingness to divulge this, although most of her reactions were muted.

"You aren't exactly subtle." She nodded toward the insignia embroidered upon his chest.

"Ah, well. In truth this is my only warm cloak, so I have to make do," he said, frowning down at the garment. It was too fine for their normal rounds and Tamora was right, it drew many eyes. His arguments for something more in line with the clothing of the locals had fallen short, however. Not Sabina's fault; the Council had been very insistent that they should be keeping up appearances.

The part of the city, the Harbor District in his notes, had a reputation for being boisterous and consistently providing the unexpected. According to Della, anyway. Racynth took in the quiet street and noted shuttered windows and what seemed to be boarded up doorways. It was far from what he'd expected.

"Is Erengate falling on difficult times?" he asked, eying one of the closer doors pointedly. Tamora glanced over to it and shrugged.

"No more than usual. I wouldn't really know, don't get into town much."

"When was the last time you were here?" he asked out of curiosity, smiling slightly when she eyed him with suspicion. "I'm not interrogating you, I promise. I would need my Commander for that."

"I expect I can look forward to that visit shortly then?" When he didn't reply she sighed. "A week ago, for an emergency, but before that it had been a few months. I don't usually leave the forest during the cold season."

He nodded, glancing back at the boarded up door of the building. It seemed to have been an inn of some kind, once. "In your condition I imagine that is quite smart," he said.

"My condition?"

He paused at her sudden defensiveness. *I have to tread carefully*, he reminded himself. *If she doesn't already like Sentinels it won't do any good to antagonize her.* "I see your limp, Miss Asken," he said, slowly and not unkindly. "It would be easy to assume that you met with some terrible accident, and I would also go so far as to say that I expect the cold season is difficult for you. I know my shoulder gets quite sore in the cold."

He swung his arm around as though to demonstrate and was relieved to see her glare recede. She hadn't quite smiled, but he supposed that was the closest he'd get.

"Ah. You're observant," she said.

Racynth refrained from noting that it would be impossible not to notice her injuries. Even in the dim light of the infrequent torches he could see the deep scars that crossed her hands and crept up her neck. She had Iokan markings there as well, ending just below her chin, but they'd become ragged when whatever had happened to the woman had healed. Not to mention, she dragged her left leg. *It would be terribly easy to take her down*, he thought, *like taking sweets from a baby. Well, a baby that could burn your face off if you upset them.* He didn't feel inclined to try.

"I do have my moments," he said instead, rubbing his hand down his beard. Her eyes followed his movement for a moment before realizing he watched her as well.

"How many are in your Sentinella?" she asked, as though to change the subject. Eloise pulled her down a street, one that thankfully opened up into something larger than an alley, and he followed suit. He could see a wall jutting up over the buildings ahead and he assumed it was one of the gates Della had told them about.

"You'll meet them shortly, I'm sure of it," he said. She continued to watch him, her eyes calculating, and he became acutely aware of how long he'd allowed his beard to get. If she asked about his heritage he'd have no subtle way of redirecting her, and those were questions he didn't feel inclined to address. *Joien* were not as rare as some might think, but they were still far from accepted in most circles.

.....

The guard at the gate didn't look at them as they stepped through. In fact, Racynth noted with disgust, he appeared to be sleeping. He pursed his lips and said nothing. That report would wait for the lord of this city. The streets in this district were significantly worse off than the ones they'd left, the falling snow turning gray as soon as it hit the ground. Which, he noticed, was no longer fully cobbled. Nearly half the street was simply packed dirt and was quickly turning to mud.

"I live just around the corner," Eloise started, her gaze darting from Miss Asken to Racynth. "My... my parents will be wondering where I was." She had a pleading look in her eye as she gripped at Miss Asken's arm.

It wasn't difficult to pick out what she was asking. "I'll remain here," Racynth said, looking around as though he couldn't think of a better place to keep watch. "I hope you have a safe night, Miss Eloise." He'd have to look into her, of course, but he saw no issue with letting her return home unquestioned on this night. It had been difficult enough for her as it was.

They rounded the corner and, when he could no longer see them, Racynth tracked them with his sense of Eiyer. Another skill that was relatively unique to his training. They were joined by two other people, who's Eiyer pulsed more subtly. He recognized them as Human. As he focused, however, he was surprised to feel that Tamora Asken's Eiyer seemed fractured, for lack of a better word. It wasn't nearly as strong as he would have expected from an Ahza of her age and, according to their records, supposed strength. It also wasn't entirely Azha — part of her felt different, more similar to Aspen, who was a Mago. *Something to note*, he thought to himself for what seemed the hundredth time in their short encounter.

The healer said nothing as they left the district and continued on toward the gate. Racynth had half a mind to ask about the girl and her family, but decided against it. Still, the silence grated on him. The sound of their boots crunching through the newly fallen snow might be calming to some, but he found it off-putting. Snow could muffle sounds and reveal your own location, and he didn't have the gifts of hearing that full-blooded Eilvyn enjoyed.

"Thank you for your escort," Tamora finally said, after what was likely ten minutes but felt more like an hour. Racynth exhaled slowly, relieved for the opportunity to speak.

"It's my duty to ensure the safety of Tunsealior's citizens," he said. "I could not simply allow you to continue on alone, knowing what had already happened." Besides, it allowed him to introduce himself. He saw no reason for this conflict between Tamora and the rotating Sentinellas to continue. From what he'd already read, the younger Karkas had had it coming.

"With the state that group is in I'm not sure it was needed... but the gesture is appreciated," she said, somewhat reluctantly.

"You are certain that I can't escort you home? It is not so out of the way that—"

"Yes. I'm sure you have better things to do that escort a crippled Azha around," she said sharply. He fell silent, recognizing when he overstepped.

They reached the wall, looming darkly overhead, and Racynth stopped short. He bowed, seeing her discomfort but ignoring it. "It was a pleasure to meet you, Miss Asken. I'm sure I will be seeing you shortly," he said.

"Thanks for the reminder," she said dryly. "Wela be with you."

He made sure to watch her through the gate, not really expecting anything to get in her way. Still, he followed her Eiyer for a time before turning back the way they had come. He had business to attend to.

.....

Racynth strolled back to where the men still hung and appraised the sorry lot. One of the Eilvyn was openly crying, snot running messily down his face, and the others had resigned to simply staring down the dark street. Upon noticing his arrival, however, one of the Eilvyn perked up.

"Hey, hey. You're gonna let us down now, right? Now that she's gone? You don't have to pretend with us, we know you're busy and we won't do anything like that again," he chattered, visibly shaking as a gust of cold wind blew down the small street. Racynth sighed.

"Look, *friend*. I am busy. But you're the fools who decided it would be a good idea to break the law and attack an Azha.

What kind of Wela-forsaken idiot does that? Did you have a death wish? I don't really care. Come on now, we're getting out of this damned wind," he said, glaring at the man who'd tried to interrupt.

He waved and the men fell from the wall, but were far from released. Before their feet could touch the ground they were yanked upward. Racynth made sure to leave them hovering there for a moment, to feel well and truly helpless. He'd seen how they'd pinned the Human against the wall, hitting her back with an efficient rage that made him sick. He ignored their yelps of pain and looked around the street to get his bearings. After a moment he shrugged. Either he'd find the jail or he wouldn't, it didn't matter much to him.

As he made his way toward where he thought the jail cells were, ironically retracing much of his earlier path but this time with his motley band of floating misfits behind him, Racynth found he had made a decision on what he thought of this barren city. He'd rather be somewhere warmer. Why anyone might choose to live in such a place was a mystery. He'd even take Toglor over this, despite their constant border skirmishes with Adbeter. At least it was warm there.

This train of thought brought him back to the Azha he'd only just left. She was clearly a person who had chosen to stay here, despite the misery the weather brought. He imagined it could only be worse for her, as warm-blooded as her kind were, although he realized he'd never thought to ask an Azha what they thought of the cold. *Maybe they don't care,* he pondered. *It's not important. She's hiding from something, that's clear enough. There's no other reason to stay here, the whole country is a wasteland.*

The guard at the district gate was awake this time, something that brought him some measure of satisfaction.

"Sir- sir." The guard managed to get out some semblance of a greeting, giving him pause.

Racynth ignored the break in protocol, though it pained him. *All that work to be a Sentinel, and I get a 'sir'? This city needs to step up their training.* "Where's the jail? I seem to remember it was somewhere in this district."

He nodded rapidly and pointed, stammering through directions. The Eilfe seemed to be devoting quite a bit of his mental capacity to ignoring the hovering men above them. As it was, they were shoved together through the small opening of the gate so it was quite difficult not to notice. And, Racynth realized with disgust, they reeked of ale. *Probably why they behaved so recklessly. Although it doesn't explain the Azha, I thought they couldn't get drunk.* He'd watched Jordan, one of his fellow Sentinels, challenge one to a drinking contest once, years prior. He'd lost, unsurprisingly, and it had ended with them all being thoroughly reprimanded by Sabina.

Racynth rolled his eyes as he turned away and waved his shivering companions forward, following the shoddy directions as best he could. Some people just didn't know what to do in a Sentinel's presence; having a reputation that precedes you could be a boon to some but if you were trying to pass unnoticed, it proved extremely troublesome. *However*, he mused as he looked upon the crumbling buildings of the Lower District, *the healer hadn't seemed intimidated.* She had cared, that much was clear. As soon as she saw what he was she'd clammed up. But it wasn't out of fear like most people.

He pulled up short as he noticed he'd nearly missed the street. Just out of sight were blaring torches, framing a wooden door to a depressingly run-down structure. *For such a major port,* he thought, *their regulations are severely lacking.* He could only hope that the cells in the Upper District were of higher quality.

"Announce your purp— oh," the guard said, the man briefly stepping in his way before seeing the emblem. "My apologies, sir, I didn't—"

"It's really quite alright," Racynth said smoothly. He gestured to the men behind him; they fell into the hard packed dirt and groaned as they rubbed feeling into their hands. "These men were caught attacking an Azha, a clear violation of the will of the Council. Please see to it that they are held for a minimum of five days."

"Five days! We're sailors, man, they'll be shipping back out soon!"

Racynth turned sharply toward them, glaring at their outspoken leader. "You should have thought of that before you decided to attack someone, *man*." He looked back to the guard who was gazing at the group with something akin to pity. "Make it six for him. I'll return in the morning for a more traditional appraisal."

The guard bowed shortly and rapped on the door. Another two came out to inspect and he explained the situation. Racynth turned away. He'd wasted too much time on this detour. The lord of this frozen heap waited.

Chapter 8

Marin

She paced, as she often found herself doing when Lark had decided to dedicate himself to doing something abominably stupid. This time, however, it was more out of worry than frustration.

"You've been holding something back from me," she finally said, looking at her youngest son. His hair was still sticking up at odd angles from the wind outside and he'd draped himself over the chair Tamora had only recently been sitting in.

"Everyone hides things from their mother," he said. He yelped as she lashed out with what little Eiyer she had, essentially knocking him over the back of head from across the room. "Ow! Alright, alright, yeah I am but it isn't a big deal!"

"Why were you home so late? You could have been hurt!"

"Well, I wasn't, alright? It's fine, really. I was just out with some friends from the docks." He sat a little more upright as her eyes narrowed.

"'Out'? Just what does 'out' mean?" she asked as she stepped closer. He looked anywhere but at her.

"Just lay off, Mother," Sorrell called from his bedroom. Without Eloise distracting him he was clearly listening closely. "He's home now, does it really matter?"

They're are up to something, she thought, her eyes darting between Lark and the son she knew was stuck in bed. *Something that they clearly have been hiding.* She'd seen the way that Lark and Sorrell looked up to Tamora, the way they listened to her every word. She didn't think that the healer would lead them down a path she wouldn't approve of; Marin knew that Tamora valued their friendship more than that. *But they could have gotten themselves into trouble, thinking they were following Tamora's advice. That would be too dangerous.* They were getting older, older than most middle-aged Humans, but they were still her sons. They might not realize it but she knew they'd lived sheltered lives. They had no idea what the city was really like. Or the continent, for that matter.

Marin sat in her chair, wishing she could talk with William. He'd always known what to say and how to convince their sons that their parents might actually know what they were talking about. She'd never found the right time to tell Lark and Sorrell why she'd left her home, just that she was happy she had because otherwise she'd have never met their father. It wasn't a lie, but it was far from the whole story. Lark and Sorrell came from a long line of successful Agata merchants, and their name was well known in Glojoemar. That lineage had been stifling, full of responsibility that Marin hadn't wanted and the duty to maintain relationships with people she thought foul. It simply hadn't been for her.

"It matters, Sorrell, because one of these days you're going to find yourselves in the middle of something serious and I'm not going to be able to help you," she finally said, sparing a glare at the wall between her and her eldest. "I know something is going on, I'm not daft."

"Lark, help me up," he replied. When the two reappeared Sorrell was hanging awkwardly off of his younger brother's shoulder. He was taller than Lark by at least a few inches, Lark instead inheriting his father's broad shoulders and stocky nature, but they both looked so much like William in their own way that it sometimes took Marin's breath away.

"Just… just tell me what's going on," she said, dropping her face in her hands. "I'm in the dark and you keep running off, and then Sorrell's leg… I can't help but imagine the worst. I don't think I could take it if you got hurt anymore," she whispered into her fingers. She knew they'd heard her. They always did.

"I, uh." Lark let Sorrell down into the armchair, pointedly ignoring his brother's look. "Look, we had some things to wrap up. When Sorrell got hurt… well, people were relying on us and it's hard to do the job alone so—"

"What job?" she asked sharply, sitting up. "Not your errands in the Lower District?"

Lark shook his head. "No, no, not that. We… we, uh…" he looked at Sorrell pleadingly.

"We've been helping get some of the Humans out of the city," Sorrell said quietly, sighing.

Marin froze, feeling her brow furrow. That wasn't what she'd expected at all, nor did she really know what they were talking about. "What do you mean, 'out'? Why?"

"You know how bad it's gotten, Mother, it's hardly a secret that Karkas and Zavalynn are making life miserable down in the Lower District," Lark said, his nose curling as he said their names. She did know, although she hadn't realized they'd been so aware. After all, she'd been feeding the Humans who lived there longer than they'd been alive. But no one had said anything about leaving the city.

"But why are they leaving? Where are they going?"

Lark shrugged, but Sorrell was the one with the answers. "South, at first, towards Ozhansa. The Azha are more accepting of Human settlements, especially if they have any skill with harvesting. Most are trying to get to Adbeter eventually, although I don't know much about that. Our job was just to get them out, simple as that." He sighed. "We weren't supposed to know more than that because of Zavalynn. His Foxes are up to no good, Mother, it's getting really bad."

She didn't need her sons to tell her that. Zavalynn had changed, and not for the better. The Foxes, his ridiculous group of followers, had started up a few decades earlier and she was sure the power had gone to his head.

"You didn't fall, did you?" she asked, hoping she was wrong. Tamora had warned her that the break was too severe to simply be from a fall but she hadn't wanted to listen. Now, though, she needed to know. "Who did it? I swear to the Wela —"

"We were coming back from a run, a family of six that was a rush job. Their mother was being followed around by one of Zavalynn's runners, and they were getting nervous so they just wanted to get out. We didn't think we'd been seen..." Sorrell sighed heavily, rubbing at his shoulder and refusing to meet her eye. This was obviously something he'd never intended her to know. "We were wrong..."

Marin looked at Lark. Sorrell was stubborn and embarrassed; she'd never get it out of him now. Lark, for all his talk, was a softie when it came to her. "Lark, who was it?"

"Mother—"

"Tell me who it was!" she shouted, hearing the screech of her own voice in her ears. Their eyes widened and Lark even took a step back. Marin felt an immediate pang of regret but pushed it aside.

"The guy wasn't someone we recognized, but he knew who we were and he knew you. He said... he said terrible things about Dad," Lark said, looking at the floor as he got the words out. "He said we should stop poking around, that'd we'd gotten into more than we could handle. We didn't think he'd be any trouble, but he wasn't alone and they had better control of their Eiyer." He seemed frozen in his story, the truth spilling from him like water from a hose. Sorrell's face was set in a grimace, his hand unconsciously digging into his thigh.

"He had a fox tail tattoo on his arm," Sorrell said, his voice cutting through Lark's. "There's only one group in the city with that mark."

Marin held back the urge to cry; her throat was full of rage as she put pieces together that had been dangling in front of her for years. *Of course it was Silas*, she thought, her eyes looking straight through her boys. He'd been the first person she'd really met when she'd arrived in Erengate and he hadn't laughed when she'd told him she was going to open a bakery in the Harbor District. Everyone else had warned her that she'd lose money, that her goods were too fine for the clientele she'd receive, that she'd be robbed or worse living where she was. Instead, he'd offered to back her. It was with his help that she'd gotten her footing; she'd more than paid him back. Money wasn't what he'd wanted though.

Marin could still remember clearly the day she and William had publicly announced their wedding. It had been a beautiful ceremony, and private, but she had insisted on sending handwritten letters to her own family and friends. Her father had even come, despite his misgivings. Silas hadn't responded. Still, not even two days passed before she found the ripped shreds on her stoop, her own careful penmanship hardly recognizable, and a single rose dripping with black pitch. They hadn't spoken again until after William's death. She'd hoped he'd forgotten or moved on. Clearly, he hadn't.

"Mother, are you alright?" Lark asked, his voice soft. Marin snapped her gaze to him, her return from the past abrupt and disheartening. *Zavalynn has been planning this for years*, she realized with a heavy heart. *He wants to ruin me, and for what? A relationship that never truly existed in the first place? Their actions gave him the opportunity he needed to make his first move.*

"I'm fine," she said, lying through her teeth, and from their shared glance they knew it as well. "I'm not fine. I thought... I'm sorry that my past has hurt you," she admitted.

"It was our fault—"

"No, Lark, it wasn't," she said, shaking her head. "I'm deeply afraid that this has little to do with either of you, although you're the ones who have been hurt and threatened. I... I need some time." She stood abruptly, feeling a touch of haze from the Azha liquor that hadn't yet worn off. *That's good,* she thought, looking at the side table. The bottle still rested there, its harsh liquid still and threatening. She grabbed the bottle, and her glass, and closed the door as she entered her private room.

Marin could hear Lark and Sorrell talking; Sorrell was angry with his brother for revealing too much. Both didn't want to see her upset and that did nothing to quell the frustration and sadness she so desperately wanted to silence. The *puhu* was more successful.

Chapter 9

Racynth

As Racynth made his way through the Harbor and Trading Districts he wasn't thinking about his impending meeting with Lord Severo Karkas, nor of the numerous groups of wandering Eilvyn and Iokan guards he passed. His mind had instead drifted back toward the appearance of the Azha healer, Tamora Asken. He'd seen the tattoos on her neck, even marred as they were, and they gave him pause. His Sentinella had two Iokans, a Mago named Aspen whose control over earth was notable, and a young Veden named Jordan whose skills with water were close to unmatched. Long ago, when they were still stuck at their last post, Aspen and her Guardian Petro had taken pity on the Eilvyn in their group and explained some of the nuances of Iokan culture. It differed, naturally, between Iokans, but the broad strokes were the same.

Tattoos were given to those who achieved great deeds or passed certain checkpoints during their schooling. It was normal, Aspen had said, for an Iokan to receive their first marking around the age of ten, when it is expected that they should be able to summon a handful of their respective element with ease. Aspen had shown them some of her markings, although many were deemed too personal to reveal, and had explained that a fellow Iokan should be able to easily perceive the skill of any Iokan whose markings they saw. As such, few Iokans revealed their markings in public and they rarely extended beyond their clothing. It was considered cocky, or foolish, to allow potential enemies to read your achievements as if from a page in a book.

Tamora, however, had quite a few visible markings. *She doesn't strike me as particularly foolish*, he mused. *Each Sentinella has mentioned her reluctance to discuss her past, I would imagine the injuries are reason enough for that. More so, if she were very powerful.*

Racynth turned down a wide street, running from the Trading District's central square toward the Upper Gate, and focused his mind on the task at hand. Tamora Asken, although an interesting puzzle, could wait. Della, the Sentinella's historian, had made sure to mention the rumors that the Karkas family was at risk of losing their tightly held influence over the city. There were other families moving north, seeing opportunity in the export of inqu, and tension had been brewing for many years as the market grew more competitive. While he had been in the city earlier today he'd confirmed those suspicions. Not to mention, Soren Karkas was a problem. He was brash and violent, motivated by spite and petty revenge rather than any actual strategy.

No doubt his father is aware of today's incident, he thought. It had been all the guards were talking about as he'd entered through the main gate; Soren Karkas had been attacked by a Human, supposedly. It hadn't taken more than a few questions to poke holes in that rumor, but it seemed to have stuck with the Eilvyn merchants and their customers.

The streets in this frozen city were chaotic in arrangement and Racynth had to clearly visualize the maps that Della had drawn just to get his bearings straight. Still, only a blind man would have missed the entrance to the Upper District. The gate here was taller and far finer than that of the Lower District, lined with what appeared to be marble and glass-encased torches and patrolled by a team of guards whose armor was distinct from that of the rest of the city guard. It was light, almost white, and the Karkas crest was emblazoned on their chest beside that of Erengate itself. They wore cloaks as well, attached at the shoulders, which Racynth deemed ridiculous. Their mobility would be greatly reduced and they'd lose precious time dealing with the heavy thing, as it looked to be a fine velvet. Still, the image they presented was impressive enough.

"Who's there?" a sharp voice rang out, a man gesturing at him to approach. He raised his arm in greeting, although the gesture likely went unappreciated in the gloom.

"Sentinel Racynth Naewynn, second-in-command of the Fifth Sentinella, here to speak with Lord Karkas on behalf of Commander Sabina Miayra," he announced. The formalities rolled off his tongue; he'd said them often enough over the decades. These scenarios often played out in the same way. He'd greet them, they'd be standoffish, he'd explain his purpose, and they'd fall over themselves apologizing for any offense and probably offer a drink or two. Which, he thought, he'd happily take them up on after his meeting with Lord Karkas.

The guard stood atop the wall, on a ledge that jutted out just above the metal gate. It was like a balcony, Racynth noticed, recalling children's tales of damsels in distress in desperate need of saving. He snorted. That would make this guard the damsel, surely.

"Let him through," the Eilvyn damsel said finally, stepping back out of sight. Racynth heard the grinding of metal and watched as the gate rose upward, eight massive spikes rising out of the street before shuddering to a stop far above his head. The same guard was already waiting inside the Upper District, watching the gate rise with a bored expression.

Seeing that Racynth had failed to immediately jump into motion he gestured with his arm impatiently. "We've been expecting your arrival for some time, Sentinel Naewynn," he said as Racynth stepped over the threshold.

Were you now? Racynth wondered, deciding he had no doubt been recognized when he first entered the city. While he wasn't on their timeline, he now worried that he may have stepped on some toes by not announcing his presence immediately.

"I was caught up in a small matter upon my arrival, which took some time to resolve," he replied. The man had already started to walk but Racynth held out his hand, waiting for him to turn.

It took a moment, enough that Racynth began to feel decidedly uncomfortable. When the man did turn, his frustration and urgency were replaced with confusion. "Ah, I forget myself," he said with a stiff smile. His shake was too firm and exceedingly brief; Racynth felt more brushed off than he had before. "Sir Abalian Ularan, Commander of the Guard. We are needed elsewhere."

Sir Ularan continued on, checking only once to ensure Racynth was following.

"Commander of the Guard, impressive. I hope they didn't have you waiting for me this whole time," he said quietly, knowing the Eilfe would hear.

"I did," he replied, "although I did not shirk my other duties."

"Of course not." Racynth wouldn't have expected it, but still, having a man of his station sitting at the gate all day was hardly a good use of his time.

The man seemed exhausted, no doubt a result of his position. Sir Ularan hardly spoke as they walked the quiet streets, and Racynth was able to use the opportunity to get a good look at the Upper District. It was a difference of night and day between this district and the others. The streets were clear of all debris, the walls were smooth and frequently washed, and the shutters on the windows were all thrown open to reveal panes of clean glass. Some doors were painted and decorated; he noticed that one in particular belonged to a jeweler, who had placed an engraved plaque on his stoop and embedded a few precious stones into the surface, which caught the torchlight as he passed.

"Most of these are nobles?" he asked, looking at Sir Ularan.

The commander nodded, his gait quickening. "Yes sir, for the most part. You have some of the more well-off merchants and entertainers in another part of the district, but they're few and far between on this street. The rest are over there, to the north of the palace," he said, gesturing. "Many of these homes belong to members of Lord Karkas's council, or members of the court."

Racynth nodded; it was what he'd expected.

"How far off do you expect the rest of your Sentinella to be?" Sir Ularan asked after a few moments, sneaking another glance.

"A week, maybe less." Something about his tone gave Racynth pause. "Why?"

The knight shrugged. "Always good to know when the Sentinella will be here — no offense. It's just that one man can't be expected to get much done."

"I would think it's more than enough. It is only a week, after all," Racynth said. He could send word to Sabina, as well, if there were an emergency and the full Sentinella was needed sooner. They were only in Vasna; a few days' hard ride to the south.

Sir Ularan seemed troubled, his mouth set in a wobbly

line. "Ah... maybe it's best if you just talk to Lord Karkas."

Racynth shrugged. "Very well. I do find it best to talk to the soldiers on the ground, actually patrolling the streets. You'd be that man, wouldn't you? I sense you to be a man of action," he said casually, noting how the commander puffed up.

"It's good of you to notice, Sentinel. Sometimes I do feel that I can be overlooked... well. I admit it can sometimes be difficult here, what with the people sticking their noses into everything. Makes it hard to keep the peace," he said with a nod, a habit that seemed to accompany anything that he expected should be agreed with.

"Seems the perfect time for a Sentinella to patrol," Racynth said. Sir Ularan nodded sharply. The palace wasn't far now, maybe a few hundred feet up a sharp set of stairs that stretched across the entire road. Side streets broke off, circling around the palace entrance, and Racynth knew from the maps he'd seen that the palace took up the easternmost half of the Upper District. It rose up against the wall like a beacon, each of the palace windows flickering with individual candles. Lanterns were placed at regular intervals up the steps, ensuring that you never stood in complete shadow. It was beautiful and effective, Racynth noted, nodding to the guards he came closest to.

"I'm sure you'll find more than enough to keep yourselves occupied," Sir Ularan agreed, stopping just short of the steps. "This is where I leave you, much to do. Wela be with you, Sentinel Naewynn."

Sir Ularan nodded and turned on his heel, walking with the determination of a man accustomed to drills and years of strict orders. Racynth watched him go curiously for a moment before turning back to the steps and bracing himself for a meeting with nobility and, not for the first time, wished that Sabina had been able to come ahead in his stead. She was far better suited for such things.

.....

The first thing that came to his attention was that every guard in the palace was an Eilfe, not even a single Iokan among them. He ignored their curious looks, rubbing his beard absent-mindedly. *I should shave it; it draws attention*, he thought, frowning. Thinking back, he recognized that this uniformity was unique to the Upper District. He distinctly remembered being questioned by a Veden at the main gate. In fact, out of any of the guards, she'd been the most thorough. *And she only asked three questions.*

He was allowed inside the palace, the guards carefully swinging the doors on smooth hinges, and he was as mindful as possible not to tread too much dirt on the cold and pristine marble floors.

"Stop, *Joien*," spoke a voice. Racynth hadn't made it more than five feet inside. The announcement came as a surprise and he turned to the left, looking for the source of the commanding voice. Another Eilfe, this one in more ornate clothing. His ageless face was encircled with white fur, the cloak itself ending just below the knees, and his white leather boots drew added attention to his long frame. "I said stop!" he repeated, his voice frustrated and losing its previous resolve.

"I have a meeting with Lord Karkas," Racynth said with some forced consideration, nodding stiffly and continuing on his way. Simply referring to him as *Joien* could be, in the right company, enough to make an arrest for disrespect. Not that he'd ever done so, despite being tempted many times. He would never hear the end of it from Sabina. Still, it was tempting.

"*Joien*, none may speak with Lord Karkas without first addressing me," said the man, as he took a few more steps forward. He was quickly breaching the space between them and Racynth could almost feel the disdain wafting from him. Racynth came to a stop and turned fully. The man's eyes caught the emblem and his brow furrowed. "You're the Sentinel then. Interesting. I never thought they would allow any *Joien* to join the Sentinels," he said slowly. He shook his head. "My point stands, regardless of your title."

"Who are you?" Racynth asked, his patience all but gone.

The frown deepened. "Lord Marcus Kelleth Enzana, advisor to Lord Karkas," he said proudly. *Pompous prick*, Racynth thought, careful to keep his expression neutral. That this man would use his full name was arrogant in the extreme, and not in keeping with Eilvyn tradition. Your second name was personal, private, and rarely spoken outside the family. Some had begun to go against tradition in recent years, believing the second name to be a powerful indicator of class and sophistication. It wasn't something Racynth was inclined to believe in.

"Sentinel Racynth Naewynn, at your city's service. I come ahead on behalf of Commander Sabina Miayra of the Fifth Sentinella, due to arrive in a week's time."

"Miayra? Hm."

Racynth waited a moment, feeling worn from the day and wanting desperately for this interrogation to end.

"My Lord, I really must be meeting with Lord Karkas," he said when the advisor did not elaborate.

Lord Enzana frowned up at him. "Your kind really are quite impatient, aren't they? Very well. Follow," he said. *My kind? Does he mean Sentinels, or Humans?* Racynth paused, staring daggers at the back of the man's head for a moment, before continuing the way he had been before this interruption. *It would be wrong to arrest him, and make our time here even more unpleasant*, he reminded himself, watching the advisor stroll down the hall. It was tempting, however.

They turned, Lord Enzana moving with the ease of someone who traveled these halls every day. "Lord Karkas has retired for the evening, *Sentinel*. It is quite late," he said without looking back.

Racynth remained silent; he owed no explanation to this man. They passed many doors and half a dozen halls and he realized that the architects of the city must have designed this building as well, as it was a maze. He made a mental note to ask Della who had built Erengate; he'd like to have a name in mind when he cursed them for their insanity. Finally they reached a door that was solid, closed, and quite imposing. It was ten feet in height and carved oak, stained dark and set seamlessly into the stone. On its surface was an ornately carved boar, the Karkas symbol, lunging toward whatever poor soul reached for the handle.

"Impressive, no?" Lord Enzana asked. When Racynth turned to him, the Eilfe was looking at him closely.

Racynth arched his brow. "It's well crafted. May I?" he asked. The Eilfe's face was pulled down by a frown and he rapped his knuckles on the boar's tusk. Without waiting for an answer he twisted the handle and stepped inside. Racynth caught the door to follow, biting back a swear.

The smell of garlic assaulted his senses and he was temporarily overcome, blinking as his mouth watered and his stomach growled. *I missed dinner*, he realized too late, searching for the source. There was a desk sitting beside a massive fireplace, within which a few logs still burned. Upon the desk were papers and a set of ink and quills, but more notable was the plate of bread, cheese, dried meat, and a small bowl of what Racynth assumed was a garlic spread.

The man behind the desk was an unassuming older Eilfe, his mottled silver hair cropped short and a surprisingly wrinkled face smiling tightly. "Ah, Sentinel. Welcome," he said, his voice flat as he rose to his feet.

Racynth bowed shortly.

"Lord Karkas, Sentinel Racynth Naewynn. Reporting on behalf of—"

"Yes, yes, Commander Miayra. I'm aware," he said, waving his hand and sitting heavily.

Racynth paused. "Sir, I have come to report—"

"Your presence in the city, I assume. Welcome to Erengate," Lord Karkas sighed dismissively. It was oddly disconcerting, Racynth realized, to see an elderly Eilfe. They existed, naturally. But one rarely remained in the social eye after four centuries or so.

He resolved to try again. "There are matters—"

"For us to discuss, yes. Thank you for broaching the subject, there is much for me to enlighten you on," said Lord Karkas as he picked up his quill from where he had placed it. Racynth's eyes narrowed. "Please, Sentinel, sit down and do not look at me so darkly. Are you hungry?"

"I'm fine," he said, remaining standing. There was no seat offered and Lord Karkas's advisor stood off to one side, closer to the warmth of the fire, his face set into a vaguely disapproving mask.

"Then we can get to business, so that you can begin to resolve a matter I am most concerned with. I am saddened to inform you," Lord Severo Karkas said, his voice measured, never rising in tone or pitch, "we have reports of traitors in our midst."

"I'm sorry? Traitors to the Council, here in Erengate?"

Lord Severo Karkas shook his head, ink dripping from his quill as he gestured with it. "Oh Wela no, no. Against the Karkas line! Against my own flesh and blood! It is a mutiny," he finished in a mutter. "A mutiny that will no doubt end with my head if they get what they want."

"Ah," Racynth said, pausing as he thought of what to say, and how to not offend. "Who leads this mutiny, then?"

"Humans." The lord spat out the word with such venom Racynth's eyes widened instinctually. "They are trying to ruin me and injure my son. My only son, you understand. Just today they attacked him in the streets — this cannot be allowed to stand. I need your help."

"While I agree your son's claims are concerning—"

"We are going to be rounding up all of those Humans in the Lower District, anyone who has been noted on record in the last decade," said Lord Karkas, as though he hadn't heard the man before him. "They will be held and questioned, and if they are innocent they may be released. This is the only way to be sure."

"Hold on just a moment—"

"You believe your judgment to be of greater value than Lord Karkas's?" Lord Enzana peeled himself from the bench he had been perched upon. Racynth glared at him briefly, hoping it was enough to get the message across.

"No. I do recommend caution, however. A mass arrest of the people would surely only provoke your enemies, rather than calm them," Racynth said.

"I'm not looking to calm them," Lord Karkas scoffed. His advisor nodded pleasantly along with him, saving his sharp look for Racynth. *Is he trying to start a war?* Racynth thought, blinking and realizing he may be. Some people, Eilvyn mostly, had not moved past the last uprising. It only ended ninety-three years ago after all. The approaching hundred-year anniversary of the final battle was already raising concern in Koren. "If we proceed with caution we are at risk and I will not have it. The arrests begin tomorrow." He gestured with sharp finality. "Thank you, Sentinel. Your wisdom has contributed much to my peace of mind on this matter."

Racynth frowned outwardly then. "I don't—"

"I will escort you to your rooms, if you would like," Lord Enzana said smoothly, cutting him off. Racynth raised a hand, knowing that he should push back against this treatment but feeling very alone at the moment.

"No, but thank you. Commander Miayra sent a messenger ahead and reserved a set of rooms in the city. We like to have an on-the-ground view of the situation, you understand." His things were already there, in fact, bundled into the room he'd taken the liberty of claiming. It had the best view, in his opinion. "Lord Karkas, I thank you for your hospitality. I do recommend restraint in these times. Often it is during times of great stress when we must look inward and choose peace instead of further violence," he said. Lord Karkas looked as though he had not heard him.

"Your services are a boon to our city, Sentinel. Wela be with you."

Racynth knew when he was dismissed and he took his leave gratefully. *Those morning rounds sound like the perfect opportunity to observe the guards when the arrests begin,* he thought. The prospect of the rest of the Sentinella arriving a week after mass incarcerations made his skin crawl.

He picked up his pace, anxious to leave these gaudy walls and return to their rooms. There was an urgent message that needed sending.

Chapter 10

Tamora

The forest was dark and heavy with its usual sense of foreboding when she finally reached its edge. Tamora looked to the sky; the clouds had separated just enough that she could catch a glimpse of the crescent moon. Nearly midnight, she wagered. Lovely. She sped into the thick tree cover and found the small footpath as fast as her hip could manage. It was hardly a path; no one even dared hunt beneath these trees. Not officially, anyway. There'd been the odd hunter here and there, desperate people trying in vain to feed starving families. It was rare. The old stories held these people tight in their clutches.

The tall and crooked trees twisted over the path and nearly blocked out the sun entirely and their black bark made the forest feel deeper and more vast at night. Nearly everything not covered by snow was coated in a layer of reddish moss, that made it look as though the ground were bleeding. The water on the ground turned the path into a mucky mess and Tamora half expected a Kit'ak to snake their way past, so deep were the pools amongst the trees. She'd never seen one willingly come this far north. Not outside the city walls, where they were kept as amusements. A water-dwelling people, half-fish and half-man, that the Eilvyn were both captivated and horrified by. They delighted in parading them about in the summer months. She had no idea where they went come winter; she didn't think they would do well once all but the sea froze solid.

Tamora's boots were soaked through by the time she saw the low wall that surrounded her cottage. Her home was small, not at all the homestead Marin often assumed it was. She never visited to prove herself wrong; she was under the impression the forest was possessed by spirits that would haunt her dreams. Tamora had no such qualms, and had experienced no such dreams.

She pushed open the gate and said a quiet hello to the figures carved and placed carefully on their posts at either side. Makmo and Ioka, King and Queen of the Shimmering Plane and rules of the Wela. Tamora paused, brushing off a few twigs and leaves that had gathered atop their heads. They almost looked the way they were supposed to. Her old attempts to carve had largely been in vain, an attempt to prove to Selena that she could do more than just fight, and she'd burned most of what she'd done decades ago. She hadn't been able to bring herself to do the same for these two. Makmo's greatsword was far from straight and Ioka's war-scythe looked more like a curved spoon. Her fingers lingered on the woman's rough hewn head and hoped her deeds today did her proud.

Her kitchen was as disheveled as she had left it. Ashes lay in the hearth. The leak at the back wall was creating another puddle. She sighed, ignored it all, and sat heavily in her chair.

This was far from the first execution she'd seen. Still, Tamora stewed over what she'd seen today. Karkas had been different from his usual insulting self. He'd spouted these inflammatory accusations before, but they'd never felt so real, or so violent. People had never actually taken him seriously. *Wrong.* She shocked herself with her own thoughts. *They listened to his grandfather. What if it happens again?* Tamora snorted.

"Impossible. No one is that stupid." Her muttered voice echoed and she felt far more alone than she had in a long time. "Great. I'm talking to myself. That's healthy."

Tamora stared at the hearth. She needed a fire; a chill had settled in while she'd been away. She looked at her hands, her eyes tracing the deep scars. The temptation to call up her flames was almost overwhelming. There'd been a time when she could have had the fire blazing in a heartbeat — Dalka help her, she could have lit a thousand hearths with a snap of her fingers. It would have been for amusement, or for Selena's comfort. In those days the cold hadn't ever touched her; now all she felt was cold.

"Ugh, what am I doing?" she muttered, dropping her head in her hands. The old her wouldn't have gone quietly back to her home after seeing what she'd seen, whether that was Karkas or those idiots in the street. As for the Sentinel, she was certain he was going to be a problem. They always poked and prodded when they came through; a solitary Iokan in the woods playing healer wasn't exactly common fare. This one seemed especially observant though and she hadn't made a competent first impression. Not to mention the fact that he was going to talk to Lord Karkas sooner or later and she was far from popular in court. He'd be visiting, she was sure of it.

In the meantime, though, she needed firewood. Tamora groaned and pushed herself to her feet, trudging toward the door.

Chapter 11

Marin

Morning came and found Marin still deep asleep, the now empty bottle of puhu at her side. She jolted upright at the light push of a finger on her cheek, blinking rapidly up at Lark as he backed away. Daylight was peeking through the window and she could hear patrons downstairs.

"Oh my Wela, what time is it?" She jumped to her feet and swayed as spots sprang in front of her eyes. "Damn the Azha that invented this," she groaned, pushing uselessly against the bridge of her nose and praying for her dizziness to go away.

"Mid-morning," Lark said, eyeing her with thinly veiled appraisal. "Never seen you drink so much in one go."

She held up a finger. "Please, Lark, I'm not in the mood. Is —"

"Eloise is running the show, yeah, and Sorrell's propped up down there in the corner and telling off anyone who tries any funny business. Not that there's much going on. We figured you needed the sleep," he said with a smirk. Marin would have rolled her eyes if she hadn't known it would hurt.

"Just... give me a minute," she muttered, ushering him outside and firmly closing the door behind him. She let out a breath, knowing full well he could still hear her. *That was stupid, Marin. Reckless, embarrassing, entirely unbefitting a woman of your reputation*— she cut into her thoughts and shook her head free of them, instantly regretting the movement.

She gathered another skirt and quickly got ready, pinching the skin on her cheeks to try to bring a little more life into her face. Lark was still in the other room when she emerged and he shrugged at the sight of her. "There's no need to rush, we've got this."

"Did anyone come by while I was asleep?"

Lark nodded. "A few people, but I sent them off. At dawn something started up outside — soldiers are patrolling the streets, telling everyone to stay inside. Not sure we're going to have any customers today." Marin couldn't get rid of the sinking feeling in her chest.

"What?" she asked. "What do you mean, soldiers?"

He waved her to follow, looking back to ensure she was fit to do so. Marin stared after him for a moment, hand on her hip. *What in Dalka's name is going on?* The bakery was empty, all her carefully prepared goods waiting for nonexistent customers, and Eloise and Sorrell leapt apart from each other as she came into view.

"Ma'am," Eloise said softly, a blush creeping across her face. A purplish bruise stretched across the bridge of her nose and Marin paused.

"Are you alright?" she asked, and Eloise nodded.

"There were some men last night that gave us trouble, but Tamora helped me." Marin was filled with a rush of anger that did nothing to help her pounding headache. *We should have kept her home*, she realized, *it would have been safer*.

"What's going on?" she asked, frowning out the door. What she could see of the streets were also entirely devoid of people, but Lark stopped her as she put her hand on the handle.

"This was slipped underneath the door when we came down," he said, handing her a piece of paper. It was freshly printed, she could still smell the warmth of the ink, and she blinked at the words for a few moments before they registered.

"'Under order of Lord Karkas, any individual with a history of disorder or record of abuse against the Karkas family will be detained for questioning'— what in Dalka's name is this?" she said, looking back up at the three young faces watching her. Waiting for her reaction, she realized. Her eyes flitted over the words again and she couldn't help but snort. "This is because of that business with the Human yesterday. Lord Karkas, the younger Lord, mind you—must have been embarrassed." She sighed. *That would be Tamora's doing, of course.*

"Embarrassed or not, he's dangerous like this. His father is looking for villains, and they've started with the Lower District from what I heard earlier," Sorrell said, grasping Eloise's hand comfortingly.

"Your parents?"

She frowned. "Fine, ma'am. T—hey've gone to our neighbors for the night, hoping it'll pass. They told me to come straight here, that they didn't want me to get caught up in it all." Marin couldn't blame them but the air of stress that surrounded the poor girl was palpable.

"I'm sure they'll be fine, love," she assured her, her own worry needling its way into her mind. Her parents were kind people but they'd drawn some attention to themselves a year back; nothing they'd done, per say, but it had been enough to ensure that Bear was never far from the guard's minds. "All right, we'll stay inside. If any customers do come in we'll obviously help them... no matter what they may need."

She looked directly at Lark and Sorrell, hoping they'd

understand. From what they'd shared last night, they were more than equipped to handle any small problem that might come to their door. If it was anything bigger than that she hoped they'd come to her.

First, though, she needed to make some tea to try to rid herself of this Wela-forsaken headache.

.....

Only a single customer stopped in before midday, a small Tri woman who took some of their rye loaves off their hands and quickly bundled herself back up to head outside. *Not the priority I would have at a time like this but I suppose I can't blame her*, Marin thought, pressing her fingers to the bridge of her nose. The pain had subsided somewhat, and she'd rejoined her sons and Eloise down in the bakery.

She reread the missive Lord Karkas had sent out and rolled her eyes. This would pass, she was sure of it, but it wouldn't be as easily forgotten by Erengate's Humans. A 'history of disorder' could mean anything and most working Humans had been reprimanded for one thing or another over the years. It was nearly impossible not to be with the requirements the city had placed on them.

The issue with Zavalynn weighed heavily on her mind and combined with this ridiculous order from Karkas, it was all becoming too much. She was sure he'd had something to do with it. Marin glanced at the clock, seeing that it was just after noon. Zavalynn always took his lunch with Madame Lucrezia — their friendship was one of the more unsettling things about her inn. *I could go and speak with him... well, scream is more like it*, she thought, tapping the paper on the countertop.

"I'm going out," she said sharply, drawing the others' attention.

"What? Now?" Lark asked, leaping to his feet. "But the order says—"

"The order says that those who are enemies of the city will be questioned — I am hardly an enemy of the city. We all know what this means, Lark, and they aren't talking about Eilvyn bakers who have been here nearly a century. I have some business to attend to, I'll be back soon," she assured him, wiping her skirt out of habit. "Stay inside, all three of you, and close the shop. We'll keep the extra goods for the Lower District once it's safe to send Eloise back."

"If you're going to do something because of what we shared last night—"

Marin cut off Sorrell. "If I am, it's my responsibility as your mother. It will be alright, I promise," she said, going for her overcoat and bracing herself for the afternoon's cold air.

.....

The streets around her bakery were deserted save for a few guards, who walked towards her until they recognized her as Eilvyn and backed off. She ran into a few more people, Eilvyn and Iokans who seemed to be going about their normal days, just a few streets on and from there to The Dancing Clover she encountered more and more people as it became clear that the flyers were only impacting the Harbor and Lower Districts. The Dancing Clover's building was painted red, chipping around the edges and so gaudy it almost hurt to look at. She felt her scowl deepen and her anger grow as she pushed her way into the inn, immediately bumping into two of the dozens of lunch patrons.

It stank of perfume and sickly flowers, the drapery clogged with it and the tables all had sticky sheen that never quite came up. Drinks were being ushered around by their imposing Madame, who lingered at the foot of the stairs just inside the inn. She smiled broadly as people drank and ate, not seeing Marin step inside. It was for the best, as Marin knew the two weren't on the best terms. Her referral to Tamora all those years ago hadn't turned out well; Tamora had nearly burned down the third floor. Entirely accidentally, but Madame Lucrezia had a long memory.

Zavalynn sat at his usual table, a group of his Foxes surrounding him. She had to shove down the anger that threatened to strangle her from the inside as she saw his face. He had a swollen lip, likely from that Human he'd help to arrest, and the thought of her fate only added to Marin's anger. His blank look of disdain dissipated as he saw her approach.

"Marin," he said, partially standing and motioning for her to be let through the crowd.

"What did you do to my boys? To Sorrell?" she asked, shocking even herself with her voice's coldness. He froze and his smile looked painful.

"Marin, be reasonable—"

"Why did you do it, Silas? Was it one of these goons, did one of them do it? Or did you just hire someone new to do your dirty work?" She pointed her finger at his chest as she approached. One of the goons, as she so eloquently put it, made to step between them but Zavalynn pushed him aside.

"Marin, I have no idea what you're talking about," he said, his hands out to his sides in a display of innocence. She didn't believe it. *He's mocking me, I know it.* She stopped short of his table, looking at the sprawl of food before him. *So much, just for lunch. Meanwhile the people who live down the street were near starving all season.*

"You have no idea," she said, her voice quiet. She looked down, seeing the ridiculous fox tail tattoo on the back of his hand and scowled. "Did you try to have my sons killed?" She didn't have to look up to hear him swallow and pause.

"Marin. Why would I—"

"To get them out of the way. To punish me for not marrying you. That's what you've wanted all this time," she said, feeling the immediate wrongness of this conversation. It was too soon, too public, and she had no proof. But she was so angry she couldn't stop. Her head hurt and her heart was heavy as a stone, threatening to pull her into a spiral of doubt if she let it. "Tell me I'm wrong, Silas. Please. I thought you were my friend."

He had the sense to give her a moment. She looked at him then, hoping to see something of the man she'd met when she came to this frozen land. He'd been charming then and the Karkas family had been nothing but a distant influence. That had changed so quickly when he'd met Soren, and he'd started the Foxes and then her marriage to William had been the final straw between them.

"You—" he was interrupted by an argument at the bar that reached a crescendo, grimacing as it distracted him a moment.

"Are you the reason Sorrell can't walk?" she asked pointedly, glaring across at him. She instinctively gathered Eiyer to her and the Foxes around him stood, drawing their weapons. The inn fell silent as they drew attention and Marin became distinctly aware at how many people seemed focused on her and Zavalynn. He blanched, glancing around as he walked around the table. While he stood over her by a few inches she wasn't a small woman and she refused to step away as he approached her.

"Marin, perhaps we should continue this conversation elsewhere," he said, reaching for her arm.

"No, I don't think so." She pulled away, feeling her heart beating in her chest. "I shouldn't have come," she said quietly, the anger in her chest fizzling as it was replaced by a rush of embarrassment. Never had she made so much of a scene, and never would she have dared talk to him in this way before. It was time to go home.

She breathed in deeply through her nose, shaking her head. "I don't want you anywhere near my family, do you hear me? There is nothing left between us, that's been clear enough for years. Stay away from my boys, stay away from Eloise, stay away from my home. Do I make myself clear?"

Zavalynn blinked at her, dumbfounded. The two Eilvyn he'd brought with him stared anywhere but at him, unwilling to look at their boss. "I think there's been a misunderstanding. In my role with Lord Karkas you cannot—"

Marin turned to step away, trying to dismiss him, and her eye caught that of one of the men at the bar as he took a few steps closer. An Iokan, his tattooed skin deeply tanned, with the distinct broad look of an Azha about him. He grinned wildly, holding his full glass up to her, before slamming it over the head of one of Zavalynn's men.

Absolute chaos sprang from thin air.

The Azha disappeared, his form engulfed by the brawl that piled atop him. Marin, only ten feet from the door, was thrown to the side as previously quiet patrons leapt to their feet to join the fray. She gasped as an elbow caught her in the ribs and she stumbled, losing her breath entirely. *I have to get out of here*, she thought, unable to concentrate on anything else. The sudden violence had frozen her mind. She crouched as she tried to avoid flying fists but someone fell backward in front of her and kicked out, hitting her just above the knee and throwing her to the floor.

Rough hands grabbed her by the shoulders and she flailed at the man wildly, her only thought that Zavalynn had sent someone to grab her. The man swore and readjusted his grip, his hands curving under her arms and pulling her to her feet. "Enough,— I'm just trying to help," he bit out, his accent far from local. He pushed through the crowd towards the door. Marin gave up her resistance and hid her face against him. She wasn't a fighter. She never had been. William had teased her incessantly for her consistent refusal to engage in anything that might provoke danger. *What in the world am I doing here then?*

A flood of people rushed out of the Dancing Clover with them, breaking off and running down the street. A few guards had heard the chaos and were using Eiyer to force their way through the doorway to silence the fight inside. Her rescuer refused to put her down outside, instead making a run for an alley a few streets down where it was calmer. She winced as she was set down and looked up at the man. It was the man who had started this whole mess. He wore a fine fur-lined coat, the black fur blending into thick fabric that looked foreign. *It's probably from Ozhansa*, she realized, blinking up at his wide and mischievous face.

"I don't know if I should thank you or curse you," she said, looking anxiously past him at the brightly lit street.

He shrugged, stretching out the shoulder he'd supported her with. "You're the one who wandered into my operation, little lady," he said, grinning down at her. He, like all Azha, was so tall he could easily look down at her.

"Operation? You— you attacked Zavalynn!" Yesterday she wouldn't have believed that anyone would be foolish enough to try; then again, that Human had hit him as well so maybe he wasn't as well protected as he'd believed.

"Is that a problem?" he asked, his voice like gravel.

"I... no," she said, realizing as she said it that she wasn't lying. "I think I came here to do the same thing."

He chuckled at her admission, a rumbling sound that threatened to draw attention. "You set quite the stage for me, I should thank you for that." He rested his hands on his waist, drawing her eye to the broadsword that hung there. His legs were so long it wasn't even close to grazing the ground, a mind-boggling realization.

"I... I wasn't involved with this. I should go," she said, feeling uncomfortably small. "The guards will be swarming the street soon enough. Is he still alive?"

"Zavalynn? Looked to be, when we left. His little friends were protecting him." He frowned, spitting on the cobblestones. "You're right, though, you should go home. Your great frozen wasteland is about to get a little heated," he said with a grin, fiddling with a small flame that danced along his fingertips.

"What are you going to do?" she asked, unable to look away from the fire that lit his face from below. She'd never met an Azha, other than Tamora — she never used her fire though, so sometimes she may as well not be one.

"Just having a little fun, that's all," he said, closing his palm and quenching the playful fire.

She opened her mouth to ask another question but paused, slowly closing it. *It's probably best if I don't know anything. I've already done too much.* "Well... thank you," she said, looking behind her. This alley connected through to another major road, she knew where she was well enough. He bowed his head slightly.

"It was my pleasure."

Marin rushed down the alley and paused, looking for guards. She breathed a sigh of relief at the sight of an empty street and glanced back, still wondering what the Azha was planning. All she found was an empty alley, the street beyond loud and unruly as The Dancing Clover cleared out.

Racynth

He had seen all he needed to. The morning had been bad enough, with what he could only call raids in the Lower District, but those had lost much of their momentum by mid-afternoon. Too many Humans had been arrested for nothing or harassed for deeds committed decades before. The group he'd shadowed had been prepared to break into their homes, and although he had stopped them he was certain others had carried out their intentions. *Is no one worried about the impact this might have? What might come of it?* He'd seen this before, although it had been far from Sienma. When the last rebellion had broken out nearly a century ago he had been in Lathmo, the capital city of the continent's central country of Tomerta. It had been a tumultuous time. Only a week's travel from Koren, the city had quickly become a hotbed of rebellion, led in no small part by the organizer himself. Krystopher Reene had been his name.

Krys's Rebellion, as it came to be known, weighed heavily on Racynth's mind as he made his way back to the inn. The guards had been called away; it seemed the younger Lord Karkas's lackey had been attacked by a mob while eating his lunch. It was far from surprising and Racynth feared this would not be the end of the people's retaliation.

Coming to the inn, a modest establishment far from the prying eyes of the palace, Racynth stopped abruptly at the sight of a shorter man stationed outside the door. He leaned casually against the stained wood, his cropped blonde hair hidden beneath a wool hat and the insignia on his cloak hidden by a dirty brown scarf. But he knew it was there all the same. The man straightened at his approach and grinned, coming over to clasp his hand.

"Jordan,— I thought you were still in Vasna. I wasn't expecting to see you so soon," Racynth said, inwardly relieved. He'd only been in the city a day and already the place was falling apart around him. "You look like shit." Dark circles dug out beneath his normally bright blue eyes, and the ragged scar that peeped out from his collar was stark against his wintery pale skin.

"Tell me about it. We left Vasna just two days behind you — Sabina was getting tired of their rambling. You know how it is. She insisted we pick up the pace after the two of you spoke. It nearly killed the horses but we arrived not even an hour ago," he said, his smile fading to a pained grimace. "I was worried I wouldn't be able to walk, if I'm being honest… you don't want to know how chapped my damn thighs are."

"I thought you'd be used to this by now," chuckled Racynth, shaking his head and leading him inside. It appeared as though they'd shown the other Sentinels to his rooms, which was fine by him. "It's been a year, after all."

"I'm used to a normal ride, sure. But have you done what should have been a two-day leisurely ride, overnight?"

Racynth thought a moment on it as they climbed the stairs. "A handful of times, during the rebellion." The thought soured his mind and brought his thoughts back to the morning's events. It was too similar. "You've only been in the city an hour?"

"Just about — seems like we're just in time for the fun," Jordan said, his drawling voice artificially chipper. Racynth didn't knock on the door, his key moving smoothly in the lock, and he found the others speaking quietly in the main room. The inn was used to hosting Sentinels, it seemed, and well prepared to house the group. A main room with four smaller bedrooms was perfectly suited for the seven of them; Racynth was, as usual, alone in his own space. It was a small perk to their odd arrangement, as a Sentinella normally had eight members. Sabina had been searching for a replacement for years, without much luck, and he figured she'd finally given up the cause. It wouldn't be the only thing strange about her

Sentinella.

"Racynth," she said, standing smoothly. Her blonde hair was pulled back as she always did for travel, the severe bun highlighting the sharpness of her features. Della, sitting as usual beside her, gave him a small wave in greeting and turned back to her maps.

"I hadn't expected you so soon."

Sabina cocked her brow. "Did you really think I'd leave you to handle this alone after that report?" She shook her head, glancing at the window. "I've sent Aspen and Petro to get the lay of the land — you couldn't possibly be everywhere at once."

Racynth nodded, grateful that she'd already been on her way. Grateful, too, for the force that allowed them to communicate over long distances. After nearly eighty years stationed at the library, they had befriended quite a few of the scholars there. Their parting gift had been two stones, that they called runes, that allowed the users to speak even when separated. It only worked, of course, if the user could manipulated Eiyer, and their existence was highly secretive. Only the High Council could lend them out, so Sabina having another set was something they didn't want to draw attention to.

"They should avoid the Lower District, did you tell them? Petro will be noticed," Racynth said, catching Bealantin's eye as he stepped in from the room he and Jordan had claimed. A Human, as all Guardians were, he was almost identical to Jordan in a way that was truly unnerving. The two were clearly made for each other, in some design only the Wela knew. "You too, Beal. It's not safe for Humans, even Guardians."

Jordan snorted. "Like anyone would touch a Sentinel."

Racynth wanted to agree with him, but he'd gotten enough snark and pushback from the guards today to know otherwise. Sabina beat him to it though. "Be careful, all the same. Tensions are high and we don't want to add any problems to our list," she said.

The door opened behind him and they all turned in surprise; Racynth felt as Sabina whipped up the Eiyer around her and held it at the ready. It dissipated as Aspen stepped through, her brown face grim and weary. Petro followed close behind, shutting the door and locking it firmly.

"What are you doing back so soon?"

Aspen's mouth was tight as she replied. "Sorry, Sabina, but we didn't get far. Seems a lord was attacked at an inn in the Harbor District. The place is swarming with guards, and they didn't want anything to do with us," she said, flopping down on the floor and stretching out her legs. "You'll love this though; it wasn't a Human that did it. From the reports, it was an Azha."

Racynth frowned, feeling his body tense and not entirely understanding why. "A woman?"

"No," Aspen said, eying him curiously. "Witnesses said he was tall, dark haired, broad. No one was giving him trouble and out of nowhere he attacked one of the lord's men. Do you know who Lord Zavalynn is?"

"Lackey for the city lord's son," he replied, still shaken at his own reaction. If it had been the healer he would have kicked himself for letting her go so easily. He'd had no reason to hold her, of course, but he'd heard enough of the old reports to know she was one to look out for.

"He's the one with the… what do they call themselves? The bears?" Sabina asked, looking back at Della.

"Foxes," she said, barely looking up from her documents.

"Sure. Well, that's odd, but I can't imagine he's made himself popular." Sabina shrugged. "If they didn't catch him there's not much we can do about it."

"It won't help matters though. Lord Karkas is on edge and thinks he's under attack, and then it comes true. His son's most trusted advisor assaulted in broad daylight. It'll rile things up and make it complicated for all of us. Were any Humans involved?"

"It was mostly Humans," Petro said, his voice gravelly from the cold. He rubbed his pale hands together and blew into them. "I asked the bartender and he said they'd come in with the Azha and no one dared say anything. He threw the first punch but they turned it into a riot."

"How'd that many Humans get in?" Sabina's question was blunt, as usual, but fair.

Petro shrugged; he'd been around long enough now to understand she wasn't being malicious. Bealantin, him and Jordan having only been with them a year, still struggled to hide his frustration. Racynth watched out of the corner of his eye as he turned abruptly to look out the window. "The Azha vouched for them. Doesn't seem like anyone wanted any trouble with him."

Racynth couldn't blame them. Azha could be terrifying, more than most of the Iokans. Jordan could drown you and Aspen could strangle you with vines, but he couldn't think of a worse enemy than one that could burn you alive with the snap of their fingers. Which was why the attack on the healer had been so unusual. "I ran into another Azha just last night.— Tamora Asken."

That got Della's attention. "The healer?" she asked, pushing her short, cropped hair out of her eyes. She rifled through her papers. "We have reports on her."

"Yeah, she knows. I had to save her from some sailors who decided it'd be fun to jump an Azha," he said. That drew surprise from everyone present.

"You think she knows something?" Sabina asked.

"I mean —"

"We can't assume that they know each other just because they're Azha," Aspen said, frowning up at both of them from the floor.

"I'm not saying that. She had a run in with Zavalynn and Karkas as well. She was there when that Human was arrested yesterday," Racynth said, his heart racing as he backtracked. "It's not out of the question that she'd want something done, from what I heard she was pretty involved."

Sabina was tapping her foot, frowning as she thought. "We should talk to her," she said finally. "If only to rule her out. From what I remember, the last Sentinella didn't think she was a threat. A thorn in their side, maybe, but hardly what I'd call dangerous."

"She's injured," Racynth agreed. "Walks with a limp and didn't defend herself against the sailors."

"That's odd," Aspen said, glancing at Jordan. He merely shrugged. "I mean,— I'd do something if some jackass decided to play the bully."

"Who knows what the Azha think," Jordan drawled. "But can we go tomorrow? We've got more than enough to do here that doesn't involve chasing down some reclusive lead."

Sabina nodded, straightening. "Tomorrow. I need to speak with Lord Karkas and we will need to be present in the city tonight. If the day was this much of a problem, I can only imagine what some brave idiots will try in the dark. You'll have your posts and I expect you to keep your eyes open." They all nodded and were dismissed. Racynth found himself glad to have them back. It had been quiet and calming traveling alone, to be sure, but he'd missed their company. They fell into their usual routines, despite the strangeness of the situation. Della briefed the group on the lay of the land, pulling from snippets and observations left to them by the last Sentinella stationed in the region, with Sabina sitting at her side looking over her shoulder. Jordan went to nap, having not beaten Bealantin to the bathtub, and Aspen and Petro stretched and meditated, respectively.

It was, for a brief moment, peaceful.

Chapter 12

Tamora

She refused to allow herself to think about the city — she had her own things to look after. There were balms and tonics to replenish; her personal store was running low, not to mention all that she needed for the dozens who filtered through her door. Tamora tried to assure herself that she had no time for whatever Karkas was scheming up. With each new Human, however, it was growing harder and harder to ignore what was taking place only a few miles from her stoop. The elder Lord Karkas was more vindictive than she'd thought. Most were bruised and battered, and she patched more than a few broken noses, but some who came in were carried by relatives and those she spent the most time with. Many had bruises and a rash she knew could only come from long exposure to Eiyer restraints. For two hours she worked with a young man, his shoulder violently dislocated, listening to his mother explain how he'd tried to stop the guards from rifling through the few remaining possessions his father had left behind. She sent them off with clear instructions on how they could leave the city unnoticed. There was a network, after all, of understanding folk within the city. She only knew a few names but it had been enough; occasionally over the decades she'd received a few words of thanks or an anonymous package with Ozhansan goods. That had been a good week, as she'd savored the spiced jam and enjoyed memories of home. Strictly censored memories, though, as there was still so much she refused to dwell on. She might miss Ozhansa, but it never failed to remind her of who she'd lost.

Tamora woke early the next morning stiff and exhausted, the trees still protecting her small home from the morning sun and keeping her comfortably in shadow. Her sleep had been fitful and interrupted, with strange howling coming from the northern stretches of the forest that had woken her repeatedly, and she was left with a mood as sour as the tea she limped out of her room to prepare. *Damn it, I'm low on wood. Probably better to do it now, who knows who will keep me busy later*, she thought with a scowl. She donned her cloak and went to the door, finding that she hesitated before pulling it inward. She shook her head and stepped outside.

Her woodshed was just past her entryway, a small structure she'd thrown together that she'd been meaning to reinforce for years now. Each passing snowstorm seemed to weaken it and at this point it was just barely doing its job. As she bent to pick up a few of the drier logs, a sharp screech from deeper within the forest froze her spine and her lungs solid. It droned on through the forest, a pained and twisted sound that belonged to nothing she recognized. She'd seen wolves, deer, even rarer beasts she hadn't known existed before she moved so far north. Sienma had a native creature that the locals called a mountain lion but it looked nothing like the sorts she'd seen during her travels. One had been curious when she'd built her cottage, lurking just beyond her low wall and watching her during the nights a few decades back. It was long dead, naturally, but she'd had the opportunity to see its dark coloring around the face, tufted ears, and short horns and it had been like no mountain lion she'd seen before.

This didn't sound like that and it sent a chill of fear through her that kickstarted her breath and sent her quickly inside. She felt a little more secure with the door closed and immediately ridiculous. *I'm not a child*, she scolded herself. *It's just an animal — nothing to be concerned over.* Still, it was a few hours before she stopped glancing out her windows, looking for the creature.

All the time, grinding herbs and packing together some quick remedies she may need for bruises in particular, she couldn't help but wonder how Marin was doing. She imagined it would be difficult for Eloise to get to the bakery, or to get home once she'd arrived, and Sorrell's leg would need to be looked at soon.

"Damn it," she muttered, looking at the dreary day that lurked outside. *I never did check on that... and I promised Marin I would. I'll have to go back in, there's nothing for it. My mind won't let me rest otherwise. Perhaps I can stay with her until the trial... not that I have to go*, she reminded herself. Ultimately, she packed light. She knew how the ordeal would go, and what the result would be. It was no use trying to help the woman, her fate was sealed.

Cutting through the forest was simple enough; she couldn't stop herself from looking around for the creature she'd heard that morning. It had sounded tortured and in such pain she didn't know if she'd help it or put it out of its misery if she did find it. Nothing stepped out from the undergrowth, however, and she reached the tree line unmolested. She paused, catching her breath, and looked out over the fields. It was turning into a bright day, almost warm, and the sun lit the small bits of grass that peeked out from the melting muddy snow drifts. They'd start the planting soon enough and it would transform from the frozen midland it currently was into a hopefully lush landscape. It was her favorite time of the year here. Everything smelled fresh; life, it seemed, had been secreted away over the long winter and was now finding its way back. It always reminded her of the first spring she'd spent with Selena. The first one that really counted, she reminded herself. They'd already known each other and been Paired for three years before they'd ever managed to have an actual conversation. She remembered being so frustrated to have to be with a Human, and Selena's whole life had been uprooted in order to be her Guardian.

That spring, though, had been one for the ages. They'd been at Brist, the school all Azha were required to attend, and they'd been able to take the afternoon and go out to the lake. They had swum out to the middle and floated in the salt water, talking about their dreams for the future. It'd been the first time, really, that they had been open with each other. She'd learned then that Selena had almost been married, before they'd met, and Selena learned that Tamora had a younger brother who'd taken more to his earth element than his fire who she hadn't seen since they'd been taken from their parents.

Tamora looked down at her hands and frowned. The scars were a constant reminder of all she'd lost, and how much she'd fought to survive. Sometimes, though, she thought the price had been too high. Maybe she would have been happier going when Selena did.

As she approached the city's outer walls, Tamora realized with disappointment that even their magnificence could not bolster her mood. They rose above the city, gleaming gray stone, in massive blocks. Each exceeded her in height and weight more than she liked to think about. It would be difficult even for a well-practiced Mago to bring it all down. It was reinforced with Eiyer and she could feel it radiating off the surface more than she felt the draw of the stone itself.

She ignored the footpath that connected with the road; she wasn't interested in trying to get through the main gate this time. Cut out into the side of the wall was a small archway which housed a sturdy wooden door, the abrupt absence of Eiyer allowing her to catch her breath. She didn't understand how Eilvyn could stand being so sensitive to it; it always felt to her like a heavy force, restraining her and raising the pressure in the air to uncomfortable levels.

She banged on the small door at the northern wall of the city. It was a service door, meant for those inhabitants and workers who needed to discreetly exit the city. The Human farmers and servants who worked in the fields used it, as the main gate had proven difficult to navigate throughout the busy growing season. Nobles didn't like seeing the workers as they came into the city for their own business, so it had been easier for Lord Karkas to make the side gate available to them. Tamora liked it because it was quiet and unassuming, and while the Human guard was old and mean he knew Tamora well. He'd been opening the door for her his whole life, as his father had when she'd first arrived. She gave the man a coin, as usual, and was let into the port city without much trouble.

With the abrupt change in weather, the sky was a beautiful dazzling blue, the city seemed transformed. People filled the streets, carts and hundreds of footsteps racketing between the buildings. They bartered and gossiped, laughed, and yelled at one another. Tamora felt, as usual, out of place. These were not her people. She could still clearly recall the warm streets of Iralt, the mountain looming over her as she would stroll through the paved streets. Erengate was nothing like that. Even on these rare boisterous days it felt flat and muted, like everyone was just biding their time before the chill of winter rolled back in.

Before she knew it, she was standing before the metal lined steps, the smell of bread again wafting around her. Tamora sighed with contentment and reached for the door, which suddenly opened onto her and drove her down a step. She glared up at the cloaked figure and froze, meeting the unfortunately familiar eyes of the Sentinel. Behind him stood a woman, her hair cropped short and brushing her petite jawline, a Sentinel's insignia embroidered on her breast.

"Miss Asken," he said, surprise clear in his voice. "This is an odd coincidence."

"Why are you bothering Marin?" she asked, straightening her shoulders. "She hardly deserves it."

His brow arched. "She's an excellent baker," he said, lifting the small, wrapped parcel he held. "You?"

"Am I not allowed to have friends?"

"Who is this?" the woman behind him asked curiously. He stepped to the side to allow her to come closer.

"Ah, Della. This is Tamora Asken—"

"The healer," the Eilfe said with a small smile. She looked surprisingly frail for a Sentinel, tall and thin and wide-eyed, her cloak doing little to hide her lankiness. She reminded Tamora of a deer but was sure she was anything but fragile. They didn't let just anyone become a Sentinel, after all, and she would have had decades of training simply to apply.

"I thought your Sentinella wasn't arriving for another week," she said. This new Sentinel, Della, arched her brow.

"We decided to pick up our pace," she said, glancing at Racynth. "You're right, she is touchy." He winced at that.

"Miss Asken, it was a pleasure seeing you again. Sentinel Keylynn and I were taking stock of the city... There's been a lot going on. I'm sure you've heard." His voice was measured, calm.

"Unfortunately."

"You'll want to take care," he said, seeming to want to say more but stopping himself. "We'll be seeing you shortly." Tamora couldn't tell if he meant to be reassuring or threatening, but let them pass. Della followed him closely, her footsteps light as she eyed Tamora with thinly veiled curiosity. Tamora noticed how Racynth's hand trailed along the iron rail gently and turned to watch them walk down the street. He pulled his purchase from its wrapping and ripped off a piece as they rounded the corner.

"Miss Tamora?"

She turned back at Eloise's voice, smiling and quieting her sudden anxieties. "Eloise, good morning. Is Marin here?" The girl smiled with uncertainty. She had a bruise from their encounter with the sailors, something Tamora deeply regretted.

"Yes ma'am, just inside."

"Fantastic. How's your father?" she asked as she stepped around her. Eloise beamed.

"When I left yesterday morning he was home and safe... he'll be with neighbors now. I haven't been back since — but thank you. If you hadn't done what you did he'd still be in that jail," she said, trying as usual to take her bags off of her and holding her hands awkwardly when Tamora waved her off.

"I was happy to help. One of the only good things I did that day," she ended, a little more bitterly than she'd meant to. The memory of that frigid walk back to her cottage would take a few more days to go away, not to mention the business with Karkas.

Marin rushed around the counter as she stepped through the door, throwing her arms around Tamora before she could say anything in greeting. "Tamora, it's good to see you," she said, her voice muffled. Tamora felt frozen and stiff, but patted her back in what she hoped was a comforting manner. She was released and Marin was smiling, but it was strained and off.

"Are you alright?" she asked, setting her bag down on the small table.

"I went to see Zavalynn," Marin said. A rush of adrenaline and nerves ran down Tamora's spine and she gaped.

"What? When — *why*?" For months now Marin had been avoiding the man, or so she'd thought. After William had died he had started to come around again, as he had when Tamora had first arrived in the city,

She hopped on her feet nervously and looked around her small bakery. "Upstairs?"

It was Eloise who shook her head. "Miss, I'm sorry, but everyone already knows. It was the talk of the street — some of the morning's customers asked after you," she admitted. "If it makes you feel better, they thought you were very brave."

Marin sighed but a small smile did inch its way across her lips. "Foolish more like — it was reckless," she said, looking nervously as the door opened and a few of her usual customers stepped in. She gestured for Tamora to sit and she obliged, grateful for the respite on her legs.

"I don't think you're foolish... but I don't understand why you'd willingly see the man," Tamora said. Marin stared at her hands.

"He's responsible for Sorrell's injury," she said quietly. Tamora had to concentrate on her voice and stifle the burning rage within her. "He didn't fall off a dock; he's been... well, both of them have been more rebellious than I'd ever thought." The customers had thinned. Eloise may have had a small part in that, Tamora realized as she noticed the girl quickly packaging food and quietly ushering them outside.

"Is that why the Sentinels were here?" she asked, her mind still lingering on him. Them, she thought with a frown. The whole Sentinella was here, from the sound of it.

"No, they just came in. They heard I was at The Dancing Clover, I guess, and wanted to check in on me. I can't imagine what Zavalynn was telling them. I thought he might have sent them but they seemed more concerned for my safety than anything else. Asking about the Azha I saw and I just told them everything. I'm not about to lie to a Sentinel," she admitted, laughing nervously.

Tamora frowned. This was moving very fast, and she'd only been gone a day. "Wait... what? I think you need to start from the beginning."

.....

When Marin had finished Tamora was grateful that Eloise had already closed the door, the 'come back later' sign flipped around for all to see. They'd gone upstairs, seeking more privacy, after a few customers had knocked on the door after seeing them. Tamora checked on Sorrell's leg, giving her a good opportunity to scold him for not telling her the truth. He just shrugged as though she wouldn't understand. *Oh but I do, more than you realize, and I also know just how lucky you are*, she thought, allowing herself to be escorted back to Marin's kitchen and sinking heavily into the armchair there.

"This is troubling," Tamora finally said, feeling it for the understatement it was. "For more reasons than one. The business with the boys... they're doing good work, Marin, even if you don't like it. They need to be more careful though. Zavalynn's not the only person who's angry about the Humans going south, but he's one of the more dangerous ones out there."

Marin's voice was small. "I'm going to tell the Sentinels."

Tamora rapped her fingers on the worn arm. "I'm not sure—"

"They helped you and Eloise! Yes, she told me, after some pressing. What did you expect?"

"We don't know them yet! You never go to a new Sentinella when they've just arrived, you know that as well as I do." There was no way of knowing where they stood or what sides they would take; you had to feel it out. It was guaranteed that they'd already spoken with Lord Karkas, and who knew what they'd been told, and Tamora didn't have the same confidence in them Marin seemed to hold.

"They seemed nice... oh, I don't know," Marin sighed unhappily.

"They asked about the Azha, right? I'm not sure it was the altruistic checkup you thought it was," she said, rapping her fingers as she thought. "What was he like anyway?"

Marin shrugged. "Big, dark hair, deep voice. I don't know... he was surprisingly cool about the whole ordeal, even after the fight broke out. I think he was having a great time with it all." She glanced at the door and looked for her clock. It was a bulky thing, taller than both of them, hidden haphazardly in the corner where she could see it from behind the counter. "If you're looking to go to this trial, you should head there now."

Tamora sat up and turned sharply. "The trial? It's not until tomorrow I thought?"

"Lord Karkas moved it up a day after the business with Zavalynn, he didn't want to give people the chance to organize something." She sighed. "This is not the start to spring I was hoping for."

Tamora reached over and clasped her hands. "I'm sorry Marin, I really am." She stood and grabbed her bag, feeling her heart pounding in her chest. She wasn't sure why she felt such an urge to go, but it wasn't a choice for her. The Human deserved an audience, no matter what Lord Karkas might try, and she hadn't done enough to help her before. The least she could do was be present for her sentencing.

.....

Tamora walked into the main square of the Trading District and grimaced at what was unfolding. The stage that stood at the far end was filled with Karkas allies and family members, with the elder Lord Karkas sitting calmly in his padded chair. *The old man must be nearing seven centuries now,* she thought as she took in his long white hair, braided back as was the custom in Koren. Not quite elderly yet, not for an Eilfe, but he was quickly approaching the time when he would need to step down. That didn't bode well for her, what with the history between her and Soren.

He was not the only Karkas family member to have made the journey from the safety of the Upper District. Soren lurked at the side of the stage, his imperious grimace never failing to set her on edge. His sister was also present, hovering opposite him. She already appeared bored. Tamora's mood was slightly lifted when she caught sight of Zavalynn, his face mottled and swollen, with a broken nose and a black eye. He hardly looked at the crowd, wrapping a coat around himself tightly as though it would protect him from the masses.

Tamora went as close as she dared, although it was not Soren she wanted to avoid. Before the stage was the Pit. History and legend alike said it was bottomless and, naturally, it was a staple in executions. Instead of hanging, which was popular in many cities, justice's victims simply were dropped into nothingness. It was impossible to know if there was a bottom. Even the most gifted Mago had never been able to sense it, and the gifts of Ioka and those of the Eilvyn were useless in its presence. She knew it wasn't the only Pit in Tunsealior; she'd seen the one in Ozhansa, seemingly dug by the Wela into the side of a volcano, and had read of at least ten others spread across the continent. The Pit in Koren had been the final resting place of many of her allies, back during Krys's rebellion.

The thought of such a fate sent a shiver up her spine. She watched as the younger Karkas carefully stepped along the stage, eyeing the edge. There was no rail along the Pit, only open air between him and death. Tamora wished she were a Tri. She'd happily whip up a breeze strong enough to push him in.

The clock tower began to ring; it was high noon. Lord Karkas rose to his feet and the crowd quieted. It was busier than she'd expected, even for the first trial of the season and one that was moved forward at that.

"Welcome all, to the Lord's Square," the elder Eilfe announced, raising his hands to the people and gesturing about. The plaza was lined with statues of various lords and ladies, many falling into disrepair as the years had gone on. It had been used for these public audiences for centuries and each time, Tamora felt sick to her stomach. She hardly imagined it was what those people had pictured for their city; although, if they were anything like their descendants they may have enjoyed such a thing. A few people cheered and Tamora looked for them with a readied glare. This was not the time.

"Today, we gather for the trial of this woman," Lord Severo Karkas continued, gesturing for a group of guards to step up from behind the stage. Between them they dragged a small shape; Tamora winced as she caught sight of the Human. What skin was visible was mottled purple and red, her face nearly unrecognizable. There was a brief muttering in the crowd but it faded as their lord continued his speech.

Tamora looked around as Lord Karkas continued to open the trial; she'd heard his words before. Soon enough his son would bring forward his charges and the Human would be sentenced to the Pit. It was hardly an unexpected result, her fate had been sealed the moment she'd mentioned her forbidden goddess. Guards lined the stage and the square, that too was surprising. She hadn't seen this many out in some time. She looked for the Azha Marin had described but couldn't see anyone out of place. She had to admit, it was odd for them to be so far north this time of year. If she hadn't had her own reasons for the move she never would have stayed through that first frigid winter. If his assault on Zavalynn hadn't been enough, his mere presence could only signal trouble.

"Thank you, father," Soren Karkas said as his father sat in his chair and looked askance. The young lord propped up his chest and smiled out at what Tamora could only hope were deadpan faces. "It is my honor today to bring forward the charges against this spy. Do not be deceived by her appearance, my good people, for that would lead you astray. This woman, as frail as she may be, is a weapon of the enemy. For two days we have questioned her as to why she assaulted my own person so violently in the street, why she would attempt my life so publicly, despite knowing what the good people of Erengate would do. For two days, we received no answer. Finally, this very morning, the truth was told. A spy, in our very midst. Not for the people of Adbeter, as was previously feared. But for an uprising in our own home!"

A murmur rippled through the crowd. "That's a load of shit," the man beside Tamora muttered. She had to agree with him there.

"This uprising is a brazen attempt at disrupting the peace we have worked so hard to achieve here in the north. We may be far from Koren but we must remember that our strength is integral to the strength of the Coalition. If it is revealed that there is support for this ill-advised revolt, the full power of the Coalition will be brought down upon those responsible," Karkas continued to drone on, seemingly blind to the shifting opinions of the crowd. At the mention of a revolt there were uneasy exchanges, but the thought of the power of the Coalition brought only bitter glances. Tamora knew the people of Sienma were no great defenders of Koren. As the capital of Tunsealior, it was the stronghold of the Coalition and a source of great frustration. The Council's tax collectors visited the capital biannually and the threat of rescinded support left the country raw.

"Fuck the Council!" Heads turned to search for the disembodied voice from the crowd. Karkas's sermon ground to a halt.

"The next person to speak such heresy will be arrested!" he shouted, but he'd lost parts of the crowd. That same cry went out again and more cheers followed. The guards stepped closer. As the people were shuffled around, squeezed together, Tamora caught sight of a Human, dark-haired and wrapped in thick furs. He looked rapt with attention at the stage, his hand on his side clutching what she thought from afar was a sword.

"Excuse me," she muttered to the people around her, pushing past them all the same. They paid her little mind, too concerned with being wrapped up in the guards' business. Most of these onlookers had come for a show and they were certainly getting one. "I hope you're not about to do anything reckless," Tamora said quietly, coming up beside the man. He looked down at her, creases forming around his eyes.

"Mind your business."

She raised her eyebrow. "Bold words, coming from you," she said, fully aware of what those words said to anyone else would bring the man. He'd be turned into the guards without question, but he didn't seem to care. "You aren't from here, what brings you to the city?"

He frowned. "What do you care?"

Her mouth opened but Karkas began to shout again, preaching about the woman's misdeeds. They were apparently numerous. He'd moved past the treachery of the crowd with such a mindless ease that she was certain he hadn't cared in the first place. His sister looked bored, his father appearing to nap in his chair. *Where are the Sentinels*, she wondered for the first time, her eyes searching. She'd expect them on the stage, in full view, so that Karkas could make a show of power. But they were nowhere to be seen. *They have to be watching somehow, this is too big not to.* After all, the entire Karkas family had deigned to leave their cushy district.

The woman, to her credit, was watching the people's rising unease with what looked to be a slight smile. Tamora couldn't be sure but she looked satisfied. She supposed it came down to the little things, when one was about to be sentenced to death.

Tamora turned back to the man but, far too quietly for someone of his size—let alone a Human—he'd slipped away. She could just see the fur of his collar, yards away, dozens of people between them. She sighed. Dragging her leg, she made her way back to the edge of the throng of onlookers. They were getting too excited for her liking and she wanted nothing to do with their chaotic glee or morose muttering.

Soren Karkas had been preaching for at least five minutes now and his family had clearly had enough. His father, roused from his nap by a tap on the shoulder from a guard sent by his daughter, sat up in his chair. "I believe your point has been made, Lord Karkas," the elder Karkas announced, taking advantage of his son needing to take a breath. His voice rang out, clear and loud and surprising from a man of his apparent frailty. "I have heard your testimony and now, for the sake of this trial's sanctity, I will hear from the accused."

The crowd fell silent. She looked out over them all and smiled, her broken teeth and many bruises giving her a malicious air. When she did speak Tamora was struck by the venom on her tongue. It was nothing like she'd seen in the market. "When the sea brings with it a hot wind, that is when you will know you have fallen. Erengate will burn and the Mother will laugh at your corpse," she said, spitting at the elder lord viciously. His gaze was inscrutable.

"I sentence you to die," he said simply, gesturing with his hand to a guard. "At high noon on Misa, three days from now, you will be sacrificed to the Pit. Wela rest your soul."

The crowd roared, whether it was a cheer or a shout of anger Tamora couldn't be certain. Regardless, her stomach was in knots.

Toward the front, closest to the stage but well away from the Pit that sprawled before it, a fight had broken out. Or rather, Tamora realized as she peered around people's heads and tried to get a better look, someone was pushing their way through the wall of those in front of them. A tall Azha man, dark hair and skin the same color as the deep brown coat he wore. He had gray eyes, but Tamora couldn't see them. She knew. Her mouth gaped open as she took in Aodhan shoving aside smaller men, a little gentler with the women but not much. What he was doing so far north, she had no idea, but suddenly everything Marin had said made sense.

His mouth was opening, clearly shouting, his grin so wide she'd bet he could hardly contain it. He loved this kind of chaos. Over the din of everything else she couldn't hear a word. She did see the object he threw toward the stage and recognized it immediately. It was a book, one of a limited batch she'd helped to print. How he still had one, she had no idea. Lord Karkas ducked out of the way but his guards surrounded him as other objects were launched over the Pit towards them. The men surrounding the square stepped forward, their badges gleaming in the sun as they broke up the crowd and searched for those responsible.

Aodhan had disappeared as quickly as he had popped up. He'd always been good at that, Tamora knew. She stepped out of the way up against a building, in the shadow of an old statue, her eyes scanning the square. The Karkas family was leaving as quickly as they were able but she didn't pay them any mind. Their guards made it impossible for anyone to reach them. The woman had gone from the stage, escorted back into the jail.

She was distracted by her search for the familiar frame but it was impossible not to notice when people started running. Guards swarmed into the crowd, grasping at anyone they thought had thrown a book toward the stage and breaking up the mass of people. They were drastically outnumbered, however, and it didn't take her long to realize that not everyone here was a simple onlooker. *Aodhan's doing, no doubt.* Despite their numbers, however, they carried only daggers and knives. This wasn't something they were supposed to win, and she doubted they were supposed to put up much of a fight. She and Aodhan had planned many such uprisings, back when she'd had the strength to do anything. Usually they were told to flee after the initial burst but these people weren't doing that.

She could see more guards heading their way. At their head was a man dressed in an obnoxious indigo cloak, the gold lining on the collar nearly gleaming against the dark fabric. Regardless of what these men—these attempted rebels —wanted to do they were going to be slaughtered. Tamora looked around, seeing little that she could do to distract or help. Her eye caught the crumbling stone of the statue she stood closest to. A moment of inspiration struck.

Her hand ran along the rough surface as she looked up at the old and largely forgotten lord. There were clear weaknesses in the rock, cracks deep in the carving that years had extended through the piece. The urge to tap into her elements was so great she spared only a moment to consider the possible outcome. It had been so long since she'd used either that the temptation was impossible to resist.

She reached deep inside herself carefully, touching on the earth that she'd stowed there. Her fire she was careful to keep away from; still it leapt toward her touch. It took all her willpower to turn from it, to tell it no, and instead coax out the little earth she possessed. Her hands tingled and shook as she laid her palm against the stone and pushed. Earth crumbled from beneath her fingertips and whether it was from the stone or her hands, she didn't know. She pushed harder, already conscious of her slipping control. Even this little touch was almost too much. Her breath sucked in a short burst, her heart pounded in her ears.

An audible crack snapped through the cold, dry air. Tamora stumbled back, quickly forcing the earth back within herself and locking it in place. Her knees were weak and she fell to the ground. The statue groaned and slipped forward so slowly she feared it wouldn't actually do it. But it tipped past the point of no return and she stumbled back as rock went flying, the forgotten lord smashed upon the paving stones.

Everyone turned to look at her. To look at the statue, she knew, but the effect was the same. Tamora swore under her breath and scrambled back with a look of surprise. The few men who had been fighting paused long enough to look her way and when they turned back, they saw the reinforcements approaching. She watched as they fled into the streets and breathed a small sigh of relief.

"You there!" The man in the resplendent cloak rushed forward, his eyes darting around the square. He gestured towards the fleeing men and a handful of guards made chase before glaring down at her. "What in the Wela's name happened?"

Tamora looked up at him, putting on a wide-eyed look. "It fell... I—"

"You did this, I saw you lurking about. How? How did you push it?" he snapped, stepping closer. She pulled herself to her feet and fixed her clothes, brushing down the cloth before looking back at him. *You should be lucky I'm not in better condition*, she thought, wanting to match his fury then and there.

"I have no idea what you're talking about," she said. The man didn't appear to have heard her.

"You're under arrest," he said, snapping his fingers and gesturing at two of the men near her.

Tamora spluttered. "For what? I'm an Azha, this is nowhere near my element!" She raised her hands, as if to show them, and they all flinched. Two took steps backward that put an arm's length between them.

"We just witnessed an attack on Lord Karkas and his family, a clear breach in our city's protection. You'll receive no allowances from me, healer," the man said. He almost sounded sad but, then again, his nasally voice could be the simple explanation.

"What's going on here?" a voice said, one that Tamora was coming to recognize. They all turned, some more sharply than others, to greet the Sentinel. *So they had been watching*, Tamora thought as the group walked closer. She recognized Sentinel Racynth and the woman he'd been with earlier, but it became clear that they were a Sentinella of seven. As they crossed the square from where they'd put themselves she took some time in cementing their faces in her mind.

There was Racynth, tall and broad, with his wide nose and long braided black hair. The Eilfe he'd been with—Della, he'd called her—was short for her kind and had hair that barely grazed the tops of her shoulders. She was quick to smile and was doing so now as they approached, something that Tamora found deeply off-putting. Striding ahead of Racynth was another Eilfe, this woman much taller than the other with narrow eyes and willowy features. She was harsh and striking and the stern set of her mouth seemed much more appropriate for the situation at hand. Behind the Eilvyn were Iokan, two of them, and their Guardians. A Mago, judging from the woman's build and the glimpse of markings Tamora could see, and a Veden. He and his Guardian could have been twins.

"Sentinel Naewynn, a pleasure," the guard said, jolting Tamora from her observations. The man looked grateful to see the Sentinels; he was the only one.

"Why are you not following those men? Get them, now, and bring them back for questioning," the taller woman snapped, gesturing at the guards. They ran off almost gratefully.

"What has Miss Asken done?" Racynth asked, drawing her attention. The others looked at him as well, the blonde Eilfe looking at Tamora as though she was suddenly of value. She bristled at the familiarity but said nothing; it may actually work in her favor.

"Saw her knock over the statue," the guard said. He bumbled over the words, his mouth tight at the corners and his eyes following his retreating men.

Sentinel Racynth raised an eyebrow. "And that is important... why? The men responsible for this are fleeing as we speak, sir, and I do believe we are wasting time."

"But—"

"I see no evidence of fire and as Miss Asken is an Azha, I find it difficult to believe she can do what you are claiming. Sentinel Miayra is right, we should be following those men," he said, jutting his thumb in the direction Aodhan and the Humans had fled in. Tamora felt as though her stomach were in her throat but said nothing.

"This woman is dangerous," said the guard, eying her mistrustfully even as he released her arm.

"So we've heard," Sentinel Racynth said. Tamora frowned at him. *Who has he been talking to? Or is it in their reports?* She had no idea what the last Sentinella had written about her but she was certain there'd been nothing good. "Aspen, Petro — please go help the guards. I will escort Miss Asken back to the northern gate."

The Sentinels nodded and split from the group, gesturing impatiently to Sir Ularan before striding across the square. There was no urgency in their pace; clearly they did not imagine the culprits would get far. *Or perhaps they simply don't care as much as they are letting on,* Tamora thought, the idea giving her pause. Why wouldn't they care? They'd interrupted legal proceedings — no matter how much she disagreed with them, she had to admit the sentencing was technically legal — and a claim could easily be made finding them guilty of creating panic.

Racynth took her elbow, jolting her from her thoughts. "Excuse me," she said, shaking him off. "Thank you, but I really don't need an escort."

He smiled tersely. "It really isn't an option, Miss Asken."

"I'm not going home. I need to make sure Marin is alright," she said, starting to walk in that direction.

"I will check on your baker, I assure you of that. She will be well taken care of," he said. She frowned at him and, as her eyes left the ground, her foot caught a stone and she stumbled and fell heavily onto the cobblestones. He bent to help but she waved him off, reaching for her fallen bag and looked accusingly at the object that had tripped her, pulling her pant leg back down to her ankle and trying to put herself together. It wasn't a stone, however, and she quickly scooped up the book and stuffed it into her knapsack. Rising as steadily as she could to her feet, she prayed that Racynth hadn't noticed.

"Fine," she said stiffly, now wanting nothing more than to confirm her suspicions. Marin would be alright, she could take care of herself. She allowed the Sentinel to lead her to the gate with little more than a sentence shared between them and left him behind as she began her painful journey to the forest.

Letters of a New Age, the book was called. By Krystopher Reene. Tamora's hand shook as she unlatched her gate and she dropped into her chair. The bag lay on the floor, out of sight but weighing heavily on her mind. The book inside it may as well have been made of lead. She had no idea how Aodhan had gotten a hold of so many copies; she'd thought they'd all been burned decades ago. It hadn't mattered for her, she knew every word within those gilded pages by heart. She'd helped to write some of them, after all.

Racynth

Lost in thought as he returned from the gate, Racynth almost didn't notice Sabina as he returned to the square. "Why are you protecting that woman?" Sabina rounded on him as soon as he returned from patrol, catching him just past the palace district gate. Racynth frowned at her. "She's already involved and now she does this — does she want Karkas to come for her?"

"The healer? I doubt she actually had anything to do with this. She's an Azha, after all," he said, shrugging. He remembered the feeling her Eiyer had and paused, but shook the thought away. "If Karkas wants to do something he'll have to go out of his way, she lives well outside of the city."

"We'll have to keep an eye on the situation all the same," she said, her glare receding. "Did you see what they threw?" She gestured at him with a small book and he sighed when he caught a glimpse of the cover. He'd thought that all remaining copies had been destroyed decades ago. News of this would travel quickly if they didn't take care.

"Interesting. We'll have to inform your father." The thought did nothing to lift his mood.

"The council, Racynth. Not just him," she said, her tone as sullen as he felt. The two hadn't been on good terms since the rebellion and the situation with her nephew. She looked around the square for a moment, taking it all in, before heading off toward the Palace District. "I've sent Bealantin and Jordan to gather as many as they can. It's best to keep this quiet for now. I'd thought this portion of our watch would be relatively relaxing, didn't you? Instead we find rebels waiting in the shadows."

"A few books hardly make a rebellion, no matter their contents. Although I don't see how you can keep that quiet for long," he said, his eyes on the guards. Many had dispersed, chasing down shadows, but there were more roaming around here than he'd seen even during the trial itself. Not that it could truly be called that; the outcome had been decided for days.

"This is a dangerous situation, Racynth, I'm not going to pretend otherwise. If we added any remnants of Krystopher Reene to the mix... Well, I have no intention of allowing things to get that far. You are not to tell my father about this, do you understand?"

Racynth didn't have to say anything, knowing she'd see his agreement. At their old post, before they'd been sent on rotation, he'd enjoyed the opportunity the libraries of Tunsealior had given him to broaden his understanding of their history on this continent. Some of the Eilvyn's greatest philosophers lived on in those walls, long after their final days had passed. Interestingly, so did the thoughts of their lifetime's greatest dissenter. Krystopher Reene had printed many copies of his musings and sermons but very few official copies remained. He'd found it sad, thought-provoking, and disturbingly inspiring at the time. Now, seeing it printed anew, he understood Sabina's fear of it.

She hadn't finished her own musing, speaking even as she frowned across the square at the bottomless pit at its heart. "If the Karkas boy— what's his name?"

"Soren."

"Yes, Soren. If he starts a true conflict up here, reinforcements are too far away to help. From Della's reports the closest Sentinella is in Vasna and they would take at least three days to reach us, if the weather is kind. I wouldn't expect them to make the time we did, not on the behalf of the Humans here. Who knows how many people would be hurt in the meantime," she said, her voice deep with worry. He followed her gaze to the Pit and tried to ignore the shiver it provoked within him.

"You think it would go that far? His father is... well, I don't think there's much his son does that he doesn't know about," Racynth noted. "For all his talk, he doesn't appear to want conflict. I do think he recognizes that things have already —" he was cut off by shouts and the reappearance of Aspen and Petro. Between them, hands bound behind his back, was a Human and the source of the noise.

"The guards caught up with the group by the docks. I think they were trying to get around the wall and head north. This is the only one they could get," Petro said, his voice strained as the man thrashed. The Human's cheek was bruised and a cut above his eye poured blood down his face but he seemed healthy enough to put up a fight.

"They all look like that?" Racynth asked. Aspen glared behind her at the few guards making a reappearance.

"Enough of them — they don't seem to realize that you can't question someone who is dead," she said, shaking her head. The tie in her hair had come undone, lost somewhere between them and the harbor, and her dreadlocks hung loose past her shoulders. The Human kicked at her and she hissed out a breath, yanking on his arm. "Wela curse it, that's enough. Relax. We just want to talk."

Sabina held up the book she still had out, holding it in front of the man. "We'll start with this." Aspen and Petro both winced when they saw it, eyeing Sabina uneasily.

The man blanched. "I have no idea what that is." Sabina only had to wait a moment in silence before he visibly collapsed under the weight of her stare. "Look, I don't know where they got them. I just joined up! All he said was to throw them at the stage, cause a distraction, and pass them around."

"Who? Who said that?"

"How many copies did you hand out?" Racynth asked at the same time, feeling an uncomfortable mountain of work piling before them. Sabina shot him a glare.

"I don't know his name, we were just doing what we were told. I think he had maybe a handful of copies, I just got a few loose pages myself. Handed them out in the Lower District." He stepped from foot to foot but hardly moved, so securely were Aspen and Petro holding him. "Can I go now? I told you everything."

"Of course not," Sabina snapped, rubbing at her temple and sighing. "This is a mess. Aspen, Petro, take this man to a cell. I expect to know everything he does by dinner. Racynth, you're coming with me to the palace. First we need to stop those guards from arresting anyone else. It'd be a waste of all of our time to try holding them all." The man began sobbing, repeating that he knew nothing as the two walked him out of the courtyard.

.....

The guards were disturbingly reluctant to head back to their normal posts. It took Racynth and Sabina at least an hour to order the majority to release the remaining citizens they'd yet to put in chains. Most had unfortunately dispersed before they could be reasoned with, and on their own way back to the palace Racynth could still hear the panic and chaos that had taken hold of the lower city.

.....

Seemingly the entire palace guard were lingering on the front steps around the central building, some standing watch while others merely paced and watched the gate distrustfully. On their way through, after being questioned until Sabina snapped her cloak's sigil in the face of the man hounding her, Racynth overheard Sir Abalian give his orders. No one was allowed entry who hadn't been explicitly named by Lord Karkas as a friend or ally. It was lucky for them, then, that a Sentinella still held influence as the elder Lord Karkas had failed to include their names on his dangerously short list.

"Seems like trust is a short commodity here," Racynth said, glancing at the page tacked to the gate's wall. Close family, a few advisors, and names he recognized as the family's most valuable backers. Della had been careful to go over all of the reports with them and those names had popped up more than a few times over the years.

"It's of his own doing, of course," Sabina said brusquely, continuing through the massive doorway and turning down the first hall. "The man spends too much time listening to his son. I haven't heard such a ridiculously paranoid speech since —"

"I know. There are too many parallels here, Commander," he said, cutting her off before she could name her father's predecessor on the Council.

The late Lord Karkas had died during Krystopher Reene's rebellion but not before whipping up most of Koren into a murderous frenzy and, intentionally or otherwise, causing a riot that killed hundreds over the course of just a few days. It was that series of events that had led to their Sentinella's dismissal from their post, officially ending what had been for years a sham assignment. Sabina's father had not taken kindly to her continued disobedience and it had resulted in all of them being sent, with no small measure of public shame, to a decades-long and quiet posting at the Coalition libraries in Saltrol. He'd thought he would die from sheer boredom at the time. Now, however, a little less chaos was sounding pretty good.

She glanced at him, her lips pursed. "This is not the same, though."

He shrugged, even as he looked for eavesdroppers. Between the show at the sentencing and what he'd seen before the rest of the Sentinella's arrival, Soren was a disaster waiting to happen. If he went after the traitors he saw around every corner, in every Human, he was going to create a panic that would be difficult to contain. Not to mention the book. Such a little thing, to cause such chaos.

"I have a feeling," Sabina continued, almost musing, "that our new Azha friend has something to do with this. The one that baker mentioned from that business with Silas Zavalynn. She didn't know anything?"

"No, I think she was just in the wrong place at the wrong time," Racynth said, watching the hallway carefully, keeping his ears open. "She was angry with Lord Zavalynn for her own reasons, and I believed her to be truthful."

"Fine, fine. Then there's only the healer to worry about — it's too much of a coincidence, having two Azha up this far north. It's unlikely even in the warmest months. And those damned papers... When we are finished here, you should go to the head of the guard. I will need you to gather as many copies as you can — I don't want this getting out," she said quietly. He only needed to nod, confident she knew it would be done. A few Human servants stepped out ahead of them, walking in the opposite direction but in earshot, and that was the end of that.

Sabina was heading directly for Lord Karkas's wing and people soon noticed. Most were quick to step out of their way, especially after a good look at Sabina, but once the doorway to his receiving rooms were in sight the guards had more nerve.

"I'm sorry, ma'am, but you cannot proceed." Two guards, Eilvyn, stepped in front of them. Their hands were closed around their swords' hilts and Racynth's drifted to his own out of habit. Between the four of them were no signs of anger or distress, trained calm facades hiding whatever lay beneath. For Racynth, those were annoyance and impatience, pure and simple. These were the times when it should be helpful to be a Sentinel; the position tended to gain one access to people even in the most pressing of times. Especially in those times. But

Karkas had shut down, as Della had warned he had a tendency to do.

"We need to speak to Lord Karkas," Sabina said, her voice quiet in a way that only her Sentinella meant danger. "It is urgent."

"Lord Karkas is in a meeting with the Commander of the Guard and is not receiving visitors at the moment," the man said, bowing slightly. "We can escort you to your rooms and notify you when he is available."

"If he is with Sir Ularan, then that is the perfect opportunity to speak with them both," she said, taking a step forward. Clearly despite himself, the guard stepped back. Racynth almost smiled at the flash of apprehension in the man's eyes. Eilvyn couldn't hide their emotions for long, it was one of their more amusing traits as a people. Not for the first time, Racynth was grateful for his father's heritage. It allowed him a great many things that the Eilvyn were denied, even if it had created a world of pain for him as a child.

"He is unavailable," the man stuttered, but he'd lost all power over their situation. Sabina made a disgusted noise in the back of her throat.

"Are you denying the Sentinella access?" she asked. "In the absence of the Council we are their voice and any action we take should be considered as that of the High Council. I would recommend you rethink what you are about to say."

The guard looked at his companion with thinly veiled panic, and Racynth could almost sympathize. Denying Sabina was no small feat, but he was sure that Lord Karkas would make the man's life miserable if he did comply.

"Perhaps we should simply go in?" Racynth asked conversationally, stepping forward. He heard a shocked gasp from the other side of the door and it opened slightly, a small head popping out. A Human servant, eyes wide and pale, gazed out at them before turning around and muttering.

"They really are the Sentinels—"

"Oh, open it, open it. Let them in," a voice from inside exclaimed. The Human stepped aside with the heavy door with her head down and the guards stepped to the side.

"Thank you," Racynth drawled, aiming a slow smile at the guard as they passed. The man gripped his sword hilt tighter and Racynth almost wished he'd draw it. All of this talking was not his way. The people were fine enough, and he enjoyed figuring things out. But give him a sword fight any day over these tedious and bureaucratic verbal dances. He was happy to leave that to Sabina.

Lord Karkas was seated on a large velvet chaise, the ruby fabric aged and faded in spots that revealed how frequently it was used. His advisor, Lord Enzana, loomed over his shoulder and glared at Sabina as she approached. The Lord of Erengate had been wrapped in a velvet cloak and in his position he looked like an under stuffed cushion. Before him, on a large but short table, was a veritable feast. Racynth saw dried and candied fruits alongside a pitcher of what was likely wine, and roasted meat sliced and presented on a platter and surrounded by herbs. It didn't appear that he'd touched any of it.

"Commander Miayra, welcome," he said, his sweet tone failing to soften the sharpness of his gaze as they entered the room. "Forgive my reluctance, I was simply so shocked by the attack on my person and that of my children I had to leave. My darling Adelina was so shaken that she needed a dose of valerian root, can you believe it?"

Sabina, to her never-ending credit, simply nodded. It was all Racynth could do not to roll his eyes at the lord. "It was certainly an unexpected development. I had hoped to speak with you regarding our course of action to calm the people and restore order. We have discovered—"

"Soren is handling it, my dear, have no fear," Lord Karkas interrupted. Sabina's eyes narrowed.

"Handling it, how? Where is he?"

Lord Karkas looked across his long table at her with heavily lidded eyes. Perhaps his daughter was not the only one with valerian running through her veins, Racynth thought.

"He's gone out, of course. To catch our attackers and those disgusting rebels," Lord Karkas said simply. "Now —"

"Down into the city?" Sabina cut in, drawing quick looks from the servants and guards. There were six in the room with them; a bit much for an audience with Sentinels, Racynth thought.

"Where else? He's leading the men, delivering justice," Lord Karkas puffed himself up, the movement highlighting how little motor control he had. His hand slipped from the table, bringing with it a plate of roast pork and root vegetables. "This will all be sorted by morning."

"Lord Karkas." Sabina spoke slowly, with careful measure. "This situation is delicate. Clearly your citizens are upset about the arrest of the Human, and I don't believe that your guards continued presence in the Lower District will improve matters —"

"I don't see your point, Commander," Lord Enzana said with a small sneer, setting a comforting hand on Lord Karkas's shoulder. "Criminals are arrested, it is the natural order of things. Lord Soren will return after settling the issue and ensuring that those responsible are brought in to face the proper justice."

Racynth sighed and leaned closer to Sabina, clasping his hands behind his back. The guards kept eying his sword and he wanted to give them no reason to do something they'd regret. "Commander, he will need to be intercepted," he said. They were wasting time with dodging questions and unnecessary pleasantries.

She eyed him without turning her head. "Please notify Sentinel Jordan and Sentinel Bealantin. I would hope that they have returned to the palace by now — if they haven't, please go into the city to bring them back here as soon as possible." She turned to Lord Karkas, who was sinking lower in the chaise seemingly without realizing. "My lord, how many soldiers did your son bring with him?"

"Hmm? Oh... um, how many? That is a marvelous question..." he turned to Lord Enzana and gestured lazily. "How many was it?"

"A dozen, my lord," his advisor replied, and Racynth nearly groaned. Thirteen trained and armed Eilvyn, for there were surely only Eilvyn in Soren's company, loose in a district of Humans did not bode well.

"Meet me in our rooms. I shall be there shortly," she said before turning back to Lord Karkas.

Racynth nodded and left without another word, the guards moving out of his way as though his mere presence repelled them. He was grateful for it, feeling a palpable sense of relief as he left the gaudy district gate behind him.

.....

The inn itself was rather empty, not unusual this time of year, but today those who worked there were buzzing with a heady mix of excitement and nerves. All the conversations he passed, most whispered and charged with anxiety, were either about the riot at the sentencing or the upcoming execution.

"If it was that bad simply for the charge, what'll they do when she's dead?" one Eilvyn woman asked, her Iokan companion shaking her head and leaning closer. Her Guardian lingered behind; his expression unreadable.

"I heard that they're planning to overthrow the Family,"

she whispered. "Did you hear that Lord Zavalynn was laid low by a band of rebels, not even a day ago? This wasn't something that just happened out of the blue, they're plotting." She nodded knowledgeably, and then Racynth had moved beyond them. He frowned but said nothing, stowing the rumors away in his memory.

Jordan, Bealantin, and Della were in the rooms, Bealantin staring out the window as Jordan poured himself a considerable glass from a decanter Racynth hadn't seen the last time he was in here. Della was busying herself with her reports and maps, having spread them out across the table in the corner of the room. She glanced up as he entered, but turned back to her documents fast. He latched the three locks and turned to face them, eying Jordan until he put the glass down with a sheepish frown.

"Now is hardly the time."

"It's not enough to do anything anyway," he said, eyeing the glass. Still, he didn't pick it back up. "What's going on?"

Racynth briefly explained the situation. Della set down her papers as Bealantin, stepping away from the window and letting the heavy navy curtain fall back into place, nodded. "I'd heard the same, as we came back. Got as many of those papers as we could, from the guards as well as the Humans. The guards ran off — we'd assumed they were heading back to the palace, but I'm sure they joined Soren as soon as they heard. They sure were angry," he said, shaking his blonde head. "It's going to be a bloodbath."

"To be fair, it already is," Jordan said. He looked exhausted and his cloak was muddy and streaks of dirt marred his clear face. Racynth almost let him have that drink; he looked like he'd earned it. "At least five people were trampled during that little show back there, dozens more injured. If he isn't brought back soon he'll have destroyed all of the Lower District through sheer panic alone."

"How many of the guards went to join him?" Racynth asked, feeling the dread building in his chest.

Bealantin looked at Jordan, frowning. "Ah, six. Maybe eight."

"So there are twenty of them now, at least, roaming the streets," Racynth groaned, sitting heavily and rubbing his face. "He'll pick up more as he goes, I'd bet on it if it weren't so grim."

They'd all be Eilvyn too, he knew. Some of the Iokans in the city might agree with him, sure, but he knew from watching Jordan and Aspen that too much anti-Human sentiment got under their skin. He'd always assumed that the necessity of having a Human Guardian prevented most from going too far, but he'd heard of the atrocities committed by Iokans during the last rebellion and he knew that they were just as capable of cruelty. Some Guardians didn't seem to mind; those he'd met through other Sentinellas had been just as ruthless as their *viluno*. Still, Soren Karkas wouldn't allow Iokans to join his group. From all the rumors, he was almost as hateful of them as he was of Humans.

The door handle shook and a light rapping sounded from the other side. Bealantin crossed the room swiftly, beating Jordan to the door and unlatching it, shooting a grin at his *viluno*. "Too slow."

Aspen poked her head through the door, her dark hair swinging as she moved and frowned at Bealantin.

"Are you two doing this again?" Aspen asked, her pert voice belying her serious expression. "Jordan, I'm sorry, but Bealantin will always be faster than you. It's a law of nature at this point." She entered and patted Bealantin on the shoulder as she passed, Petro in her wake.

"Done so soon?" Racynth asked, gesturing at one of the armchairs. This inn had no shortage of seating, which was handy when you booked a room for seven.

Petro scoffed. "The man knew next to nothing, couldn't even tell us his leader's name. Just repeated 'captain' every time we asked." Aspen nodded, her upper lip turning as she scowled.

"And he vomited at least ten times. We didn't even touch him," she said, shuddering slightly. "It was truly disgusting. We left him in a cell, but instructed the jailer that they weren't to do anything to harm the man just in case Sabina wanted to go back and question him herself." Della made a small sound at her table and Racynth looked over just in time to see her, paler than usual, turn away. Blood, she was fine with. Anything else sent her stomach roiling.

Racynth almost groaned. "So we learned nothing then," he said, staring up at the ceiling. "And Soren is on a rampage."

"I heard about that," Aspen said, shrugging at Racynth's quick look. "The guards were talking. Some went down to join him, and a few came back to spread the news. It seems his plan is to go door to door and interrogate people in the Lower District about their involvement, and arrest the guilty. No idea what his criteria is."

Probably just that they were Human, Racynth thought bitterly. Or part Human — he'd met enough Eilvyn like Soren to know they didn't see a difference. He clenched and released his fist, unable to keep his thoughts from drifting back to his own encounters with people he'd known in the past. Before his gift with Eiyer had come in, he'd been close to helpless against them and they'd made sure he'd known it.

"Isn't this all a bit of an overreaction?" Della asked, glancing around as she sat back from her maps. "The woman was arrested — things like that happen every day, all over Tunsealior. Their jail is full to the brim. Why this one? Why go to these lengths?"

"He's impulsive, and probably bored after a long winter. It sounds like this is routine from him, but I think that the people here have finally decided that they're tired of his cruelty. I know I would be," Aspen said, shrugging and trying to look nonchalant. But from the way she held her jaw, and the white-knuckled grip she had on the seat before her, Racynth was certain her feelings were stronger than she let on. "I don't think we can pretend to understand this man. But he could be using it as an opportunity to gain more power. His father is hardly the sort to intervene, and I'm sure Soren has allies among the other noble families here."

"Friends? I wouldn't give him that much credit," Petro said, his voice quiet but carrying his usual reserved strength.

Racynth snorted. "In any case, it's our responsibility to do something. Sabina will be back soon enough... I can't imagine her conversation with the elder Lord Karkas is going to go on for much longer. He fully supports his son; that'll be a dead end. We're going to have to find another way to stop him from arresting half the city," he said, feeling the impossibility of the situation. They had no idea how many allies Soren Karkas had, nor did they know how many enemies truly lay within the city. Someone was orchestrating a plan of rebellion, the presence of Reene's book made that very clear. He turned to Della.

"Have you read Krystopher Reene's pamphlet? *Letters of a New Age*?" he asked. She sat up a little straighter even as her brows pulled down.

"You know it's treasonous to do so." She paused. "But of course I have. Why?"

He nodded at Jordan, who had sprawled across an empty armchair. "The Human they interrogated, he said they were throwing copies at the stage. Sabina has one on her... and I think I saw Tamora pick one up as well," he said, frowning. That healer kept getting herself involved in things much bigger than herself, and she always seemed to be in the wrong place at the wrong time. He knew more than to say it was all intentional, but there was a point where it became too unlikely that she was accidentally getting between the Karkas family and their goals.

Della winced. "Reene was one of the most persuasive writers I've ever seen. You can very easily see how he gathered so many to the cause, he speaks in such plain and relatable terms about the issues that plague most citizens of Tunsealior. The villain of his story is always the Council and, by extension, most of the ruling families across all seven countries. So, naturally, they all want it destroyed. Do you know how many copies got out?" she asked, turning to Jordan and Bealantin.

They shook their heads in unison, almost making Racynth smile. Aspen and Petro had a habit of doing the same, and the bond that both pairs shared was almost enough to make him jealous. From what he remembered of his father's stories, an uncle a few times removed had been a Guardian. The rest of the family had hoped for another Pairing but it had never happened. Still, the relationship between an Iokan and their Guardian was something he'd never understand, not even after the centuries he'd worked with Aspen and Petro.

"No idea, but we rounded up as many as we could." Jordan sighed. "I'd like to know how they got a copy of that to begin with. I thought they were all destroyed a century ago."

"We may never know how many were created —" Della said, putting on the tone that she always got when she was about to explain history, but was interrupted by a loud knock.

"Oh, thank the Wela," Jordan said, leaping to his feet and, for once, beating Bealantin to the target. He opened the door and smiled at Sabina. "Saved by the commander."

"Was Della lecturing again?" she asked, smiling softly across the room at the woman in question. Della rolled her eyes, but returned the smile all the same. "Lord Karkas is a dead end, he'll stand by his son. The most I could arrange was that he'd call him back at daybreak, but who knows what damage he'll do in the meantime."

"We should go out and stop them then," Jordan said, pulling out a dagger and inspecting the edge. "It shouldn't be too difficult."

Racynth scoffed. "Yeah, just twenty or more trained Eilvyn guards and one ridiculously anger-prone Eilvyn noble. Don't see how that could go wrong at all."

"Twenty?" Sabina asked with an increasingly deepening frown. Racynth sometimes worried that someday she'd never be able to smooth out those grooves she carved into her skin.

He summarized all that had been shared and she shook her head as she breathed deeply. "I honestly don't see what more we can do. They aren't listening to me, even when I pull rank. I... if this gets any worse, I'll have to consult the Council," she said, her voice dropping.

"Well, let's hope it doesn't come to that," Racynth said.

Sabina's hand had fallen to her pocket, almost of its own accord, and he knew what she was thinking. Though she had one set of runestones that she shared with him, the other pair allowed her to speak directly with her father in Koren. The small glossy rock, barely the size of his palm, could be imbued with Eiyer and allow the holder to see through to the other side. The symbols, carved deep into the surface, were meaningless to most and a terrifying new power. Racynth knew that Sabina was reluctant to use it and that she feared revealing its power to those outside the Council. Most of all, they all feared what might happen if the Council had unfettered access to see through her stone. It was best to keep many of their actions, and discussions, private. As such, the runestone remained safely wrapped in leather in her pocket, on her person at all times.

"They'll purge the city looking for these Humans," Aspen said, drawing them all back to the task at hand. "Innocent people are going to be caught in the chaos. We need to help them."

Sabina exhaled sharply. "For now, we will have to just wait to see. Racynth's right, there are too many of them for us — they aren't following rank. That would make this too easy," she muttered. "If things get too out of hand we can reassess. I want all of you to go out. Aspen and Petro, Jordan and Bealantin, and Della you can go with Racynth. If you see anything that concerns you, report back to me. We will meet again at sundown. Then, and only then, will we decide on a course of action."

She didn't look up as they all left, even when Della kissed the top of her head in farewell, and not for the first time Racynth was struck by the difficulty of her position. Her orders, if she'd sought the instruction of the Council, would be to focus on the pamphlets and nothing else. The work of Krystopher Reene was too dangerous, too persuasive, to allow it to reach the general public. But the sounds of panic, and the silence left in its wake, flooded the streets as they set out on their mission and he knew that those weren't the orders any of them wanted to follow.

Chapter 13

Tamora

Her cottage was dark, cold, and the opposite of where she wanted to be at that moment. If it hadn't been for that Wela-forsaken book she would have gone straight to Marin. As it was, simply having it in her possession could get her arrested and she would be damned if she was about to bring that upon Marin's household. She had enough trouble already.

Having little better to do, Tamora made a fire. She made dough, which turned out too dense to rise properly, and she made tea, set out some herbs to dry, chopped and boiled and mixed balms. She stripped linens for bandages. None of these monotonous tasks did anything to quiet her mind and the day was dragging on and on, as though it would never end. The sun hadn't yet set and her mind wouldn't stop churning over itself and digging rabbit holes of a strange conspiracy she had no way of confirming. *What in Dalka's name was Aodhan doing there? Why would he come all this way for a Human's trial?* Clearly something had been in the works before the events of the other day; there would have been no way for him to get here under such short notice. *Not that I know where he lives… but I'll eat my shoe if it's anywhere near snow.* Last she'd heard he was still in Ozhansa, trying to go legit. This was so far from that, though, she felt as though she'd missed something. *Seventy years can really put you out of the loop.*

A knock at her door told her that she'd been right to prepare.

"A moment," she called, biting her lip with a frown. She wasn't sure if she wanted to know what had happened in the hours since she'd left the city walls. But she couldn't turn them away, not when they'd come all the way out.

"Healer, please, we need your help," a male voice spoke, muffled through the wood but recognizable all the same. She froze a moment before leaping toward the door, hitting her small table and rattling her mug as she struggled.

Tamora whipped the door open, glaring out into the darkness. "Aodhan," she said. It was as much of a greeting as he was going to get. The man loomed in her doorway, his enormous shoulders nearly taking up the width of the space and he crooked his head down to get a quick glimpse inside.

"Any company? No? That's good," he said, smiling cheekily at her as he grasped her by the shoulders and bodily moved her aside. At least half a dozen Humans had huddled behind him and they poured in through the gap he'd created.

"What do you think you're doing?" she shouted, slapping his hands off her and glaring up at him. "Aodhan Trikel, I don't see you in over seventy years and you think you can just barge in here—"

"Quiet, Tamora, you don't want the whole country to hear you," he said, his normally booming voice brought low. He looked down at her, his hands still clasped around her shoulders. "You don't look half bad. For a cripple."

Her eyes narrowed so small she could hardly see through them and if she'd been able to use her fire she would have scorched him there and then. "You're still an imbecile." She looked at her new guests, her frown morphing from anger to concern. Nearly all of them had blackened eyes and she saw more than a few swollen jaws; two in particular were in rough shape. One was unconscious and the other was held up by two companions. Someone had clearly tried to bandage them both, with little success. "What in Ioka's name have you done to yourselves?"

"We really need your help, healer," one of the men said. It was the one who'd been wrapped in furs back at the trial, she would recognize that cloak anywhere. He looked as though someone had hit him in the face with the blunt end of a hammer and, knowing how the city guard usually operated, she feared that was just what had happened. He was clearly favoring his left leg as well and leaning heavily on her table.

"That much is obvious," she said, shaking her head. She pointed sharply at Aodhan. "We're not through. I know this is your fault — once I patch these men up you're going to explain yourself." He shrugged. Compared to the others he was practically untouched. She thought she saw the shadow of a bruise on his cheekbone but it could have been the light.

"Get on with it then. You go around calling yourself a healer, I hope you've learned a thing or two since I knew you." Tamora rolled her eyes as she turned from him.

"Get off your feet, you fools. Lay him down by the fire — wait, don't touch that. Don't touch anything," she said. Soon the only thing she allowed herself to think about were these men's wounds and how to alleviate their pain.

Once cleaned, few of the wounds were as bad as they'd first appeared. Not to say that the men were in the clear or that Tamora's treatments were painless. The unconscious man was her first concern; he'd been cut up his thigh so deeply that she could see bone. It was hours of cleaning and stitching before she felt it safe to attend to the others. She was grateful that some hadn't been injured more than a bruise or two; most others had been rendered useless by their injuries and the cold trek into the forest.

The man wearing the cloak still hadn't followed her instructions to sit and he was swaying on his feet, watching the others nervously. "You're a fool," she said, not as scathingly as she may have liked. "What on earth were you thinking?" His jaw was clearly broken but he'd been speaking to the others all the same. His eyes were swollen from the shattered nose as well. He was hardly the pretty picture he'd been last she'd seen him.

"They forced us —"

"Because of the mess you made of their ridiculous trial, yes I know," she cut him off, more to stop him from moving his jaw than anything else. "Stop speaking. I saw what you did and I saw the book too. It's a death sentence to even own a page of that." She shot a glare at Aodhan, who had moved into her kitchen and was currently downing the last of her stew. He looked pointedly at the door leading to her bedroom and, with a final scoop of boiled potato, let himself in.

Tamora looked at the man in front of her, and those now scattered around her living room. They were all so young, the oldest might have been thirty. She sighed. "Just go sit by the fire now. You're in good hands; try to get some rest."

.....

When she stalked into her bedroom she found Aodhan spread out on her covers. She threw the first thing she could reach at him, a metal plate that clanged loudly against the wall as he brushed it away.

"Is that any way to greet a friend?" he asked, a lopsided smile sprawled across his face.

"A friend? Oh, that's rich," she snapped. "Where were you, back then? I haven't seen or heard from you for years and now we're friends?"

He frowned. "I wasn't the one who ran, Tamora—"

"I had to!" Tamora slammed her bedroom door shut. It wasn't likely to block out any of their racket but she at least wanted to think that the Humans couldn't hear everything. " I was injured and if you didn't remember, *Aodhan*, there was a price on my head!"

"And there wasn't one on mine? Come on, Tamora. I couldn't exactly go 'round asking where you'd ended up, could I?" He sat up. He was comically big in this small space. "Look, I'm sorry I didn't come find you but it was a fucked up time, if I'm being honest. Everyone was either scrambling to turn one another in or trying to hide, and those who were still loyal were trying to find Krys and you—"

"He was dead, Aodhan. You knew that," she said sharply. Aodhan sighed, running his hand over his head and loosening strands of hair.

"Yeah, I knew. But no one wanted to believe it could happen so they just didn't, alright? And with you gone... well, someone had to pick up what was left."

Tamora peered across the small room at him. He looked... nervous. Not for his safety; they both knew she couldn't take him on in this state. They'd been pretty evenly matched back then but plenty had changed. No, he was looking at her like a child who'd taken a parent's sword or dagger and been found playing soldier. "I didn't realize that you'd be the one left with all that," she finally admitted, leaning back against the door. "I thought you holed up with the king, back in Ozhansa."

"Yeah, I did. Your mother did reach out, you know. I knew where you were. But... I just couldn't. Innogen had seen you and said that you were just... well, I guess you know. I'm sorry. I couldn't see you that way," he said.

"I don't remember that," she said. She'd been broken, that's what he wasn't saying. She knew, logically, that Innogen, his Guardian, had been on the Plains that day. It was all a terrible blur now. She looked down at her hands, at the scars that covered them, and clenched her fist.

"She's the one who carried you off the plains," he said, his voice falling to a whisper. It was all he needed to say. That last battle had been the worst day of her life and should have ended it; she was grateful she only remembered pieces. Tamora sighed but it came out more strangled than she'd meant.

"Well, she saw the worst of it then," she said. The chuckle that erupted from her lungs was dark but it was enough, and even Aodhan snorted.

"Yeah, I suppose so. She didn't sleep for weeks... don't think that was just 'cause of you but it certainly didn't help. You'd give anyone nightmares," he said, a hint of a tease in his voice.

"True enough."

A silence filled the room but it didn't have the same animosity as it had before. It wasn't his fault, she knew, that she'd ended up this way. She couldn't even blame the man who'd killed Selena, not really. They'd been at war and he had taken his shot; it didn't make it easier. Being so far away from it all had made it all seem a more distant memory.

"What are you doing here, Aodhan?" she asked, breaking that silence. He sighed.

"I thought it was obvious. I'm trying to start a war, Tamora. Want to help?"

Tamora scoffed. "We helped Krys start a war and it ended with more blood than I ever thought I'd have to see. So forgive me if I don't want to repeat history. Why are you roping in these children?" He fixed her with a telling stare she knew she deserved, but she looked aside all the same.

"They haven't been 'roped in', and they're grown men that are more than willing to try this without me. I'm not the one driving this particular mission so don't blame me for this mess," he said, shaking his head. "They call the one out there 'Captain', and he's got the direct orders right now. I'm really just hired muscle."

She gave him a long look. His mouth was fixed in a half smile and his eyes were wide; he was telling the truth. Tamora sighed heavily, the events of the day weighing on her. "Alright, we'll say I believe you. Who's giving the orders then, if not you? I'd imagine you're the most senior member of this... this group." She gestured at the door, toward the broken Humans. "Where's Innogen anyway? I can't imagine she'd let you do this alone."

He shrugged. "They had different orders for her. I didn't like it, believe me, but it meant she'd be safe home in Iralt." Tamora nodded, understanding all too well. She and Selena had been offered something similar and they hadn't taken it. Look where that had gotten them.

"She's always been the smart one. So, spill it. Who's giving the orders?" she asked. But Aodhan shook his head.

"Not without knowing for sure that you're with us. You're an old ally, sure, but it's been years. They could have gotten to you," he said, frowning over at her. She snorted.

"Yeah, I'd go through everything I did and then betray you now, nearly a century later. Come on, Aodhan. I'm a cripple, not a traitor." She shook her head, kicking at the floor. There were scorch marks on the wood and she couldn't tell if it were from this conversation or one of her older outbursts. He hadn't said anything but, then again, he wouldn't have brought it up. That's not how Aodhan was. "Really? You think I'd turn?"

"You were pretty friendly with the Sentinel, honestly — but no, I don't. I still can't just go around sharing our secrets. I have no idea who might be listening," he said.

"But—" a pounding on the bedroom door interrupted

them.

"Aodhan? Healer? Why don't y'all keep this door open for now?" the one Aodhan had called Captain called. She narrowed her eyes.

"They're really trusting."

"Would you be in their situation?" Aodhan asked. His perpetual nonchalant attitude had seemed amusing, when they'd practically shared a brain. Now it was only frustrating.

"What *is* that situation?" she asked, stepping forward as he went to open the door. He loomed over her but this power struggle could go either way. He rubbed his neck as he looked down at her.

"As far as I know, they don't like the Karkas family and want them out. I guess there's someone that's sympathetic to the cause, on the inside?" he said, more of a question than a statement. He clearly didn't have all the answers himself.

"Do you have a name?" she asked as he reached past and opened the door.

"What are you talking about?" Captain mumbled, pushing into the space the door had occupied. Tamora turned with a scowl.

"You need to sit down, you idiot. You've got a broken jaw and a twisted ankle. Do you want to ever eat solid foods again?" she asked, guiding the man bodily to the fire. Aodhan chuckled.

"Your bedside manner hasn't improved, I see," he said.

He'd earned himself another glare. "I've been doing this for long enough I don't think it really matters what I say," she said. She turned to Captain. "I was asking Aodhan here what you were up to. I didn't think it was anything good but if you're trying to assassinate the Karkas heir, well, I don't think it's going to the way you'd planned."

"You'll turn us in?" he asked, jutting out his chin.

Tamora rolled her eyes. "No, I wouldn't. But you'd have a rough time trying to get close enough to do any damage. Look, I want to help you. Soren Karkas is an ass and deserves whatever is coming his way. What have you done, other than throw a few books at him?"

Captain shrugged, gesturing to Aodhan, who stopped fiddling with the flame he'd had flickering between his fingers. Tamora was glad for it; he truly was in no state to speak. "Oh, well we got a few of our friends out of the jail down in the Lower District, I went up to the palace to try to speak with the elder Karkas but was turned away — did you know his daughter is actually quite beautiful? I was surprised... sorry, not important. We planted a few people around the palace prison as well as the lower jail, just in case they tried to arrest anyone else. Heard about you stopping by, doing what you do. Nicely done, by the way, I love the health scare with the guard. Soren's right hand man was making an ass of himself and we dealt with him—"

"I heard about that. If you were going to do something, you should have finished the job. The man's a menace, and it's going to get worse now that his pride has been injured," she said. Aodhan just shrugged.

"He was dragged away before we could finish the job. But he's in no shape to help his dear master either, didn't you see him running like a coward earlier?"

"They all were." She busied herself with the man's bandages as she mulled it over. "You still haven't told me what your actual plan is here. Just raising a bit of trouble is going to get you killed, along with anyone who seems close enough to want to help."

"They were already doing that," Captain said. She hit his shoulder and he gasped out a wince.

"Stop talking, Wela help me. You're going to lose your damned jaw," she snapped.

"He's right," one of the other young men roused himself enough to say. He was staring up at the ceiling with his eyes glazed over, a dreamy smile on his narrow face. That'd be her tonic taking effect. "It's already happening. Sorry, healer, you're going to be busy."

She looked over them all; they certainly looked like they'd been through one hell of a fight. "What's the boy mean?" she asked Aodhan. Captain interrupted him.

"He's twenty five, hardly a boy——oof." He didn't back up fast enough to avoid Tamora.

"Good for him, I'm two hundred years his elder. If you don't stop talking I'm going to knock you out — for your own good," she snarled.

"I'd listen to her if I were you," Aodhan said lightly. "She's done it more than a few times. No, after the trial they started going door to door in the Lower District. Anyone who's ap threat, or someone they don't particularly like, is going to be arrested."

She pinched the bridge of her nose, trying to rub away the headache that was building again. "I can't believe you'd come here and — oh Wela help me," she said, dropping her hand with the sudden realization. She turned to Aodhan. "I need to go back in. A friend, she lives in the Harbor District and I shouldn't have left her there in the first place."

He shook his head and crossed his arms. "Oh no, definitely not. With your reputation you'd be one of the first to be arrested. It's the young Karkas lord that's leading them, I heard."

She groaned. "That's worse, much worse. My friend, she went to see Zavalynn yesterday when you started your damn fight and they might think she was involved."

"She blonde? That cute plump Eilvyn woman?" Aodhan asked, straightening when she gave him a bewildered nod. "I saw her. Does he know her name?"

"Oh yeah, he courted her for a decade. She married a Human instead."

He swore. "I still can't let you do that, Tamora, I'm sorry. You look dead on your feet, and these men need your help. If we leave them here they'll try to run off and get up to Dalka knows what, and without you some of them may not make it through tomorrow." She meant to protest, but one glance at the men sprawled around her living room told her exactly what she needed to do. She swore, worse than Aodhan had, and it turned Captain's ears pink.

"Fine. I'll tend to these *boys*, and you better hope she's alright. You've started this — if something happens to her, I'm blaming you," she said, leveling a finger at him. Captain, whatever his real name was, deserved some of the blame at least but he looked like he was suffering enough.

"I'd be sorry if she got hurt, she seemed like a nice woman. But I'm not going to apologize for what we've done here; I hardly started it," Aodhan said firmly. For that, Tamora had no reply. She had a few choice words for him but it wouldn't help. With one last glare, and a sweeping look over her drugged patients, Tamora stalked into her small bedroom. She didn't intend on sleeping, not really. If the guards came calling they were done, and it wouldn't matter if she hadn't really been involved before this point. There was already room for suspicion with her actions with the statue; they didn't know she was half Mago but if they ever found out, she'd be arrested for interference. Or endangering the guard, whichever had the highest sentence.

She went quickly to the small panel beside her bed and pulled it up, revealing a thin and long case beneath the floorboards. Her fingertips ran over the wood. There had been a time when she'd pulled these open daily for maintenance and keeping up whatever skill she had left. Now it was more like weekly, less than that if she were truly honest with herself. She was out of practice. Still, as she revealed her two black swords to the dim light and picked them up carefully, her fingers rested perfectly in the worn indentations and she felt a little more at ease. One practice swing proved that her arms were not what they used to be, but they felt right.

She sat in bed, her blades at her side. If someone came that shouldn't, she'd be as ready as she could hope to be.

Marin

"Lark, I'm serious. I won't tell you again," Marin said, waving her arm as she looked back down at the dough she was kneading, baking in her own private kitchen for once. The shop downstairs was closed to the public but being that close to the outside was not something she was comfortable with at the moment. Nor was there really a need for any more baked goods in this house but she baked when she was stressed, always had. Lark stepped back from the window that he'd been peering out for the tenth time in the last hour but she knew it was only temporary; there was no way to satisfy his curiosity for long. If he'd had his way he would have gone out when the ruckus started. Now, having listened to it through the night, she knew that would have been a terrible mistake. Instead she'd had him board up the windows, barricade the bakery door, and stay up on watch with her. Sorrell had insisted on coming out to the main room as well and he sat, leg propped up, on the tufted armchair.

"They aren't in the district, I think we'll be alright," he said, speaking for the first time in hours but saying the exact same thing he had when this started. His fingers were wrapped tightly around Eloise's, who had been a bundle of nerves since daybreak. Marin felt for the girl, not wanting to think about what her parents might be going through out there. She prayed to the Wela that they were safe.

She couldn't sit down, couldn't keep her hands from shaking. The bread would be dense and overworked. "I don't think that really matters, Sorrell," she said, "because they know exactly who we are. If Zavalynn is with them—"

"Why would he come here now? He loves you, that's the problem," said Lark, flopping on the chair opposite his brother. "And besides — if Zavalynn comes within a foot of this place I'll beat him bloody, I've told him so."

"You're a child, Lark—"

"I'm fifty-three! If I were Human I'd be going gray," he said, slamming his hand into the window frame. He turned back and she saw true anger there. "Stop treating me like I'm still too young to understand! Sorrell and I, we know what's happening. We've been out there, we've seen it. *We're* the *Joien*, Mother, not you."

Sorrell wouldn't look up from his hands and that's how she knew he felt the same. She set aside the bread and brushed the flour from her fingers, removing her apron. Taking her time with this gave her permission to think. He was right, of course. She wasn't *Joien*. She'd made this decision for them and had kept them here far too long. But she'd also seen far more of the world than they had.

She was seated in her own chair, beside Sorrell and Eloise, before she spoke again. To their credit neither had tried to rush her; they'd been with her long enough, their whole lives, that they knew better than that. "You're right, I could not imagine what you, on your own, have seen or heard from the people here. I know they are not always kind. But... you don't know how bad it could be, how bad it was." She paused, looking for the words. "This is not — Zavalynn is a very powerful man here in Erengate. You cannot insult him and bring his attention down upon you. He's not the man I once knew and he's not someone you want as an enemy so early in your lives. And I doubt you'd do more than annoy him, to be perfectly honest. You've never trained with weapons and he is over three hundred years old and has had plenty of practice." The clamor outside, dim but still audible, punctuated her words.

"I can insult who I want, especially when they're a no-good, brutish, pathetic—"

Lark's words were cut off by pounding on the bakery door, a loud banging that was muffled by walls and stairs. They looked at each other; Lark and Sorrell's eyes had gone wide in very different ways. Sorrell, incapacitated as he was, looked nervous. Lark, however, had become jittery with sudden excitement. Just as suddenly, however, Sorrell sat up straighter.

"It's Miss Davina, I can hear her," he said. Marin and Eloise both were on their feet in moments. "It's her and Bear!" Sorrell shouted after them, stuck in his chair as the two rushed down into the bakery.

"Mistress?" she heard Davina call; not a shout, per say, but a very panicked sounding plea that made her heart ache. *I should have sent Lark*, she thought as she pulled chairs out of the way and unbolted the door as fast as she could. *We could have gotten them here sooner.*

Eloise's parents stood on the stoop, thinning coats wrapped around their shoulders and each with a bag in hand. They looked utterly exhausted and they embraced their daughter, Davina looking at Marin over Eloise's shoulder. "Mistress, we're so sorry to intrude—"

"No, come in, come in," she ushered them all inside before securing the door and looking pointedly at Lark, who had followed them down. "Secure that. Please, come upstairs. And it's good to see you both. Please, call me Marin." The two Humans looked shell-shocked and stumbled up the steps, with their daughter guiding them forward. Her father fit into his name nicely, Marin noticed, realizing she hadn't actually met him yet. Eloise talked about them both constantly but neither had ever stopped by while Marin had been in; she'd only met Davina a handful of times when she had been much younger. It boggled her mind that her own children were older than Eloise's parents — it was always strange to think about the differences between their people. Even when she'd been with William she hadn't liked to think on it.

Sorrell was clearly trying to get out of his chair when they all entered the room. "Um, my son, Sorrell."

"We've heard a lot about him, about you all," Davina

said, not unkindly but there was something else in her face when she looked over at their children. Hesitation, Marin thought. Her daughter was a spitting image of her, with the same stunning dark hair and light, downturned eyes. "We're so sorry to—"

"We're happy to have you, and glad to see you safe. What's going on out there?" Marin said, guiding the two Humans to chairs where she handed them a warm blanket. Their hands were frozen and their coats far too flimsy for this time of year.

Bear sighed and opened his mouth to speak, but jumped when the door creaked open and Lark let himself back in. He chuckled at himself before rubbing his jaw. "Sorry, it's been a night. Well, it's been a week if I'm being entirely honest. Did Eloise tell you?" Marin nodded.

"I'm glad to see you're still a free man."

He nodded, staring at his wife and gripping her hand. "As am I. You have Healer Tamora to thank for that, the woman is truly a gift. But tonight is something else, something I've never seen. We had to leave. They were a few buildings away, just pulling people from their houses—"

"They're arresting people? I thought they were patrolling?" Marin asked, feeling sick to her stomach. Bear frowned.

"I don't really see the difference, ma'am. They started in the Trading District earlier today, shutting down stalls and storefronts and telling everyone to go home. That upset more than a few folks, as you might imagine. I think someone threw a rock; I even heard that they ran over a guard with their cart but no one knows what was going on, they just know that the guards started to fight so they cleared out, ran for the Lower." He sighed again, visibly swaying in the chair. Davina wrapped her arm around his shoulders and looked pointedly at Marin.

"Sorry, we've been up all night. The Lower was bad enough last night before the trial, I didn't think it was going to get worse," she said, her voice strained.

Marin shook her head. "No, no it's alright. I don't want to interrogate you; if you need to sleep, we'll go downstairs. We're far enough from the Lower that I'm sure we'll be safe." She hoped so, at the very least. Brushing her apron, knowing there was still loose flour there, she stood and nodded to Lark. "Help me get some things together, blankets and the like."

He trailed after her until they were out of earshot of the Humans, but not of Sorrell. "You really think they won't come this far?" he asked; his eyes still held too much excitement over the prospect.

"I hope they won't, but I doubt it. Many of these shops are owned by Humans, it's why your father and I were able to settle here. If they're going through the Lower, and no one stops them, they'll come here next," she said, handing him their two remaining blankets. They were scratchy and pulled out only on the coldest of nights, but they'd do. "We aren't sleeping, you understand? We'll let them rest because they clearly need it. But I need you to pack whatever you can comfortably carry, for the both of you. Do you understand?"

"Where would we go? The Respite?" he asked. She glanced around him, seeing how Sorrell watched them even as he spoke quietly to Eloise. *Good,* she thought sadly. *At least we'll all be somewhat prepared.*

"No, we'd have to go through the district gate and they probably have guards there now. I'd like to get to Tamora's... it's far enough away that we'd have some room to breathe." She was thinking out loud. "There's a gate involved there too, though, so I don't know—"

"I have a way around that, we don't have to use the gate. There's a door, a false bit of wall, that someone put up years ago down by the water's edge," Lark said. For once, she wasn't sad to hear that he'd been snooping places he shouldn't.

"Please never tell me why you know that. But good, we'll go there. Only if we need to," she said, pushing him back to the main room. "Now go, and make our guests as comfortable as they can be. I'll come back soon." Marin watched him go, all smiles, and hand out blankets and set a pot over the coals for tea. He was a good host and growing up well, they both were. After a moment that she wished she could freeze in her mind, she turned and went to pack a bag she hoped she wouldn't need.

.....

She must have dozed off because when she opened her eyes, Lark was shaking her by the shoulders. "Mother? There's someone at the door," he whispered. There was little excitement in his eyes now, it had faded into what she sleepily recognized as fear.

"What? Here? What time is it?" she said, groping around for her bag. She remembered packing it, leaving it beside her and getting tea and then... she must have slept. It was still dark out, so it hadn't been long.

"I'm not sure, it's almost light. What are we going to do?" he asked. She heard the pounding at the door now, more forceful than when Eloise's had arrived. Eloise. She looked at the couch but her parents were nowhere to be seen, and neither were Sorrell or Eloise.

"Where are they? Where's Sorrell?"

He waved nervously. "Getting his things, Eloise is trying to help him. He asked about weapons—"

"Mistress, I'm sorry but I'm going to be taking this," Bear said, walking back into the room hefting a rake that she didn't remember owning. Davina held a small paring knife in her hands and was as pale as a sheet.

"No matter to me," Marin said, jumping to her feet. "I... we should go." The urge to see what they wanted was strong but she knew it would be useless, she could imagine what they'd say. Better to not risk it at all. "The back stairs, Lark. Now. Get your bags."

"What's going on?" Eloise asked as they all came together in the main room; her head jerked when she heard the noise from the bakery below. "Are they here for us?" Her voice shook and she grasped Sorrell's arm.

"They don't know you're here. I think they're here for me," Marin said, hoping she sounded braver than she felt.

"Why?"

The sound of cracking wood cut off whatever reason Marin was going to give and she felt the blood drain from her face. "Out the back, now," she said, waving her hand and throwing her bag over her shoulder. "Now, now!" She could hear their footsteps and then they were at the door. It shook in the hinges and wouldn't last long. Marin looked around for anything that would slow them down. "Bear, help me—" she said, pointing at the chairs. He was there before he finished her sentence, throwing the cushioned armchair in front of the door. It was quickly followed by another, and the small kitchen table for good measure. She hoped it would buy them time; even a few seconds would matter.

Lark pried open the window that directly faced the neighboring building; a rickety wooden staircase traced the wall. It was more of a ladder than anything else and had been ignored for years. He looked down it for a second before sliding down, hardly even touching the individual rungs. Marin and Bear rushed to the group.

"Davina, you next," Bear said quickly. "Don't look at me like that, just go." He couldn't stop glancing back at the door, all that was between them and the very angry group pursuing them. His wife visibly braced herself and began a slow descent.

The air pressure in the room began to change. There were Eilvyn in the bakery and they were trying to break through using their Eiyer. Marin felt her ears pop and stretched her jaw.

"That's a damn good door," Bear said, after ushering his wife on.

"I had it reinforced— it's not important," Marin said, shaking her head. It was about to break anyway, regardless of all her efforts. "Eloise, go now!"

"This is insane," she gasped, looking down at the rickety set-up.

"Go, Eloise. I'll be right behind you," Sorrell said, a brave smile on his face. Marin felt a ball settle in the pit of her stomach. He'd have to try to control his fall, because it could only be a fall with his leg in the condition it was.

The girl shook her head fiercely. "I can't—"

"You'll die. Go, careful now." Marin pushed her forward and watched with bated breath and Eloise stooped out the window and down the tilted ladder. It shuddered beneath her with every movement.

She hadn't reached the bottom before Marin gestured for Davina to go. She shot her an uneasy glance and stepped out on the first rung. The whole thing shook like a leaf in the wind. It hadn't gotten this much use in over thirty years, not since William died. He'd always maintained the house, and the bakery, and it had just seemed a chore after he'd gone. Marin bit her lip as the women went down; Eloise thankfully reached the bottom and held the ladder for her mother.

"Alright, Sorrell. You next," she said, looking at her son. It worried her, how he'd have to do this. But he had a set to his jaw that she rarely saw and determination written all over him. He threw down his bag; it was nothing but clothes, hardly breakable. But when he got to the edge Marin leapt forward. He was just too unsteady on his feet. "I'm going to hold your hands, alright? Just hop down, rung by rung."

"Mother—"

"Don't 'mother' me, just do it."

Sorrell grasped her hands, one final glare the only protest he dared give, and swung his bad leg out into the air and prepared himself to jump down. Marin heard Eloise gasp, and the door behind them shake, but she was entirely focused on Sorrell. He pushed out a final breath and was airborne. He came down on the rung hard enough to shake the entire flimsy construct and Marin braced herself. On the second rung she was pulled outward, bending lower to keep her grasp.

"Just keep going," she urged him, looking over her shoulder inside the window. The door wouldn't hold long.

On the third rung, she was hanging half out the window. He was still ten feet above the ground, too far to simply jump into the waiting arms of his brother. The sill dug into her stomach and she stifled a groan; it would do no good here. At that moment the door behind her burst open and chaos erupted.

Bear paused for only a moment before he rushed away from her. "Go, go now!" he shouted, swinging the rake wildly at the men who flooded into her home. Marin swore, Sorrell jumped, and both of them plummeted toward the ground below.

Marin swung herself forward, twisting Sorrell above her, and landed on her left side hard enough that she heard, as well as felt, the crack that radiated out from her ribs as she and then Sorrell hit the ground. The air was pushed from her lungs and she gasped up at the sky. He rolled off of her as fast as he could manage, with Lark jumping to pull him up and Eloise rushing to her side.

"Oh my Wela, are you alright?" the young woman cried, helping Marin to sit.

"Where is Bear?" Davina asked, her face appearing in Marin's line of sight. She felt her lungs finally, thankfully, fill and coughed so hard she feared more ribs would break.

"We need to get out of here," she managed to say. "Bear... Bear stayed to fight—"

"What?" Davina cried, standing and staring up at the window.

"He's buying us time— we need to go."

"Eloise, please take my arm," Sorrell said, pushing Lark towards Marin. "Help her up, lead the way. Miss Davina... I'm sorry." It was all they had time to say as yells emanated from above. Marin's heart was in her throat as Lark took her hand and pulled her down the short alley; she looked back and saw that Eloise was pulling her mother with her, tears streaming down their faces, as she struggled to support Sorrell's weight.

"Lark, Lark, I'm fine," she wheezed, pulling him to a stop just short of the alley's entrance. "Please just get your brother... she, she can't—" She didn't have to say more. He peered around the corner and motioned them forward, moving faster than Marin had thought possible. It was both a blessing and a curse that the streets were so empty; it felt like they were more exposed than if they'd been shouting their position from the rooftops.

He moved fast, often too fast for them to reasonably catch up. Her chest burned and she worried that her lungs were damaged in some way, as each breath brought with it a stab of pain. Twice she called out for Lark to be careful and not go too far ahead. The second time, when he paused enough for them to reach him, she pulled him by the arm and gripped tightly.

"You want to run into the guards now?" she snapped at him. His eyes went wide. "Or anyone, for that matter? Either the guards will kill us or others will be too scared not to react on instinct. Stick to the damned walls like your life depends on it."

"Yes, ma'am," he said quietly, eyes on the ground. "Sorry."

"How far?" She could smell the fish-logged stench of the docks and see the wall looming over the buildings.

"Just a few streets; the wall breaks near the water's edge." When he led this time, it was at a slower pace and with each glance Marin could see renewed caution in his eyes. Sorrell was clearly muttering in his ear.

The last open stretch they had to run was to the edge of the sea; Marin glanced around the corner with Lark. It was deserted.

"This must have been where they started, right? Most of the Humans work down here," Sorrell said, looking back past his mother at Eloise. "Are you alright?"

"I can't talk about this here," she replied, her voice cracking and tears very clearly being held back with all her remaining force of will. Marin squeezed her hand and turned back.

"Alright, let's go."

They all rushed from the wall to the very edge of the bricked road. It dropped down to the rough beach, small stones and twigs all that made up the water's edge, the docks stretched out to their left. From this perspective they looked very close together, like you could hop easily from one to the other. The wall that jutted up to their right stretched out a dozen yards into the sea and looked as impenetrable as it always did. Lark lowered Sorrell down, apologizing under his breath as his brother landed on his bad leg and swore, and then turned to help each of them down in turn. The surf kicked up and sprayed her, sending a chill down her spine. She looked around. They were terribly exposed here, if anyone dared leave their shops. If anyone was left to see.

"I thought you said there was an opening?" she snapped.

"There is," he muttered, feeling the rocks. "They put it together so the guards don't- ah, here." He pushed against a smaller rock and it fell through to the other side. Marin rushed forward and helped him pull it down. It was a thin false wall, a few bricks thick, and beyond that a tunnel of darkness through the city's outer wall.

"It opens on the other side too?" Lark and Sorrell both nodded. Marin sighed.

"I really hate that you know this." She ushered for the group to get into the darkness. "Come now. Lark, help me put this back up."

He frowned at her. "But—"

"We can't let them see that it's broken. I'd like to have them think we stayed inside the walls for a little while longer." He huffed but helped her pile the rocks carefully up. Some were glued together, forming larger patches, and it didn't take as long as she'd feared to enclose them again into darkness. "Alright," she whispered, the blackness seeming to require silence, "let's go open up the other side."

Racynth

"I'm done with waiting," Petro said, huffing and sitting up from the position of meditation he'd taken on the floor. They had all returned well after dark, despite Sabina's orders. Karkas's men were raiding the Lower District and it had taken all of their will to keep most of the Humans they'd come across from ending up in jail cells or worse. It had taken little encouragement to get windows boarded and doors locked, and the city had looked nothing like what Racynth had first been greeted with upon his arrival only days earlier.

"For once, I agree with him," said Racynth, ignoring the man's raised eyebrows and looking at Sabina. "We've been here too long."

"I don't see what you expect us to do," Sabina snapped, running her hands through her braided hair and loosening it. She frowned at it before beginning to braid, her hands moving swiftly. "The 'little lord' can't be arrested for this, not yet. He has every right to restore peace to his city and the Council would come down on us for interfering."

Her father had been clear when they'd left Koren; the Sentinella was not to interfere in peace-keeping. Clearly, he knew his daughter well enough to specify that she was to keep her nose out of the business of others, especially nobility. Anything more than this would lead to a reprimand — nothing formal, but Councilman Miayra was known for his more creative punishments. Hence their nearly eighty-year post at the remote libraries of the east.

"They're not restoring anything, they're destroying it," said Petro, looking out the window. "Bensa forgive me, but he's in the wrong here."

Racynth couldn't hold back the sigh. It was always 'Bensa this' and 'Itrodo that' with Petro. "We know he's in the wrong," he said, "but it doesn't matter. We can't arrest a city lord's son on such flimsy charges."

"Hunting Humans, a flimsy charge?" Petro said. Racynth shot him a look but it was impossible to ignore the pain in his face.

"We all know it's not, Petro," Aspen said, her voice soft. It wouldn't stand up in court, not one run entirely by the Karkas family and their allies. And if they tried to bring charges against them in Koren, they'd be laughed out of the city.

"What can we do then?" Petro asked, leaning against the wall. "Just sit here and let them arrest people? Or kill people? No one is keeping track of this and I hardly think he'll be too bothered by a few 'accidents'."

Racynth frowned at him. He'd never seen Petro this worked up before. He was always the quietest of their Sentinella, with a stony face that Racynth often found himself jealous of. Too much Eilvyn blood in his system, he thought, made it difficult to hide his truest feelings.

"What do you want us to do then? Arrest him in front of all his men and hope that they just let us?" Racynth asked. "Please, give us an option here." Petro shook his head and shrugged, glancing at Aspen.

"I don't know, all right? I just think it's wrong," he muttered. "But it's not like anyone else in the city cares."

Going off Aspen's slight shake of the head, Racynth thought it best not to pry. He sighed and looked at the window; from behind the curtain he could tell the sun was close to rising. It had been a long night of tense frustration and they were all antsy. "We could go to the healer," he said, the thought coming to him unprovoked. "She has a copy, I saw her pick it up. And you wanted to speak with her anyway."

Sabina looked pensive, and the others straightened at something to do besides sit and wait.

Aspen cocked her head. "I think she's a Mago."

They all looked at her sharply.

"What?" Racynth scowled. "Impossible. She's clearly an Azha. The... the hair and the eyes." He gestured at his own face, frowning. He remembered the feel of her Eiyer, and it had been off. But that couldn't be true. Aspen rolled her eyes.

"Azha aren't the only ones with reddish hair, Racynth, nor gray eyes. Still, she's obviously part Azha. But when she fell in the square yesterday her pant leg pulled up, and I saw a marking there only a Mago would have," she said. She reached down to reveal her own ankle and pointed at the tattoo there. It was faded and in a curiously angular shape; the black ink almost looked like a tent to Racynth's untrained eye. A malformed and jagged tent, with swirls and points darting off at strange angles, but it was close enough. "You get this when you're early in your schooling. They have you live in the forest for a week and you have to survive on your own. I don't believe any other Iokans do this." She looked to Jordan for confirmation, and he shrugged.

"Definitely not the Veden, at the very least. So she's a *Pikvul* then," he said, grinning suddenly. "That's new."

Racynth knew what *Pikvul* meant, although he'd never met one. From what he'd heard, the four Iokan peoples weren't banned from relationships with one another, but the resulting children tended to be unpredictable and, in all reported cases, barren. While that hadn't prevented *pikvul* children from being born it had made them just as rare as he was as a *Joien*. He tried to stifle the sudden kinship he felt; it was unwarranted. The healer was hardly a friend, and she definitely didn't want any sort of bond between them. She hadn't wanted his help when he'd offered it either.

"It isn't in any report," Della said slowly, turning to Racynth, "but it would make sense. That means she probably collapsed the statue yesterday, just as the guard said. She may actually have more of a role in this little uprising than we thought."

Sabina detached her arm from where it was intertwined with Della's. "Then we question the healer," she said, looking at her partner. It softened her, being with Della. Racynth much preferred this version of his commander to the one he'd worked with before Della had joined as their navigator and records keeper. The old Sabina had been sharp and intentional with her words, often in ways meant to harm. That side of her rarely showed now. "What were you saying earlier, Del, about the records?"

Della snorted and ran her now free hand through her short hair. "The last Sentinella, and practically every group before them, weren't interested in this city and found it very boring. The sole exception was that healer. She threatened to kill one of them, according to the report, and they thought her to be a part of the last major rebellion... so it may be worth our while to speak with her."

Racynth snorted unintentionally. "And we all know how reliable those reports are. She doesn't look like she could actually hurt anyone, despite what Karkas said." Racynth tried to shrug off their looks. Among other things that the drug-influenced lord had rambled about, Sabina had explained that Soren Karkas and Tamora Asken had long been pitted against one another. Consistently restoring his victims to health had put her squarely in his sights years ago. "Did you see her scars? I'd be willing to bet they're on more than her hands, judging from that limp."

Everything about her was odd, he'd give the last Sentinella that much, but he wouldn't take any threat from her seriously.

"None of that means she wasn't more dangerous before whatever happened to her," Aspen said, twisting a section of her hair around her fingers. "*Pikvul* are rare, and like *Joien* they aren't readily accepted in most Iokan cities. It wouldn't have been a stretch for her to have joined up with Reene a hundred years ago — she may even have gotten those scars from battle."

"Or she was attacked because someone assumed that," Racynth said, feeling his temper rise despite himself. "Not every *Joien* or *Pikvul* joined the rebellion."

Petro flushed on Aspen's behalf, but Sabina cut both of them off before they could speak. "We won't know for sure without speaking with her," Sabina said, looking pointedly at Racynth and standing. "It's odd for a number of reasons that an Azha would be here in Erengate, although I won't jump to connect her with what's going on now. She's been here too long. If she were set on stirring something up I imagine she would have done it by now. Jordan, could you and Bealantin stay behind to go to the palace and see if the guards on the wall logged any recent arrivals in the city? I doubt someone with actual ties here would try to disturb the peace to this extent."

"Not this time of year," Della agreed, her hands flying as she put papers she'd been reading back in her pack. "The thaw hasn't fully come in, so if anything big came of these riots anyone trying to flee would be stuck in potentially life-threatening weather."

"I'm not sure if rebels think too critically of weather conditions, Della, but I get your point," Jordan said with a shrug. "We're fine to stick around, right Beal?"

"I suppose." His Guardian mirrored his movement, the two so similar they could have been twins. "I want to help here, in the city. This Iokan sounds interesting enough, but she's only one person."

"Can we even get out of the city right now?" Della asked, frowning suddenly. "Isn't it locked down?"

Sabina shook her head. "Del, we're Sentinels. Who is going to stop us?"

. . . . .

213

In truth, there was no one readily available to get in their way even if they'd wanted to. All remaining guards not tasked with protecting Lord Karkas had been pulled to the Upper Gate, as the elder Lord Karkas was fearful of an attack. The streets were deserted and a cold wind whipped through them. It brought with it the smell of rancid mud and the sea, and Racynth could see why it was one of the least popular postings among Sentinellas.

"You know I didn't mean anything by what I said," Aspen said quietly, walking beside Racynth as they headed toward the northern gate. She glanced over at him.

He nodded, focusing more on their surroundings than his feelings on the matter. "I know," he said, confident that she understood that the matter was done. Aspen had a good sense of the world, and he'd gotten defensive. It was something he'd struggled with since childhood; his mother's family had never once let him forget his heritage. He'd hoped that would change when he became a Sentinel, one of the most respected positions a warrior could achieve in the Coalition, but it had never had the effect he'd hoped.

Della pointed at a grated patch in the northern wall, a shift in texture that was barely visible. She had, being who she was, scoured all available documents before their arrival and had noted many of the older access points in and out of the city. This one was hidden in a small alley between the shadows of the towering outer wall and the surrounding buildings. Racynth would have walked past it without a second glance as it was entirely invisible as the sun rose above the horizon and cast long shadows through the streets.

"Nicely done," he admired, and Della beamed with pride.

"Allow me," Aspen said, stepping up to the opening. She closed her eyes for a moment and laid her hands on two of the stones on either side of the metal bars. Racynth always marveled that he couldn't tell if an Iokan was using their gift;

if it were *Eiyer* he'd know in a heartbeat that something was being altered. But as the stones crumbled away, taking the grate's support with it, he felt nothing. She caught the grate before it fell, grunting under the sudden heavy load, and set it as gently as possible on the ground beside them.

"Thank you," Sabina said, stepping through the opening and under the outer wall. Racynth watched as Aspen reassembled the grate as they stepped through, until it appeared as though nothing had changed. It was disturbing, he decided, that any Mago could do the same. Sneaking into any city must have been as easy as breathing for some people. Aspen caught his look and must have read his mind, because she smiled and shrugged.

"Not all of us need pretty words to get us into places we shouldn't be," she said, striding past. Racynth shook his head and followed. The fields outside the city walls cropped up from the salty shore, mostly tall grass and barely tamed shrubs this time of year. They hadn't gone far at all when Aspen, her eyes towards the west and following the shore, motioned for them to stop.

"Hey, you see that?" she asked, pointing toward the water. Racynth followed her line of sight and, to his surprise, saw a small group of people edging carefully along the shoreline. Two were clearly wounded, one hanging off another figure and the second limping on their own. It was also evident that they were trying, and failing, to not be seen.

"Follow me," he said, waving for Aspen and Petro to join him. "If they're in trouble, we'll bring them back here." Sabina nodded, her arms crossed.

"And if they *are* trouble, I suggest you take care of it." He shot her a look but she was staring past him. "Five. Two wounded. Shouldn't be much to handle."

He shrugged. "Then I hardly imagine they'll be trouble," he said, beginning to walk towards the small, ragged group.

It was impossible not to be noticed crossing such an empty space and he saw when they tried to pick up the pace, but it was simple for the three Sentinels to span the distance. When they were within five yards he nearly stopped in surprise as he recognized one of the figures. "Miss Agata?" he called out, seeing her stop and turn back to peer at him.

"Who?"

"A baker," he murmured to Aspen, shushing her. One of the men, boys really, reached back and tried to grab the baker's arm and pull her forward but he was supporting one of the others and the move nearly toppled them both.

"Miss Agata, do you need help?" he asked, as the three came up to the group. Her face was tear stained and dusty, her clothes a mottled mess, and the others fared little better. Two Humans, the baker, and — Racynth paused. "Are these your sons?"

She looked back at them nervously and then at the Sentinels, clearly wishing they were anywhere but there. "Yes-yes they are. And... we're just going to Tamora's..."

"What's happened here?" Aspen asked, waving Petro to the Humans. A smart move, it seemed, as they let him get near while still shooting Racynth and Aspen looks that could kill. "Why aren't you in your homes? It isn't safe."

"That's the problem," one of the young men, the one supporting his brother, spoke shortly. "They broke in and tried to kill us. We couldn't exactly stay behind."

"Who is 'they'?" Racynth asked, but the sharp sob that burst from one of the Humans was enough to silence any questioning he might have otherwise pursued. Petro spoke with her and the younger woman quietly before returning to Racynth and Aspen.

"Her husband held them off while they escaped. A group of Eilvyn, it seems, a mix of the city guard and others, attacked the bakery," he explained. "They're trying to reach the healer, they think she can help."

Feeling almost flushed with sudden anger, it took only a moment to decide upon their course of action. "Well, they could use an escort then," Racynth said. Aspen glanced at him, a small frown on her lips.

"I… do you think that's wise? Clearly they need protection, I'm not sure if this healer is capable—"

"I don't know that we could easily convince these people to come back to the city, not after what's happened to them. Especially not if the guard was involved," he said, looking back toward the stone walls. "I'm not sure how they got out, but it's best to keep them calm."

He stepped closer, holding his hands out peacefully, and looped the baker's arm over his shoulder. She was average height for an Eilfe, putting them at nearly eye level, so it was an easy task. "We're heading to Miss Asken's home as well. It seems someone is looking out for you."

"What do you want with Miss Tamora?" the young man asked, his voice rising as he gripped his mother tighter. Racynth caught a good look at him, and his injured brother, and made a judgment he hoped he wouldn't regret.

"We had a few questions for her — she was in the square when the Human was arrested, and was present for the sentencing as well. Both resulted in… well, let's just say it's a good time to leave the city for a few hours. And you're lucky we did," he said, eying him meaningfully. The young man looked exhausted. "It would have been a long walk and it's getting light — you've nearly lost the cover of darkness."

The young man muttered under his breath, hissing in pain as his brother elbowed him in the ribs. "Fine, fine. I do know the way," he said, wincing as his brother hit him again.

Racynth held back a smile as he turned and led them

back toward Sabina, gesturing for Aspen and Petro to help the Humans.

"You're like them, right?" the baker, Marin Agata, whispered.

Racynth could have told her it didn't matter, or asked how she'd known. He decided against it, his earlier thoughts about his kind's reputation still weighing heavily on his mind.

"Have they ever met another *Joien*?" he asked, sighing when she shook her head. "I'm not surprised. We're few and far between."

"How old are you?" The question seemed to slip out and she snapped her mouth shut. "I mean...— I'm sorry. That was terribly rude. I only want to know what to expect... you know... if they'll take after their father—"

"I'm four hundred and sixty-two this year, and I've met others who are older still. They should be fine," he said, cutting her off before she could continue on her rambling train of thought. He was keenly aware that her sons had fallen extraordinarily quiet behind them, and Sabina was not far off now.

He felt her small sigh of relief more than he heard it.

Sabina and Della came to meet them, a frown firmly in place on Sabina's face as she took in the condition of the ragged group. "Who are these people? Why are they not in their homes?" Aspen went to her side and whispered in her ear. When she finished Sabina straightened and her frown had only grown deeper. Still, she merely gestured toward the forest's edge. "Come on, we are wasting precious daylight."

"She's chatty," one of the boys said. Miss Agata whipped around, pulling Racynth around with her in a surprising show of strength.

"You will show your elders respect, Lark, or I swear to Afina I will lock you in your room for a month!" she snapped.

The boy, Lark, went as red as a fresh tomato and Racynth didn't bother hiding his smile.

"Come now, we best follow closely." Despite the circumstances, he felt this bode well for their conversation with the healer. At the very least, it was sure to be an interesting day.

Chapter 14

Tamora

The forest was quiet and peaceful, which wouldn't have been surprising if the last few nights hadn't been so unnerving. If it hadn't been so frigid, and if the trees didn't have their own terrible reputation, it might have been a pleasant evening for a walk beneath the no longer snow-laden boughs. With the city gates locked tight, no one was on their way looking for a quick remedy or salve. Inside the cottage structure, however, was a different story.

"If you don't stay down, I will knock you out. Do you understand?" Tamora snarled into a man's face, pushing him backwards for what felt like the hundredth time since their arrival. He glanced over at Aodhan, his eyes wide, but Tamora snapped her fingers in front of him. "He will let me, don't you dare look at him. I'm in charge here. This is my house. Your leg has been slashed open and if you put weight on it you'll ruin all my good work and you may never walk again. Do you want that to happen? No, I didn't think so." This time he stayed back on his elbows and Tamora shook her head, almost ready to get up and leave herself.

"Remember what I said about that bedside manner—"

"I swear to the Wela, Aodhan, if you say another word I will rip out your tongue," Tamora snapped, pushing herself to her feet and stalking to her kitchen. She wished desperately for privacy so that she could bash her face against the wooden countertop but instead, she glared at her old friend from across the room. He looked entirely too sympathetic for her liking.

Aodhan had watched her outburst silently but said a few words to his Human companions before he joined her.

"I'm in no mood to be lectured," she said, able to find her words. "This is all your doing, and if you've ruined this small peace I've found—"

"She'll be alright, you know," Aodhan said, his voice falling low enough to go underheard by the men sprawled around her fireplace. "Your baker friend, I mean."

"How do you know that? You don't understand what this place is like," she said, shaking her head again. If she didn't have something to hold onto, she was going to lose her temper. She found a sturdy mug did the trick, even if it was empty.

"Don't I?" he asked, crossing his arms across his broad chest. It made him look like a bear, which only caused her think of her friends in the city more. *Friends*, she thought sadly. It wasn't something she'd ever thought she'd have again, back when she'd first arrived in the north. *I hope they're all right.* "Name a single a place on this whole continent that isn't like this. Where Eilvyn don't run the show, and Iokans don't help enforce their ridiculous and small-minded laws, and everyone else isn't left behind. Where those Humans over there wouldn't be forced into the worst of jobs or left to hope that a kind Eilfe might take them under their wing. We've been doing this a long time, Tamora, so it's no good pretending that it isn't worth it."

Tamora frowned, running her fingers over the mug's rough surface. "I know what you're trying to do but it won't work. I've done what you're doing — or don't you remember why I'm like this?" she asked, gesturing down her body. "I swore not to get caught up in this again. Not when it nearly killed me the first time."

"I had no intention of dragging you back into this," he admitted, before shrugging. "It's never the right time, but we must do something. There's still a chance here to save that Human and prove to Karkas, and everyone in their court, that there are people who won't bend to their will anymore."

Tamora thought about the Pit, about what it would be like to stand on its edge and know you were going to die and shivered despite the warmth of her cottage. The tradition of executing people by dropping them into the Pit was barbaric — no one knew how long it took people to fall, or to die. They just never came back.

"I can't be involved; not like I once was. What can I even do?" she asked, frowning down at her scarred hands. They were a constant reminder of what she had once been, what she had once accomplished. She hadn't needed help then and she'd never hesitated. It tore at her, and part of her fought to throw herself back into the fray, but she knew better now. She'd never survive it if she did.

He arched a brow down at her. "Tamora, I've only been here a week and even I have heard of the rogue healer who keeps emptying out the prison. There's an underground movement here to get Humans out and move them south, and another that keeps the Lower District fed through the winter months. Knowing you, you're already more involved than you even know."

She opened her mouth to reply but was interrupted by a wave from the Human at the door, who recoiled from the window and let the curtain fall limp.

"Healer, there's a Sentinella coming. Five of 'em, and they've brought company," he whispered, his voice catching.

Captain, the fool, made to stand but Tamora stepped stiffly forward and pointed at him.

"Don't you move," she pointed at Captain. "You know you won't get far."

Aodhan spoke at the same time. "Trust Tamora, Cap, she's more than capable."

She shot him a grateful look and breathed in deeply. Her hands felt clammy as she reached for the knob. *Of all the times for them to make their damn visit, they have to come when I'm harboring rebel fugitives in my living room.*

Tamora pulled the door open a foot and was dimly aware of the five Sentinels outside her door. Racynth was closest, huddled under her small, stooped roof, and the blonde Eilfe was at his side with her hood pulled up against the chill.

What truly shocked her was the sight of Marin leaning heavily on Racynth's arm, her breath labored and pained. Lark and Sorrell leaned on each other behind them, and Eloise and Davina stood beside the Mago Sentinel and her Guardian.

"What's going on?" she exclaimed, stepping out and reaching for Marin. The blonde Eilfe, however, stepped between them.

"Miss Asken, I am Commander Miayra of the Fifth Sentinella. Will you invite us into your home?" she asked, far too formal for Tamora's liking. She narrowed her eyes, knowing her fingers were only inches from reaching Marin.

"Would you take her away with you if I said no?" she asked. She refused to simply allow this woman to take control here, as she had so easily done back after the ridiculous sentencing. Commander or no, this was her home and these were her friends.

The woman peered down at her. "No," she finally said, stepping out of the way. "There is, though, a certain necessity for formalities. Will you allow us inside your home?"

Tamora needed only to glance at Marin before she nodded and opened the door to let them pass. As they did she found herself shocked at the condition of the boys, not to mention whatever was wrong with Marin. *What in the Wela happened to them?* They all looked like they'd been to the Underworld and back and had barely scraped by.

As Davina passed, supported by the Human Sentinel, she reached out to take her by the shoulder.

"Where's Bear?" she asked quietly, guiding her to her armchair and motioning two of Aodhan's men out of the way with a jerk of her head. Davina stiffened and tears rushed to fill her eyes.

"He stayed behind. We were attacked, Tamora. We tried to hide with Marin where it was safe, but they came for her too," she whispered, staring up at her as she sat back.

"I'm going to get you some tea, Davina," she said, grasping her hands. "We'll find Bear again, I promise you."

Her eyes were very wide and had entirely lost their usual luster. "I think he's dead," she said flatly. "All that I'll get is a burial now. If that." She pulled her hands away and looked at the fire. Tamora found she had no response and simply looked at her for what felt like a long, uncomfortable time as she struggled to find the words.

Realizing they wouldn't come, she turned to the Sentinella. Not the entire group, she knew, but still enough to pose a problem if they put together the obvious dots that were sprawled around her living room. Aodhan hadn't tried to hide but instead was leaning casually against her counter and inspecting their new arrivals. Racynth still held Marin, but had turned to look at all the men who filled Tamora's home with a suspicious furrow in his brow.

She went to her friend, ignoring Racynth entirely and settling Marin by the warm hearth. "Marin, are you alright?" she said, trying to see where she was injured. Marin looked like she was still in a deep state of shock, but lucid.

"Fine, fine, Tamora, really. Lark, please let Sorrell down, you'll hurt yourself," she said, pushing Tamora's hands away as her voice wavered. She motioned to Lark to do as she'd told him but winced and pressed her hand firmly back into her side. "Really, I'm alright."

Aodhan leaned forward a hair, just coming off the counter enough to peer over at Lark as he slowly lowered his brother to the floor. He didn't say anything, looking at the Sentinels, and Tamora was far too preoccupied with Marin's injuries to question him now.

"What happened? Please let me help you," Tamora insisted, helping her remove her soaked cloak.

The Sentinels also adjusted their own thick woven cloaks as the heat that rolled through the small room settled on them. Tamora felt it was important to keep her home warm to keep any further sickness at bay. It also kept her comfortable and gave the Humans something to do. Captain still refused to relax and had insisted on lugging in more wood than he could reasonably handle.

She lifted the edge of Marin's shirt and inspected her side. "Nothing broke the skin... does it hurt to breathe? What happened?" she asked, reaching for some bandages to make a compress. She already saw a bruise forming beneath the skin, although it couldn't have been more than a few hours from the time of injury. "Aodhan, get me some ice. Wrap it in this, please."

The Sentinella watched him carefully as he stepped out and returned. Marin's breath hissed between her teeth when the now frozen wrap touched her skin.

"I jumped out a window," Marin explained, and Tamora's eyes widened in shock.

"And I landed on her," Sorrell interjected, wincing as he looked across the room at his mother.

Tamora paused, looking between all of them. "And why did you do that?"

Marin sighed, then winced. "Because a group of Eilvyn were trying to arrest us, or worse. I just need to rest, Tamora, I'm fine. Please just... deal with this. We'll still be here when you've finished," she said, gesturing vaguely at the Sentinels.

Racynth cleared his throat and bowed shortly to Marin.

"I know to take a cue when I am given one. I believe introductions are in order, as we did not have the time yesterday. Aspen Crayg, Petro Equerry, and Della Keylynn." They all bowed in turn. Tamora nodded to each and noticed Marin snapping at her boys to ensure they did the same. As expected, neither Aodhan nor his Humans made any moves.

"Thank you for escorting—"

"That's not why we are here, although it was a happy coincidence," Commander Miayra interrupted, resting her hands on her belt. With her cloak unfastened, Tamora could see that she wore traveling armor; it was leather and sturdy, but flexible. The Sentinels that usually came through Erengate had reveled in formality and their social standing; she'd never seen any without embellished metal armor and finery. She couldn't decide if this boded well for her opinion of this particular Sentinella.

"Sentinel Naewynn made his report of what has occurred here in Erengate over the past two days and, somehow, you are at the center of most of it. How would you care to explain that? I'm in a hurry to see this resolved, and I don't feel the need for more pleasantries or for your excuses. I'd also like to know how it is that this group of Humans, some with clear signs of violence, came to be in your home," Commander Miayra said.

"Well, I—"

Tamora again opened her mouth but it was Aodhan

who spoke, drawing the eyes of everyone. "That was me, Commander. I brought them here," he said. Tamora frowned at him but he hardly looked her way.

"And who are you?" Commander Miayra asked, her eyes narrowing.

"Friend of Tamora's. I was in town when that whole riot started and these boys were in some clear trouble. Helped them get out of the city, same as you did for Miss Marin over there," he gestured, smiling in that crooked way he did when he wanted to look like a simpler man. Tamora wanted to groan and throw herself into her fire; it would make this whole situation so much simpler.

"Hmm. Well." Commander Miayra's eyes were so narrowed as she took him in it seemed impossible that she could see out of them. "If I said I believed you, would you be more inclined to explain why they so closely resemble the group of Humans we saw flee the scene of yesterday's riots?"

Aodhan shrugged, keeping his arms firmly crossed. "I'd say I wasn't there and, from what I did see of the city, they're victims more than anything else," he said. Commander Miayra glanced at Aspen and Petro for a moment, but they said nothing as they all looked closely at the Humans sprawled across the room.

"I'm not an idiot, 'friend of Tamora's', and I don't like being treated as such. It doesn't look like any of you are in a position to go anywhere, however, so I have no reservations about leaving you here. Under supervision," Commander Miayra said, cracking her knuckles as she spoke. She didn't seem to realize she was doing it. Tamora refused to look at Aodhan; he'd brought this mess to her doorstep. Seventy years, a hundred really, of avoiding any accusations of treason and now it had all come back to haunt her.

The commander still hadn't finished her thoughts. "We will need a few of these Humans to make a statement, at the very least. Aspen, Petro, please help them outside. One at a time," she said, gesturing first at Captain. He stiffened and looked desperately at Aodhan, but Tamora watched her friend just shake his head. Now was not the time to put up a fight — not with seven well-armed and uninjured Sentinels in her living room. She was sure they'd gone over some sort of plan for interrogations. She could only hope, for their sake, that they'd practiced well.

She said nothing as the two Sentinels helped Captain roughly to his feet and walked him out her front door. They didn't go far, she could see them through her small window, but it would be impossible to hear from this distance.

Commander Miayra watched the stilted questioning for a moment before turning back to the room, a small grimace on her face. "Miss Agata, I am sorry you and your family were attacked today. We know some of Erengate's residents have taken it upon themselves to deliver their own form of justice... however misguided that may be. Do you think you can identify the Eilvyn who entered your home?"

"That may be difficult," Marin said. "I didn't recognize any of them — well, I didn't have time to look very hard. It may have been anyone... I never expected something like this might have happened." She looked at Tamora with wide eyes. "Tamora thought I might be in danger, but I didn't believe her."

"Marin is well liked in the city, or so we thought," Tamora added. "There has never been vandalism, or rumors even."

"That's not entirely true," Marin said, looking quickly between Tamora and the Sentinels. "I never reported it, we didn't think it was serious. But there have been messages left at my shop before."

"Threats?" Racynth prodded.

Marin shook her head. "Nothing specific. Usually just

something crass about Humans, or my sons. They were more common when my husband was still alive, but they'd grown scarce in recent years. I did get one last week but I destroyed it before anyone else could see — I just didn't think it was important."

Tamora's heart seemed to be beating at twice the pace.

"You never mentioned this," she whispered, looking at her friend. "How many have you had to destroy?"

"I didn't want you to worry, you have your own problems." Marin smiled, but it disappeared as soon as it popped up. "I didn't think they would do anything. Some people just have a lot to say."

"Why did they send you these threats?" Commander Miayra asked. Tamora did respect her for her attention; if their roles had been reversed, she would have been far too concentrated on the weapons Captain and the others still had in hand.

"My sons are *Joien* and my late husband was Human. I am well-liked by most but I've never really been able to overcome that," she said pertly. Tamora glanced at her; this was more pointed than anything she'd ever heard Marin say before. All those years of subtly trying to convince her to move to a safer area— Tamora wished it didn't have to take an attack to convince her of the truth. Racynth had grown very still, his face furrowed in quiet concentration, while the other Sentinels looked truly frustrated for the first time.

"We will investigate upon our return to the city. There is no doubt in my mind that this should not have happened," Commander Miayra said, a short glance all she gave to her second-in-command. "Is there somewhere private in this place?" she asked Tamora, gesturing vaguely at the room around them.

Tamora elected to ignore her tone.

"The back bedroom is fine," she said, pointing toward the door reluctantly.

"Good. Aspen, Petro, please help Miss Agata and her sons to the bedroom. We will need to go over the threats you've received, and your sons may have heard rumors during their time at the docks," she said. Lark jumped at the mention of the docks, but Tamora wasn't surprised at the woman's knowledge. It would have been foolish to think that she hadn't been informed, especially of those close to Tamora. She had no doubt that the last Sentinella's notes had mentioned the bakery and those who lived there.

As the Mago, Aspen, and her Guardian helped Marin up, Tamora was left under the commander's full scrutiny. "I still have questions for you, Miss Asken, and I would request that you answer me truthfully. Are you *pikvul?*"

Tamora stiffened, feeling a rush of adrenaline course through her for a moment before she locked it down. No one, not even Marin, had ever guessed that. "I don't see how that's relevant—"

The commander rolled her eyes, the first real gesture she'd made since stepping through the doorway. "Please, tell me the truth. Are you half Mago? Did you truly collapse that statue in the square?"

Tamora chewed the inside of her cheek and concentrated on not burning through the soles of her shoes. "I am, yes, and I did," she finally admitted. "How did you know that?"

"Sentinel Aspen saw the tattooed markings on your ankles when you were on the ground, when the guard tried to arrest you," Commander Miayra said, smiling slightly. "Apparently they are unique to Mago rituals."

Tamora looked down at the offending ankles, safely hidden within her pant legs for now.

"You interfered in an arrest, Miss Asken, and that is a crime in every Coalition territory," Commander Miayra continued, tapping the pads of her fingers against her belt. "The arrest of these Humans, in fact." Tamora was fully aware of the tension in the room as it spiked, with all of the Humans and Aodhan waiting to see what the Sentinel might do.

"You have no way to prove that. Besides, regardless of who they were, can you tell me with certainty that the city guards would have given these men a fair trial? After what they've done in the city, to people like Marin? I don't regret doing what I believe to be right," Tamora said, crossing her arms. If this was how everything was going to come to light, so be it. There were few options left, once the Sentinella had shown up on her doorstep.

The commander looked unsurprised, if a little frustrated. "It's not up to a single citizen to decide what is lawful and what is not. If you had a complaint, it should have been brought to the Council's ambassador here in Erengate," she replied tersely.

Tamora almost laughed. "Ambassador Ademaro is a hard man to reach."

Truly he was only available to the upper class of Erengate. Any complaints from the rest of the city were funneled through the guards at the Palace District's gate and they were as likely to arrest you as listen. The Sentinella knew that as well as she did.

"That doesn't mean that you should take the law into your own hands. They exist for a reason — as it stands, the riot that they caused led to destruction of city and private property, and harm to the citizens of Erengate. Not to mention the distribution of illegal documents," she added, almost as an afterthought.

That, more than anything else, gave Tamora pause. "Are you arresting these men for a crime?" she asked, watching the commander closely. For a woman with all the power, she was doing a lot of beating around the bush.

Commander Miayra glared at the men for a moment, but it took her long enough to respond that Tamora knew her instincts were right. For whatever reason, the commander was going to let them go. What that reason might be, however, was still up in the air.

"Even without knowing that these men are here, your name is already being circulated. The Karkas Family wants someone to blame and a group of injured Humans is hardly enough at this point," Commander Miayra said.

"Then am *I* under arrest?" Tamora felt cold and flushed at the same time. She shot a glance at Aodhan but he motioned subtly for her to do nothing. She had to hope that if worse came to worst, he'd help her out of this mess. He always had in the past.

"We would prefer not to arrest you," Racynth said quickly, looking pointedly at his commander as he spoke. "The community trusts you and bringing you in would do more harm than good. No matter what Karkas might want."

"The person at the heart of this is Soren Karkas," Aodhan said. They all turned to him in surprise. Tamora wondered, silently, what else he'd share. She'd assumed he was going to play the role of innocent bystander in all of this. "He and Silas Zavalynn are brutal and, from what I've heard, have been taunting the people in the Lower District for years. I wouldn't be surprised if they'd wanted something like this to happen."

"And how long have you been here, exactly?" Commander Miayra asked, her eyebrows raised.

Aodhan counted on his fingers. "One, two, three... five days," he said with a wide grin.

Racynth snorted, but it was his Commander who spoke. "Mhm. In that case you are certainly an expert on the matter."

She turned back to Tamora. "Despite what you may think, I'm not the enemy here. We are not blind — we do see what Lord Karkas is doing. I know this may seem difficult to understand but the purpose of a Sentinella is to uphold the law, and nobility are not above that. Not to me. I don't like what we've found here in Erengate and I will be putting a stop to it. This little charade, however, with the rioting and statues and everything else — it isn't helping." She glared at them all.

"I'm glad you can see reason." It slipped out before Tamora could stop herself. She clamped her jaw shut.

The Commander's glare sharpened and Tamora felt the Eiyer in the room build as she did. It pressed against her skin and felt almost suffocating. "You will not speak out of turn again, Miss Asken, or I might turn you into the Karkas family, power games aside." She recollected herself, lowering the room's pressure, and Tamora bowed in slight apology. "We can provide safe housing for Miss Agata, her family, and her servants —"

"They are welcome to stay," Tamora said quickly. "I don't want them going back into Erengate, not when those Eilvyn are still roaming the streets. You should look for Bear Wyatt, though — he is Eloise's father. He may still be alive, maybe in the lower prison." She gestured to Eloise and her mother, who looked tearfully at the Sentinella. It was likely the first time they'd hoped a Sentinel noticed them at all.

Commander Miayra's expression softened, just for a moment, and she nodded. "Very well, we will do our best. For now, I believe it best if Sentinel Naewynn remains here, at least for today, to ensure your continued safety while we work out this issue with the Karkas Family."

The other Eilfe, the petite brunette named Della, stepped away toward the bedroom, likely to inform the others that they were leaving. Racynth dropped his cloak on the counter with a small sigh, sitting carefully on the rickety stool by the door. He nodded to Aodhan as he did so, his expression almost pleasant. To his credit, Aodhan was trying to look unimposing. It was very difficult to do when you towered over everyone else in the room.

"Ah... very well," Tamora said, unable to see a way to refuse the offer. It was, on the surface, a kind one. She had a full house on her hands and a crazed noble out for her head — most people would be hard-pressed to turn down protection under those circumstances. It was bound to get a little dicey in a few hours though. She couldn't help but look at the Humans; they were miserable already. When this business with Soren Karkas was finished, would they be arrested?

The Sentinella wasted no time in gathering their things. The Sentinels Aspen and Petro returned, helping Captain. He sat shakily and his face was pale, but he wasn't in chains. Yet again, Tamora found herself confused. There was no good reason not to arrest them, not if they knew about the pamphlets.

The commander paused to give her one final glare before they left.

"Miss Asken... I would recommend you do not leave your home for any reason over these next few days," Commander Miayra said tersely. "Racynth, I'll send word." She stepped out before either could respond, shutting the door firmly behind her.

Tamora let out a stiff sigh and glared at the unmoving Racynth, whose face was placid. Now she was out in the cold woods, useless, with a handful of rebels and a Sentinel under her roof. What could possibly go wrong?

.....

Racynth was apparently happy to busy himself anywhere but in the main room. First, he inspected the cottage's feeble outer defenses, then the few windows she'd put in, before finally sitting and going over the state of Erengate with an increasingly tired Marin. Happy to ignore his presence for now, Tamora tended to Sorrell, ensuring that his injuries were more cosmetic than serious. Sorrell's binding had loosened considerably over their race north and she found herself apologizing more than a few times for the pain that rewrapping it caused him. She also set him and Lark up in her own bed, ignoring their protests, as soon as Eloise mentioned that neither had slept for at least a full day.

When Tamora finally rejoined the others in her crowded main room, she found that the Sentinel had run into an impasse with the Humans and with Marin. His polite interrogation wasn't getting him far, but he didn't seem perturbed. He turned to her as she walked through the doorway.

"So, Tamora—"

She groaned and wagged a finger at him. "Are you done learning the name of every baker, butcher, and vintner in the city?" she asked, looking pointedly at Marin.

She'd been doing such a good job keeping him busy. The baker smiled nervously between the two of them, sitting up against the doorway between Tamora's room and the main space. She'd insisted on staying where she could see her sons, and had her fingers threaded through Eloise's as they sat together in the doorway. Davina refused to be more than a few feet from her daughter at any given time but had finally fallen asleep just inside the bedroom's entrance. Eloise had covered her in one of Tamora's spare blankets; with all her new guests, she had only one or two left at this point.

"As it happens, I am. Thank you." He leaned against the windowsill, for lack of better seating. "So you are *pikvul* then. I imagine that makes us rather similar."

Tamora rubbed her shoulder and sat on the hearth before really inspecting Racynth. He seemed kind enough, for a Sentinel. His expressions tended to be clear and honest, even when he was withholding information, and he had good strong features. His hair was tied back with a strong cord, same as one of the other Sentinels had.

"I suppose."

"Azha and Mago?"

"That's what I said, yes."

"Did you attend Brist or Hirne?"

"I'm a little surprised you know what those are," she said, arching her brow.

He responded in kind. "I have been around, Tamora. *I'm* not a hermit," he drawled, eying her pointedly. Aodhan snorted and quickly turned away when Tamora whipped around to glare.

"I went to Brist," she snapped. "That's where I met this idiot."

"What was your name again?" Racynth asked, turning to Aodhan. "I don't recall you mentioning it."

Aodhan stiffened slightly; he hadn't moved much from his place in the kitchen, avoiding the Sentinel as much as possible and speaking infrequently. As much as he clearly wanted to be ignored, it was hard to do with someone his size. "It's Aodhan," he said finally. "Tamora and I have known each other for a long time. I came to visit."

Racynth nodded, a small smile on his face. "Alright. Nice to meet you, Aodhan," he said before turning his smile on "Aspen—Sentinel Aspen—told me about Hirne once. She talks a lot as we travel, she thinks it fills the time. Unfortunately, I don't know as much about Brist."

"It's been a long time since I've been at either," Tamora said, scratching absent-mindedly at the edge of a scrape on her knee. She'd almost forgotten those months at Hirne, actually, until he'd mentioned the school. Her control over earth had never been worth much so her time there had been short-lived — just long enough to suffer through the ridiculous camping exercise. Her brother Julien had always been better with earth. He'd dreamed of having her control over fire though. Or at least, he had when they'd still been on speaking terms. "My time at Brist wasn't noteworthy."

Aodhan arched his brow at that, from behind Racynth's back, and rolled his eyes.

"Sure. You seem like someone who likes to stay behind the scenes," Racynth drawled, shaking his head. For a moment she thought he'd be content to leave it there, but it wasn't two minutes later that he spoke.

"Is it true that these woods are haunted?" he asked, the change of subject throwing Tamora off. *Naturally I'd be stuck with the curious Sentinel*, she thought sourly. She'd never met one who seemed so easy-going.

"Uh, no. It's not."

"The locals believe it to hold spirits of the dead, led by one of Dalka's five Grand Lords," Marin said, her voice unwavering for the first time since her arrival. She'd always loved the stories. If it got her out of this mental fog she was in, Tamora was happy to indulge her. "There was a battalion from a war that had almost been lost to history — apparently they all disappeared and were never seen alive again."

"I'm not sure the battalion existed, but I'd be hard pressed to stick around the place I died," Tamora muttered.

"It did exist!" she exclaimed, perking up a bit. She had a watchful audience now, as even the few Humans that were awake eyed her with interest. "The records exist, my William saw them after he promised to bring some of my sweet cakes to——well, it was after a friend, who cleaned in the archives of the palace, showed him. That's not the interesting part of the story. The battalion fought for Lord Gatin, who he said was a Veden lord who ruled the southern portion of Sienma many, many centuries ago, against the people who lived in the far northern reaches of the country. They were probably the Bolsi, or the people they came from. Maybe an unusually large settlement of Tri, but they don't usually live so far north, right?" She paused, looking at Tamora for confirmation, but she just shrugged.

"I've never known any Tri well enough to ask many specifics," she said. "But if it was a force of Veden, I don't think they'd go out of their way to fight Tri."

The two Iokan people hadn't been friendly until relatively recent history, namely the forced comradery the Coalition had placed upon them. A fight with the Bolsi, on the other hand, was likely. They were Humans, originally from the far northern reaches of the world, who had been cast adrift after their lands had been taken. Their ancestors had fought and resisted Iokans, Eilvyn, and Kit'ak alike. In school Tamora hadn't learned much about them, but Selena had made sure that she knew their true history. They had been her people, after all. Tamora waited for Marin to say something off about them, as people usually did, but instead she just nodded.

"Probably Bolsi then. In any case, this lord went with his army through the forest, rather than along the base of the mountains to the east, in the hopes of sneaking up on the settlement. Only a few survivors came back out, fleeing south with claims of living, moving trees and beasts the size of mountains that could melt weapons and bones with their breath. And ever since people have reported hearing voices and seeing shapes in the trees that they believe to be the lord and his army," she finished suddenly, pulling her knees into her chest and allowing her thick skirts to fall over her feet.

Racynth pulled lightly on his beard as he thought, but it was actually Captain who spoke up. "Where does Dalka come in?" he asked, his jaw even stiffer than it had been last night and the words slightly garbled. Some of his men paled at the name and moved their hands quickly into the symbol of the Wela, to ward off her gaze. Marin didn't react, but thought for a moment.

"Uh... I'm not sure. I assume it's because they're all dead. She'd never just let someone leave her realm after all," she said, nodding at her own logic.

"In any case, it's not haunted. That's just old history," Tamora said, leaning back against the hearth's edge.

"You're sure?" Captain asked. Tamora snorted at the hint of nerves in his gaze. He may not have known the tales before coming out here. She wondered if he'd have made the journey if he had.

"I've lived here just over seventy years; I think I'd have seen something by now. A stray howl, some odd rustling. Nothing worth mentioning," she said, smiling in a way she hoped was reassuring. It had been years since she'd last seen any sort of beast. Those first few months when her cottage was still being built had been difficult, but she'd been a foreigner in an isolated and new countryside. Of course she'd been uneasy.

Racynth opened his mouth to speak, a small smile on his lips, but he paused, half turning to the window. Just as he did, it shattered inward, and he threw his body back from the shards of brittle glass. Tamora swore, throwing herself to the ground, and both Aodhan and Racynth were armed—with blade and fire respectively—in the span of a few seconds. She scrambled forward down to see what had come through the glass; one of her own idols. Makmo stared sternly up at her, a small chip in his aged wooden face.

Racynth stared out the window, sword at the ready, not even sparing a glance her way. The Human who'd made Dalka's symbol, though, muttered something she didn't quite hear as he stared at her hands. "They should know not to disrespect the Wela," he said more loudly, drawing a few other looks.

"I don't see anyone," Racynth said, looking at Aodhan. "You?"

Aodhan stalked from the kitchen to the window, his palms filled with flickering flame, and looked briefly out the hole in the glass. Tamora stared at the fire in his hands and her own fingers clenched around her idol as her chest swelled with a black envy she could do nothing about.

"Nothing."

"They aren't speaking," Marin said, on her feet now, "but I can hear some of them going south, the mud is squelching under their boots."

"I'll get them," Aodhan said, making for the door, but Racynth put his arm out to stop him.

"No one is leaving," he said, his voice low.

"I can take care—"

"I believe you, but we have no idea who's out there. Tamora is not popular right now and someone could have found out that she's harboring these Humans. Could you fight off Karkas's people single handedly? Maybe one or two, but more?" he asked, frowning up at Aodhan's face. Tamora believed whole-heartedly that he could, but she wasn't about to announce that. Neither, it seemed, was Aodhan.

"Fine," he snapped, looking again out the window. "I hope they're Eilvyn because if they can hear me, I want them to know that I'll set their asses on fire if they do that again. I'll piss off these cursed spirits by lighting the damned forest on fire, I don't care."

Racynth eyed him sideways but said nothing. Tamora, though, stood on sore legs. "I hardly think that's necessary," she said, putting Makmo's idol carefully on her mantle, "and if you light my house on fire, I'll kill you myself."

Aodhan frowned. "Can you get somewhere safe? In the bedroom with the baker?" Tamora glared back at him.

"I can take care of myself, asshole. Where are they?" She turned to Racynth, who had lowered his weapon.

"I... I don't know. I think they've left." He turned to Marin for confirmation, and, after a moment, she nodded. "It's unlikely they knew I was here, or that you were not alone. If they come back, I'll be ready."

"Lovely. I'm going to make tea then," she said, setting the kettle on the hook. When she turned back, Racynth and Aodhan were looking at her with identical expressions of disbelief. "What? You said they'd gone, so there's nothing else to really do. Anyone want some?"

They all refused, even Marin, and Tamora shrugged. More for her then. She dropped a heavy amount of her tonic, pulled from the bottle within her jacket pocket, within the swirling hot water once it had boiled and felt immediately that some of her aches had faded.

Racynth's look turned to curiosity and he took a slight step towards the hearth. "What was that, just now? It didn't look like tea."

"It's a tonic for pain I created a few years ago," Tamora said, reluctantly handing over the mug so he could sniff it. He recoiled and gave it back quickly.

"It smells foul."

"It doesn't taste much better," admitted Tamora. She sighed. It was going to be a long night, with them all cooped up and on edge like this. "How long do you usually stay in one place? As a Sentinella, I mean." She surprised herself by wanting to know, although she thought she had a good idea already from all the surveillance she and Selena had been assigned. Who knew, though, protocol could change over a hundred years.

"A few weeks usually, a month or so at the very most. Our next post is Tuannu, we need to be there before Basana," he replied, glancing out the window again.

"Basana?" she said with surprise. "That's not much time for such a long journey." It was still early Kana now, the end of winter, so they had two and a half months to get halfway across the continent.

"We stop over in a few villages here and there, but for the most part it's a hard ride. Our post there is longer I think, about two months. Tuannu is our last stop before heading home to Koren," he explained. The Humans were grumbling to one another. Tamora shot them a warning look but Racynth just smiled again. It was a quick thing, something that seemed to come very easily to him.

"I never realized you were on rotation for so long," she admitted. Aodhan, too, looked surprised. Maybe this would be helpful for him, for whatever plans he had bouncing around in that thick skull.

"It's been about a year now, but I wouldn't change it. This is our first rotation, as a Sentinella," he said, adding it almost as an afterthought.

She cocked her head. "Your first rotation?" Racynth was old, she was sure of it, and Commander Miayra was clearly accustomed to being in charge. There was no reason for them not to have been on rotation for decades now, going off what she'd learned of Sentinels years before.

He frowned. "We... Well, we were on a different assignment for many years, and we have some new members. We were hoping for some excitement, and Erengate has certainly given us that."

Tamora had nothing to say to that. What he was describing was different from Erengate's previous Sentinellas, as they had all been posted here for far longer than a few months. It reminded her of the group she and Aodhan had ridden in all those years ago when they'd been in the prince of Ozhansa's Guard. They'd moved around a lot and he and Innogen had always been antsy any time a mission went longer than expected. Aodhan caught her look and she wondered if he too had gotten swept up by memories before he turned away to stare out into the forest.

Racynth sheathed his weapon, giving a final glance out the small window. "I don't think they're coming back, and we've got an awfully long afternoon ahead of us now." He looked around the room and rested his hands on his sword belt. "Look, I want to be clear about something. We had every right to arrest the lot of you and haul you back to Erengate. We didn't, and I truly don't think it would help anyone to do that, but if I don't get some answers here I'm not going to have any guarantees come morning. So, let's have a bit of honesty, alright?"

He was focused on Tamora but he didn't spare anyone else, even Eloise and Davina hiding in the bedroom doorway.

"I'm not in the mood to talk, Racynth, but ask your questions. I won't promise an answer and that's the best you're going to get," Tamora said, staring him down.

He paused for a moment but nodded finally. "Very well. You live here alone? No Guardian?"

"She died." Tamora set her mug down on the mantel harder than she'd intended, looking into Makmo's dented face. Aodhan, of course, already knew and said nothing, but she felt the others' eyes on her intensely.

"Ah— how? Did you Spiral?" Racynth asked. His voice sounded strangled and uncomfortable. Tamora didn't turn around to look, instead staring down into the fire. Of course he would know what a Guardian's death meant, what it inevitably did to their *viluno*. Being paired to a Human rewrote your very being and made you entirely dependent upon their lifeforce as well as your own. Having that ripped from you so suddenly destroyed you, without question. Well, she'd always been taught that it would. Clearly, she'd survived.

"I did and I expect you to understand that I don't like speaking of it," she replied, throwing a log onto the dying flames.

"I don't really want to ask, believe me," he said quietly. "But now that I know, I need to ensure you aren't a threat."

"A threat?" Tamora laughed and turned back to him. It was an angry and painful sound. "How could I possibly be a threat like this?" Racynth's expression was too much like pity for her liking, and Aodhan's wasn't any better. She bitterly hated them both at that moment.

"You could still drop that statue yesterday, and I've seen how forcefully your anger affects you. Are you a danger to others?" he asked, not once looking away. She was almost flattered that he thought that much of her abilities, even now.

"I've been in control for decades, I'm not going to lose it now," she finally replied.

"Do you have trouble controlling your anger?" he continued, looking around her cottage. Tamora was immensely thankful she'd dragged blankets and mats over the floorboards she'd singed over the years. Some of the decades had been more difficult than others.

"I am fine, and perfectly in control. Thank you for your concern," she said with as much grace as she could muster when all she wanted to do was rip his head off. Aodhan's too, as he was watching her a little too closely.

"Clearly," he sighed. "Look, Tamora, I see no reason for there to be a problem between you and Sentinels any longer. I don't believe that the other Sentinella knew of your Guardian... they would have put it in the records they left us. If you truly are not a threat I am inclined to believe you and let this be." It was a branch of peace, Tamora saw that clear enough.

"They didn't know because I never told them, but I think you overestimate your comrades' compassion," she replied curtly. "I don't want trouble; I just want to continue living here."

"Then why consistently get yourself involved? We have records, going back decades, of you putting yourself squarely in Soren Karkas's way. If you really didn't want any trouble you'd do more to stay out of it," he said, his voice sitting somewhere between frustrated and understanding.

She glanced at the Humans around her, all of them battered and bruised. She knew Aodhan was listening, although he continued to stare out the window with a mask of careful indifference. "I don't think preventing the loss of more life was the wrong choice. I feel you would have done the same, in my place."

"Of course I would have but I am a Sentinel! You are just some cripple in the forest. I'm sorry, but it's true." He shook his head at Marin's murmur of protest, a faint hint of red on his cheeks. "You do realize it is behavior like this that gets people sent to Koren? Or Rookland Island? Do you want to be imprisoned as a traitor? That goes for all of you, by the way."

Tamora knew it was wrong but she almost chuckled. They'd tried that once; she'd never been caught. "Obviously not. Now, if you are done berating me, I'd like to continue on with my evening. I assume that's acceptable."

"No, you can't get out of this that easily. You've clearly demonstrated that you're willing to take action which, in some cases, I could support. I know that's hard to believe but I don't always agree with what's happening either. But it won't end well here. You know as well as I that this city of yours is a powder keg." Racynth spoke vigorously, ignoring the looks of surprise he was getting. Tamora had to give him credit, she'd never expected a Sentinel to admit such a thing. "This is not the way to fix things. Sabina— Commander Miayra—has a plan and I think it could work. Will you let her try before doing anything rash?"

She waited a beat before answering. Her plan was likely something political, something nuanced that wouldn't get her in trouble with the Council. She knew all the Sentinels had to report back at some point, and that they rarely interfered with local matters. Soren Karkas would never respect something so soft. "You don't have anything to worry about from me," she said, gesturing around. "I'm a little busy here, and they're far from capable of doing anything more."

Racynth stared at her for long enough that she began to think she'd said something wrong. "Good, it's settled," he finally said. He looked out the window again. "I'm going to take a loop to make sure they've all gone." He opened the door, letting a rush of cold air in, before disappearing into the early evening gloom.

Still staring out the window, Aodhan watched him. "Well, that was uncomfortable," he drawled, sparing a moment to look back at Tamora and, past her, at Captain.

She shook her head. "You're an idiot. You're all idiots," she snapped and walked to the bedroom, gesturing for the women to step out of the way and shutting the door firmly.

Chapter 15

Racynth

The forest was quiet and their surprise visitors had disappeared, but he'd expected that. They were not with Soren Karkas or they'd have stayed to have a little more fun. No, they were probably just Eilvyn, or Iokans, from Erengate who thought they'd take the opportunity to cause some trouble for a lonely, crippled healer. He made a cursory look around but what Racynth had really been looking for when he left the overheated cottage was a moment of fresh air and silence in which to think. He'd said too much. Sabina would've throttled him if she'd heard. Those thoughts he'd expressed, to a room full of Humans who had certainly committed acts of rebellion, were things the Sentinella had only admitted to one another in brief moments of honesty after years of living together. He hardly knew these people. Most were nameless to him, and he suspected five of the Humans hadn't had much say in what they had participated in. No, he had no doubt that it was arranged by the Azha, Aodhan. He was friendly with Tamora so the story that they'd met during their schooling could be true, but he didn't believe for a moment that he'd just run into the Humans after the riot and offered a helping hand. And that one who Aspen had questioned had been referring to a Captain, and that was a title he'd heard muttered from the fireplace.

He sighed. Tamora may not have been involved from the beginning — in fact, he strongly doubted that. She was involved now.

Despite the cold, Racynth remained outside for more than two hours. He still felt on edge after the incident with the window. His mind went over every possibility. It could have been reconnaissance to see if Tamora was home, to seek her out just as they had Marin in her bakery. It was dangerous being a friend to Humans on the best of days, and it seemed Soren Karkas had given free rein to every bigoted Eilvyn in Erengate. It was at least midday by the time his fingers were numb enough that he could stand the cold no longer. When he opened the door, it was clear that Tamora and the others were concentrating on ignoring his presence. That did no harm, and he resumed his position by the window. If their unwelcome guests returned, he would be the first to notice. After another hour or two, however, he found himself tired of doing nothing. The trees weren't moving, and the most action he'd seen was a rabbit clambering under Tamora's small wooden gate. A full night awake, plotting and fearing for the city's future with Sabina and Della especially, had not left much time for rest.

"Healer." The Human named Captain, who Racynth was trying to figure out what to do with, whispered to Tamora as she doled out the meal she'd spent the morning putting together, a rough looking stew that he himself feared to try. The smell alone was enough for him to wish he had remained outside; it had too much similarity to that tonic of hers. "We cannot stay here."

Racynth looked pointedly out the window, ignoring Tamora's rushed gaze in his direction.

"Don't be foolish," she snapped. "You can't run out from beneath a Sentinel. And be quiet, an Eilfe's ear is better than you think."

"If we stay we'll be arrested, it's certain."

"Nothing is certain," she said, but Racynth could hear her own hesitation.

He knew little more than she did, if he were being honest with himself. Sabina's orders were her own and she often strayed toward harsher punishment than he would have chosen if left to his own devices. These men had surely played some role in the city's grievance, that much was painfully clear. He didn't doubt that some of their wounds had been at the hands of Aspen and Petro, received as they'd fled the scene. But he didn't know that he would want them to face imprisonment for their actions. The city was a nightmare for Humans – that much was perfectly clear. At the hands of the Karkas family they would be executed, and Racynth had tired of constant reports of death. It wouldn't help the anger brewing in Erengate, either. All they had done was reveal something that had been brewing within the city for months, if not years.

Tamora had continued to mutter, and Racynth turned his head slightly towards them. "Your man there can't even walk, how far do you expect to get?" she asked, her mouth hardly moving. Any attempt at hiding their conversation was in vain, though, as he could have heard a pin drop in the tight quarters.

"You've done your job well, he'll be fine. He assures me he can move at a moment's notice," he said, bracing himself as he sat up.

"Of course he does," she said dryly, and Racynth could practically feel her glare at the young man. "Captain, it's not happening."

Racynth pushed himself from the windowsill. "What isn't happening?" he asked. Tamora shot up so fast her back audibly cracked.

"Wela be damned— he wants to help patrol the house. I told him it was out of the question," she said quickly. He frowned at the group. They knew he'd heard everything; it was impossible to disguise it in this small cottage. Tamora hovered over the Humans with her repugnant stew in her arms and matched his gaze. He decided to let it go.

He snorted and shook his head. "A commendable intention, but foolish. You can barely move."

Tamora nodded. "Exactly what I—"

"Please, leave the guarding to the professionals," he continued, glancing at her. "It will do you no good to work yourselves into a frenzy."

He turned, seeing that Aodhan also watched him, as well as the baker and her Human assistant. The woman's mother had moved little since her arrival, her daughter had wrapped her in the blanket she now had draped over her shoulders, and her face was a numb mask of grief he did not expect to see changed. He'd seen people caught in sorrow's throes, and when it was this thick it rarely lifted without help. No one here seemed well equipped to play that role today.

Racynth cleared his throat. He didn't want to see these men arrested, nor be responsible for their executions. There was only one way to avoid that fate, and he was surprised to find that he wasn't opposed to simply letting them free. No one knew they were here, only the Sentinella. Sabina would feel the same, he was certain of it, although he'd get a verbal lashing for his foolishness. It was a price he was willing to pay.

"You know, it is a pity that we have met under these circumstances. I... I would not be surprised if we shared the same opinion regarding many of your concerns," he said, pausing and not entirely knowing where he was going with this. "I understand you were all injured in the riots. It's a pity that you didn't see the men who started it all. I've heard that they all escaped into the forest to the north."

Tamora looked at him sharply, as did her friend Aodhan,

but the Humans had not quite caught on. Racynth winced, staring at the ceiling. Sabina was going to reprimand him but this wasn't right, this whole city wasn't right. She hadn't arrested them immediately for a reason and he had to believe that this was why.

"A true shame," Aodhan nodded stiffly. Racynth looked at him; the Azha was a massive man. He barely cleared the doorway and with his arms crossed as they were he looked as immovable as a mountain. He'd protect them well enough as they got out of the city's long reach, hopefully well south of even Vasna. If they didn't cause any additional trouble on their way, they'd be free men after that.

"I am going to rest my eyes," Racynth said, feeling the need for it deep in his bones. It had been a long night, and he knew dawn was approaching fast. He shook his head, wishing that Sabina had left someone else here with them all. "I am going straight to Dalka's court for this," he muttered, sitting by the door and wrapping his cloak around himself. The baker eyed him, but he ignored her.

He turned to Tamora. "I trust that you will wake me should I oversleep, yes?" She nodded minutely and he turned away, giving one last glance at the bandaged and near-panicked Humans lying at her hearth. He knew he was in the right. And if he wasn't, he thought as he closed his eyes, so be it.

Tamora

Tamora bunched up the hand towel she held, setting down the pot as she stalked back to her small kitchen, glancing at the apparently sleeping Sentinel as she passed. His face was smooth, the dark circles under his eyes deep and heavy, and he hardly moved as she stepped past his feet. Aodhan waited for her and to his credit he whispered when he spoke. "Was that what I think it was?"

"You need to go now," she said, raising her hand to quiet him.

"Tamora, come now. This is a trick—"

"This is not a discussion," she snapped. She looked again at the Sentinel, but he seemed to have truly fallen asleep. An unnatural power if she had ever seen one. "He's given you a chance, Aodhan, and I don't think you're going to get another."

He grimaced. "This is only because they know they can't prove anything—"

"You know they don't need proof!" Tamora grasped his arm. "Go now, while you still can." He looked at her, and she could see the struggle behind his eyes. But this wasn't time for self-sacrificing and he needed to take Captain and these poor men somewhere safe. "Those men don't deserve whatever Karkas is going to have in store for them. He knows that, and so do you," she said, pointing at the Sentinel.

Aodhan nodded stiffly, taking his first step toward the Humans. Captain rose to his feet as well, meeting their gaze, but he froze as Racynth suddenly stiffened and stood, his hand on the hilt of his sword.

"What? Is something wrong?" Tamora asked sharply and the Humans grasped at what few weapons they had. It would have been their only saving grace in the city, if they'd been caught, to be unarmed. The only way to prevent being murdered in the streets by guards. Racynth shook his head, clearly confused as he cocked his head and listened.

"Quiet. Something is outside." He drew his blade and looked past her at Aodhan, then at the Humans. "I'm sorry, I really am," he said, the lines in his face deepening as he frowned.

"Is it the Sentinella?" she asked, watching the lines of his face.

"No," he said grimly, and the expression on his face was all she needed. She rushed to Marin, pushing her inside her bedroom door. "Go inside, stay with the boys. Bar the door after me," she said, stepping past her. Her swords lay on the small stool beside her bed where she'd left them upon Aodhan's arrival. They felt right in her hands, and she ignored Racynth's lingering gaze on them as she closed the bedroom door behind her.

"What's going on?" Captain asked as he pulled himself painfully to his feet. "Why are you armed? Are we under arrest?"

"No, you fool, sit down—" a boom shook the walls of her cottage and Tamora fell silent, staring at her front door. "Back up," she whispered, holding one of her blades aloft.

"What—"

"To the back wall," she snapped, and as she turned to wave him back a second boom echoed through her home and set her teeth on edge. The Humans scrambled back, a fire blazed in Aodhan's hands, and Racynth ran his sword through the air before him as he loosened the muscles of his arm. She knew the movement well as she had done the same many times, moments before a fight. Her bedroom door cracked open but she shouted at Marin to stay inside.

"Aren't you going to do something?" she yelled at Racynth, but he'd beaten her to it.

He threw open the front door and peered into the

forest, his sword in one hand and the other curled into a fist as he gathered Eiyer to him. "Show yourselves!" he shouted. "I am Racynth Naewynn of the Fifth Sentinella, know that any action against me is a crime punishable by—" he huffed in surprise as he was thrown backward and landed bodily on the hard flooring. Aodhan leapt across him, sparing only the briefest look at the Sentinel, and put himself in front of Tamora.

"You cannot face this as you are," he said, pure white fire billowing from his palms. Tamora felt the pressure of *Eiyer* inside her cottage continue to build and knew there was another Eilfe outside. She didn't know what it felt like to the Eilvyn, but it was like she was submerged underwater and barely able to breathe through the now dense air.

"You need to go," she whispered, looking up at Aodhan.

"But you—"

"I can protect myself," she said, holding her blackened blades aloft. She waved them at the Humans, who Captain was pulling carefully to their feet. "Get them out of here."

Racynth rolled up from where he'd landed and crouched, his sword before him as he glanced back at where she stood. "I don't know who these people are," he said, "but they will hunt you down if you leave now."

"That's a risk they'll have to take, I think," Tamora barked back, feeling the walls of her poor cottage shiver as whoever was outside built to their full strength. They didn't have long. "Out the windows, go now."

Racynth swore as another boom shattered all her windows, showering him and the floor in glass shards. Tamora heard shrieks from her bedroom and prayed that Marin and her family were unharmed. Aodhan growled in frustration but picked up the closest Human, the most injured, and led him to the back window. It looked out in the still dark wood and led west; they would have to bear north to get around whoever these attackers were and then head east before dipping back south toward Ozhansa. Assuming, of course, that was where they wanted to go. Tamora realized she had no idea what Aodhan's plans truly were; they'd been interrupted by the Sentinella before she could ask.

"Tamora, I'll find you—" he said, lifting Captain through the shattered glass still stuck in the frame.

"Get out of my damned house and thank me later!" Tamora said, helping the next man climb out of the window. She threw her elbow through the glass, wincing as it sliced through her skin, and helped the more injured Humans through.

"I'll meet you in Jorolkar, I'll be there in a month," he promised, lifting the last of the Humans back through and onto the ground. She nodded, making a mental note of the city. It was on the border of Ozhansa; he was heading south after all.

"I'll be there," she promised, glancing back to the front and realizing that the bedroom door had again cracked open. "Marin, get back inside!" she screamed, running from the last of the men as she tried to reach the bedroom. A heady blast of *Eiyer* threw her off her feet as it poured through her open doorway, curving around the frame and rushing at her and Racynth. She hovered midair for a long moment, making eye contact with a panicked Eloise before her entire body slammed against the floor.

She heard a snap deep in her chest and lost her breath at the pain of it; the only thought in her mind was keeping that room's door closed. As she crawled forward a voice she recognized rang out from her yard and she groaned, both from the pain and the realization of who was at her doorstep. She was going to die, she realized with chagrin. To have made it so far, and through so much, to be killed by someone so insignificant as Soren Karkas.

"We expected only the healer. Leave and you won't be harmed."

Tamora sneered into her floorboards, and she lifted herself to her knees.

"Threats will do you no good, my lord. Leave while you still can!" Racynth shouted back. The last blast of pure energy had left him with a scrape on his forehead that bled readily. He wiped it from his eye. "I will say it again, I am Sentinel Racynth Naewynn and you must—"

"I am Soren Karkas, son of Lord Karkas of Erengate, and I must do nothing," he said. Tamora groaned as she got to her feet, standing just under the doorframe. He could hit her now with a bow or *Eiyer* but she didn't care. She just wanted him off her land, and out of her forest. Seventy years she'd been here, and it would take more than an uptight cruel lordling to drive her out. She glared out her broken window at Karkas, meeting his gaze. He smiled widely as he saw her, likely taking in how she was bruised and sore from his previous assaults.

"Get out of my house."

"This is no house," he scoffed, looking it over with undisguised scorn. "A hovel, perhaps. I want the justice I am due."

She sneered and spat in his direction. "I have no idea what you're talking about."

"You insult me, attack my steward, incite violence — you are a plague on this city! It's been decades dealing with your insolence and this is too far. You even lie to the Sentinels and set them against me. What did you tell them?" he shouted, spit flying from his mouth. She could just see him through her door as he glared into her home. He seemed to jump from rage and panic to absolute calm. He'd finally snapped, she realized. All these decades of prodding and mocking and he'd finally tipped over the edge of sanity.

"Nothing they didn't already know," she said and watched him pace in her trampled yard. Snow and dirt mixed into a thick and frigid mud, sticking to the boots and cloaks of Soren and the four Eilvyn men he had brought. Guards, from the look of them, and they watched the house closely for any signs of movement.

"And what would that be?" he hissed, smiling grimly and stalking outside her door. She hated the sight of him in her garden, within her small wall. No purifying ritual would be enough to erase the presence of him, she thought with disgust.

"You overreacted and sentenced a woman to death for an insignificant slight, and you dishonored our city by breaking the laws of the High Council. You deserve to be punished," she growled at him. Racynth coughed, crouched beside her.

"That's not exactly—"

Soren laughed sharply. "She's just a Human, it doesn't matter."

"Lord Karkas, lay down your weapons," Racynth said, raising his voice so that it carried. It held a ring of power that only a Sentinel could wield.

"I will do no such thing," he said with a laugh, earning taunts and jeers from his friends. There were fewer of them than she'd expected but she supposed he'd had no intention of having so many witnesses. He looked around at her cottage again. "You, go after the Humans they let escape and bring them back to me." The closest man he'd gestured to ran out of sight and Tamora hoped that Aodhan could fend him off. The Aodhan she'd known would have made mincemeat out of a single Eilfe, though, so she allowed herself to cast the concern from her mind.

Racynth stood and stepped before Tamora. "I am a Sentinel and you will obey—"

"Enough," Karkas screeched. With a wave of his hand the air in the room seemed to pause in anticipation, even the air taking a moment, before an immense pressure crashed down around them with a strength Tamora had not faced in years. Her door collapsed in on itself, the blast too strong for the sturdy hardwood, and it tore down parts of the walls with it.

Racynth shouted and threw himself to the side. Tamora, unable to dodge, was tossed back against her fireplace. The edge of the stone dug into her back and she hissed in pain as her head hit the floor. Screams came from the back room and she blinked away tears as the bedroom door was thrown open and Karkas's men dragged Marin and the others out into the main room, sharp knives at their throats. A rush of frigid air surged through the broken wall, shimmering particles of ice already crossing over into her home.

"Protecting more traitors, are we? Who is this?" Karkas said, his voice carrying even as the dust settled and Tamora hazily took in her ruined home, willing the blinding pain in her spine to give her at least a moment of clarity. Karkas glanced at Lark and Sorrell, his face a twisted grimace. "*Joien,* I see. Blood traitors then."

"Get away from them," she groaned and dragged herself forward off the hearth. She made it only a few feet before he stepped up to meet her, his muddy boots inches from her nose.

"If you are friends with this woman you must all be criminals. Arrest them."

"You can't do this," Marin cried, whimpering as one of Karkas's men hit her with the hilt of his drawn sword. Her boys threw themselves towards the man, snarling, but it was no use.

"I am an Iokan, that means something," Tamora snapped. Clearly, it didn't mean anything to him. Marin was an Eilfe, after all, and still they'd driven her from her home. Racynth, though, should have mattered more to him. If Karkas couldn't see it through his hate then surely one of the others would. "You can't do this to us. He's a Sentinel! You'll all be thrown in the Pit for this, it's a crime against the Council."

She hated that she had dragged their authority into this twice now, but there was no other way to get through to them. Karkas had brought his most vehemently loyal guards, though, and they hardly spared her or the Sentinel a glance.

Karkas shrugged, glancing at Racynth. "I see no Sentinels. It was an accident, a terrible and tragic accident. I will mourn for you, you know. Driven mad by the spirits in these trees and killing one another — such a brutal way to go but it's been known to happen, hasn't it?" He looked at the men he'd brought and a few nodded, not even flinching at the thought. It was cold blooded murder. Tamora figured Karkas may have just come himself, if she'd been alone, but whoever had broken her window must have reported back to him.

Racynth stood, shaking his cloak from his shoulders and brandishing his broadsword. His armor was thick and dull, the material beaten down by some masterful technique in a way that allowed it to disguise the wearer while still remaining a stunning work of craftsmanship.

"I'll see you arrested for this, Karkas," he snapped. "I don't care who you are, threatening a Sentinel is a capital offense."

Karkas, forgoing all reasonable conversation, roared a wordless screech that drowned out the rest of Racynth's words. The Sentinel gripped his sword with a grimace, and Tamora could see his knuckles pale under the pressure.

"Quiet, you Wela-forsaken half-breed!" he shrieked, his eyes manic as his nostrils flared and spit flew from his mouth. Even the men he had brought took a step back at his sudden plunge into insanity. "If you say another damnable word, I'll run you through."

Racynth's face was as cold as ice, his tanned skin pulled tight. "I'd like to see you try," he replied and bared his teeth. Tamora dragged herself to her feet and grasped at her blades. If they all attacked, Sentinel or not, she and Racynth were going to die. There were too many of them, and Marin could hardly use her Eiyer. Tamora had no idea if Lark or Sorrell had even been formally trained; it had never felt like her place to pry. Now it seemed like a glaring oversight.

Karkas took a step forward but paused as the men around him hesitated to come any closer. It seemed, once push came to shove, they weren't so confident they could win.

"What?" he yelled at them, turning and waving his sword around. "You think this traitorous bitch should live!" He was fuming and she could have sworn he was foaming at the mouth.

"Sentinels are off limits—"

"We'll be executed," one finished, his mouth drawn into a thin nervous line as he looked at the others. If they'd been Human they would have been pale as snow.

Karkas cackled. "Fine! Fine! I'll kill the lot of you when I'm done with her, you traitors!" he shouted. He took a menacing step toward Tamora, and she raised her blade. Its weight burned in her shoulders but she held it firm, willing it not to waver.

If she was going to die, she'd rather do so with a weapon in hand.

"You will not," a voice, one she'd never thought she'd be glad to hear, rang out from the dark trees. Tamora realized that the sun was rising as Commander Miayra stepped into view, her own twin swords drawn and the dawning sunlight reflected from their surface. Close behind her were Aspen and Petro, him with a short blade and her with a ring of earth rising behind her.

Karkas's men immediately dropped their weapons at the sight of her fierce glare. The one holding Marin threw her to the ground and raised his hands, practically shaking in his boots.

"How dare you disobey a direct order from your superiors," Commander Miayra said, her voice deathly calm. She wrenched command over the room in a heartbeat, stepping through the broken wall, and Tamora had to strain to listen to catch what she said next. "How dare you attack a Coalition citizen, an Iokan, in her home. How dare you threaten a Sentinel, one of *my* Sentinella. How dare you bully and blackmail your way out of our custody."

With every breath she stepped closer, until her face was even with Karkas's.

"You have no right—" Karkas squeaked.

Sabina snapped her arm out, the blade tilted away, and the crack that the back of her hand made against his cheek reverberated through the small room. Marin gasped, clutching her mouth as the sound escaped, and Karkas's men looked like they were going to be sick.

"I have every right!" she shouted back at him, before quickly regaining her composure. It was as though she'd never moved and Tamora became acutely aware of how dangerous this woman could be, watching her face flash from deadly to still in an instant. "You are all under arrest, under my authority as leader of the Fifth Sentinella sanctioned by the rule of the High Council. You will be held in Coalition cells, in the Lower District. You will have no visitors and your trials will be in three days."

One of the men fell to his knees, but she paid him no mind. With a single gesture from her, Sentinel Aspen restrained the men within claws of still frozen earth and dragged them outside. Karkas hardly had time to yelp at the unyielding grip of Aspen's element before Petro shoved a small rag into his mouth and silenced his wretched tongue.

The Commander watched him go for a moment before turning to Racynth, her eyebrow raised. "You are alright?" Sabina asked Racynth.

"Fine, he was mostly talk," he laughed shakily, sheathing his weapon.

"True. But there were too many of them for one person to take on," Commander Miayra said, sparing a glance at Tamora. "No offense, healer, but you hardly look as though you could handle a fight. I am sorry... this shouldn't have happened. He slipped from our grasp in the city."

"He was in your custody?" Tamora asked, swinging her blades loosely at her sides. She knew the Commander watched them curiously and could predict what thoughts were going through the woman's head. They were her most valuable possessions and had once played an important role in identifying her in her role as Jakela of Krys's Rebellion, back when that had matter. It was one of the reasons she usually kept them tucked away from prying eyes.

Commander Miayra nodded, looking sharply away from Tamora's weapons. "When we returned to the city, Soren had come back to the palace district. It seems a few nobles spoke in a way he believed was... well, to summarize, he assaulted them quite brutally, in public, in front of their families. It became a simple matter to arrest him then."

"You arrested him for hitting a noble," Tamora replied, deadpan. "What about that Human woman? Or all the people he terrorized last night?"

The commander sighed and glanced between her and Racynth. "As of now she is still under arrest... Miss Asken, there is only so much—"

"Not enough, clearly! Her execution is tomorrow!"

The Commander's eyes pierced her. "I am aware of that,

Miss Asken. Let me remind you that I have been preoccupied, chasing a ridiculous young lord as he tried to track you down and murder you in your home," she said stiffly. She turned slightly down toward Marin. "You and your family, and your servants there, will follow me. We have guaranteed you safe boarding at The Outpost."

Marin narrowed her eyes. "That's pricey. Why wouldn't I just stay here?" she asked. Tamora sunk down in front of her fireplace, and Marin looked over at her a little nervously from where she still sat on the floor. "Aren't we safe enough here?"

Commander Miayra shrugged, looking around what was left of the living room. "I'm offering out of kindness, Miss Agata, you don't have to come. It will be paid in full by the Sentinella. But I imagine a room with all four walls would be more comfortable for your family."

Tamora looked in mute shock at the remnants of her front wall. It would take weeks, at least, to simply get the materials. Not to mention the fact that Karkas had just single-handedly run most of Erengate's workers into hiding.

"And Tamora?" Marin continued, gingerly lifting herself to her feet.

"Miss Asken will remain here, where she is safest. She will not be bothered again," she said. She looked hard at Tamora, making it clear how much she meant it. "I'll be outside, Miss Agata, when you decide."

She left without another word. Tamora sighed and leaned back against the stone.

"Are... is it alright..." Marin asked, turning to her but her mind clearly elsewhere. Tamora couldn't blame her. A warm, safe room would be much better than this mess. If she hadn't been clearly not invited, she might have even been willing to make the trek into the city herself. As it was, she had enough to do tonight. The wall would need to be patched, or at the very least she'd have to get a roaring fire going to counteract the wind that would no doubt rip right through her home.

"Go, follow them before they leave," Tamora said, realizing Marin was still waiting. "I'll be fine here."

"But..."

"Really, it's fine. Take care of the others. I'll come to see you tomorrow," she sighed. It had been a chaotic week, and one she never wanted to repeat. Hopefully now that he was securely in custody Soren would find it more difficult to cause so much trouble. She doubted he'd be gone for good; he was too well connected for that.

Marin mirrored her sigh, more of exhaustion than anything else, but she went to the bedroom door all the same and allowed Eloise to help her out of the cottage. Davina trailed closely behind, her eyes wide as she took in the destruction of Tamora's living room, and Lark supported Sorrell as they left.

Racynth turned his head to watch Tamora for a moment, until she raised her brow at him in question. "Yes?" He shook his head.

"Nothing. Be safe, Tamora. Don't hesitate to come to the inn if you need us." She rolled her eyes but kept a mental note of where they were staying—The Outpost. He let himself out, walking leisurely behind Marin's stumbling group, and Tamora watched until their forms disappeared down the break in the trees.

She folded her swords over her lap and sat still, trying to take a moment of peace before getting to her task. There was firewood to gather and stew to make now that her last was spilled across her floorboards.

"It's a start, I suppose," she said out loud, savoring the final sight of Karkas encased in earth as he was dragged back toward Erengate. A small start, but it was something.

Marin

The worst part about the long walk back across the fields was the strict silence the Sentinels kept as they moved. All five of them, Lark and Sorrell trailing behind even the slow pace that she was setting, kept a good distance between themselves and Soren Karkas. He had thrashed against the hard earth that had formed his cage but when he'd discovered there was no use, that not even his Eiyer would make it move, he'd fallen eerily silent. His men had been properly cowed as well by the Sentinella's commander and merely stared at the ground ahead of them as their prone forms were pulled through the earth, kicking up rocks and dragging mud behind them. Marin gripped her side tightly, ignoring the thrums of pain that radiated from her ribs, and tensed as she saw Racynth pick up his pace to fall in step beside him.

"Are you hurt?" he asked quietly, but not quietly enough. She was not going to let Lark and Sorrell know how badly she hurt, not when there had been no other way out of the city. Too much had happened for them to have to bear any guilt.

"You're just going to leave her there?" she gasped out instead, keeping her eyes straight ahead.

He paused, and she could feel his gaze on her. "It's for the best, Miss Agata," he said finally. "She isn't safe in the city at this time, not after what's happened. Soren would have other allies there who would want to put themselves in his favor, and she's too good of a target for that."

"Are any of us safe?" she asked, shaking her head. "You've arrested Soren. But what difference does that truly make? Silas ——Zavalynn—is still in the city, and Soren has allies. He'll be out of whatever cell you put him in by the end of the day."

Racynth shook his head. She could see his thick hair swing along his back, even tied as it was. "I understand your concern, Miss Agata, I really do. But there's nothing for it.

You're right, we will not be able to keep him imprisoned for very long. His father will see to that. That's even more reason for Tamora to remain where she is."

She glared up at him, her eyes darting away only to be sure that Lark and Sorrell were still moving with them. "She's alone," she insisted. "Her friend, that Azhan man, he's gone. If Soren came for her once he is going to do it again, I don't see how leaving her out here defenseless is going to help anyone."

"I don't think we can spare anyone, Miss Agata. When Lord Karkas is released we will need to monitor him. With the execution still scheduled for tomorrow the city will need all the help it can get to keep things from getting out of hand." He held up her hand as she opened her mouth, effectively silencing her. "She could come to the city, but that's likely to do more harm than good. No, she must stay out here for now. When it's safe, I'll come back to get her. You have my word."

Chapter 16

Racynth

Despite what he'd hoped to be calming words, Miss Agata was anything but a relaxed traveling companion. She and her sons constantly bickered about little things like Sorrell's leg and the tightness of his bandages, as well as whether she herself should be carried over the fields. He wasn't even sure they knew that they were talking. It seemed more habitual, a way to remind themselves that the other was there. The two Humans observed silently as though this were a common occurrence. As he watched, though, Racynth became more and more doubtful that the girl's mother had had much experience with the small family. She looked more shocked by their chattering than anything that had happened in the cottage, and the lower stakes arguing seemed to put her at ease. Perhaps that was a small blessing. Still, when they finally made it to the small side gate and Sabina turned on the group with a silencing glare, Racynth was grateful.

The door creaked open as Sabina pounded on it, the grim face that peered out wizened and clearly belonging to a Human in a foul mood. He glowered down at them and Racynth truly didn't believe he was going to open the door further. Finally, he stepped aside. "Thought maybe you wouldn't come back," he said, glumly. Sabina stepped up, suddenly towering above him.

"Sorry to disappoint," she said, waving the rest through. The Human perked up considerably when he saw Soren and the others escorted past him.

"Is that the little lord?" he asked, his expression impish. "Is he going to be executed?" Racynth looked down at him in surprise.

"Ah, no. He is under arrest," he said, frowning as the man returned to his glum state. *Why is everyone here so set on execution?* It was a decidedly northern condition, he decided. It happened elsewhere, of course, but not with nearly so much excitement. Perhaps they got too bored as the winter dragged on.

"Bah. He'll be out before nightfall," the man muttered, waving them past and shuttering the door behind them. Miss Agata glanced at him, her thoughts clearly in agreement with the man, but both she and her sons remained blessedly silent.

Sabina cleared her throat. "Aspen, Petro, I imagine you can handle our 'little lord' and escort him to prison?" As she spoke, Soren gathered *Eiyer* to him and attempted to throw himself from his captors, but he was nowhere near as skilled as he thought and he lacked a certain degree of nuance. Sabina reached out and clenched her fist, evaporating any *Eiyer* he may have accumulated and casting it firmly out of his reach. She stepped up to him calmly.

"Lord Karkas, I would recommend that you not struggle. I have been at this far longer than you and it is entirely within Sentinel Aspen's power to fully encase you in stone for more convenient travel to the Upper District. Would you like that?" He shook his head, biting down so hard on his gag that Racynth imagined his teeth might snap. "I thought not. Please, Aspen, show these men the way." Petro waved for the others to follow, carrying his bow freely, and they went with no protest.

They had passed just out of view when Racynth again felt the tell-tale change in *Eiyer* pressure. The rumble and yelp that followed implied that Aspen had indeed been forced to act accordingly. Sabina winced.

"I'm sure that will be fun to explain to his father," he said wryly, and she just sighed. Still, she couldn't hide the small smile of satisfaction.

Sabina gestured at Marin and her family. "Set them up, and then meet me in the palace. Tell Jordan and Bealantin that one of them is to guard their rooms until further notice. They are not to leave," she said, turning on her heel and following after Aspen and Petro.

.....

They traveled slowly through the city, largely because Miss Agata was clearly more injured than she was letting on. She moved as though every breath hurt and Racynth knew that she must have hidden it from Tamora; the woman would never have allowed them to leave so easily if she'd known. Looking at her pale face, Racynth wasn't sure it had been the right decision either. Leaving them all in the wood may have been easiest. He sighed, rubbing his face. Actually sleeping would have been nice.

He swore suddenly, drawing startled looks from the others. "Sorry, sorry. It's nothing," he muttered. Inwardly he swore again. He hadn't recovered the pamphlet from Tamora. Sabina had clearly forgotten in her anger, but there was now at least one copy of the work out there for anyone to find. *Wela curse them, it was her friend who distributed them in the first place. There are probably more anyway*, he sighed. It didn't do him any favors to dwell on it; he was sure he had bigger problems waiting for him just around the corner.

.....

Once the baker, her sons, and the Humans were safely in the rooms and under the watchful eye of Bealantin, who they all decided might get along better with the group, Jordan and Racynth headed out to the palace. Along the way Jordan peppered him with questions but Racynth was careful only to answer what was absolutely necessary; there was no way to know how many Eilvyn had been posted nearby. Lord Karkas would have already heard of his son's arrest and he highly doubted they were as welcome as they once had been. They hadn't exactly rolled out the welcome party then either. The outer gates were firmly secured and it took some time for the guards to respond to their arrival. Jordan stepped uneasily from foot to foot as they waited.

"This doesn't feel right, Racynth," he said quietly. "They're usually more... Well, Sabina usually doesn't have to work this hard."

Racynth snorted but felt no real amusement. "I know," he replied simply, waving up to the guard who eventually cranked open the gates for them. Within, the district had the feeling of a bubble just about to pop or the air just before a thunderstorm. Either way, the *Eiyer* around them was so charged that Racynth began to feel lightheaded as they made their way to the palace.

Guards lined the walls of the palace, and the sides of the grand steps, facing out toward the rest of the city. They did not acknowledge the Sentinels as they approached. "Spooky," Jordan quipped as they stepped up and walked past the first row.

"Keep your comments to yourself," Racynth replied, earning a shrug from Jordan.

"Just trying to relieve some tension."

"It isn't helping," he snapped back, nodding to the mute guards at attention as they passed. Just within the great door stood Sabina, still as a statue, and Jordan nearly walked into him as he stopped short. "Commander," he bowed respectfully, mindful of keeping up appearances. Their friendliness was all well and good on the road, but this was not the time. "I thought you would be with Lord Karkas."

Her face was serene and placid, but he knew her well enough to see the rage that was simmering behind the facade. "Lord Karkas has refused an audience and he has ordered our Sentinella to leave the city as soon as things have calmed down," she said. Racynth felt Jordan smother his gasp of surprise more than he heard it.

"The Council will not be pleased—"

She shook her head. "I told him as much, but he doesn't seem to care. We have until the day after tomorrow and the execution is continuing as scheduled. As we speak, palace guards are on their way to release Soren Karkas and escort him here, upon which time we are forbidden from speaking with him." She paused, frowning at the wall opposite her. "Sentinel Naewynn... I will need you to take over from here. I have a report to make to the Council, and I don't expect it to go well."

The nod was automatic. "Of course. Jordan, we're going to inspect and secure the execution site," he said, gesturing for him to follow him out. Sabina left with them, and they split as they approached the Trading District. Racynth paused to watch her stride down the street, grateful that she hadn't insisted he join her.

"That," Jordan said slowly, "is why I never want to be Commander. You think we'll be reprimanded?"

Racynth sighed. "She'll take the brunt of it — Councilman Miayra won't be pleased, and I'd hate to be on his bad side again," he said, running a hand down his beard. Sabina's father was a real piece of work. Being pulled from active duty and told to guard dusty old tomes, had been insulting enough that few other Sentinellas had bothered communicating with them even after they'd been reinstated. Sabina had needed to work hard to regain any connections she'd once had. Hopefully this business with Karkas didn't put them back to square one.

"Let's just make sure there isn't another riot, yeah?" Jordan said, his voice finding its usual chipperness. "I'm sure Karkas won't make it easy on us."

Tamora

The rest of the day passed with eerie laziness as the wind whistled through the massive hole in the wall and revealed every threadbare patch in Tamora's clothing. She tried to keep the fire lit, tried to keep some semblance of normalcy. She threw on another layer of long-sleeved black clothes beneath her cloak and wrapped it around herself again, and then a third on top of that. With the Sentinella gone, Marin gone, and Aodhan off to Dalka knows where, she refused to give up the moment of peace she had been granted. She swept away the dirt and wood that littered her floor and spent some time staring at the damage and trying to decide if it was something she could even begin to repair on her own. Eventually she gave up on it all and huddled before her hearth.

Hours passed, and night fell. Every crack and movement through the trees outside made her stiff and on edge. "Could have gone with Marin," she muttered under her breath, stacking what seemed like the hundredth log on the fire. "But the Sentinels didn't seem keen on that. Maybe I could've holed up in the bakery; no one would expect that." No one would expect her to stay in her cottage, destroyed as it was, either. She still could head into the city, she supposed, and break into the bakery. At least that would be warm.

As yet another gust blew in through where her door had been Tamora pushed herself to her feet and stalked into her bedroom, searching for an extra blanket. "This was stupid," she said to no one. "Utterly, completely, stu—" she stopped as an object fell from the blanket she pulled from the bed, hitting her floorboards with a thud. It was Krys's pamphlet, and not where she'd left it. She looked down at it, feeling as though it were searing a brand in the ground. It must have been Lark; she knew for a fact she'd hidden it in here. Tamora looked on the opposite side of the bed and, sure enough, the hole she'd thought she'd been so clever in hiding was uncovered just enough. "That little —" she swore, calming herself just enough to keep from lighting her boots on fire.

She bent to pick up the book and looked at it carefully. It was well made, for a reprint. His name was hardly legible below the massive title and it reminded her of how proud he'd been to have it out there at all. *This*, he'd said, holding it aloft and grinning, *is going to be how we do it. How we get the word out. The Council will never know what hit them, not when everyone in Tunsealior knows the truth.*

She dropped the book on the bed and slammed the door behind her as she left the room. He'd died only a few months later. Tamora wrapped the blanket around herself and tried to keep the image of his melting face from her mind. It was impossible, she knew that. She saw it every night. His beautiful face contorted in pain and Selena's blank stare up at the bloody sky, along with thousands of bodies turned to ash around her. The memory of that day haunted her every moment and she knew she'd never be able to make up for what she'd done, even if it had been accidental. A terrible accident, her mother had called it. A tragedy. She'd been wrong, of course. Tamora had put herself in that situation, squarely in the middle of the rebellion's bloodiest battle, and Selena had been at her side. They'd always known the risks. Iokan Guardians didn't get in the middle of the fray for very good reasons but Selena never would have let herself be put to the side. Tamora had loved her for it and had respected her choice. She'd never once thought that it would be their ruin.

As night fell, her thoughts only turned darker. Sleep refused to come and her fire grew dim. The forest was filled with rustling and insects seemingly coming back from the dead, and she heard small animals poking around outside. Her mind concentrated only on the past. She could almost smell the stench of scorched skin, the heady feeling of knowing that she'd been the one to create it. That day, so many years ago, she'd killed hundreds. Thousands, with the wall of fire she'd thrown across the entirety of the plains. That was before she'd lost control completely, before Krys had melted in her arms, before Selena had collapsed and she'd spiraled.

A crack broke the silence outside.

Tamora shot to her feet, her blades scratching across the stone hearth as she gripped them so tightly her knuckles paled. "Who's there?" she shouted, her voice muffled. She stared out past her broken wall and into the soft darkness of the forest. "I'm warning you, I will hurt you." Her threats felt false, even to her own ears.

When had she allowed herself to become so weak? She shook her head. Thoughts like that would do her no good, she couldn't question herself. The swords were still sharp, she'd kept them up well enough. She could catch someone by surprise.

She waited, feeling her heart beat slow as her body realized that nothing was happening.

"It must have been a rabbit," she said, her voice feeling too loud and too shaky. She went to sit, her muscles begging for her to rest, when another branch cracked and she straightened abruptly.

Tamora edged forward and crouched in her doorway. She'd had some trouble out here before her cottage was built, but it had always turned out to be a curious animal. The bears didn't come this close to the city, years of hunting had taught them better. There were wild cats that she'd heard could be the size of a small horse but that had never been confirmed. This didn't feel like an animal. She didn't know how to explain it, even to herself. It weighed on her mind like an outsider, as though an Eilfe had dropped a great load of *Eiyer* upon her.

"If you're here to fuck with me, just come out here and do it!" she shouted, staring into the dark. "It's been a long day and I'm tired of your bullshit!" The wind blew right through her, making her teeth rattle. She was either burning hot or freezing, there was no in between. Tense minutes passed; Tamora didn't even dare to pull her cloak tighter around her. Nothing moved, and nothing responded to her challenge.

Finally, when it seemed like she'd been kneeling there for so long that her knees were going to collapse in on themselves, she sighed. "I need to sleep," she muttered to herself. She pulled herself up and turned her back to the wood, eying her warm hearth.

Behind her cottage, to the north, there was a sudden unnatural screech.

Tamora whipped around.

The howl—no, scream—was indescribably horrible. A baby's cry, a hiss, a roar — all in one, deeper and more primal than any animal she'd ever come across. It chilled her to her core.

Seeing nothing outside she rushed to her bedroom and threw open the door.

"No, no, not staying here." She shook her head, her voice thin and panicked. Whatever that thing was out there, it hadn't sounded very far.

She felt for her bag and started throwing things inside. Everything she'd kept in the hidden panel went in. Some clothes, her old standbys, the remaining knives, and she already held her swords. A ragged old book caught her eye then, the history of Tunsealior. She groaned and threw it in the bag. Her father's Guardian had gifted it to her before she'd been Paired with Selena; she couldn't simply leave it. It had been the last time she'd seen either of them. The other book was leather bound and soft with age and she shoved Selena's diary under the clothes, even as she dreaded the added weight. The rest had to stay, there was simply no time.

She felt her hands shake as the screeching echoed again

through the trees; it was much closer now. That was new to this forest, it must be. There had never been anything like that out here before. She stepped outside and crept to the gate, trying to let her eyes adjust to the complete darkness. She hit the wooden door with a grunt and a muttered swear and rubbed the remaining carved head for luck. May the Wela guide her out of these gods-forsaken woods. A third cry came from the north and sounded so close that Tamora imagined she might see the creature leap out at her any moment. She had no idea what to expect and she wasn't about to let herself be eaten by a beast. She swore and stepped past her wall, stumbling into a blind run.

There was nothing to guide her, not a shred of light. Dawn was many hours away but she hoped she could follow the path by memory. She couldn't hear over the sound of her own ragged breathing but the thought of something giving chase was enough to push her forward. Soon enough her worn out lungs burned and her legs felt like they would fall clean off.

The tree line appeared suddenly, and she was out in the field. Tamora bent over, falling to her knees and coughing so loudly she feared she'd draw whatever creature was in the wood straight to her. A glance behind her revealed nothing as the air itself looked thick and muddy in the darkness. She crawled forward in the mud and heard branches snapping behind her. The sharp pang of fear was more than enough to pull her to her feet and send her running toward the distant city walls.

.....

Tamora stumbled into the city, ignoring the angry grumbles of the man at the gate and making a beeline for The Outpost. The streets were terribly packed, most of those she saw were trying to sleep and bundled against the cold. Humans, for the most part, with the occasional Eilfe or Iokan who looked just as shocked and worn as the rest of them.

She couldn't spare them a moment; she needed to get to the Sentinels. If Marin had been put up there, maybe one or two of them would be watching over her. Although, she thought darkly, they have more important things to worry about right now than something terrifying lurking in the trees. It wouldn't get past Erengate's walls; they'd stood for centuries now, and with the Eiyer reinforcing them they were effectively indestructible.

A hand grasped at her leg, nearly sending her flying. "What—" she snapped, turning back and holding out a sword. The Human backed up, hands in the air. He was dirty and covered in mud; she felt she didn't look much better.

"I— I'm sorry. Do you have anything to spare?" he asked, stumbling over his words and staring at her blackened blade.

Tamora lowered it, but shook her head. "I'm sorry," she muttered, thrusting her hand in her pocket and tossing the first coin she found at him. She didn't see any guards at all on this street, only Humans who all looked as though they'd been through much worse than her. The crowds stopped completely at the Trading District wall, the guards holding her back until she could pull her crumpled pass from her pocket. The streets afterward were empty and quiet.

She pounded her fist against the wood on the front door, and a face appeared through the crack. "Can I help you?"

"Ah... are the Sentinels here? The Sentinella. Are they here?" she muttered, glancing down the dark street.

"What do you want with them?"

"So they are here. Let me in."

"I can't just—"

"Move." She shoved at the door, pushing him backwards into the main room. "They'll arrest me if I'm not supposed to be here." He muttered a room number after her and she stumbled up the stairs.

Another door, more pounding. Tamora leaned against the doorframe and closed her eyes as she waited. Over a full day without sleep; perhaps she'd imagined the creature. She sighed. She didn't know if that was wishful thinking or another sign of a delusion. The door opened a crack and the face beyond was the Mago Sentinel, Aspen. "Tamora? Why are you here?"

"There's something in the northern wood." She knew she looked and sounded crazy.

Aspen's eyes narrowed and took in her appearance. "Have you slept at all? You had a rough day—"

"That's not it, I know what I heard. There's something, a creature — I don't know — it's in the forest," she insisted, stepping closer. Aspen held the door stiffly.

"Look, Tamora. Go somewhere safe and get some rest."

"I'm at an inn that's safe enough. Look, I need your help."

"Then get a room and go to bed. It's still hours till dawn, you've been up all night," Aspen said, shaking her head. "Get some sleep." She shut the door and Tamora stared at the wood grain.

She leaned her head against the smooth surface. Weariness weighed on her mind and body. She could go get a room. That was probably a good idea, something that Selena would have insisted on. Tamora found, though, that she just couldn't move. Her thoughts raced and she felt too jumpy to do anything but pace.

She hobbled over to the stairs and forced herself to sit heavily on the lower stoop, resting her chin in her hand. "I'll just stay here then," she muttered, closing her eyes. "You can't make me wait forever."

.....

"Have you been sitting here all night?" Tamora startled

at the voice, wincing up at Racynth as the light darted between her eyelids. "Were you asleep?" he asked, frowning.

"I don't think so..." she trailed off as she looked around. Light streamed through the windows, the door was propped open. "It would seem that way. What time is it?" She pushed herself to her feet, ignoring the hand that Racynth offered.

"Just after sunrise," he said, looking her up and down. "Why do you look like you rolled in a bog?" Tamora wanted to glare, she really did, but she was still so exhausted.

"I told your friend, the Mago—"

"Aspen, yes. Something about a creature in the forest," he said, crossing his arms. "Starting a career in storytelling, are we?"

The look on his face made her bristle. "I'm not making this up," she snapped. He looked past her, down the stairs, and sighed.

"Come in," he gestured toward the door. "Quickly, please. You're well known in the city and there's a price on your head."

That shocked her out of her anger. "What?" He held the door open and she saw a plush room beyond, with what looked to be an armory's worth of weapons laid out on the table and the rest of the Sentinella staring at her. She walked through, slowly, and took it in. "Are you preparing for a war?"

"She shouldn't be here," said the Commander, who only spared a glare at her before turning to Racynth. "Take care of this. I'm going to the square and I expect you there before any crowds." She grasped her own blades, sneering at Tamora as she left. "If she's going to stay, she needs a bath."

The door closed behind her and Racynth pushed her toward an open chair. "Sit, try not to pass out. You look like death," he drawled. Tamora followed his instructions reluctantly, folding her blades in her lap and searching for an understanding face.

"Look, there's something—"

"What, a monster?" Racynth snapped. He rubbed his face. "Tamora, Lord Karkas has already released his son and we're preparing for the worst to happen today. You set that man off like a flame to oil, forgive me for the analogy," he said, shaking his head at Bealantin as the man snorted. "Coming here was a mistake—"

"Tamora?" a familiar, and very welcome, head poked out from an adjoining room. "Is Tamora here?" Marin's face lit up as she saw her and then promptly fell when she got a better look. "No, don't you dare get up, what in the Wela's name happened to you? Are you alright?"

"Marin, I—"

Lark pushed past his mother, making her wince and grasp her side, and rushed out. Sentinel Petro stepped out in front of him, keeping him at an arm's distance. "I heard something about a monster?" he exclaimed, nearly hopping from foot to foot in excitement. "What happened?"

Racynth swore and Tamora thought she heard him mutter something about Eilvyn hearing, but she was watching Marin catch her breath with narrowing eyes. "Ah, well I heard something howling and it was... well, it was unnatural," she admitted. Saying it out loud felt foolish and from the look the Sentinels were sharing she knew they thought the same.

Racynth sighed. "I don't have time for this, Miss Asken, we have an execution to prepare for." He gestured at the others, who rose to their feet and gathered their gear. "You will stay here, with Miss Agata, until we return. Do not open the door for anyone, do you understand?" he said, staring at her with such intensity that Tamora feared he may be able to read her mind.

"I can help—"

"That is so far from a good idea, I cannot truly put words

to it," he said, shaking his head. "I've reported everything to the rest of the Sentinella, they know that you helped the rioters escape."

"You let me," she snapped. His expression stiffened so fast that it was as though he'd turned to stone.

"Yes," he bit out, "I've explained that as well. I have... I have no good reason for doing so, other than that I felt their presence would do no good here. More Humans being executed is hardly what this city needs. Regardless, you made a scene at both the arrest and the sentencing for this woman. I won't have you creating more panic by being at the execution."

Tamora opened her mouth, but Marin shook her head from behind the Sentinels pointedly, smiling innocently when they looked her way. Slowly, Tamora nodded.

"Fine, I'll stay here. I'm tired and it's not like I actually want to see Karkas again," she said, wincing what she felt was the appropriate amount.

Racynth frowned, but the other Sentinels were beginning to leave. "Fine." He turned but looked back before closing the door. "If I see you outside this room, I'm arresting you, understand?"

She bit her tongue to keep from retorting and just nodded. When the door closed she turned to Marin and Lark, whose head was cocked to the side as he listened intently.

After a few minutes, he grinned. "They're gone," he said, turning to his mother. "We can speak freely, I don't hear anyone nearby."

"Yes, thank the Wela," Marin muttered, walking out to sit beside Tamora. "You ran all the way here, in the night? What did you hear?"

Instead of replying immediately Tamora looked closely at Marin, noting the paleness of her skin and the perspiration on her face. "You didn't tell me you were this injured," she said quietly, reaching out to where Marin's hand pressed against her ribs. She recoiled before Tamora could reach.

"Please, I'm fine. Just tell me what you heard," Marin insisted, not meeting Tamora's eyes. Tamora bit her lip, restraining herself from yelling. She was clearly not fine, and hadn't been fine for a full day now, but fighting about it would not help.

"It was in the north, the far north, and it screamed like no animal I've ever heard before. It came up fast too — I think it heard me running. I... it frightened me," she admitted. "I thought that maybe you'd heard some old stories." Marin grasped at her hands, releasing her fingers from their tight hold on her swords, and her grip was more comforting than Tamora wanted to admit.

"I don't know about monsters, Tamora, it's really just those old ghost tales," she said quietly, turning to Lark. "Could you go check on Sorrell and ask him. He's better at listening for these sorts of things than I am." She waited for him to go before looking back, her face full of undeserved kindness. "You need to sleep. The Sentinel may not have been particularly kind, but he was right. Just rest and we'll talk about this when you wake, alright?"

Tamora let Marin take her blades and set them to the side of the chair, and when she pulled her to her feet she didn't resist either. "Fine," she murmured, "fine. I'll rest now. But I'm going to the execution." Marin sighed.

"I know. But that's not for a few hours yet," she said, smiling at her. "You aren't as tough as you like to pretend you are. Please, just rest." Tamora laid down on the couch that Marin pointed her at, admiring the softness of the fabric with a kind of dull envy that she didn't know what to do with. Marin settled onto the floor beside her and Tamora fell asleep, her hand still grasping Marin's.

Chapter 17

Tamora

It was about eleven when she woke to Marin's gentle prodding. Sorrell's potential knowledge had been a dead end and she felt like a fool for making up monsters in the trees. It was probably a wild cat or a mountain lion — she didn't even believe herself, though, when she repeated it wordlessly. Something unnatural had been out there, but now was not the time to dwell on it.

"No, no, I'm going," Tamora insisted as Marin protested her getting up from the couch, firmly putting her hands on her friend's shoulders and moving her to the side. "Thank you for your concern, but I have to go."

"Why? You don't owe her anything," Marin said, even as she let Tamora sheath her swords and shrug her bag across her shoulders. She still moved with the slow stiffness of pain and Tamora eyed her a moment, assessing.

"I think I do," she said finally. "I was there, I tried to help her. Twice. It seems the least I can do to be there to watch her die."

"That's morbid and unnecessary," Marin said. "Dangerous, too — Karkas will be there, with all his guards! They'll take one look at you and arrest you on the spot."

"And that's why you aren't coming with me. I'll come

right back, it's not like I want Karkas to see me either. It'll be fine," she promised, smiling and opening the door. "Oh, and please rest. Your ribs are definitely broken, and you've been moving around way too much — they'll take ages to heal if you keep going the way you are." Marin nodded mutely and closed the door firmly behind her. She waited a moment to hear the satisfying click of the locks before heading out.

The streets in the Trading District were not nearly as empty as they had been the night before; people crowded here as they made their way to the square and the Pit that awaited them. Tamora watched everyone in her path, carefully hiding her dual scabbards beneath her cloak. There was no need to raise any alarm and while it wasn't uncommon for people to be armed, it would do her no favors now. Despite what she'd told Marin she had no intention of standing by. The simple fact that Karkas had gotten out was bad enough but that they would continue on with this plan was outrageous; people were going to get hurt. There was no need for an innocent woman to die today. Seeming to sense her determination, people moved from her path with little more than a glance in their direction.

It was odd, she realized, that this section of the city seemed to have returned to normal. As normal as Erengate had ever been. Shops were open and shouting at the people streaming by, trying to sell their wares to the growing crowd. Tamora shuffled past it all and scowled. Why did these people get to ignore what had happened, when people like Marin and Eloise were driven from their homes? She knew why, and that made it even more frustrating. Very few Humans worked long-term in the Trading District; the docks were the closest most got to leaving the Lower District. These people were all too happy to forget and ignore what had happened to the hundreds she'd passed on the street the night before.

The Pit sat in the center of the square as it always had and seemed to radiate an especially foul energy today. The group that had gathered in the square, refusing to get within a few feet of even the rails that surrounded the pit, was even larger than it had been for the sentencing. Chatter filled the air as though they didn't have a care in the world; only excitement thrummed through the crowd.

A sneer curled her lip. This nameless woman's execution would begin a season of them, she was sure of it. From the riot alone, and that night's chaos, they'd amassed a jail-full of future victims to torment. She turned to look around and caught a good look at the stage. The Sentinella stood there this time, dressed in their iconic cloaks and all sharing the same stony look of disdain that she'd come to associate with any visiting Sentinel. Sabina carried this responsibility especially well, looking out at the crowd with a sneer that bordered on hatred. Racynth, for his part, simply looked bored. His mask was almost perfect, but she could see his hand fiddling with his belt all the same. So, they didn't like this either. They were still there. She huffed, keeping her head down.

The time crept closer to noon, the sun rising in the sky even as the crowd grew louder. She could pick out the individual threads of conversation easily enough; they were all the same. Who would be presiding? Wasn't Soren arrested? And the Sentinella, when did they get here? All of this seemed ready to be answered when the clock tower, looming over the Pit like a gravestone, began to announce midday. Tamora turned again to face the stage and her stomach twisted into knots.

Soren Karkas was stepping out onto the flat surface, just as he had only days earlier. He looked pale, a little bruised, but unfortunately intact. Following him was his father, a prim look of sophistication plastered across his features. Neither spared a glance at the Sentinella and it seemed that they were determined to ignore their presence altogether.

Tamora almost laughed when Silas Zavalynn appeared behind the rest of the Karkas family and their individual guards, looking as though he'd been on Dalka's doorstep and resurrected purely for the occasion. His face was mottled purple and green, bruises beginning to heal but just barely, and one eye was completely swollen shut. He had a limp worse than Tamora's, and it gave her more pleasure than she would have admitted out loud to see him hobble over to his place behind his lord. She'd have to tell Marin later, and hopefully she'd find it just as amusing.

Karkas raised his hands in greeting, effectively silencing the crowd.

"Welcome, citizens of Erengate!" he shouted, stepping closer to the edge of the stage. It dropped off abruptly at the edge of the Pit, not even a railing erected to stop anyone from stumbling off. She saw the faint twinge of fear in his posture as he glanced down into the depths but it brought her no satisfaction. It was a feeling they all shared.

A few people cheered and those around them muttered darkly until they fell silent.

"Today, on this beautiful Misa, we honor the Eight with justice righteously served." A scattering of shouts, even less than before. Tamora was quietly proud in the harshness of the crowd. She knew, however, that the tension was only going to build. There were too many people here for this to end well; she saw that same thought in the stiffness of the Sentinella upon the stage. Sabina made a small gesture and the Sentinels Aspen and Petro split off from the sides, both making their way along the square's edge. A few moments later a barred carriage, brought out from the barricaded side street behind the clock tower, was opened and the Human emerged. The crowd jeered but not all of it was directed at her. Tamora looked around at the dozens of downcast and downright angry faces around her.

The woman was now huddled, shivering, on the stage and surrounded by heavily armored Eilvyn guards. She looked so small. Karkas stalked around her, giddy in his delight at the cheering. He was spewing the same vitriol he had at her sentencing, something about a great conspiracy and how he'd overcome it. His father was grimacing out at the crowd and speaking with one of the men beside him, the rest of the family secluded at the back of the stage. This was Soren's big moment, after all. His hatred was all too clear but Tamora knew it had nothing to do with the woman. He was utterly deranged and always had been; the past few days had just put an ugly spin on his already disturbing behavior.

He didn't see the discontent of the crowd, but she did, and the Sentinels as well. They all had their hands on their weapons as they noted the sharp glint of knives throughout the gathering and the determination in people's eyes. Tamora took a step back, suddenly realizing how bad of an idea this was. The Sentinella stepped forward and drew their weapons, but they were too late.

A solitary yell rang out from the back of the crowd and those closer to the far left and right of the stage leapt atop its worn surface. They rushed the guards and Tamora was pushed sharply to the side as the mob ebbed in a burst of sudden panic. She touched the hilt of one of her blades but did not draw it. She'd only bring attention to herself and right now, she was more at risk of being trampled.

The roar of hundreds of running feet was nearly deafening on its own and the thrashing of bodies as they suddenly tried to leave blocked her line of sight completely. She stumbled as someone ran into her and threw her to the ground. Tamora could hear the clanging of metal on metal and knew the city guard had gotten involved, and that they were being met with resistance. Feet trampled her hands and legs kicked at her body as she tried and failed to stand. She crawled, pushing herself back onto her knees each time she was knocked back and gasping for air as it was pushed from her lungs.

Finally she broke through the edge and grasped the stone wall of the closest building, hauling herself to her feet. Her left hand was swollen painfully and her fingers would barely move as she pulled up on the stone's edge. She winced as she shoved it into her cloak's pocket. *Best not to move it, I'll set it later*, she resolved, gazing into the square. It was still packed but held merely a fraction of the people as before, as many had fled into the streets and the civilians had left behind the much smaller group of true rebels. She was grateful not to see Aodhan or Captain among them.

Tamora searched the crowd for the Sentinels, trying to follow their movements, and her eyes finally focused on Commander Miayra. She pushed a Human back with the flat of her blade, loosening his grip before grabbing and throwing his weapon aside. The others, when she found them, were carrying out similar maneuvers and clearly opting to disarm and injure rather than kill. It was a far cry from what Soren Karkas and the city's guards were doing. She looked at the stage and gasped, taking in the brutality of what Karkas had done. The elder lord and his family seemed to have fled, or had been escorted away, and Soren and Zavalynn were the only nobles remaining. Zavalynn was cowering, unsurprisingly, but Karkas was grappling with a Human man. They were precariously close to the Pit and she watched the man push Karkas towards it with bated breath. It seemed he would succeed in throwing him down but at the last moment Karkas flipped him overhead with his legs, pushing the Human over the edge while he himself rolled back to safety. The man disappeared into the darkness and Tamora felt her chest seize up at the thought of that fate.

The Human woman, the root of all this chaos, was still shackled to the stage. Her chains shook as she fought against them, pulling up at the lock as she watched Karkas lie prone on his back only a few feet away. He seemed too shaken by his near death to do much against her, but Tamora knew it was only a matter of time. She had to get to the stage. If Karkas saw the woman, and realized that she was still alive, he'd kill her anyway. If Tamora could move fast enough she truly could prevent this woman's death.

She ran along the edge of the mob and tried not to get pulled back into the fray. People were running for their lives from the guards while others rushed in to protect them. A few were thrown bodily into her, the surge of Eiyer filling her mind as it was thrust out from the closest Eilvyn guard, and she was pushed into the stone building as the Human collapsed on top of her. She groaned as she pushed the man aside, checking briefly to make sure he was still breathing, and continued on. Her lungs burned worse than her crushed hand as she reached the stage and hauled herself atop it, pausing only a moment to catch her breath before scrambling to the woman. Karkas hadn't moved and was just breathing heavily as he stared across at the Pit. She could see the whites of his eyes as she passed, but he barely acknowledged her. He looked utterly broken, more so than what she'd seen in the forest.

The woman scrambled away from her with a shriek, her eyes wide, visibly weakened by her ordeal.

"Stop, stop. It's okay, I'm going to help you," she said quickly, not knowing if she was calming the woman. It didn't seem like it, as the woman stretched the chains as far away from her, and the Pit, as they would go.

"Hey!" Tamora looked sharply up, hearing Zavalynn shout as he saw her appear. She spared him only a glare, looking around for something heavy enough to use. There wasn't much time; she knew the easiest solution was to brave her elements, but she knew in her heart that she couldn't use them. Her fire would be useless here as she couldn't control it, not anymore. Her earth was more of a possibility but she needed to have the energy to escape this mess and it was just as likely to grow out of control as it was to help. The guards probably had the key, or Karkas, but one wrong move around him and she'd follow that Human right over and into the darkness that loomed behind her. One of the rioters who had made it up on the stage, his body sprawled across the wooden surface and his face gazing glassy-eyed up at the blue sky, had been using an axe before he'd fallen. It would have to do.

"Lean back," she warned the woman before she brought the axe down upon the lock. The force of it reverberated through her shoulder and she had to grit her teeth against the pain. She didn't stop. The second hit did slightly more damage, and by the fourth painful strike the lock cracked in half.

"You need to go," Tamora said, panting.

"But you—" she began. Tamora pushed her shoulder and she stumbled back.

"Go, now. Before he realizes." She spoke of Karkas, but she wasn't sure if he would even remember the woman existed after the scare he suffered. The Human's eyes darted quickly between the two of them; the Eilfe on the ground and the Azha crouched before her trying to help. Tamora knew how it looked, especially after all the woman had been through. "Please, you have to go now," she urged her, sparing a glance at Karkas.

In that crucial moment, Tamora didn't see Zavalynn. But she felt the energy around her shift and her own body began to move against her and she whipped her head around to face him. Too late, she realized.

He wasn't the best at wielding his *Eiyer* in his condition, but she was weak. He threw Tamora backwards and held her against the stage with the force of his will, even as she struggled to touch her hand to one of the swords in her belt. It was all she could do to lift her arm and she cursed her own weakness. The Human tried to run but she was too slow, too unimaginably Human. She was thrown down, but she rolled across the polished wood and right up against the edge of the Pit and Tamora watched her chest heave as she stared in panic down at the abyss. Tamora struggled against the bonds of energy that wrapped around her, entirely invisible but pressing into her skin with the force of physical restraints. Zavalynn rushed to Karkas' side and lifted him to his knees.

Karkas finally did see the woman and a small glint of terrible recognition flared in his eyes. Tamora screamed out in a rage as he stumbled closer to her and nudged the woman with his foot. She scrambled at the wood as she was pushed even closer to the edge, her back leg dangling over the precipice.

The woman glared up at Karkas and spat at him, saying something that Tamora couldn't hear, and threw herself backwards and tumbled out of sight into the darkness below.

Karkas, his face pale with shock and rage, stumbled back. Zavalynn pulled him bodily from the Pit and as they ran from the stage Tamora felt the bonds of *Eiyer* release her. She crawled frantically to the edge and bile rose in her throat as she looked down into the darkness, hoping to see the frail woman clinging on.

There was nothing in the depths, only a sickening pull of silence. Fear rose within her, fear that she might willingly succumb to its call as the Human had. It felt as though her very soul were being erased; everything about being Iokan meant nothing, and she was left utterly defenseless as her elements fell away. She understood now why Karkas had frozen for so long, and Tamora wrenched herself from the edge and fell back on the wooden stage, a hacking sob the only sound she was able to make.

Hands pulled her backwards, slivers of wood stabbing at her back as she was dragged across the surface. "Tamora — Tamora!" The voice was familiar and she looked up at the source, Racynth glaring down at her. She gazed through him as though he were not there, seeing only the deep source of darkness that was the Pit. "Are you insane? I told you to stay with Marin. Do you *want* to die?"

"Where is he?" she muttered, seeing him at last and shaking off his hands. "Where is Karkas?" She fought against his grasp.

"Gone! Stop, you're going to—" he cut himself off and turned away, pausing as he looked toward away from the Pit. Tamora pulled herself from his arms and finally unsheathed a sword, scrambling to her feet and fully intending on going after Karkas and Zavalynn. Their faces swam in her vision and all she could think of was the sweet satisfaction of running them through and dragging them both to the Pit to watch them fall.

She didn't know what stopped her. It wasn't something she was fully aware of, just a growing sensation that something was terribly wrong.

"What was that?" she heard the Sentinel, Della, shout as she climbed up the stairs to the far left of the stage. Tamora stumbled in her direction, the direction Soren had gone, and was vaguely aware of her own confusion.

What was that noise? It thumped in her chest and she looked down, thinking it could only be the beating of her own heart. *Am I dying? Why is it beating so loud?*

"Racynth?" she whispered as she turned to him. His expression was frozen but it was not the stony resolve she'd seen before. It was fear.

Chapter 18

Racynth

The air itself seemed to have grown thick and heavy and it was not the work of some Tri, nor was it the unmistakable pressure of Eiyer. His heart beat in his chest so loudly that he almost feared it would injure itself. The square had grown empty, the guards too brutal for the rioters and those few Humans who remained had begun to flee. Chaos had broken out, just as Sabina had feared, but that was not what had stopped him in his tracks.

He could hear a dull and repetitive drone so deep it was no longer a sound; it was this that he was feeling in his chest, that he'd mistaken for his own heartbeat. Sabina, across the square and still holding the weapon she'd taken from the guard huddled on the ground before her, froze in place and her head snapped to look towards the harbor just as he was. Della, stepping up on the stage, had stopped just before Tamora and had grown as pale as an Eilfe could.

Those around them looked between them and the guards with unmasked confusion as all the Eilvyn stopped in their tracks. Many Humans took it as their opportunity to escape but their movements were confused, feeling the noise in their bones. Panes on the windows around them began to rattle with the booming noise as it grew closer, some high in the tower shattering and falling upon the back of the stage like violent rain. The sharp sound shocked Racynth out of his stupor and he turned to Tamora.

"You need to get out of the city," he said, watching her wrench herself from her discomfort and grimace at him.

"Over my dead body."

"Go get Marin and anyone else you can find, and get out of the city," he repeated, hefting his blade experimentally. He had no idea what this was, or if he had any chance of defeating it.

She stiffened as he moved away from her, confusion marring her face. "Why? What's happened?" He spared her only a look as he stepped off the stage.

"I have no idea," he admitted, breaking into a run. He heard her trying to follow but falling behind as the other Sentinels snapped to attention and joined him. As he left the square and turned down a side road, what he hoped would cut him around some of the panicked crowd, he finally realized what the sound was. It was a drum, but he'd never heard its equal. Even during the rebellion, when he'd been amid the heat of battle, nothing had ever shaken him like this.

As he grew closer to the harbor, cutting through streets and pushing around groups of people, he could see smoke beginning to rise, black as night and clogging the air as it swirled over the buildings.

"What is this?" Sabina asked, catching up to him as they rounded another corner. He looked at her sideways; she'd always been the fastest. Della would be close behind as well.

"An attack?" he huffed, cursing inwardly. There were pirates, of course, but no one would attack Erengate directly. Its walls were impenetrable and the Karkas family had developed a reputation—one he'd experienced very clearly since his arrival. Besides, pirates usually went for isolated ships, small towns, or at most a small island community.

"There were no reports of any—" Sabina was cut off as a group of people rushed out from a building, piles of belongings in their arms. She jumped over one, jumping off the side of a building to evade them, but ran bodily into another, his bundle scattering across the cobblestones as he fell to the ground. He scrambled to catch up to his family, leaving behind everything he'd been carrying. Racynth didn't stop to help her; she was already getting up and cursing boldly as she sprinted to catch up.

Marin

The booming drone shook the walls and she froze in place, her heart seeming to slow to match its pace. Only a few minutes later, as the drone wore on, she heard the ringing of bells. The palace. Something awful had happened, she realized, and the palace was taking in survivors. In all her years in the city, they'd never done that. If it was bad enough they were willing to bring in the public for their own safety, it would have to be truly terrible.

"What is that?" Lark asked quietly, clutching his own chest. "Are we under attack?"

"Get your things," she said, not willing to wait for an answer. It was time to leave the city. It was long past the time when Lark and Sorrell should have started their own lives and Erengate was no longer safe. She'd take them to her family back home and hope that they'd be accepted; even if they weren't, anywhere was better than this.

Sorrell was moving slowly, even with Eloise's help, and the droning drumbeats had gone on for no more than ten minutes when the sound of someone running up the stairs made Marin rush to the door. She peeked out and gasped when she saw Tamora, covered in blood and dirt, and pulled her into the room.

"What in the Wela—"

Lark rushed from the side room, bags in his arms, and came to an abrupt stop in the doorway. Marin could hear Sorrell yelling for Eloise to help him move faster.

Tamora just held up a hand, the other stuffed into her pocket. "We're leaving— now. Eloise!" Her voice rang out in the small space as Eloise's face appeared behind Lark. "Get your mother. Lark, you're taking Sorrell. We need to get to the woods, or the main road. There's no time." The thrumming drone had only grown louder.

"What is that?" Marin's voice cracked. Her boys were following Tamora's orders without question, but the only thing she could see were the wounds, the clear signs of a fight. "What happened to you? I thought—"

"I have no idea and it isn't important because we're not staying long enough to find out. We're going to the road, south to Ozhansa—"

"What are you talking about? What's out there? Tamora?" Marin went to her, grasping her arm and pulling her around to face her. "Don't ignore me, Tamora, please."

Tamora's breath was heavy and sounded pained and Marin looked down into her face and found more despair there than she'd ever seen before. Ever been allowed to see, she realized. Tamora had kept so many secrets, from her friends to her murky past, and the blackened blades that hung from her waist were evidence of a life before Erengate that Marin wasn't sure she wanted to know the details of.

"I... I have no idea," she said finally, her voice cracking. "But something happened, I think it's in the harbor. The Sentinels are on their way, and you need to get out of Erengate. Please."

"Are you coming?" Marin asked, her voice small. She already knew the answer. In the past day she'd seen more resolve from Tamora than she'd seen in the last seventy years. This was what she thrived on, what she'd needed. And it wasn't anything that Marin felt comfortable sharing with her.

"No," Tamora said, shaking her head. "This is different, I've never felt anything like it. This much power... I need to see it." She was set, that much was clear. Marin released her arm and stepped back.

"Fine. Lark, get your brother. Eloise, you and Davina are coming with us, alright? Don't fall behind," she said, making eye contact with them all to be sure they understood.

Whatever happened, she was going to keep these people safe. She felt the power of whatever the source of the noise was; it wasn't *Eiyer*. She had never been the most talented with her gift, but she knew enough to know that this was as far from it as you could get.

They were outside in minutes. Tamora stumbled behind them and was clearly in rough shape. Marin almost laughed. That seemed to be the only thing they shared right now. Her friend had a steely look in her eye that she hardly recognized. Screams could be heard clearly through the streets and people were running, scrambling down the street as fast as their legs could take them. Most seemed to be rushing to the gates while others fled deeper into the city. Everyone was escaping the harbor. Marin stumbled as half a dozen people sprinted between them and pushed their small group apart for a moment before disappearing down a side street.

"Go, get to the road! I'll find you!" Tamora shouted as they were separated again, and she was pushed out into the center of the street. Marin nodded, hoping that she had been seen, and then she was gone.

Marin grasped Lark by the shoulder, careful not to jostle Sorrell too much, and pointed. "The main gate, let's go!" she said, shouting over the screams around them. She led the way, looking back to see that Sorrell had Eloise firmly by the hand and that Davina too had not been lost. The last look that she'd seen in Tamora's eye had been fear and excitement; Marin tried to cement it in her mind. It was the most alive she'd ever see her.

They came to a major road and stopped short, the wall looming ahead of them, and a problem suddenly became very clear. Everyone in the city was running in the same direction and there was no way that they were going to get to the wall from here. The streets were packed like canned fish and they could clearly see the bodies of those who had already been trampled by the panicked crowd; they lay motionless under the hundreds of feet that still ran atop them.

"Wela help us," Eloise said, not bothering to be quiet about it. Marin turned to her, and to Lark and Sorrell, but found their faces pale and their eyes wide as dinner plates. This time, they were not able to lead. This was more than they could manage. She straightened, her grip tightening on Lark's shoulder. She'd get them to safety.

Marin waited a moment, staring at the rush of people, and tried to think of how they'd make it to the gate. As she did, though, something about the rush of people changed. Fear and confusion turned to pure unadulterated panic, and the crowd's violence escalated so much that she pushed the others back into the alley another few feet. Lark gasped, his breath catching in his throat, and as Marin turned to look back toward the harbor she thought her chest might explode from the sudden burst of terror that struck her.

The back of the crowd was being completely overrun, thrown to the side and crushed underfoot as something massive lumbered up the street. Four creatures spread out across the road. Writhing masses of darkness and shadow. That was all that was truly comprehensible. *This is impossible*, she told herself, squeezing her eyes together before staring back at the monstrosities. They were still there, throwing people aside as easily as a child did a doll. Each was enormous, eight or nine feet at least, and from their breadth she knew they could crush her without a thought.

There was no hesitation as they removed the obstacles from their path. They simply cleaved through people and continued forward. Marin held her breath as they passed the alley her family stood in and never even acknowledged their presence. The creatures smelled of rotten meat and despair, of death. The crumpled bodies they left in their wake made her stomach roil and Davina collapsed behind her, silently retching up her breakfast.

"We... we have to get out of here," she finally said, allowing Eloise to help her back to her feet. She grasped Marin's arm and pulled urgently. "We need to get out of here *now*."

Marin stepped out after the creatures, watching them lumber through the crowd ahead of them, and ran across the now blood-soaked road. Many of the bodies they passed she recognized, as they were customers, old friends she hadn't spoken to in years. They'd been mown down as if they were nothing. She couldn't comprehend what it meant, what those monsters were. They were something out of a terrible storybook, something locked away from children lest it cause nightmares. As it was, she didn't think she'd ever be able to sleep again. Not when the blood from Eilvyn, Iokans, and Humans was beginning to soak through her boots. The street here was packed with people choosing to hunker down and wait out the attack rather than to flee. Marin wept for them, knowing what was coming.

Davina gasped out a sob when they stopped for breath, the end of the street seeming as good a place as any. The wall still loomed above them but they were far from the gate, and those creatures were between them and their escape. "We're going to die," the woman cried softly, grasping at her daughter. "We're all going to die."

"That's enough," Marin snapped. She turned on the Human, taking her chin in her hands. "We are not going to die here, do you understand? We're going to the palace. They rang the bell, they're taking people in." She stared at them all, hoping her words sounded confident enough.

"What are they?" Lark asked, even his voice shaky. Her brave boy, she thought with a sad smile.

"Dalka's army, or some creation of the High Council... I don't know," she said, wincing as she looked out into the street. There were fewer people, now that so many had died. She didn't smell the creatures and that seemed to be important; she hoped it meant that they were far enough away. She had no idea if that was right or not. "I don't think it matters. What matters is that they're dangerous and we need to find safety, and the palace is as good a place as any."

They ran as fast as they were able, quickly running to a wall of people trying to get out of the front gate. This lay to the northeast and the crowds backed up through the streets and clogged them. The air was thick with fear and panic, and there were more than a few Eilvyn manipulating the Eiyer here as well. Some pushed themselves into the air, rising above the crowd with their own force of will. Others opted to shove people out of the way; one hit Lark and sent both him and Sorrell flying. Marin screamed, reaching out with her own *Eiyer* to try to stop their fall but watching all the same as they crashed into the stone pavers. Sorrell landed on his bad leg and cried out, Lark rolling to the side and leaping to his feet at the same moment.

Marin pulled Eloise and Davina to the side as a Mago and their Guardian flew past atop a massive chunk of stone that they sent flying through the air with the gift of their element. They both screamed as rubble fell from it, the Iokan not even sparing a glance at those left behind as they hovered overhead. Those who could were going to get themselves out, one way or another, Marin realized. They had no real way of doing the same and their only option was to rely on the Karkas family, if they were still alive. The thought made her sick. Still, as she reached Sorrell and helped Lark pull him to his feet, she knew there was no other way.

Tears ran silently down Sorrell's face but he gritted his teeth and allowed Lark to support him. He pulled Eloise close and pressing his face into her cheek, reassuring himself that she was alright, and then nodded to Marin, blowing his next breath through his clenched teeth. "I'm fine, really."

Those were the last words spoken in their group as they made their way to the palace. A monstrous roar sounded from the north, when they were only a few streets farther than they'd been, and it threw the people around them into more of a panic. Davina and Eloise were shoved down when a group pushed past, only Sorrell's grasp keeping them on their feet, and Iokans and Eilvyn alike were taking every advantage to get to the gates first. Marin felt like she was in a daze. Her ribs burned and if she didn't know better she'd have thought her heart was giving out instead of her ribs. Her feet felt like they weren't connected to the rest of her body, dragging and catching on the cobblestone below.

Still, they made it to the gates. Privately, she dreaded what lay ahead. The Palace District. She'd rarely been inside the palace proper; very few people, after all, made it from the lower city to these pristine streets. The crowd, however, was determined. It would take the entire city guard to stop them now. Their small group went with the flow, rushing past guards and through the lacquered gates, and she sighed with relief as the palace came into view.

"We're going to be alright," she said, hoping that she wasn't lying.

Chapter 19

Tamora

She hugged the wall as she turned against the crowd. People streamed past her. Crying, soot-covered, wearing expressions she knew all too well. Tamora realized she had absolutely no idea what she was pushing toward. Another riot? It seemed too drastic; there were too many innocent victims. It wasn't something that Aodhan would do. All she could hope was that the Sentinels could handle it, and that Marin was able to get to safety.

The bells in the Palace District began to chime again, clearly audible even from this distance. A warning; at least some of the city would be prepared. She breathed deeply and stepped out into the larger street ahead, coming straight out from the harbor. Hundreds of people rushed past. Tamora rocked on her heels as someone hit her in the shoulder, nearly sending her to the ground. She stabilized herself as best she could, knowing that falling would be the death of her. There was no way anyone would stop long enough to help. She looked up to see that many people were pulling their shutters closed and hoping to wait out whatever was creating the panic. The realization that she'd never make it through to the harbor was glaringly obvious.

After she'd gone no more than a few hundred paces, those taking an immeasurable amount of time, the energy of the crowd changed. What had been fear and distress became pure panic. Those who were in the back, closest to the shore, pushed violently and threw themselves into the people ahead of them. Tamora was tossed backward and shoved at the woman in front of her, jumping to the side to get out of the raging path and reaching the wall and grasping onto a windowsill. It felt like she was in open water during a storm, a rising wave threatening to plow through her. She crouched and watched, hunkered beside a stone water drain that allowed for the smallest of reprieve from the crushing of boots.

She glanced around the drain, realizing that those at the back who weren't throwing themselves forward were falling. They were being killed—crushed—by something coming up behind the crowd.

Tamora leaned back into the stone, wrapping her cloak around her and now praying for the gift of invisibility. Her eyes widened as the creature responsible came into sight and her mind immediately denied its existence; such a thing was impossible and unnatural and yet, it lumbered forward at a leisurely, terrible pace.

Four creatures were making quick work of Humans, Eilvyn, and Iokans as they all tried to flee from their impending deaths. She could barely comprehend what they were; she could only see undulating shadows and brief glimpses of terrible wiry forms that lay beneath. There was no pause, no hesitation as they removed the obstacles from their path. They simply cleaved through people and continued forward.

The creatures passed by where Tamora crouched and never looked in her direction, as though they would not pursue anything not worth the effort. She caught a whiff of them and gagged. Rotten flesh, death and decay. It wafted from their bodies and it transported her thoughts to those weeks after a battle if the fallen were not properly cleared away. She coughed, covering her mouth frantically lest they hear her, but they went on without pause. Her relief was brief, erased by the sight of the carnage left in their wake. There were audible cracks as their victims hit the paved stone; most did not move again.

She stumbled to her feet, small hunching steps. Slowly, she drew a blade in her good hand but had no idea how she'd fare and no intention of finding out now.

When she was out of sight of the road, no longer able to smell their stench or feel their evil, she collapsed against a wall and allowed herself to breathe fully. This was something she had never seen, an evil that didn't exist. She'd just watched dozens of people die instantly, with no effort on the part of their attackers. There was no time to rest. Smoke still billowed and she had no idea how many of these things there were, or if the Sentinella still lived. She'd counted four in the street and that had been more than enough to clear the mass of people who'd been trying to escape them.

The alley she chose to run down was deserted. It gave her little hope, only reinforcing her fear that these things had been sent to kill them all. Adrenaline helped her forget her own pain, her limp all but disappeared in the heat of the moment. She knew it would come back with a vengeance but the thought almost made her laugh; who even knew if she'd live long enough to regret this. The next road came too fast, she was still in her head and every instinct told her to fight but she was so weak. Her body would never be able to handle the strain of battle.

She froze in the opening, watching as stragglers ran by. The harbor was just around the bend and there were bodies everywhere. Did she want to see what ruin was left? For years after the battle in the Gwen Plains she'd had nightmares of death, of burned and mutilated bodies. If this left her in the same state, she wasn't sure her mind would be able to stand it.

Indecision and fear rooted her to the ground.

As Tamora stood still, wavering between the alley and the road ahead, a familiar figure ran down what little of the road she could see. Aspen. Her Guardian Petro was close behind, bow in hand.

The other Sentinels had to be close.

It was their disappearing figures that lifted her feet. This city was her home. It was flawed and corrupt, but she would fight to save it from these monstrosities. She'd been here too long to see it burn.

.....

The waterfront was ablaze and her breath caught in her throat as she gazed at the carnage before her. The docks she'd seen only a few days ago were burnt to a blackened crisp. Smoke billowed in the air and disguised the figures stepping out from the depths of the shoreline. Tamora ducked behind the remains of a building, the fire warming her to the core. Her clothes were not fireproof, she'd have to be careful.

There were ships. She could just see them through the haze. Two had landed and three lurked in the distance. Their hulls had broken on the docks they'd rammed into and the shadow creatures poured from the wreckage. Smoke clung to their frames and all that was truly visible were misplaced and grotesque limbs. They slashed at the city's defenders with claws and weapons equal in numbers and vicious design.

Tamora yelped as she saw a shape from the corner of her eye barreling toward her. She leapt back and brandished her blade but the creature was distracted. Two Eilvyn guards, their armor clearly showing the city's insignia, followed and taunted it. They seemed like children beside it as they dodged its misshapen weapon. She scrambled back out of their way and fell to the ground, too close to one of the burning buildings. Her bag and clothes smoked in the heat.

The two guards were well trained, they worked in deadly unison. Not unusual for their kind, long lives lend themselves well to mastery. It all meant nothing in the face of this creature. The fight seemed lost from the beginning. With an enraged bellow the creature swung its decrepit weapon. With a single blow the man's face was in ruin and his body fell lifelessly to the ground. The other shrieked in anger and charged; his life was similarly cut short. Tamora did not dare make a sound. The two had fallen in such a way that she had a clear view of their corpses, it seemed to her they looked at her through the smoldering haze. Centuries of life, gone. Their attacks had proved meaningless. The creature turned back to the shore.

Tamora looked at its path. The Sentinels were there, fighting their own battles. To her shock and amazement she saw a creature fall to the ground. She had no idea who dealt the killing blow as they were obscured by distance and smoke. But it was possible, she realized. These things could die.

She swung her bag over her back and wished that her left hand could grasp a blade. Hopefully it would not get in the way.

Tamora stood on shaky legs, not from exertion, she realized, but fear. She pushed the feeling down with a skill she'd learned two hundred years prior, from the instructor at Brist who'd been tasked with creating an Azha army. Fear, worry, decades of anxieties — none of it would do her any good here.

Before the closest creature could sense her presence and before it could come within striking distance of the Sentinels, Tamora leapt from her cover. She slashed at its back, close enough to the shadowy mist that surrounded it to see its true form. To her surprise it was covered in black hair, thick in some places but nearly bare in others. The muscles beneath were deformed and bloated, bubbles clearly visible just beneath the surface. It looked diseased.

It swung at her as it turned faster than she'd anticipated. Things of that size should be slower. She dove to the side and slashed again, this time at its neck. It was clearly stronger than her; she would have to be faster. Her body was weak, however, and she knew her limits were closer than she could allow. She swung at its legs, cutting the tendons before diving out of its reach. Its bellows were bone-chilling and seemed to reverberate in her skull.

It stumbled.

Teeth protruded from its face like enormous fangs, half the length of her forearm.

Tamora fell back, her foot caught on something. She glanced down; the destroyed face of the Eilfe stared blankly up at her. She came down hard beside the body and immediately rolled to the side, knowing any hesitation on her part would mean her death. This was higher stakes than any battle she had fought in the rebellion. Those enemies had all been people. The massive weapon swung down at her and smashed through the corpse, easily cleaving it in two. It was followed by the fangs, the creature lunging at her like a bear at its prey. She slashed at its face, its neck, any opening she could find.

It seemed like an hour had passed but it could only have been a few moments. Already her arms were tired and she knew she couldn't go on. This was a foolish attempt at playing the hero. The realization dawned on her slowly.

She was going to die.

Tamora knew she'd failed but she raised her arm to block the blow that would end her. It came for her side and she'd seen enough of their strength to know it would cut clean through. A fitting end, she thought. No one would know who to tell. Her brother might hear of her death if the Sentinels lived to tell Erengate's tale. They didn't know him but maybe he listened to mere rumors, maybe they'd think her important enough to mention her by name. Perhaps he might even tell their mother, and she could mourn her.

Tamora closed her eyes and waited the millisecond it would take for the creature to end her life.

The blow didn't land. Before she could open her eyes, or even move, she was thrown aside and to the ground by a body that wrapped around her, shielding her from the brunt of the fall.

"Are you trying to die?" Racynth spat at her, repeating his earlier words as he leapt away. The creature growled in anger and spun on them both. She stared up at it and at Racynth, who stood above her. Her ability to move had vanished entirely, her muscles seizing.

Racynth was in his own class of warriors. He moved faster than even other Sentinels she'd seen; perhaps even faster than she had once been. The creature was wounded, she'd done that much at least. It slowed as Racynth beat it into submission, before burying his blade into its skull. Its blood ran black as it poured into the dirt.

"Thank you—"

"You're a fool," he snapped and dragged her to her feet. "What in the Wela's name do you think you're doing here? I tell you to stay put, and you run into a riot. I tell you to find safety, and you run straight towards death."

She stared at him, her mouth working to form words. *Is he right?* The thought leapt into her mind. *Do I want to die? Is that what I've been doing all this time?* Everything told her that he was wrong, that she had a reason to be there. But she couldn't even think of what that might be.

"I just—"

"You what? Thought you'd relive whatever glory you once had?" His eyes blazed as he pushed her back. "You want to take those black swords of yours out for one last fight? You're a fool," he repeated, and she felt the words echo in her head.

Her heart thundered in her ears and she knew that it wasn't the drums, although those still droned on. They were just off shore and so close that she could feel them reverberating through her very bones. Her breathing was wild and her emotions raged with limited control. There was nothing she could do to stop it. She looked around; there were nearly a hundred of the creatures already ashore. More ships were landing.

"We're outnumbered, we've lost the city," she muttered.

Racynth kicked the thing's head. "Follow me. We have to get to the palace."

He half dragged her through what was left of the harbor, avoiding the fray. When a creature lunged at them he tossed her back and worked tirelessly to dispatch it; she could do nothing but watch. The port was beyond saving. The heat wafted off the massive crumbling structures, making the defenders slow and giving the shadows a cruel advantage. They seemed impervious to it. It would be best to gather the survivors and make a run for safety, wherever that may be. She prayed Marin had made it out, but their chances now seemed so very slim. She wished she said something else to her in their last moments together. Anything else. So many years of friendship and she couldn't think of a single kind thing she'd ever said, or anything truly personal. She'd wasted time behind angry and defeated, she realized with a pang of sorrow. Did Marin even know who she really was? She gripped her blade tighter, Racynth's words again coming to mind. *One last fight.*

The Sentinels were seeing some success but they were too outnumbered. Jordan matched Racynth in skill as he pulled water from the shore, throwing it above the defenders with all his strength at the invading creatures. It hit them with the force of a hurricane, throwing them back. With the same blow he whipped it around a group of three, drawing them into the air in a bubble of saltwater.

They hung inside the bubble and lashed out in vain with their weapons. Their movements slowed but they were not truly dead. Their struggles came to a stop and he dropped them to the ground; they were twitching and beginning to move again when he finished them all with his sword. Bealantin covered him, shooting arrows into anything that attempted to approach his *viluno*. They exploded into flames on contact, throwing the figures back with the force. Black powder from her homeland, Tamora realized, an Azha creation. They were well supplied.

Watching Jordan use his element sent ripples of pain through her mind. Her own raging emotions reigned and she shot to her feet, her body uncaring of its own pain. *One last fight*, she repeated.

The Veden saw her approach and raised his sabre in defense, but with a glimmer of recognition he instead came to her aid. She marveled at Jordan's skill with bitter jealousy; he had a mastery over water that many dreamed of. Something she had once enjoyed in her fire. Flash frozen darts impaled the invaders and disappeared just as quickly, melting away. Soon the creature was riddled with holes and it too fell.

Her fire leapt at its cage, eager to escape and join the fight. Tamora's inner struggle with her own element was beginning to break out of her grasp. She stumbled, bent over in sudden fear. "I can't," she gasped out, staring at the ground, speaking only to herself. She couldn't let it out.

"Get up," Jordan shouted at her. Tamora couldn't breathe. The fire within her burned up her air. Her feet felt rooted to the ground once again. It was burning, begging to be set free. She felt a push on her shoulder and turned her face up; Racynth stood over her. He was splattered in gore, whatever these creatures were made of. It was black and rank, a thick ichor that coated his armor and clumped in his braided hair.

"Either get up and fight or run for the palace. You can't choose both," he said, pushing her backward. Tamora gasped for air and stumbled as far as she was able. One of the buildings had not been entirely destroyed; the alcove was made of brick and it alone remained standing. It was hot to the touch as the fire still raged beyond it. The heat was refreshing, it seared away her stray thoughts. Racynth helped her kneel, watching the fight that still continued in the square in front of them. "Calm your mind, Tamora. You can't freeze here; you'll die."

"I am not freezing," she managed to gasp, pulling at her collar. "I'm burning." He recoiled as she brushed his arm away, his sleeve smoking at her touch.

Her energy faded as her exhausted mind took control once again, the fire within ebbed. It felt behind an aching hunger and emptiness. She was alone and cold once again.

"Tamora, get up." Racynth pulled her to her feet, not a moment passing. She pushed him aside.

"Don't touch me."

"Now's not the time," he snapped, pulling her with him. Tamora winced and wished he wouldn't. He'd burn. Just like everyone did. Everyone except her.

Her gaze was caught again by the ships. A third was landing. A figure stood aboard, dressed in a white cloak that was unnatural in the gloom. The frigid ocean winds whipped around the figure on their solitary perch.

A billow of smoke erupted and blocked her view, and when it dissipated the figure had gone.

A cry for help drew her attention back from the shore; a second fearful scream echoed it and even Racynth slowed. A Veden she recognized, a young woman. She held her own against the creature she struggled with.

The initial cry had not been hers. The scream, however, was.

Tamora watched her turn in horror, the ice and water she directed through the air falling to the ground, as she stumbled back toward her Guardian. The Human was only a few yards away. The bow she had been using to keep a creature at bay was at her side, broken and in pieces beside her. Tamora's feet moved of their own accord toward the woman. With an energy she didn't have she dashed forward but there was little hope — the Guardian was going to die.

She tore a dagger from her sleeve, shoved up into the hidden pocket along her forearm, and hurled it at the monstrous form. The Veden flung her hands towards the creature as well, water turning to ice shards and each embedding themselves deep into its body. The dagger struck its back; it roared in pain and anger and the Human closed her eyes.

Her final shriek was matched by her *viluno* as the Human was cleaved through and fell lifelessly to the ground. The Veden screamed, an unending wrenching cry that dried Tamora's mouth and shook her to the core.

"No!" Tamora cried out, changing her course and rushing to the young woman. Her own terrible memories reached their claws out from the depths of her mind; this was too similar. She squeezed her eyes shut and the unwanted image of Selena collapsing onto the dirt, her face caked with blood and unnaturally still, appeared behind her lids as clearly as if it had just happened. She forced her eyes open, forced herself to think of anything but Selena. She couldn't relive it, couldn't go through that again.

Water enveloped the Veden as she began to Spiral. It swirled from her feet and hands, wrapped itself around her limbs and poured from her chest.

The girl cried out, a weak and groaning scream ripping

itself from her throat, and she waved Tamora away even as she bent over in pain. Tamora ignored her; she had to reach her side. She could help, draw her back to herself. The girl didn't have to die. She just had to get there.

Tamora watched the Veden's body seize as shards of ice formed beneath her skin and pushed their way out. Blood mingled with water and ice and turned her skin an eerie pink. Hopelessness filled her; it was over. The woman was too far gone. She recognized those wounds, recognized her own ruined skin as she watched the Veden shake and scream in agony. Her fire had done the same to her. It had ripped itself from her body and tried to consume her. Tamora skidded to a halt, too fast. She fell and watched in horror as the water surrounding the woman froze solid and encased her in blood-tinged ice. Shards of it snapped and cracked as she jerked below the surface.

Tamora was mere feet away when a force exploded outwards from the Veden; it tossed her back and she rolled across the hard ground like a ragdoll.

She covered her face as the Veden shattered, consumed by the water and ice within her. It flew past her as sharp as knives. One scraped her cheekbone, leaving a razor thin and burning line just below her eye, while another needle-thin shard embedded itself in her left shoulder and immediately melted at the temperature of her own blood. Most of the Veden's body buried itself into the nearby remnants of buildings and the closest of Erengate's defenders.

Tamora lay still, stunned. Others were in a similar state of shock, as people always were after a Spiraling. They were horrendously destructive, tragic, and all too common in times of war. This, she realized, was the beginning of another war. She looked up and stared into the empty space that had been the young woman. An icy patch was all that remained, already melting under the force of a nearby fire.

A thundering sound jolted her from her stupor; she raised her left arm out of instinct and just in time. A weapon slammed down upon it. It wrenched her shoulder downward and she felt something crack. Tamora could smell the rotten stench of the creature, could feel its acrid breath hot on her face.

She cried out as she fought its strength. Her blade was inching back toward her body; her arm was at an odd angle and every bone within it felt as though it were snapping in two. Swearing, she dropped her weapon and rolled away. Her own blade was buried into the ground where she had lain; the creature roared in frustration. Tamora sprang to her feet but her muscles felt lethargic, she felt like the air was made of tar.

They couldn't do it. The fire within her leapt at its cage but she didn't dare submit. The Spiraling of the Veden had reminded her of its rage and its power and it scared her to her core. She stumbled back from the creature and scrambled for her weapon. Her back was turned, she heard it coming but could do nothing.

"Get out of here," a voice cried in her ear. There was a clang of metal on metal, a grunt of exertion. Tamora turned and watched as Racynth, again, swung back at the creature and drove it from her. He spared another moment to look her way. "Go! To the palace!" he cried.

Racynth

The Sentinella retreated. The Veden's Spiraling had not been the first he'd seen in the harbor, but it had been the closest. Jordan was especially shaken and he rushed to cover Bealantin as they fled. The others covered the few that remained and dragged who they could with them, but in truth it was a free for all. With each new street Racynth could only look around the corner in terror, waiting for a monstrosity to jump out at them and end it there. They soon came upon hordes of people desperate for protection, racing to the palace in the hopes of being saved.

Sabina leapt atop a remaining statue, one of the rulers of old Erengate, and brandished her sword overhead. "Move! Out of the way!" she shouted, her voice doing next to nothing.

"The wall," Tamora muttered. Racynth twisted to hear her. He held her up as they edged along the eastern wall, seeing people try and fail to shuffle forward.

"What?"

"These people aren't going to the palace, they're trying to reach the front gate. Stay to the right," she repeated, gasping as they were pushed roughly into the wall. Racynth looked for Della, only a few feet away, and whistled.

"I heard — she's right," she shouted back. Only an Eilvyn would have been able to hear in the din.

"This is madness —" Petro began, talking to himself. There was a terrible ripple in the crowd that cut him off. Racynth knew what it meant and peered out over the people, dreading what was coming. From the left, the northern wall, came a disgusting mix of roaring and shrill screams.

Three creatures lined the street, moving forward in a destruction so complete he had never seen it's like. The carnage they left was maddening. Bloodied bodies and torn limbs, images Racynth would never clear from his mind.

"Move, move," Aspen pulled at him, turning around and pushing backward. "We have to go another way." He turned and was face to face with Petro. His face was pale as he looked out at the crowd; their screams were deafening and their panic tangible.

"We—"

"We can't save them," Aspen snapped at her Guardian and she yanked him forward. They ran, the rest of the Sentinella drawing weapons to get through the crowd, and Racynth hefted Tamora over his shoulder. The healer groaned in protest but seemed to be in no place to keep up with their pace. Her left arm was useless, that much was obvious. It hung in such a way that it was clearly dislocated and when it fell from her pocket the sight of the hand itself was enough to make Racynth's stomach turn.

At last, there were no more back alleys to hide in and no side streets to cover them. Only the main road. Before them was a group that easily numbered in the hundreds, but it was nothing like even the crowd that had gathered for the execution; it seemed many of Erengate's citizens had perished before reaching this point. Many of those who could, the Eilvyn and Iokans, used their gifts to get ahead of the crowd. Racynth had seen more than a few Tri floating through the air effortlessly with their Guardian, far above the crowds, making their way to freedom above the wall. He wondered if the air was clearer up there, if the shadowy monsters truly couldn't reach them. At least some might survive to explain the danger to Erengate's neighboring cities, and to the Council.

They reached the small square that stood before the gate to the Upper District and everyone was stopped in their tracks. It took a moment to realize why. Guards lined shoulder to shoulder atop the enormous doors and it was barricaded shut.

Sabina brandished her weapon and people dove out of her way, a few well-placed prods enough to encourage even the most panicked person to move from her path. A few did stand shoulder to shoulder with her, but they backed down when they realized what she was. Racynth set Tamora down when she began to hit him again. It wasn't worth the fight now.

"I am Sabina Miayra, Commander of the Fifth Sentinella," she shouted, her voice barely audible as she approached the doors. "I command you to allow entry to these people."

She repeated herself as many times as was necessary to catch their attention; it took far longer than Racynth had expected. People began to quiet, hope dawning as they too heard her commands.

"None will pass. We've already let enough of you through," a guard shouted. Boos and cries thundered from those gathered.

Sabina's gaze could have killed a weaker man. "I am—"

"I heard who you are and our orders are unchanged. We would not open the gate for the High Council itself."

Sabina snarled a reply but Racynth was distracted by the crowd. A woman beside Tamora had dropped to the ground, suddenly limp, and her Guardian was silently crying at her side.

"Come, we have to keep going. You can't rest here," Tamora said, kneeling beside the woman and brushing back her hair with her good hand. The woman, a Veden, was pale and her face was damp with sweat. "There is hope, we're still alive. Look, your Guardian is here. Stay strong for them."

"She was trampled," the Guardian, a short sandy-haired man, said softly. "We were trying to get my family, they were still home. But the crowd was too much... they wouldn't move and when those *things* came—"

"I understand," Tamora said. Racynth had rarely heard her speak so kindly, except in those brief hours when the baker had been in her cottage. She turned back to the woman, pressing gently on her body and searching for her wounds. There was hardly any response and he could see from her expression that Tamora feared the worst. "Darling, you need to wake up, do you hear me? Open your eyes, I know you're awake. Good, that's good."

Racynth glanced at Sabina, still shouting her threats, and the other Sentinels were quickly approaching the gate. He gave it a minute, maybe more, until they either convinced them to open it or forcibly did so themselves. He knelt beside Tamora. "We need to get ready to move."

She glared at him; the dark circles around her eyes and the bruises that were beginning to mottle much of her visible skin made her look like a walking corpse. "A moment, Racynth," she snapped, directing her attention to the Guardian. "I can't save her here," she said, "and she doesn't have much time. I... I would say your goodbyes." She looked so defeated that Racynth placed a hand on her shoulder and, for once, she didn't brush it off.

The man swallowed deeply. "It's alright." He looked at his *viluno*, his eyes filled with tears. "It's alright. I've lived a long life, much longer than I would have before I met you. Thank you, for choosing me," he said, his voice breaking as his *viluno* smiled once and closed her eyes again, growing still. He took a shaky breath in, staring at their clasped hands, before releasing it slowly. The color in his own skin was fading quickly and the lines in his face deepening; it took only a few moments for him to look decades older. He laid down, with the gentle help of Tamora, and closed his eyes. After a few breaths, he too was dead.

Tamora stood slowly, hissing as her body protested. He couldn't stop himself from staring down at the two, unsure of what had just happened. "What... what was that?" he asked. She closed her eyes and turned from the two.

"A Guardian's life is extended when they are Paired with their *viluno*," she said quietly, staring at the gate. He followed his gaze. Aspen and Petro had climbed up, her crafted footholds still jutting from the wall, and were wrestling with the guards. As he'd suspected, the gate was about to open. "If the Iokan dies first, that time will catch up to their Guardian. If you've lived past a normal Human lifetime you will die; it can be delayed, somewhat, under the right circumstances. But he wanted to go."

She spoke stiffly, as though it pained her even to speak of such things. Racynth had many questions, but this was so far from the right time. He'd seen Iokans die in battle, of course, but it had never occurred to him what might happen to their Guardian after the fact. He supposed he'd assumed it was violent, like the Spiraling, but this was far sadder than he'd expected.

The crowd was growing angry, seeing the guards struggle with the Sentinels to keep them out. Stones, debris, and blasts of Eiyer began to be thrown at them. One guard fell from atop the gate, falling on the other side with what Racynth could hear was an audible crack.

"Guards!" Sabina's voice rang out unnaturally over the crowd; she was exerting a huge amount of Eiyer. "I am Sabina Miayra—"

"That's enough —"

"I am Sabina Miayra," she grew enraged at the interruption. Racynth felt a pulsing in the air as she wrapped *Eiyer* around herself and amplified her voice. It physically pained him to stand within walking distance of the Commander. Everyone turned to face her. "I am the Commander of the Fifth Sentinella, daughter of Councilman Miayra who resides in the sixth seat of the High Council. I command you to open these gates under pain of death and treason against the High Council." Racynth sighed inwardly but made sure his expression let nothing slip. Tamora, however, visibly stiffened beside him.

The guard's frown froze before he finally sighed, a visible weight lifting from his shoulders as he waved to the guards grappling with Aspen and Petro. "Enough! Open the gates."

The relief that surged through the crowd was almost breathtaking as the gates began to slide open and the masses pushed their way through, stepping over one another in their urgency to reach the relative safety of the palace. Racynth feared that their suffering hadn't yet ended — after all, they were still trapped in the city, and those creatures would come for them.

Chapter 20

Tamora

Tamora wanted to scream in frustration at the thought of leaving the poor Veden and her Guardian out there to be trampled. But there was nothing she could do as she was dragged through the magnificent, pristine streets of the Upper District. She wasn't surprised that Sabina had been able to convince the guards, especially when she'd announced her lineage. Councilman Miayra. Tamora could have spat. She'd dreamed of killing him and of ending his terrible reign. But then Krys had died, and their movement had collapsed with him, and she'd been too broken to do anything but run and hide. Exactly what she was still doing now.

People gazed down at them from their homes, their windows thrown wide. They didn't seem to realize the city was under attack, or perhaps they thought they were safe here. Parents turned their children away from the sight of the disheveled and dirty incomers. She marveled at how untouched this part of the city was, even by the general grime of the rest of Erengate. She'd only been in this district once, many decades ago, before she'd turned herself into even more of a pariah than she'd been upon her arrival. It hadn't changed, while the other districts had gotten muddier. She wondered if these people even knew of the execution, or of the riots and what they meant. None had lost anyone, she was certain of that. Their servants might have been aware, might have wept for families, but she knew that many Human servants of these upper class families were forbidden from leaving the Upper District altogether. Only the most trusted were allowed to run errands or make deliveries, and it took many years to reach that point.

This brief moment of calm was shattered by screams behind them from the gates. The creatures were here. They had been that close to death, she realized with a shiver. As the panicked throng poured up the palace steps, beautiful carved stone veined with gleaming silver, she turned back to the gate.

Three monstrosities had made it through. They cleaved through the escapees and ravaged the street. Their weapons slammed into walls and crushed bodies beneath their weight. If they weren't stopped now they'd reach the palace, and if they made it inside all of this would have been for nothing. Marin could be in there, if she hadn't made it out of the city right at the start of the attack. If there was a chance that Tamora could save her, and everyone else, she had to take it. *One last fight.*

She stopped short, suddenly knowing what she must do. Racynth swung around as she stood still. "What are you doing?" he shouted at her but she ignored him. She pulled one of her blades from its sheath and shrugged off her pack, handing it carefully to the Sentinel.

"Watch this for me." She didn't look back as she went down the steps and straightened her spine, centering herself. *I'm not going to die. He's wrong. This isn't it for me.* It became easier with each step to ignore her pain and she knew, just for this moment, that she was going to step into her old shoes. She grinned suddenly as her fire leapt within her and even the earth that sat heavy at her center tested her resolve. All the years of frustration poured through her body. Her struggles to rebuild herself, to rebuild her life, and the looks and sneers she'd gotten every time she came into town. The silver lining of hope that she'd found in Marin, in having a friend.

She had walked down the street a ways, high on this feeling of purpose, until the creatures were only a dozen feet ahead and they noticed her, standing alone. She hoped no one had tried to follow but she didn't look, didn't dare turn her back on them.

This time, instead of pushing it aside, she drew from the fire and it answered her call.

Racynth

The pack was heavy in his grasp and he stared at it, then at the figure boldly striding toward the gate. With each step she grew more sure of herself; he could see her determination in the set of her shoulders. He looked back; the Sentinella was running into the Palace. Sabina paused, gesturing for people to follow, and met his gaze. He hefted the pack so that she'd see, and set it upon the step. Tamora had wanted him to have this; he wouldn't abandon it. But he couldn't abandon her either.

When he looked back, everything about her had changed. Flickers of live flames washed down her good arm, springing from her cloak and lashing itself to her blade. She drew the other hand from her pocket and although it was broken and weak it was wrapped in a wreath of blue fire. Sparks reacted with the black metal of her sword as waves of orange, yellow, and red came down from her fingertips. Each time she'd come close, when he'd seen the smoke rise from her touch, she'd backed down. She was scared of her own fire, he could tell from the way she cringed away from its touch. But he watched as she breathed in deeply and set her shoulders, and he smelled the crisp and dry air that her power brought with it. It reminded him of the desert, of the months the Sentinella had been posted in Ozhansa. Comforting, almost, in its destructiveness.

She swung the now fire-encased blade at the closest monstrosity.

Singed black smoke plumed from it as she made contact. Its fur burned and choked the air and her fire thrived, sending the creature thrashing backward. None of them had encountered an Azha yet, the few who lived in Erengate had largely fled when the attack had begun or lived here, in the safety of the Upper District. The creature roared in pain but she roared back, the sound from her throat guttural and violent and nothing like the weak healer he'd seen so far. Her clothes were aflame, her sleeves had already turned to ash. It didn't hold her back—if anything, it made her movements more brazen.

Tamora swung again and her blade found its mark. She stabbed deep into the thing's chest and a black ooze spurted from the open wound. Again and again she hit. It stumbled back as it clawed at its wounds. Slowly, it toppled.

Tamora

She didn't wait for the creature to hit the ground before she moved on. Killing it, successfully fighting against it, was invigorating. Her body felt more alive than it had in decades. Her joints didn't hurt as her fire rushed through them, powering her limbs with its burning lifeforce and allowing her to make each movement with deadly precision. Oh how she'd missed this. This was how she'd lived, what she'd once been able to accomplish. She'd burned thousands on the battlefield, killed dozens on missions with Selena. She'd been a legend, a nightmare, the dark flame that had haunted the minds of her enemies. It had been glorious — she had been glorious.

In the back of her mind, she knew it wasn't going to last. Her breathing slowed as she concentrated on the fight ahead of her, on the creature before her. Her heart was beating in time with the pulsating flames that roiled down her body and they were beginning to sting. She threw aside her blade as she felt the hilt mold to the heat of her hand, not willing to ruin it as she ran toward the gate.

Racynth

Tamora's sword hit the dirt, still smoking, and he felt his own blood run cold as he saw the hilt glowing slightly from the heat of her body. He knew something was very wrong. Those weapons had clearly been forged for her and would have been designed to withstand her heat — all Azha weapons were, through some strange method they had perfected over the centuries. He'd never met someone whose fire had this freedom, or contained this amount of pure power. It was boiling over within her. He could hear her heartbeat grow more erratic and knew he had to get closer, to tell her to stop. To make her stop before she killed herself.

Sprinting with sudden youth that he hadn't known she possessed, she reached the gate and the lacquered metal smoked as she approached. She was pure fire now, her clothes melting away, and it hurt to look directly upon her. It was like looking up at the sun and it encased her entirely. The creatures fell and writhed beneath her hungry flames as if they were nothing but toys, hardly a danger at all. She terrified him then; what great power had she once possessed? Who had she been? The thought of her being content with being a simple healer, back when she was not crippled, was laughable.

As if she'd read his thoughts Tamora laughed aloud, a crackling sound he felt would haunt him for years to come. The shape of her, from within her flames, looked down in wonder at her hands. He imagined that she had seen fear in the creatures' eyes; all it had taken was a touch and it had died screaming. The air around her turned back with the acrid smoke of death.

There was nothing left to fight. Racynth would have celebrated but his elation fell as she looked around and a sigh escaped her lips. She physically reached out, as though grasping her flames, and pulled her arms inward. She was trying to bring them back, he realized. She was failing. Nothing happened, her flames only grew in strength. Her control had disappeared entirely.

Racynth stepped forward, feeling the heat waft from her body like a physical assault. The stones beneath her were red, fading as she moved away but still superheated beyond what his own shoes could take. His feet were uncomfortably hot, painful pricks of burning stone melting through the soles, but he continued forward. She had saved them from death and she was suffering for it. Her smile, so clear before, had turned into a grimace as she bent down upon herself and tried to rein in her flames. Instead it rolled from her body in waves that she clearly could neither control nor diminish. The gate was beginning to melt, the golden lacquer smoking as she stumbled forward.

He broke into a run to both reach her faster and try to stop from blistering his own feet. It was useless, he knew, but he could hear her heart racing and saw as she squeezed her eyes shut in pain, opening her mouth as though she were suffocating. It was too hot; *she* was too hot. He could smell the acrid stench of burned flesh and it wasn't from the creatures, it was Tamora's own skin. He'd never seen an Azha burn too hot, he hadn't thought it was possible. *She's Spiraling*, he realized, his own heart lurching in his chest as reality set in and the fear overwhelmed him. If the Spiraling of a Veden had been so destructive, that of an Azha would raze the very city she'd tried to save. He couldn't let that happen.

A wave of heat pushed against him like a physical force but he reached for her anyway. His beard was burning off, the smell of singed hair overwhelming his nose, but he grasped her arms and shook her until her eyes opened. The scars on her hands had reopened, the flesh below the color of molten lava, and now that her clothes had melted he saw the terrible wounds on her arms and torso, tracing a cracked pattern along her entire body. She looked like a volcano ready to erupt, her skin breaking apart along her old scars as she struggled to hold herself together.

Her eyes were filled with fear as she stared at him. She tried to shake his grasp from her but he ignored it, though his palms burned. He was vaguely aware of Sabina screaming and knew how it must look. She was going to explode and he would go with her, if he couldn't help her regain control.

"No! No, no, no," Tamora moaned, pushed against him. "Go away!" Her fire pushed against him and he grimaced but refused to let go and refused to shout out.

"I'm not leaving you," he said, keeping his voice as level as he could. Although she was the one on fire he felt like he was burning, and was sure that he was. The skin on her arms felt swollen and she moved like someone drunk on pain. "You need to live, Tamora. You deserve to live. Don't go like this."

Tamora opened her eyes again and they glowed red, fire cracking through the gray color of them like a piece of metal thrown in a forge. Her legs were rooted in place by thorny vines that bit into her skin, that came from within her body, and it was impossible to move her. He smiled, hiding his own pain for her benefit, and reached out with his Eiyer. If anything could help her it was this. He imagined the fire receding, imagined his *Eiyer* shielding her from its grasp. Images of a cool breeze, the light spray of the ocean on dark rocks, or bright green fields. He tried to conjure up a fortress within her, one that they shared, that they could be protected in. Somewhere where she wasn't afraid of her fire but relished in it, somewhere she could feel joy. He felt she deserved that much.

Suddenly, he was aware of Tamora's very being. It was more than the grasp he had on her arms, the closeness of their physical bodies. The connection was mental — he could actually sense her taking control of her fire and her earth, wrapping them into a shape she could take hold of. He knew her anguish and her pain as his own. She looked at the two elements and he looked at them with her as though he were in her head, as though they were sharing this moment of consciousness. Before she had imagined them in a cage, restrained and fighting against them daily. Now instead she asked them to rest, to lay still, and to wait for when she called upon them again.

He reached out, as though he would with his own *Eiyer*, to help. He entwined his will with hers and pushed gently against her elements and they responded in kind. He felt their presence on his mind as sharply as though he'd thrust his body within a volcano and hoped to survive. But Tamora was there, helping him to understand them. They were not so different from *Eiyer*, he realized. The elements she held were raw power, just as *Eiyer* was, made in the shape of that which was all around them. He could see for the first time her true power and it startled and terrified him, but he also knew that now she could control it. With him at her side, the elements would rest.

Together, they coaxed the fire and earth down. They settled, not within Tamora, but within them both and when it was done, they stared at one another in exhaustion. Both Racynth and Tamora were burned, clutching one another, and standing shakily beneath the melted palace gate. Before either could take a breath to clear their scorched lungs, they collapsed upon the cooling stones.

Chapter 21

Marin

People swarmed, dragging Marin and the others inside as dozens of panicked citizens were allowed in the main palace. Seeing the Upper District after so long was shocking, even now, as she had grown so accustomed to the haphazard state of things in the Harbor District. Lark and Sorrell were wide-eyed as they took it all in, this part of the city they'd never been allowed to see. Davina, too, was open-mouthed in wonder at the pristine stone buildings and clean white cobbled roads. Only Eloise looked grim, her mouth tightening into a thin line as she watched the people inside the buildings peer out at the rush of people from the rest of the city. Most around them were Iokans from the Trading District; Marin recognized some from the market. There were a good amount of Humans, too, from the Lower District but most had died at the hands of those terrible creatures.

The palace was awe-inspiring in its beauty, the finest thing that her sons had ever seen. Marin had been well-traveled before arriving in Erengate so she was less impressed but she knew that Lark and Sorrell had been sheltered in comparison, even if they had found a way to fill their days with rebellious and dangerous activities. She still shuddered to think about the trouble they could have gotten themselves into; the thought that she would have had no idea what had truly happened was chilling on its own. The doors of the palace were covered in grimy handprints as people pushed them inward and rushed for safety.

Their small group followed the crowd as it surged through the halls, dimly aware of the finery around them. Tapestries and massive paintings adorned the walls, flickering candlelit scones ensuring everything was visible and on display, and even the floors themselves were so expensive she cringed to see them ill-treated. This was not the time to dwell on such things, though, and she focused on finding somewhere safe to rest. She desperately needed it, and she was terrified that Sorrell was deeply wounded.

"Come," she said as she saw a small hallway that seemed to be for servants, "this way." She pulled Lark's arm and guided them through the throng of people, and the quiet of the darkened hallway was a welcome relief.

Lark set Sorrell down, easing his good leg on the ground and helping him to sit, before leaning back himself and pushing damp hair back from his face.

"Ex—excuse me I— I don't think you're supposed to be here," a small feminine voice said, and Lark leapt back to his feet. Marin turned and saw a servant, a small Human girl no more than fifteen years old who was holding a bundle of blankets in her arms and pale at the sight of them. "Lord— Lord Karkas said that everyone was to stay in the dungeons."

Marin raised a hand to keep Lark back; he seemed ready to pounce on the girl. "We need a moment to breathe," she said, gesturing at the others. "My son is hurt, and... and there is so much death."

The girl visibly shook as she handed Marin a blanket, almost turning green as she looked down at Sorrell. "Please take this... what happened out there?"

Marin had no idea where to begin. The creatures were indescribable, the destruction they caused so horrible she never wanted to think about it again. Already she knew it would haunt her for the rest of her life. "The city is going to be destroyed," she finally said, feeling it in her bones. "The people here will need to escape, you will need to find a way out. The gates are barred — do you know of a way?"

She backed up, and behind her Marin could see a small door that led to a spiral staircase. She could flee upstairs, it seemed, to delve below the main floor of the palace. The dungeons were down there, she assumed, and that was where all the people from the lower city were being sent. Was that a way out, or a trap? There was no real way to know.

"I— I don't know. I need to go," the girl said quickly, escaping up the staircase. Marin sighed, and fell back against the wall. It was covered in soft velvet, even here where only the servants would see such luxury. The Karkas family was more well-off than she'd ever admitted to herself. How could they not be, when they employed nearly everyone in Erengate? She almost laughed at the thought — this attack had ruined them too. It was the only silver lining she could think of.

"We should stay here a while," she said, glancing out at the main hall. Most of the people fleeing had passed already, and there were worryingly few people coming down the hall now. Had so many died, that this was all that was left? "We'll wait for help, for word on what to do." The others were tired enough that they obeyed wordlessly, and they sat huddled under the blanket. Marin didn't even notice when her eyes closed and she fell into a blissfully dreamless sleep.

.....

They were close enough to the palace entrance to hear the doors bang open and as a rush of people ran inside, screaming and crying and begging for somewhere to hide. Marin jumped from sleep, her eyes sticking together painfully, and Lark leapt up to look around the corner. His exhaustion was visible; he clearly hadn't slept. Marin remained where she sat, her hand on Sorrell's shoulder. She feared she wouldn't be able to pick herself up, as her body felt like lead. He had also fallen asleep, passed out from either pain or sheer exhaustion, and Eloise and her mother sat stiffly on his other side. When Lark returned, she couldn't tell if he bore good news or bad.

"The Sentinels are here — they had to reopen the gate. Karkas had closed it," he said, crouching before them. Eloise shuffled closer, leaning over Sorrell.

"Do they have a way out?" she asked. Lark shook his head and she collapsed back with a sigh. "We're going to die here." Eloise was grim, her voice quietly resigned.

Marin said nothing. She didn't believe that the Karkas family had an escape ready. It was more likely that they were accepting people into the palace as a distraction, a way to lure the creatures here so they could slip out of one of the city gates. Now that they were here, they were trapped. People began to fill the halls with nowhere to go, more Human faces that she imagined the Karkas' had liked.

"Clear a path! Move!" Shouting rose up from the doorway and she recognized it as the Sentinel Commander.

"Help me up," Marin urged Lark, grasping his forearm and biting back a cry as she got to her feet. She hobbled to the corner and looked past the dozens of people between her and the door. Commander Miayra's blonde head appeared, her hair falling from her bun and giving her a frizzled halo, and her furiously beautiful face sent people stumbling from her path.

"I need a healer!" she yelled again, and behind her Marin saw two other Sentinels, each carrying a limp body in their arms.

There was no way she was going to move as fast as the Sentinella, who barreled through the halls as though they knew where they were going. Of course they did, they'd been here before. She snapped her fingers at Lark, pulling his attention back to her. "Get your brother. Eloise, Davina, get up. We're following them," she said urgently. "They can get us further in, where it's safe."

He picked up his brother without another word, looping Sorrell's arm around his shoulders, and staring past her where the Sentinels had gone ahead. People were frozen in place, staring after them. At whatever, whoever, they'd held. Marin tried not to think about it as she pushed her way past the shocked people and ushered her family forward. Tamora, her body naked and still steaming, had looked like she'd been ripped apart from the inside out and the other Sentinel, Racynth, had been badly burned. His beard had appeared matted and singed, the armor on his arms and torso had been removed in a hasty effort to reach hidden wounds. *They are going to be alright*, she thought mutely. It was all that kept her moving.

They shuffled along, pushing through the gap that they made in the massive gathering of survivors. *That's what we are now*, she thought mutely. *Survivors*. She hoped it would stay that way. If no one survived, if those creatures got into the palace and killed them all, there would be no one to warn the rest of Sienma. The thought of those creatures being unleashed upon the country, and Tunsealior, made her shiver in fear. It was too much to think about.

The Sentinels came up against a wall of guards and their commander was shouting again. She was so abrupt and loud but Marin could feel her fear as viscerally as if it were her own. She motioned for the others to stop and crept up, prodding one of the Sentinels in the back. He turned his head sharply, breathing out in relief when he saw her face. It was one of the Guardians, Petro.

"Miss Agata," he said quietly, drawing the attention of his *viluno* Aspen as well. In her arms was Racynth and his burns were more severe than she's realized. The hair on his face was half gone, his black braid singed and falling apart as it brushed against Aspen's clothes. His cloak had been melted and revealed the skin of his arms, with red blistering handprints wrapped around his forearms. Tamora's handprints, she realized, looking past them at the limp form of her friend. Jordan had her now, resting back against the wall as he held her as you might cradle a sleeping child. Marin looked away, a choked sob rising up through her throat.

"I—" she tried to speak, but her mouth just wasn't working. "We tried to get out," she finally managed. "I know a healer here, I've met him before. He used to help me, before William. His name is Tieren, I think. He's Veden."

Petro nodded shortly, stepping forward and clearing his throat to catch his Commander's attention. She stopped her verbal assault on the guards immediately.

"What is it? Oh, you lived," she said, seeing Marin and the others. She nodded, more to herself than anyone else, her look of relief softening her words. "Good, that's good. What do you need?" She was covered in soot and bloodied, a scrape on her temple staining her blonde hair.

"She knows someone in the Physician's Guild. Aren't they here, in the lower level?" Petro asked, turning to Marin for confirmation. She nodded, swallowing to ward off a suddenly dry mouth.

"Yes, I think so. That's why— that's why they're so selective," she said, trying not to look at Tamora. She couldn't help herself, but whenever she did she was filled with so much despair it threatened to overwhelm her. "But he, Tieren, was a customer. He should help."

His Commander's smile was sharp and toothy as she turned back to address the guards. "I will return and when I do, I expect an audience with Lord Karkas. In the meantime, you need to get everyone inside and lock the gates. The District gate is destroyed, and there are more of those creatures coming. We won't be able to hold them off for long." She turned on her heel and waved for them all, including Marin's family, to follow. "We are going to the lower level. Hurry now, I expect we'll have company shortly."

At her words the rest of the Sentinella picked their way out of the crowd, each looking as beaten down as Marin felt. Marin ushered her family along, desperate to stay with them. People fell out of their path and Marin couldn't decide if they realized who they were or if the poor people were simply too shocked to do anything else.

Marin tried to keep up with their long strides, keeping Lark's hand firmly in her own and trusting them to follow close behind. The palace seemed to be a web of fine art and elegant hallways, and it took a few minutes before they reached the stone steps downward. These were of no lesser quality but they were dark, sturdy, and as they descended she felt a sense of security wash over her. Davina stumbled in the darkness, her foot catching the edge of a stone, and Eloise had to fall back to support her.

"They can't get in here, right?" Marin asked the Eilfe closest to her, a small woman she barely remembered from her bakery, with short hair and a longbow strapped to her back.

The Sentinel winced. "I wouldn't give us much time," she admitted. "I've never seen anything like them—"

"Della," the Commander said in a warning tone, shaking her head. "That's enough. There's no need to cause more of a panic."

"It isn't a panic if it's true," Della replied. Commander Miayra turned away without another word.

Marin didn't ask any more questions after that, not wanting to hear the answers. The stairs looped in a circle, the air growing colder as they descended, before opening up into a surprisingly well-lit space with an open doorway ahead of them. The stairs continued on and Marin imagined that below them were the dungeons, but this level was wide and extended back quite a ways through the door. Above it was a sign, painted in bold strokes, claiming this to be the Physician's Guild.

"Bit of an odd place to put your healers, hidden away like this," Della noted, cocking her head. Her Commander didn't seem to have her reservations, walking Petro and Aspen through the doorway and yelling for aid. There were a handful of physicians who stood at tables covered in books, herbs, and bottles who were wide-eyed as they scrambled to attend to the Sentinella. More walked out from a back room, summoned by the noise. Marin hung back, watching it all unfold.

"They used to be in the Trading District. Now they're only meant for the Karkas family, and their friends," Marin said quietly, and Della grimaced before joining the others, who were laying Racynth and Tamora onto the first two cots.

"Is this okay?" Lark asked Marin, stepping up beside her. Sorrell had woken, though he looked bleary-eyed, and he peered out ahead of them.

"They don't seem to get many visitors," he said, blinking as if to clear his head.

"They have to know what to do, they're healers," Eloise replied, her voice hoarse with exhaustion. She was helping Davina to walk. The older woman's face was caked in dirty tears.

Marin frowned. "Let's get you in there as well. You don't need it as much as Tamora, or that Sentinel, but you should be looked at anyway." She stepped up to the doorway and peered inside curiously. Both Tamora and Racynth were still breathing, she was grateful to see, and each flanked by two of the Physicians. They didn't look like the healers she'd expected them to be. They wore long robes with cowls that edged up to the bottom of their ears, and the sleeves were cut away at the elbow to leave their arms bare. From the markings she saw at least some of them were Iokan. She didn't see Tieren, but suspected he must be around here somewhere.

A man walked up to them and frowned up at her. An Iokan, short and broad, with a shock of white hair and markings on his wrists. "Are you with them?" he asked, jutting his thumb toward the Sentinella. Marin nodded stiffly. "Alright then, get your injured on a cot. We don't have many."

She followed him, watching warily as he pointed Lark and Sorrell to a bed just a few down from Tamora. Some of the other survivors from the city had followed their cue, it seemed, and they began to come through the doorway as well. The healer eyed them as they poured through the entry and gestured toward the back. "Go on over there, we're not usually this busy. Find a bed and I'll be with you shortly — it looks like there are others more injured than you so I may be a moment."

She walked on, wanting to stay with Lark and Sorrell but knowing there was nothing she could do to help. It was best to leave it to the experts — in any case, they had Eloise and Davina with them to keep watch. She could rest. They were safe.

There were tables and instruments behind the first few rows of cots, the rest of the beds further down. It appeared that the physicians rarely treated anyone, and she guessed that they spent most of their time preoccupied with experiments and concoctions. She paused at one of the tables, staring into the pot that was propped on top. It smelled foul, almost like manure, and she couldn't think of any medical reason for such a thing. Her nose curled and she continued to the cots. Most were piled with sheets and she settled down on the closest one. She couldn't hear well over the bustle of people as they came in, crowding around the entrance, so she was content to watch the Sentinella for reactions. No one seemed more shocked or angry than they already were. Marin sighed, feeling the ache in her chest as her ribs moved. Hopefully one of the physicians could get to her soon as well.

"Now, this is a surprise," said a voice behind her,

recognition making her stomach drop. She turned sharply back to what she'd thought had been a pile of blankets on one of the back cots. Soren Karkas, his face scraped and his torso bare save the bandages wrapped around him, smirked back at her. Beside him, propped up in his chair and wrapped so tightly in a blanket she hadn't seen him, was Zavalynn. He barely moved as he registered her presence, his face swollen and mottled and his breath heavy. "You're the healer's friend, aren't you? The baker with the half-Human brats. I've heard a lot about you." He sneered as he looked past to where Tamora lay. "Isn't this a happy coincidence?"

She scrambled to her feet, wincing as her ribs protested any quick movements. *Where is the physician?* She scanned the room but the man who had sent her back here was now bending over Sorrell, and dozens of people were filling the space between them. The din was becoming almost unbearable to her sensitive ears.

She looked back at Karkas.

"Look, I know that the past few days have been hard—"

"Shut up," he snapped, pushing himself up on his elbows to look at her fully. He pointed, his hand bandaged tightly. "You don't get to talk about 'the past few days', understand? That bitch is a rebel and I swear—"

"She just saved all of our lives," Marin cut him off. She scoffed, holding her chest as it warned her against any sudden movements. "Don't you know what's happened? There are monsters attacking us—"

"I don't care. Monsters, Dalka's generals, it doesn't matter. She deserves what she got," Soren said, pointing past her and grinning. His finger hovered in the air a moment, before turning to Marin. "And you, you deserve punishment too. You harbored a criminal and you were part of her little scheme against me. You're the reason all of this happened."

She needed to get away from him. The others were too

far to hear her. "You're insane, Karkas." She shook her head and turned away, pushing her legs off the cot to reach the floor.

The *Eiyer* around her moved and although she opened her mouth to scream, the sound didn't carry. It was as though she'd swallowed it and her breath was trapped within her. She moaned, feeling the *Eiyer* yank her backwards onto her cot. The mottled face of Zavalynn appeared above her and she saw nothing of her former friend within.

"Silas, silence her. It seems her wounds are far worse than previously realized," Soren said, his voice sounding very far away under the pressure of his *Eiyer*. She thrashed against his hold, certain that someone else would feel it. *Eiyer* wasn't secretive or subtle — any Eilfe in the room should know it was being manipulated.

But they were distracted. There was too much going on, too many people in such a small space. The healers used their Eiyer to diagnose injury, it wasn't difficult to overlook a bit of rogue energy in the back of the room. No one came and Silas's hateful grimace was the last thing she saw before he dropped one of the loose blankets over her. His hands pressed down on her neck, drawing the blanket tighter, and Marin choked on the fibers.

No, no, she thought, trying in vain to push back against Karkas' *Eiyer*. She'd never had much skill for it, had never seen the need to practice, or even to teach her boys. She'd always assumed they would have even less of a gift than she had, that they would have taken after their father. She breathed in as much air as she could, feeling his hands tighten around her throat and knowing it was the last she would get. *Not like this, I'm so close. They're so close.* She pictured her boys and Eloise on a busy, happy day in the bakery. Lark would run off to get up to mischief and Sorrell would stay behind to help as he always did, casting sideways glances at Eloise that he didn't think Marin could see. She tried to scream and all that came out was a gasp. Tamora would be coming into the bakery, grinning ruefully as Marin ran to greet her. Her throat was dry and it burned, burned so badly for air that it was impossible to hold onto the thought. They'd made it to safety, she thought. They should have been safe.

Silas jerked his hands tighter and she felt something pop in her neck, feeling a rush of pain as her lungs wanted to burst and begged for air. It never came. Tears rushed from her eyes as she felt weakness overcome her, replace the burning in her chest with numbness, and her limbs go limp. The last thing she heard, over the din of the survivors begging and pleading for help, was the dry chuckle of Soren Karkas as he watched Silas kill her.

Chapter 22

Tamora

Awareness came slowly. First there were sounds; a low and stifled crackling, the sound of constant movement around her, and heavy breathing. Her own, Tamora realized. Voices that hovered close by, talking in low tones. She was not sure how she knew them, but they felt familiar. Selena? No, it couldn't be. But there was a presence that was comforting her mind in a way that she couldn't associate with anyone but Selena. Who is it? What had she done?

Next was the realization that she could feel, something she wished would come later or not at all. Numbness was a welcome reprieve from the pain she knew was coming. She'd felt this before, she knew what was coming for her. She was on her side, on top of a soft and forgiving surface that she couldn't identify. That part was fine. Her own body though, it was killing her. Her limbs felt torn from their sockets and her chest heaved as every breath brought a new pain. She knew she was riddled with deep gouges. The now familiar scars had been torn anew and she felt them all, even the shallower cuts on her neck and hands. Tamora squeezed her eyes tighter as she tried to steady her breathing. In and out. In... out. *I thought I just had to fight one last time*, she thought bitterly. *I didn't realize it would go on forever.*

A hand broke through her concentration, grabbing her shoulder. It recoiled as she winced and opening her eyes to look was a painful exercise. A face was quite nearly pressed against hers. The Eilvyn man, scrawny and mouse-like, leapt back.

"Wh—" where am I, she wanted to say. It stuck in her throat.

"S—he's awake!" the man squeaked. He was immediately joined by Aspen, who knelt by her side.

"Hush, stop trying to talk. You're badly wounded and you need to drink this. We tried... it just evaporated," she muttered, shaking her head.

The small man held out a similarly small glass and poured the warm water into her mouth. It was as sweet as candy, coating her throat like a salve. Her lips cracked into a smile that became a wince, but it was fine. Minimal, compared to the rest of her pain.

"That— that has been known to happen," Tamora croaked. Aspen chuckled.

"Wela be damned, I thought you were going to die."

"You weren't alone in that," Tamora groaned and tried to look around. She didn't dare move yet, not anything more than her head. Even that gave her a terrible headache that settled at the base of her skull. "Where are we?"

"The palace. They finally let us in and we made it down to the Physician's Guild," she said, a sad smile breaking through her grimace. "Marin... Marin helped us find it."

Tamora forced herself to really look around. The Spiraling had been hard this time from the last, although the first had hardly been gentle on her. She desperately hoped it never happened again — she wouldn't survive it a third time. The room they were in was larger than it first appeared; there was a haze of darkness further back but that was simply as far as the small lantern could reach. She saw other lights but her eyes couldn't focus on them. It wasn't musty or dank but she realized she could see her breath and Aspen was shivering slightly; Mago weren't built for the cold either. Absently, she realized that the chill didn't bother her the way it usually did. It settled against her skin but couldn't penetrate it, and she wasn't uncomfortable.

"How many?" she asked, and Aspen's brow furrowed in confusion. Tamora cleared her throat. "How many survived?"

"Not nearly enough. There are maybe a few hundred here and most lived in the Palace District to begin with. We think some made it out alive of the rest of the city... it doesn't look good. If you hadn't cleared the street and the gate this wouldn't even have been possible. No one here thought that they were in any danger," she said, her voice bitter as she shook her head. Tamora's stomach dropped. Just a few hundred, out of the entire city.

"Is Marin— she made it out? You said she was here?" she asked. Aspen winced, looking away, and the dread that pooled in her stomach felt thick and heavy.

"She... I'm sorry, Tamora," Aspen said, and Tamora's heart nearly gave out. "She went to rest and we couldn't hear her over the survivors coming in... she's dead." Her words falling over themselves like she just wanted them out as fast as possible.

Tamora stared up at her, feeling nothing. The moment passed and her eyes welled. "No... no, she was alright when I left her," she whispered, closing her eyes. "She was okay."

Aspen grasped her hand, the pain bringing her back to the moment. "I'm sorry. They said she had internal damage, that it must have happened after they left you," she said, squeezing her fingers. Tamora winced and drew her arm back, feeling as though it were still on fire as she moved it. Aspen said nothing but grimaced as she watched.

"I have to see her boys— they'll need help," Tamora said, trailing off as a figure approached. Commander Miayra looked worse than Aspen, her hair stuck to her face by dried blood and deep circles under her eyes.

The Commander had no visible reaction to the sight of her, her face barely twitched as she spoke. "You lived," she said. Was that satisfaction in her voice? Tamora couldn't believe that it would be happiness, that seemed too much of a stretch. "Can you move?"

"Not easily." Tamora raised her arm again, testing herself. She reached her limit far faster than she'd thought she would. The scars that traced her arm had been torn up from the inside; they'd cracked open like a rock under intense heat. The other was the same and she knew without looking that her body was covered in them. She'd torn herself apart.

"Please try not to move," Aspen said, not able to watch her any longer. "I don't even know how you survived."

"I've done it before—"

"Keep trying," Commander Miayra said, stretching her own arms. "We're not going to be able to stay here much longer than we already have."

"How long has it been?" she asked, trying to push herself up to the elbows. Aspen had to help and even that much made her gasp as lights dazzled behind her eyes and her head felt like it was spinning.

Commander Miayra frowned. "Racynth was out for a day and a half, and you've been unconscious for two. We've been helping the guard keep them out of the palace itself, but there's little left for us to do. Aspen, listen. They finally found where Karkas got out—"

"Karkas? What happened with Karkas?" Tamora asked, trying to focus on her breathing but everything the Commander was saying was just too much. Two days? Where were the creatures, and why were they all still here? If she'd been in charge she would have had the wounded carried out, not left here for care. They had no idea how much time they had left. "He's gone?"

She looked down at her, her eyes narrowing. "I was speaking with Sentinel Aspen. But yes, he escaped. After he'd killed his father," she said, distaste twisting her words. Tamora closed her eyes, shaking her head.

"Wait, what? When?"

Aspen kept her hand lightly on her shoulder. "No more than a day ago. Look, Tamora, you need to move more slowly. Stop trying to sit up." Tamora paused, her body grateful for the break. She couldn't let it rest for long though. They needed to get out of here, and she needed to see Lark and Sorrell. She couldn't imagine how terrible the past two days had been for them.

"More importantly, we know how he got out," Commander Miayra said, her gaze once again settling on Tamora. "We're going to follow him, all of us, and escape this Wela-forsaken city. Are you going to lose control again?" Tamora could hear the threat apparent in her question. If she did, or if the commander thought she would, they'd just leave her here.

Tamora met her steely gaze with as much resolve as she could muster. "I am in control."

"But how fast will it slip?"

"It won't, Commander." Surprisingly, she knew that to be true. She hadn't felt this much in control since her first Spiraling, since Selena.

Commander Miayra sniffed and looked at her for a moment before shaking her head. "Call me Sabina, please. You saved our sorry lives back there, it's the least I can do. In any case, you can hardly move and definitely not on your own.

You're still a liability."

"Give her some time, Sabina," Aspen said quietly.

She scoffed. "She got two days already, that's more than most. We need to gather the rest of these nobles; they're faltering without Lord Karkas and have no idea what they're doing. I don't know how anything ever got done around here," she said as she stared up at the ceiling. The Commander's hand shook slightly as she pushed back her disheveled braid. She'd been so poised and certain of herself up until now; it was unsettling to see her and Aspen this shaken. "We're secure here for now. The creatures haven't been able to get into the palace yet... well, they seem to have been drawn off back toward the harbor and the other districts. Even if they weren't, these lower levels are fortified. Della has reviewed as many records as these physician's had down here and they're as old as the city itself."

Tamora felt sick. The fact that the creatures weren't focusing on the palace didn't make her feel at ease. They were making sure they got everyone left, that's what Sabina meant. They weren't moving like mindless beasts; someone was controlling them. "So," she said, feeling the words stick in her dry throat, "how are we getting out?"

"Tunnels, ancient ones. Apparently Soren and Zavalynn escaped through one after killing his father. They were seen by at least half a dozen nobles but they were all too frightened to do anything. Of course, they claim that he immobilized them with *Eiyer*... which could be true. But I don't think any of them has ever wielded anything more powerful than a dinner knife," she said with a scowl. Tamora's heart sank.

"So after all this, he got away." She sighed. "That's just like him."

The elder Karkas was about as reasonable as his son, but he'd seemed less impulsive. Now that he was dead, and there was nothing left to tie Soren to the north, she had no idea what he'd do. Surely he had friends in the uglier parts of the world that would help him — he was resourceful, if nothing else. Sabina gestured once and Aspen left Tamora's side to listen quietly, and Tamora stared out into the rest of the room as her eyes searched for the few people she knew.

There were nobles, sure, still dressed in finery that was growing drab and grimy after days of hiding. Sadly they were most of the crowd, but there were a fair amount of Humans. They looked more worn and empty than the Eilvyn, like they had seen true horrors. She had no doubt that they had. Finally her eyes rested on a cot and a familiar crop of sandy hair, and she watched as Lark flopped his head back beside his brother. Sorrell looked pale and sickly, his leg bandaged more profusely than it had been before, but Lark looked surprisingly untouched.

"Help me up then," Tamora said, her heart thumping with sudden impatience. The two Sentinels looked at her with a jerk.

"I'm not sure that's wise," Aspen said, her frown matching her commander's. "We need to clean you up, those wounds are going to get infected. The physician they pulled over seemed fine enough but a second opinion—"

"I'll give my own opinion," she snapped. "I need to see what's going on. If I've really been laying here for two days I've had enough rest." She lifted her arm, trusting her other to keep her sitting up, and the surprising lack of pain was enough reassurance for her. Aspen stared at her outstretched hand; her eyes darted between it and whatever she saw when she looked upon the rest of Tamora's prone figure. Tamora sighed. She was tired of wondering how bad it was. If she couldn't see what had happened soon she was afraid she'd lose her mind.

Finally, the Sentinel grasped her hand and pulled her up. *Gentle,* Tamora thought as the blood rushed from her face, *please be gentle.* The dull throb of pain that had been ever-

351

present erupted and she grunted in shock, falling forward off the cot. She was far taller than Aspen and the Sentinel struggled to keep her up; she was dead weight in her arms as her limbs felt like they wanted to rip themselves from her body.

"Help," Aspen choked out. Tamora tried to stand on her own but was useless. She stumbled forward and her foot caught and they were both going down.

Sabina deftly put herself under Tamora's other arm, standing and settling them both. Tamora's breath hissed through her teeth as the movement pulled at the wounds that had already started to scab. "What in Dalka's name—" Sabina muttered. Tamora bit out a laugh.

"I can't believe I lived," she said, staring at the floor. The two Sentinels, supporting her under either arm, looked at her with matching bewildered expressions.

"You aren't going to stay that way for very long if you keep pushing yourself," Aspen finally snapped. Tamora looked at her sideways.

"Your Commander, Sabina, just said it. We have to keep moving. You can either help me do that, or get out of my way." She smiled. "If I fall a few times, what does it matter to you?"

Aspen sputtered. "I— because you saved us! You're the only reason we're all still here and I'll be damned if I let you kill yourself now," she said, standing taller. The move brought Tamora's left side higher and she winced.

"Alright, alright, your point is made," she said, looking over at Sabina. She looked like she had the same resolve, watching Tamora with a wary gaze, and Tamora just sighed. "Can you just get me over there, please?" she said, nodding to the boys. Their glares softened and she winced with each shaky step. The clothes they'd draped over her were little more than rags, and bits had stuck to her wounds as she'd slept and were now ripping off with each new movement. That alone was enough to make her light-headed, and by the time they reached the cot she was more than ready to sit down.

"Tamora!" Lark exclaimed, sitting up sharply. His eyes were swollen red and he'd clearly been crying, but he wiped his nose and pulled out his chair for her. "Please, please sit down. Sorrell — Sorrell, it's Tamora." His brother didn't seem to recognize that anything had changed, and was still sleeping. Fitfully, she realized, looking at him closer.

"What happened to you?" she asked, glancing at Lark. She looked around for Eloise and her mother. "What happened after I left?"

Lark's face fell for a moment, replaced by a falsely calm facade. "We tried to get to the northern gate but it was blocked. Then the main gate but those... Those things were everywhere so we ended up here," he gestured around them, "and I thought it was going to be okay. We followed the Sentinels down here, Sorrell was getting help... and..." he trailed off, unable to finish. Sabina muttered something to Aspen and helped her sit Tamora down before they both walked away, giving them space. Tamora wasn't going to pretend that they couldn't hear them, but the gesture was kind.

"Lark, I'm so sorry," she whispered, grasping for his hands. They were cold and clammy and she tried not to think about how long he'd been dealing with this loss alone. If Sorrell had been unconscious for all this time, he hadn't had anyone to grieve with him. "I didn't... I should have stayed with you. I don't know why I left." He shook his head, his expression snapping sharply into something more serious.

"No! You saved all of us, Tamora, you're the only reason we're alive. I heard what you did — it was amazing. It's all anyone's been talking about," he said firmly. "It was the creatures that did it. They knocked Sorrell back, and Eloise, and I didn't realize but they must have hurt Mother too—"

She looked again at Sorrell, peeling away his shirt and

inspecting what she noticed to be the biggest wounds, other than his leg. "Has he been unconscious this whole time?"

"No, just the past few hours. He hasn't said much though, Eloise was really the only one who could get him to talk."

"She's here too?" He nodded.

"She went to find a physician, they're spread pretty thin. He said his leg hurt really bad, and his chest too. He got knocked aside when we were trying to get away from one of those things, and I think he landed wrong." Tamora carefully massaged his ribs, looking for breaks. She wasn't at all surprised when she found a few.

"Aspen, he needs one of the physicians," she said, snapping her fingers back at the Sentinel. Aspen looked over at him with a small furrow in her brow.

"Again? We made sure they were seen when we arrived."

"Did they?" she asked, turning to Lark. He shrugged.

"Yeah, a bit. That's when we were separated from Mother... it was just a few minutes, and then they moved on. Everyone was rushing in," he said, his face darkening.

"If I had more strength...—" She swore, and the corner of Lark's lips lifted slightly. "Aspen, go get me that damn physician. Please."

Tamora spent the time she was gone examining Sorrell. The young man was pale and sweaty, his arm also tender to the touch and purpling, and she already knew his leg was bad. Besides the broken ribs she worried about other wounds, deeper, like the ones that had apparently killed his mother. The thought made her grit her teeth; she needed to see Marin's body. If it turned out she'd died because of something that Tamora hadn't noticed, she didn't know how she'd ever forgive herself.

The Eilvyn physician nearly fell over when he saw

Tamora up and about. "You really should be resting—"

"Stop saying that!" she shouted. Some of the other survivors, an assortment of injured and ragged people, quieted and looked their way; she ignored them entirely. "Help him."

He frowned. "I already looked at these boys, they're fine —"

"Fine? I know for a fact that Sorrell has a broken leg he's been walking on for days, and look at his skin! He's feverish! You really think he's fine? Are you insane?" The man couldn't keep her gaze as he peered at Sorrell more closely.

"I will look again," he assured her as she glared up at him.

"You will. We're going to wait here until you are done." She crossed her arms and nodded reassuringly to Lark. "Right, Aspen?" The Sentinel frowned at the small man and gestured him forward.

.....

The little physician worked quickly and hardly touched Sorrell as he inspected his wounds and felt for his pulse. Tamora watched him silently, but she was an ever-present presence behind the man. Soon enough he was taking more attentive care.

As he worked, Tamora turned to Aspen. "You said Racynth woke up? Is he alright?" she asked, scared to hear the answer. She remembered seeing him come to her, his skin blistering as he reached through her fire to help. *But I didn't kill him*, she reminded herself. There were so many parallels to the last time, but so much had changed. She was injured, yes, and everything hurt. But her fire, and her earth, they weren't caged. In fact they were thriving, spreading through her body and testing each nerve like someone greeting an old friend. Despite her wounds, she felt more at ease than she had in decades and she had no idea why.

"He's fine, given the circumstances. Would you like to

speak with him?" she asked, smiling when Tamora gave her a jerky nod. "Watch them, then." She left, and Tamora was left with Sorrell and Lark. And, soon enough, Eloise and her mother. They had no physician with them, Tamora wasn't surprised to see that, but her face lit up when she saw the man tending to Sorrell.

"Miss Tamora, you're awake," Eloise exclaimed, rushing to her side and looking as though she would hug her. Tamora raised a hand, wincing, and held her off.

"It's good to see you too, but I'm still healing," she said. Eloise's smile dimmed but she settled next to Lark, and Davina stood at her shoulder.

"He should be alright now," the physician finally said, sitting back. She wiped his hands on the edge of the cot, looking nervously at Tamora. "I'd already reset his leg— he'll need to be carried from now on as he cannot put any more weight on it. It may never set properly at this point."

"That's what I told him a week ago," Tamora muttered, shaking her head. The physician eyed her warily.

"His shoulder is secured, it's another thing he shouldn't stress. Is that all?" His eyes darted around and he fidgeted constantly.

"I suppose," Tamora said stiffly. "His chest? What did you do there?"

"He's bandaged, that's all I can do right now. You'll have to keep an eye on him," he sighed, standing. "I really do need to move on."

"If we need you again, we will let you know," Aspen's voice appeared, making Tamora turn and the man took his opportunity to leave. At her side was Racynth, the large man looking better than Tamora had expected. His cloak was gone and the leather armor he'd worn removed, and the long sleeves of the shirt he wore hid most of what she imaged were burns to his skin. What was visible of his arms was bandaged, but he waved his hand to draw her attention back to her face.

"You know, it isn't nearly as bad as it looks," he said, grinning ruefully. Seeing her expression as she wrenched her gaze from the mess she'd made of him, he shrugged. "Really, I'm alright. I'll probably always have your damned handprints though." He glanced at his forearms and Tamora did the same, remembering what had happened when she'd grabbed him. It had felt like she was in the middle of a cyclone, her fire raging out of control and about to destroy her. Then he had appeared, and he had somehow helped. Their minds had been connected, she knew that, and she also knew that there was only one way that they could have survived. She blanched at the thought. No, that was impossible. It just couldn't have happened.

"I'm so sorry—"

He cut her off. "Never mind that. Couldn't just let you go get yourself killed," he smirked. He turned to the boys, and Eloise. "If it's alright with you, I need to borrow your healer. I'll return her shortly, I promise."

Lark nodded quickly, perking up. Tamora eyed him as she carefully stood, moving more slowly this time. Aspen looked as though she wanted to jump to her side, but they both breathed a sigh of relief when Tamora realized she could support herself. She stared down at her legs. *I shouldn't be healing this quickly*, she knew. And she feared she knew why.

"Lark, you're going to have to look after your brother, alright? If anything changes or if you're worried at all, you come find me or you let one of these Sentinels know. We are not going to leave you, do you understand?" She waited for his nod before letting herself be satisfied. There was so much more she should do for him, so much more he and Sorrell deserved after what they'd been through. It would have to wait, for now. "Alright, let's go then."

Racynth

The two walked some ways away, Racynth making a beeline for the corner he'd carved out as his own personal space. Not that there was much to go around, but it seemed an injured Sentinel could get some measure of privacy even at a time like this. Despite what he'd said to Tamora, and to the others, his body hurt. The physicians had done a good job in healing his minor burns but there was only so much they could do. Eilvyn healers were the best, and that wasn't some strange preference he had. They trained for decades, some for hundreds of years, to be masters of manipulating *Eiyer* for healing purposes. It could eradicate small wounds in a matter of minutes, or smooth over painful burns. He'd never been able to piece together how it worked, but Della had tried to explain it to him once. Something about how *Eiyer* is energy harnessed for the user's purpose, and that the energy could be converted into something that the body could absorb.

Still, he would limp for a time as the soles of his feet healed and it would take a true miracle for him to not have Tamora's handprints scarred into his forearms. The armor alone had been a beast to remove from his skin, and the fresh layer on his arms itched when his shirt brushed against it. He waved off Aspen, watching her walk away before helping Tamora sit beside an overturned table he'd turned into a wall.

"I need you to tell me something," he said quietly, hoping the din was enough to cover their conversation. If it wasn't, so be it. He needed to know. "What happened? Why are we alive?"

Tamora bit her cheek, wincing more than usual, and leaned back against the table. "I was Spiraling, and you saved me."

He sat heavily across from her. "I don't mean that, I mean this," he said, gesturing at himself. "I'm healing faster than I ever have before, and it isn't because of anything the physicians have done. I should be mutilated, burned beyond recognition. You should be dead! Those wounds..." he trailed off, shuddering. He'd never seen anything so bad as he had when he'd woken up and seen the physicians working on her. All of her scars had been ripped open, and he'd never expected her to have had so many. They spread in a spiral shape out from her heart, carved deep into her skin. He hoped he never had to see such a thing ever again.

"I Spiraled," she repeated, as though that answered his question. "This is exactly what happened before." He glared at her. That was a lie, he could tell.

"But why do I feel a connection to you now?" he said, admitting it out loud for the first time. He'd noticed it immediately, a thread reaching out from himself to Tamora. Something had happened, something had bonded them together. "What is this between us?" he asked, seeing some of his own confused panic in her own eyes.

She shook her head, breaking their eye contact. "I... I have an idea but I thought it was impossible." He waited for her to continue, for her to look back at him. She had tears in her eyes. "I think we're Paired. I... I think you're a Guardian now, and I'm your *viluno*."

"That's impossible," he scoffed. Her expression didn't change. "No Eilvyn has ever been a Guardian. It just can't be done."

She rubbed her face with her good hand, her breath hissing in pain as the wounds on her arms were jostled. He winced; he too could feel her pain, in a distant way. It was another unwelcome sign of a link, evidence that she was right. "That's the only explanation I have," she said. "I feel the connection too, and it is just as it was with Selena. Somehow we were Paired out there— I didn't know it could happen without the ceremony." She paused a moment, thinking and staring at the ground. "We have to support one another now, Racynth. You may not die if I do, but it won't be pleasant, I don't really know what would happen. But if you die—" she broke off, grimacing.

"If I die, you'll Spiral again," he finished for her.

"And I wouldn't survive that," she whispered. "I can't do this again."

He sat back, looking past her at the survivors huddled together. So much had changed over the past few days, the city had been through so much. For it to all be destroyed over the course of a few hours was almost too much to bear. "I don't know if it's this bond between us or something else, but I don't want you to be hurt. I'll stand by you, Tamora, but I need honesty. We'll need to figure out what this means," he said. *And*, he thought, *we'll need to tell the Sentinella everything.* That was not a conversation he looked forward to.

"Then we'll start with Marin," she said, surprising him.

"What?"

She moved as though to push herself to her feet and he jumped to help, ignoring his own discomfort even while marveling at the rate he was healing. It wasn't something he'd ever really noticed, but he supposed that Petro and Bealantin did recover faster than most Humans should. Still, they'd never been hurt this badly. It was terrifying to know that his own body had changed so much so quickly and by some means that he didn't understand. He was sure Tamora felt the same.

"I need to see Marin's body," she said, her jaw set. "I need to know if I could have helped her."

"Tamora... there was nothing you could do, you were unconscious—"

"I don't care," she said simply. He looked at her for a moment before nodding.

Tamora

The back of the Physician's Guild had been rigged into a rough morgue as many of the survivors succumbed to wounds they'd received before arriving. Marin had been one of the first to be laid there. Tamora stood before her covered body for a long time before she was ready to lift the blanket that had been laid on top of her. Without meaning to, she drew on Racynth for strength just as she had with Selena. Perhaps just as unconsciously, he leaned toward her and she felt his energy willingly shared. Every part of her wanted to reject this bond. It was something she'd shared with Selena; she was never meant to share it with anyone else. *How can I trust myself to protect him?* she wondered. *I failed to protect Selena. He may be a Sentinel, but if he dies now...* she didn't want to think about the possibility of what may follow. It would do her no good to worry about it; she could only focus on the present.

Tamora lifted Marin's cover slowly, taking in her face. Her eyes were closed, her expression calm. She looked as though she were sleeping. If it were not for the paleness of her skin, the slight blue tinge around her eyes, Tamora might have even believed it. She drew the sheet back and frowned.

"They said she succumbed to her wounds?" she asked. Racynth nodded.

"Apparently there was bleeding internally, they said she must have sat down to rest and just drifted away." She didn't look at him, but he sounded as though he were trying to reassure her. Tamora cocked her head as she looked down at the body of her friend. If she ignored who it was, she could think about this critically. It was hard, though, to separate her feelings from her thoughts. She'd never again walk into the bakery and smell Marin's delicious creations, never again sit at her little table and listen to all the gossip Marin had heard in the week before. She pushed the thoughts away; the last thing she wanted to do was cry. Racynth might be her Guardian now, but they weren't close enough for that.

Too much jumped out at her to make sense of it at first. The odd color of Marin's neck, for one, and the fact that the wounds on her torso didn't indicate anything about severe internal bleeding. She pressed gently on Marin's side and could feel broken ribs, but nothing seemed to be so severe that she would have died. She looked closer at Marin's neck and gasped, jerking her head back.

"She was strangled," Tamora said, pulling at Racynth's arm so that he would look closer as well. "You see, those marks. Someone killed her." She stepped back then, nearly falling as her leg threatened to give out.

"But why would someone do this?" Racynth asked, leaning down to look before crouching beside her. "Who would kill her, and why now?"

She shook her head, rubbing her eyes. "I don't... I don't know but whenever I find them I'm going to kill them," she whispered, glaring at her palms. "She was good, she didn't have any enemies, she—" Tamora drifted off, gazing at her scars as her mind wandered. Karkas had been here, and Zavalynn. Sabina had said so herself. He'd killed his father, in front of everyone, and run. *What if... what if he got to Marin first? If he saw her, and recognized her — of course he'd recognize her, she knew Zavalynn. If he were angry enough, he wouldn't have even hesitated.*

The knowledge cemented itself in her mind. It was Karkas, and that pig Zavalynn, that had done this. She clenched her fist and stood, ignoring Racynth's move to help. They would have to run far to escape her now. It would never be far enough; she was going to burn them both. Her fire leapt at the bloodlust that rushed through her veins, jumping for joy and excited to be free. She grinned, laughing despite herself and earning a look of concern from her new Guardian. She could do it now, she realized. She could burn them all to the ground.

Glossary

Terminology

- **Azha**: Iokan people with power over fire and its forms.
- **Basana**: The first month of the calendar year and height of spring. The first day of Basana is a day of feasting and celebration.
- **Bolsi**: Humans descended from those native to the northernmost reaches of Tunsealior; now they live on the edges of Coalition society.
- **Caliot**: smallest value currency in Tunsealior; a semi-precious stone carved into a hexagonal shape.
- **Dakelt**: The fourth month and middle of the calendar year; the height of winter.
- **Eilvyn**: People native to Belven who settled in Tunsealior thousands of years ago; an ancient race that lives long lives and who consider themselves to be the eldest creation of the Wela.
- **Eiyer**: The life-force of the world, manipulated by Eilvyn.
- **Guardian**: A Human who is Paired, through a secretive ceremony, with an Iokan youth to share in the burden and power of wielding a natural element. This process gifts the Human with long life and strength, tying them to their *viluno* until the Iokan's death.
- **High Council**: Ruling government body of the Coalition comprised of sixteen representatives of Eilvyn and Iokan descent.
- **Human**: Native to Tunsealior, created by the Wela Bensa.
- **Inqu**: Currency made of shell, carved in a circular shape,

that is sourced off the coast of Erengate. Worth ten Caliots.

- **Iokan**: Named for the Wela Ioka, their creator, the four Iokan Peoples (Azha, Mago, Veden, and Tri) can manipulate the natural elements. They live long lives, their natural lifespan crossing multiple centuries, and are typically Paired with a Human Guardian to assist them in controlling the element within them.
- **Itro**: The third day of the week.
- **Jakela**: A title used by the General of Krystopher Reene's forces during his rebellion against the Coalition.
- **Joien**: A person who is half-Human and half-Eilvyn.
- **Kana**: The sixth month of the calendar year, the last month of winter.
- **Kit'ak**: Native to Tunsealior's rivers, lakes, and seas. Entirely scaled, with the lower body like that of a snake and an upper body like that of humans. There are four Kit'ak peoples: the Zut'ak, native to lakes, the Akki, native to rivers, the Ot'az, native to the oceans, and the Uzaku, native to marshes. They live in remote regions, away from most Iokan and Eilvyn settlements. Those who are present in Coalition cities are often kept as objects of amusement by the wealthy.
- **Kwim'wa**: one of Dalka's five Grand Lords, who help her maintain order. Kwim'wa, Tri for 'War Leader', is the highest Lord and leader of the armies of Dalka.
- **Mago**: Iokan people with power over earth and its forms.
- **Maken**: The seventh month of the calendar year, marking the end of winter and advent of spring.
- **Naturalismo**: The title of someone employed by either a city or town to predict the weather. A Veden, usually.
- **Paro**: The eighth day of the week.
- **Physician's Guild**: An organized group of healers under the rule and protection of the city in which they are housed.
- **Pikvul**: An Iokan whose parents are different Iokan People (ex. half-Azha, half-Mago)

- **Puhu**: Very alcoholic Azhan liquor, spiced with cinnamon and other potent herbs.
- **Rocklung**: A contagious illness
- **Rubbi**: the second-most valuable currency in the Coalition Merchants' Guild; a metal sphere with a hole in the center, hung on a cord for storage. One Rubbi is worth ten Caliots.
- **Sentinel**: Coalition peacekeepers who work in teams of eight, known as a Sentinella.
- **Shimmering Plane**: The Plane of the Wela, separate from the Natural Plane where the mortal races live
- **Spiraling**: Upon the violent death of a Guardian, an Iokan will Spiral – losing control of their element they are consumed, often leading to wider destruction and the disintegration of the Iokan's body. There are no recorded survivors of a Spiraling.
- **The Pit**: Bottomless Pits that appear around Tunsealior. No one knows how deep they are, or where they lead, and they seem to have a negating effect on the gifts of Iokans and Eilvyn.
- **Tri**: Iokan people with power over air and its forms.
- **Valerian Root**: a sedative
- **Veden:** Iokan people with power over water and its forms.
- **Viluno**: The Iokan in the Iokan/Guardian relationship. An Azha word, used by all Iokan People.
- **Yatés**: The fifth month of the calendar year.

Geography

The continent of Tunsealior is made up of seven countries: Glojoemor, Graenaka, Irodel, Ozhansa, Sienma, Sotwifas, and Tomerta. It is ruled by the Coalition from their seat of power in Koren, a city-state independent from the seven countries.

Separate from Coalition rule is Adbeter, an island nation to the southeast of Tunsealior, populated entirely by Humans.

Deities

Wela: The Wela are the deities of Tunsealior, descendants of the Imdite who created the world and all creatures that live within it. The Coalition only acknowledges eight of the sixteen Wela as being true deities, although worship of the "Lesser Eight" can still be found in pockets across Tunsealior.

The Eight Wela recognized by the Coalition:

Makmo: Wela of Warriors and King of the Wela. He is associated with knowledge, strength, nobility, and fatherhood.

Ioka: Wela of the Natural Elements and Queen of the Wela, wife to Makmo. She is the creator of the four Iokan Peoples, who reflect her elements within themselves, and she is associated with mothers, vengeance, and the natural elements.

Afina: Wela of Beauty, the Jewel of the Wela. She is the firstborn daughter of Makmo and Ioka and the creator of the Eilvyn, who reflect a portion of her otherworldly beauty. She is associated with beauty, *Eiyer*, gemstones, and protection.

Itrodo: Wela of Truth and Judgement, husband to Afina and firstborn of Paroi and Dalka. He helped Afina in her creation of the Eilvyn and is associated with justice and retribution.

Bensa: Wela of Fertility and Life, daughter of Afina and Itrodo. She created Humans, as well as assisting the other Wela in their creation of all life. She is associated with the earth, childbirth, farming, and nature.

Dalka: Wela of the Dead, the Deep Sea, and Darkness. Half-sister of Ioka, she is the Ruler of the Eternal Plane, where all dead rest. She is associated with death, darkness, protection, and the afterlife.

Paroi: Wela of Wind, lifelong partner to Dalka and father of Itrodo and Nen. He is associated with sailing and fishing, secrets, spies, and birds of prey.

Hepas, the Unnamed: Wela of the Hunt, brother of Makmo and former partner to Bensa. He was banished to the Black Plane by the other Wela many ages ago.

Separately from the Wela, the All-Mother is the primary goddess of the Humans in Adbeter, and many in Tunsealior. She is considered by some to be an aspect of Bensa.

Acknowledgement

I would not have been able to write this book without the support of so many phenomenal people in my life, who I am lucky to call my friends and family. I also want to thank Megan McKeever for her amazing work as my editor, your feedback was invaluable. Thank you also to My Lan Khuc – your cover art is gorgeous, and I wouldn't change a thing.

Mom and Dad – I love you! Thank you for always encouraging me to read and be creative. I've talked your ears off for years about ideas and characters, and now it feels like it's all come together. You fostered my love of reading and books and that is something I will cherish forever.

Emily and Chase – growing up with you both has made me the person I am today, and I am proud to be your sister. You are both so creative and I can only hope to be as talented as you!

Roger and Tilly – thank you for letting me crash on your couch and tap away on many visits and chatter away about my imaginary worlds.

Rachel, thank you for reading my unwieldy first draft and giving me the guidance I needed to make this book what it was always meant to be. Your feedback was so important for my journey as an author, and I will always be grateful for the time you took on my behalf.

Sean and Michael, thank you for being my amazing beta readers! The time you took to read my work meant a lot to me and without you the book wouldn't be where it is today.

To my beautiful daughter Vivian; while you aren't old enough to read this yet, you have inspired me to finally take the last leap and publish my own work. I am so excited to see the young woman you become and the stories you will tell.

Finally, my husband Ian. You've read countless drafts, named some of my most important characters, and listened to probably thousands of hours of brainstorming on long car rides. I remember on one of our earliest dates I told you about this crazy idea I had to write a story about a woman named Tamora who could throw fireballs – you've been with me every step of the way. Her story wouldn't be complete without you.

About The Author

L.a. Garnett

L.A. GARNETT has been writing stories since she was a child, and creating the world of Tunsealior for the better part of a decade. When she isn't writing she enjoys crochet, long walks, and spending time with her family.

You can find more of her work at www.l-a-garnett.com.